★ ★ A TIME TO RUN ★ ★

★ ★ A TIME TO RUN ★ ★

A NOVEL

BARBARA BOXER

with Mary-Rose Hayes

CHRONICLE BOOKS
SAN FRANCISCO

Library of Congress Cataloging-in-Publication Data available.

ISBN 0-8118-5043-9

Manufactured in the United States of America
Designed by Jay Peter Salvas
This book was typeset in Perpetua 12¼/14⅔ and Trade Gothic

Distributed in Canada by Raincoast Books
9050 Shaughnessy Street
Vancouver, British Columbia v6p 6e5

10 9 8 7 6 5 4 3 2 1

Chronicle Books llc
85 Second Street
San Francisco, California 94105
www.chroniclebooks.com

To Stewart, Nicole, Doug, and Amy, with love.
And of course, Zach.

★

2001

★

CHAPTER ONE

May 21

MONDAY

7:00 P.M.

Senator Ellen Fischer promised to call back within the hour and let him know her decision, then ended her phone conversation with the chairman of the California Democratic Party. She leaned back in her swivel chair, lacing her fingers behind her head and stretching her neck and upper back. Under her massive antique partner's desk, her feet rested on an upholstered oak stool, an office-warming gift two years ago from her chief of staff. Ellen was a petite five-foot-two, and in order to comfortably use her computer and phones, she kept her desk chair cranked to its maximum height; without the stool, her feet would be dangling.

It had been a particularly intense day in her D.C. office, with a steady stream of meetings, e-mails, and phone calls from organizations and constituents, all urging her to step up her opposition to Professor Frida Hernandez's nomination to the Supreme Court.

There was little time left for any attempt to block the confirmation of the ultra-conservative professor. The floor debate and vote were scheduled for tomorrow afternoon, and in a few minutes Ellen would hold a final meeting with her staff to map out strategy.

In many ways it was too bad, because Hernandez should have been the ideal candidate. Not only was she a first-generation American from a humble background whose appointment would be a huge source of pride for the Latino community, but she was from California, Ellen's home state. Hernandez also had impeccable credentials. She was dean of the law school at the University of California at Berkeley and a full professor, a nationally known legal expert, lecturer, and commentator. She was intelligent and articulate. She had a warmly sympathetic voice and fine dark eyes that could flash with passion. Unfortunately, that passion was invariably on the wrong side of all the issues Ellen held dear. The professor's appointment to the Court, Ellen was certain, would be disastrous.

Just last week, under hard questioning at her hearing before the Judiciary Committee, Professor Hernandez had proved to be skillfully elusive regarding her own views, particularly when Ellen, a member of the committee, had sought to challenge the nominee's strongly suspected bias against *Roe v. Wade*.

"Professor Hernandez," Ellen had asked, "do you believe a woman deserves to have her reproductive health care decisions kept private, between herself, her doctor, and her god?" To which Hernandez replied with an assured smile, "I have great respect for the past decisions of the court, but am unable to elaborate about particular cases and issues that might come before me as a Justice—should this committee decide to put its trust and faith in me."

"Are you then telling us," Ellen pressed, "that you have great respect for Court decisions involving the right to privacy?"

"I'm saying that, in general, I have great respect for the past decisions of the Court."

In response to a probing question on the environment from Senator Desmond Leary, senior Democrat on the committee, Professor Hernandez insisted on her inability to comment on the power of the federal government to regulate offshore oil drilling in state waters adjacent to federal sanctuaries and again reiterated, "because, as we all know, such a case may well come before me."

She sidestepped, gently and implacably, all questions regarding her views on sensitive issues or on how flexible her thought process would be as a Supreme Court Justice. Since Hernandez had never been a judge, there was no way to confront her with actual past decisions on cases. And, incidentally, she was charming.

But without a doubt, from earlier articles and speeches, from the political agenda of the senators and White House insiders who put forward her nomination, from views of other outspoken supporters, and from Frida Hernandez's personal advocacy for certain causes—years before she had been a law professor of Ellen's late husband, Josh—Ellen knew that, once on the Court, Hernandez would help turn back the clock on Court decisions that Ellen believed were vital to the people.

In the end, Hernandez's confirmation was approved by the Judiciary Committee, the partisan vote of 10–9 reflecting the thin Republican majority. Observing the time-tested principle of not allowing a favored nominee "to hang out there too long twisting in the wind," the majority party quickly scheduled a full Senate vote.

Ellen restlessly leafed through the unhelpful reports on her desk, gathered by her staff on the impregnable Frida Hernandez, then looked up as David Makins, her communications director, poked his head through the doorway.

"The media's clamoring," he said, "and I need to give them something on your plan for Hernandez. Any statement yet?"

"Just say I'm still weighing my options."

"And the *CBS Early Show* for tomorrow?"

"Tell them thanks but no thanks. Be nice."

"Aren't I always?"

"No comment on that, either," Ellen said, smiling. "Do me a favor and ask Vic and Derelle to come in. Maybe I'll have something more for you later."

Ellen moved to the oval table in the middle of her office as Vicente Aguilera, her Chief of Staff, and Derelle Simba, her executive aide, entered the room.

Aguilera had been her husband's Chief of Staff through his three terms as a Congressman, and he and Josh had both previously worked for Congresswoman Shirley Lester of Oakland, California. Aguilera was forty-eight, stockily built, and wore his glossy black hair—of which he was inordinately proud—just a shade too long. His hair was his one small vanity, though. Aguilera was hardworking to a fault and possessed a photographic memory, the gift of near total recall—a priceless quality in a chief of staff. Ellen imagined his mind filled with small file drawers from which he would unerringly extract the appropriate information.

Derelle Simba, in her early thirties—she herself had never known her exact age—was African American with caramel skin and golden eyes, a dusting of freckles across her nose, reddish tones to her close-cropped hair, and might almost have been beautiful were it not for a subtle misalignment of features. "Yeah," Derelle would shrug if asked, "cement floors'll do that to you when they come up and hit you. Got a lot of busted bones that way, and some of them never quite got back together in the right places." She was several inches taller than Aguilera and towered over her diminutive Senator. They'd known each other for almost twenty years, ever since Ellen had first encountered Derelle as a teenage runaway. Over time Derelle had grown fiercely protective of Ellen, her savior and mentor, until their positions occasionally seemed reversed. "You should be my bodyguard," Ellen would sometimes joke to Derelle, "instead of the Capitol police!"

To balance Vic's experience, pragmatism, and intricate memory, Derelle possessed savvy instincts second to none. She had needed those in the world she'd grown up in, a fast-moving world of violence and chaos, where, too often, a moment's hesitation could be fatal. On most issues, she could be counted on to take a more aggressive position than Aguilera—though Ellen's staff, taking their cue from their boss, prided themselves on their lack of rigidity and their ability to think outside the box.

While Derelle and Vic were still pulling up their chairs, Ellen opened the discussion. "We're down to the wire with Hernandez. Let's run through it once more, make a decision, and live with it." She asked Aguilera, "What's the word?"

"The vote will be close, but she'll do better than she did in committee," said the Chief of Staff. "It looks like she has it by a margin of six or seven. Several Democrats are crossing over, and the Republicans are holding solid."

"If she made it in committee," Derelle said, "there's not much chance of a floor debate changing anything."

"A lot of our friends are apoplectic about her getting on the Court," said Aguilera, "but not a word about any Senator leading an all-out attack on the floor. So if ever—"

"I see where this is going," Ellen said.

The Chief of Staff continued, smiling at her ability to read his mind, "So if ever there was a time for you to speak up, it's *now*. Maybe some pressure from you will change a few votes. You need to be the conscience of the liberals, even if you're the only voice in the wilderness."

Derelle spoke up with force. "Not this time, Vic." Falling into the possessive mode not unusual in a Senate office, she said, "We've already opposed two district court judges, and we're not even halfway through our first term. We only have so much political capital. Let someone else take the lead on Hernandez now; there *are* other Democrats. Let's name some." Derelle picked up the "whip card" that was sitting on the table—an alphabetical list of Democratic Senators with their office phone numbers that their Senate colleagues keep in their jacket pockets. "Let's see—"

Vic interrupted before she started to read the list. "One, just because those other judges got confirmed doesn't mean Ellen should have stayed mute. And two, Ellen's the only one with the credibility to stop dear Frida. They're both from California; they're both women."

"That's not what I'm saying here!" Derelle protested.

"Just what *are* you saying?" interjected Ellen. "You've never been one for subtlety."

Derelle laid her palms flat on the table, her eyes hard with intent. "Your bill," she declared. "That's what. It comes up in committee next week. I'm saying it's even more important than

Hernandez's confirmation, and you shouldn't risk anything that might stop it passing."

There was a pause while the three of them considered the legislation that Ellen had authored, which she and her staff had been putting together almost from the minute she was elected to the Senate: The Childhood Protection and Enforcement Act. It provided for federal funding for shelters, interventions, and training related to protecting children, and called for removing them from lethally abusive homes. States that failed to fully implement the act would lose federal funding from a variety of programs. The bill also provided for confiscation of all firearms from offending households, which was even more controversial.

"Let's prioritize here," Aguilera said. "With Hernandez on the Court, the conservatives will have enough votes—to say nothing of the inclination—to declare most of the bill's provisions unconstitutional anyway. So even if it passes, we lose in the long run. Not to mention the hit we'll take on choice, affirmative action—remember Frida's old argument 'I made it, so why can't you?'—and of course the environment. Hernandez is the only person I know of who claimed she was working pro bono by doing legal work for big oil!"

"Predicting future actions of a court is way beyond our pay grade," said Derelle. "Here's the point. Lead the opposition to Hernandez now and doom Ellen's signature bill that she ran on in her Senate campaign."

"If only we had some real ammunition we could use against Hernandez," Ellen mused, "something damning that the Judiciary Committee missed."

"Well, there's nothing," Derelle said. "Nada. Zip. Not even something small and embarrassing—though I bet there's not much would embarrass *that* lady."

"You're probably right." Ellen leaned back and ran her hands distractedly through her thick red hair. "Frida Hernandez is one tough cookie," she said bitterly. "She's made to order for the conservatives—Carl Satcher sure chose well."

★　★　★

Ex-Senator Satcher, whose seat Ellen had won in an upset, was a deeply conservative Southern California power broker and a close friend to every Republican President for the past thirty years. His political agenda and blatant self-interest were abhorrent and should have been obvious to anyone, thought Ellen, who could see his fingerprints all over this nomination.

Satcher had done his best to wreck Ellen from the outset, not just during the campaign, which was as brutal as expected, but also personally, culminating at her swearing-in ceremony that cold and blustery January day two and a half years ago. Standing beside the rostrum in the Senate chamber, she'd taken the oath of office—*Do you solemnly swear to support and defend the Constitution of the United States against all enemies foreign and domestic, so help you God?*—and accepted the Vice President's handshake and congratulations. Then, in a daze of unreality, she'd walked down the blue-carpeted center aisle, past the curving rows of one hundred historic desks (one of which was now hers), barely aware of the applause from the packed galleries above, unable to dispel the feeling that this was her husband Josh's destiny, not hers. Surely it was Josh who should now be holding the press interview in front of the historic Ohio clock in the hall outside the Senate chamber. Surely it should be Josh moving out onto the Capitol steps for the required photo op—this was all wrong. It was a terrible mistake. She was in way over her head. She'd never be able to do the job.

And then from out of the crowd appeared Carl Satcher, his mane of white hair crowning a broad, ruddy face, his bearlike frame even bulkier than usual in his black mohair overcoat. Standing too close to Ellen, looming over her, his breath steaming in the cold air, "You'll never make it up here on the Hill," he murmured. "You'll be ripped apart." Baring teeth like tombstones— with everyone else too far back to hear what he said, probably thinking what a great guy he was, so smilingly gracious in defeat—he added, "You know you only got elected because that son of a bitch husband of yours died at just the right time!"

Ellen had recoiled from his invasive presence, and for a moment, stunned and sickened, she almost lost her balance on the icy steps.

Then, suddenly, she felt her head clear of doubt and fill with a new resolve. She clenched her teeth, and her gloved hands formed fists inside her pockets. I won't let him do this to me, she swore silently. He will *not* undermine me. I can do this job.

Early the following morning, her first day, she had walked into her Senate office—which had been Satcher's office—and rid herself of every last vestige and echo of the man. She'd ordered new paint (light and sunny yellow), new carpet, new furniture, and lots of plants. She hung dozens of photographs: of herself and Josh as students; their wedding in a hillside spring garden; herself unusually elegant for her Senate swearing-in ceremony; and her all-time favorite, Josh's framed campaign poster from 1998: JOSH FISCHER FOR SENATE, FIGHTING THE BATTLES FOR YOU!

In the end, Ellen did allow Carl Satcher a presence in her Senate office. Between two bookcases, among the autographed photographs of previous California Senators, she placed a photo of Satcher culled from her election night press files. It had obviously been taken after his less than civil concession speech, and here he did not look handsome or senatorial at all but pouchy and angry—and old.

Ellen wanted that picture on the wall to remind herself that, although he might be rich and powerful, Carl Satcher was still only a human being, albeit a mean-spirited, vindictive one, and vulnerable like all humans. She wanted to remember that he, and people like him, were out there—and that because he had lost the election, Satcher now recognized his own vulnerability, making him doubly dangerous.

★ ★ ★

Derelle was still making the case for not speaking out against Hernandez. "Don't forget a third of our constituents are Latino!"

"That may be so," Aguilera snapped in a rare display of impatience, "but don't we Latinos deserve a judge who understands our issues and will *help* us? Or at least not kill us!"

Ellen forced Carl Satcher from her mind. She traced small circles on the polished tabletop with her finger, a sign her staff recognized as meaning she wanted to move things along. "Any other thoughts?"

Aguilera reminded her, "Last week, we were talking about a filibuster."

"Too heavy." Derelle was adamant. "We can't afford it. We'd be facing a toxic situation in the Senate for months. The Childhood Protection bill is the Senator's first priority, and we could lose votes we're counting on." Looking Ellen directly in the eye, she said, "If there'd been a bill like this when I was a kid, maybe I wouldn't have ended up in that parking lot with a crowbar."

Ellen felt an urge to reach out and touch that long-fingered hand so close to her own, but restrained herself. This was no time for sentiment.

"Filibustering a Supreme Court judge will definitely send tremors through the old boys' club, that's for sure." Ellen knew her Democratic colleagues were skittish about filibusters, but she had nonetheless considered it a weapon of last resort since it would reduce the number of required "no" votes to stop Hernandez from fifty-one, the majority needed to deny confirmation, to forty-one, as Hernandez's supporters would need sixty votes to end a filibuster. It would be a bold move. There hadn't been a successful filibuster against a Supreme Court nominee in recent history, not since Abe Fortas in the sixties. Ellen exhaled and told them wishfully, "Maybe one of my colleagues will decide to take the lead on this."

Aguilera said, "So where are we?"

In the silence that followed, the buzz of the intercom sounded exceptionally loud.

"I know you said you didn't want to be disturbed," said Diane from reception, "but there's this gentleman here to see the Senator."

"Does the gentleman have a name?" Ellen asked. Diane was usually meticulous at screening visitors; she must have a good reason for the interruption.

"Greg Hunter, the writer from California," Diane said in a voice of undisguised admiration.

Greg Hunter.

The name struck Ellen with a visceral thud. Beside her, she heard Derelle's hissed intake of breath.

Greg, of all people—and now of all times.

Ellen glanced at her wall of photographs, at the one to the extreme left: Josh's graduation from U.C. Berkeley in 1974, Greg standing immediately behind him—tall, handsome Greg Hunter, Josh's college roommate and best friend. Greg, who was now Carl Satcher's man.

Ellen had chosen that particular picture of Greg—once her best friend, too—because it was the only one she'd ever seen in which he looked uncertain, and even forlorn. In another small act of revenge by photograph, Greg also existed in this room on her terms.

"Not now," Ellen told Diane over the intercom.

"He says it's really urgent."

Save me from Greg's urgent business, Ellen thought, reluctantly recalling the last time Greg had confronted her. She supposed she'd have to see him, for he wouldn't show up like this, so suddenly and at such a time, without something serious on his mind. She decided it was best to know. "Okay. Bring him in." To Aguilera and Derelle she said, "We'll continue with this later. Maybe over dinner."

Derelle was last to leave the room, her face schooled to expressionlessness, a restraint she had learned over the years. She demonstrated her disgust at Greg's person only in the quietly exaggerated precision with which, on leaving the office, she closed the door behind her.

★　★　★

Greg had barely changed in three years.

His tall body was still strong and spare, his blond hair thick and only slightly tinged with gray. The grooves that ran from each nostril to the corners of his mouth were deeper, and his light blue eyes more shadowed. He wore a well-fitted, dark gray pin-stripe suit and held a slim black leather briefcase under one arm. Diane would certainly have been impressed by his looks, as well as by his reputation.

"Well," he said admiringly, "look at you. Senator Ellen."

"Welcome to D.C." Ellen had moved back behind her huge desk and nodded him toward the winged armchair a safe distance away. "Sit down. How is it in California?"

"Gorgeous. You know how May in the Bay Area can be." For a moment a memory came back, the three of them, herself, Josh, and Greg, so young, hiking through mountain meadows among golden poppies and blue-purple lupines.

Greg held out his hand to her, and she touched his fingers very briefly but did not come out from behind her desk to welcome him with more warmth. Nor, she thought, should he expect her to.

"You're looking terrific," he said. "Power suits you."

Ellen searched for a hint of mockery, detected none, and responded with a noncommittal "thank you," thinking how much she didn't want to see him, particularly right now. Bluntly, she asked, "What do you want?"

"To give you a gift," Greg said. With no apparent effort he one-handedly dragged the heavy chair up to the desk, then set his briefcase on his knees and clicked it open.

"A gift?" she asked.

He took out a manila envelope and passed it across the desk to her. "Information."

Ellen stared into his eyes, so clear and guileless, then at the envelope in her hands, addressed: E. F. Confidential.

She slit it open with a pencil and removed a thin sheaf of papers. "What is this?"

"Look and see."

She scanned them, one by one: official documents, explicit in their record of deliberately inflicted cruelty; the first from an emergency room at the Bayshore Medical Center, Hayward, California, in June 1978:

Patient presented with a mild concussion and extensive bruising across left side of chest. Claims she fell against table. Suspected parental abuse.

From the same hospital one month later:

Bruising and swelling of third and fourth fingers of left hand; claims accidentally slammed in car door. Suspected parental abuse.

From the nurse's report at Emerson Middle School, also in Hayward, February 1979:

Extensive reddened area surrounded with numerous circular blisters on inside of right forearm.

Suspect cigarette burns, though patient refuses to explain; recommend notification of police and Social Services.

And the child in question? Ellen searched one page, silent, and thought, *Oh my God.*

For that tormented little girl was Flora Hernandez, ten years old at the time, only daughter of Frida Hernandez, the same woman who tomorrow afternoon was expected to be confirmed by the Senate as a member of the Supreme Court of the United States.

Ellen looked up, stunned. "How did you get this?"

"I can't reveal my sources, but I haven't lost my touch as a reporter."

Ellen looked directly into Greg's pale eyes. She knew too well his investigative abilities and how he could use them. "I don't understand any of this. Not just where it came from but why you're giving it to me. You know what I'll do with information like this."

Greg shrugged and shifted in his seat. "Can't it be because I feel I owe you? I felt terrible that night I had to come over to your place and tell you all that ugly stuff about Josh. But you have to believe that at the time I was doing what I thought was right, to spare you finding out about him when you read about it in the paper."

"So you said."

"I tried to tell you then how truly sorry I was, but you never gave me a chance. I left messages, e-mailed you, wrote—"

"I didn't want to talk to you. I'm sure you understand."

"—so for a while I gave up trying. But ever since, I've been looking for a way to make things up to you, as much as I possibly could. When I got hold of this information, I saw a chance and took it. Now it's yours. Use it any way you want."

Ellen responded, "And exactly where am I supposed to have gotten this information? I assume you don't want me saying it was from you."

"Correct. Say what you like: the package arrived in the mail with no return address. It was dropped on your doorstep by elves— whatever. But I'm absolutely trusting you not to mention me."

"Don't worry, I can keep secrets. Where's the daughter, Flora, now?"

"She's Doctor Flora, anthropologist, working out of the University of Colorado."

"Would she verify this?"

"I assume she would."

"Seems odd she hasn't gone public with the information before."

"Family loyalties can be irrational. You know that."

"What about the father?"

"Hernandez divorced him when Flora was five. He died in '91."

"You've been thorough."

"I'm always thorough."

"Yes, indeed," Ellen said, and thought again of the last time she saw Greg and how thorough he'd been.

He said, "I already *told* you I was sorry. What else do I have to do to convince you?"

Ellen laid the documents down on her desk and rubbed her hands against her thighs, feeling suddenly contaminated by the contents. "Thank you for bringing this to me. I'll have to think about what best to do with it."

"Of course."

"And now I'd better get back to my meeting. Come," she said, getting up and extending her hand, almost ashamed of her initial coldness. "I'll walk you to the door."

She led him through the outer office to the door and offered her cheek for a good-bye kiss. Derelle and Vic both watched as he bent his head, but they couldn't see that for a fraction of a second as his lips touched her cheek, she closed her eyes.

As he was stepping away into the marble hallway, Ellen said, half in jest, "By the way, we did sweep the place for bugs after Satcher left. I hope we didn't miss anything."

Greg's face blanched beneath the tan, then the smile returned and he gave a parting wave. As the outer door closed behind him, Ellen turned to Vic and Derelle, waiting expectantly for her report.

"Well," she declared, "as our old friend Shirley Lester used to say, we just got ourselves a brand-new ball game!"

★　★　★

9:00 P.M.

In single file, Ellen, Derelle, and Vic climbed the narrow stairway of the Hunan Dynasty restaurant, its worn linoleum and ancient, cracking plaster walls belying its role as an unofficial but important Capitol Hill hangout where, against reassuring clamor, sensitive topics could be broached and high-ranking deals go down in safety.

At the desk, beneath the faded, autographed photographs of familiar faces going back at least six administrations, they accepted the laconic greeting of the maître d' and followed him to a corner table in the back room, passing, on the way, two White House staffers, the senior Senator from Minnesota, and several powerful lobbyists. The noise was tremendous, the energy palpable, the atmosphere thick with steam and savory smells from the kitchen, where waiters yelled orders and the staff crashed pots. The waiter planted their order of orange chicken, steamed broccoli, and shrimp fried rice on the lazy Susan in the middle of the table, distributed plates, and at Ellen's request, removed the vase of plastic daffodils. He poured ice water, then tea, and left them alone.

"This is much better," said Ellen. She'd decided she needed a new environment in which to ponder Greg's unbelievable revelation. It was noisy and busy in here, but it was a blanket of white noise, not involving her personally, and a good place to plan. Besides, she had missed lunch and was very hungry, and the food here was always good so long as you insisted, at least three times, *no* MSG!

While they all filled their plates, Ellen asked, "So how do we make use of this windfall?"

Before they left to eat, Derelle and Aguilera had both examined the reports in astonished silence. Now, Aguilera said, "You'll need to go public with it, of course."

"Do I have a choice?" Ellen asked.

"Pardon my skepticism," Derelle said, "but Greg Hunter is what you might call a hostile source. He's not our best friend. Can you explain why he passed this stuff on to you?"

"He said he was trying to make it up to me for what he—for what happened when Josh died. Remorse can happen."

Derelle said, "Not to Greg Hunter."

"You've never liked him, have you?"

"You got that right. Not from the minute I met him."

"That was a long time ago."

"Makes no difference. He is what he is. And his friends are who they are, too. And we know all about *them*."

"Greg's on his own here. You didn't see his face when I suggested the office might be bugged. He was scared. No way he wants Satcher to know what he's doing."

Stubbornly, Derelle said, "You still need to check this out."

"Too bad we can't reach the abused daughter," Aguilera said.

"Yeah, there you go," agreed Derelle, who had immediately called the University of Colorado and accessed the anthropologist's voice mail. "Field studies in Venezuela until mid-July. Don't you think that's a tad too convenient?"

"Come on!" Ellen said. "Give him a break. Greg had no idea she was out of the country."

"Least that's the impression he wanted to create," Derelle countered.

"Let's look at what we've got," Aguilera suggested. "Dr. Flora's not the only source. There's this clinic in California and the school. We can check the records for ourselves."

"I'll call them in the morning, but they'll tell me the information is confidential," Derelle said.

"It'll take time," Ellen said, "and there is no time. We're talking about tomorrow *afternoon,* people. With a vote by the end of the day."

"Then call Senator Leary," Derelle said, "and have him try and delay the vote."

"I could try." Ellen thought about contacting Leary, whom she knew well from their work on the Judiciary Committee. How likely was it that he could call for, and get, a delay when the timing of the vote had been set by unanimous consent, and a vote to delay would also have to be unanimous? Any attempted change would be perceived as a last-ditch, desperate ploy by the Democrats.

"Yeah, share this with Leary," Derelle said. "At least you'd cover yourself!"

"This is what we were praying for," Vic said. "Ammunition. A smoking gun no one else has found. Finally we have a real, honest-to-God reason for blocking Hernandez. I mean, we're not exactly talking illegal nannies here."

"And if Leary won't, or can't, get the vote delayed?" Ellen asked.

"Then you just vote 'no,' and don't make waves," Derelle advised. "It's way too bad, but there's no time to check it out, and we *really* can't afford to be wrong."

Ellen picked up a piece of chicken in her chopsticks, dunked it in plum sauce, looked at it, then set it down again. Her stomach felt tight with conflict and her appetite was gone. "So much at stake, such a huge opportunity," she lamented. "I hate to waste it."

Aguilera agreed. "Imagine how we'll feel if Hernandez gets confirmed, then this information checks out as true."

"Right. Imagine how I'd feel when it came out this woman had burned and tortured her young daughter," Ellen said, "*and I'd known all along and said nothing?*"

★ ★ ★

Derelle was uncharacteristically quiet during the rest of the meal, which ended with nothing resolved.

Outside in the warm night, walking to Vic's car, she suddenly gripped Ellen's arm. "I've been thinking," she said. "Listen to me. I just get this feeling about Hernandez, watching her testify, from listening to her, from everything about her. She's not a child abuser—*and I should know, of all people!* Her politics suck, that's for sure, and she runs with the wrong crowd, but she didn't do those things to her daughter."

"But it's a feeling," Ellen said, "you don't *know*. We've been over and over this thing tonight. Get some sleep."

Ellen insisted on putting Derelle in a cab. She wanted to ride back to the office with Ellen—she had a lot more to say. But Ellen was adamant, they'd talked enough. Vic was just dropping her off and going home to Virginia.

Alone at last, the phones quiet, feeling secure under the protective eye of Big Sam, her favorite Capitol policeman at the duty desk immediately outside her door—there was a distinct advantage to working at street level, front—Ellen fixed herself a cup of coffee and carried it to the window. She looked across Constitution Avenue at the Supreme Court building, imagining Professor Frida Hernandez doing her worst in there for the next twenty years or longer, and wondered exactly what to say to Senator Leary.

Senator, it has come to my attention that . . .

I've been handed documents that appear to show . . .

Join me in going out on a political limb and . . .

Ellen shrugged away her ambivalence, picked up the phone, and called Senator Leary's personal cell phone number. When, after five rings, his voice mail message clicked in, she realized she was relieved. She hung up without leaving a message.

The truth was she didn't want to speak to him.

Ellen turned to gaze at Josh's poster on the opposite wall. Although it was in shadow, she could still pick up the points of light in his deep-set, dark eyes.

"I guess, where you are," she said aloud, "you know all the answers."

Josh returned her gaze, fond but silent, offering no advice.

Ellen thought with resignation: No Josh. No Leary. My staff in conflict.

She would have to do things her way.

CHAPTER TWO

May 2 1

MONDAY

9:00 P.M.

Greg Hunter enjoyed two vodka tonics at the bar of La Brasserie—he liked the cheery bistro on Capitol Hill and chatted desultorily with the bartender and the couple to his right, then moved outside to dine on the terrace, where the dogwood blossom was softly fragrant. He had thought of going to the Hunan Dynasty simply because it was such a hangout for the movers and shakers—how *did* a place like the Hunan Dynasty establish such a reputation?—but he didn't need all that racket and preferred eating in the open air, a treat after the invariably cool evenings of the Northern California coast.

He wandered unhurriedly through the meal—home-smoked Norwegian salmon, rare filet mignon, and a crisp Caesar salad, all accompanied by appropriate wines. What was the point of stinting? As he ate he thought about Ellen and the scalding information he'd just given her, and how, Ellen being Ellen, she would do what she thought was the right thing and make it public at once. He knew that cruelty to children was the one issue guaranteed to stab directly into her heart, and into the heart of Derelle too, who, should Ellen have any doubts, would do all in her power to encourage her.

Greg had known Ellen for almost thirty years, in all stages of being—as a crusader, college activist, too briefly as a lover, then as a politician's wife. Now there was this new Ellen, still strong, confident, and capable, but in a position of power—and still with the ability to wrench at his heart.

Damn her.

Greg called for the check. It was ten o'clock here on the East Coast, but he was still on California time. Back in San Francisco it was only seven, the evening just beginning, and with the long, excellent meal over and the meeting with Ellen uneasy on his spirit, he felt restless. What was he supposed to do now? Return to the hotel and watch TV? Sleep alone in that king-size bed?

Once he had asked Ellen, Are you ever lonely? She'd deliberately misunderstood him and said she treasured her time alone. But I wasn't talking about being alone, he'd said, I was talking about lonely.

Of course, tonight he didn't have to be on his own. A seemingly inexhaustible supply of attractive, intelligent women lived in this town, working in government departments, law firms, and embassies, and he knew all the right bars and clubs where they could be found after hours. There'd been a French undersecretary not too long ago; a tawny-haired congressional aide from Texas; and a while back a sultry Brazilian cultural attaché, though by now she would surely have moved on to London, Mexico City, or even Beijing.

But tonight he wanted to relax with someone he knew better, someone familiar. Someone who cared.

Greg pulled out his phone. He'd managed to track down the private number this afternoon, with great difficulty and only after unauthorized assistance. He remembered the first time he'd taken a chance and called this woman at her home. That had been years ago, back in California, on a night when Ellen left him high and dry.

"Micaela," Greg said when she answered, "it's me. Don't hang up."

★　★　★

On the way to her apartment in the Watergate complex, Greg stopped the cab to buy a chilled bottle of Napa Valley Chardonnay. He was looking forward to seeing Micaela again and wanted to set the right tone.

She opened the door, a tall, pale, dark-eyed woman, her blunt-cut black hair swinging shoulder length. She was wearing a peach-colored tracksuit and an expression of haughty disbelief. "I don't know why I'm doing this," Micaela said. "I must be nuts." She stepped back and let him in.

Greg strode past her into the room, carrying the wine. "Old friends, old times. We had some good ones. Remember?"

"I've tried to forget."

"I wanted to see you. I had one hell of a time getting this number from the folks at the Future Mobility Institute."

She frowned. "They know better than to give out private numbers."

"Then I'll protect the privacy of the woman I had to bribe."

"Right," snorted Micaela, unimpressed. "What're you doing in D.C.?"

"Business. I'm only here for a couple of days. Flew in this afternoon."

"Satcher business?"

"Partly. You're looking good. Very good. Must be enjoying your job, this Future Mobility outfit. Do you like it more than the research you used to do for me?"

Before answering she led him into the living room, so similar to the living room she'd had in Tiburon, another walk-away-from place, down to the oatmeal-colored wall-to-wall rug, expensive, neutral furniture, and the little balcony overlooking water, this time the Potomac rather than San Francisco Bay. So little of Micaela here, just that Mexican vase, centered on the coffee table. Was that colorful weaving of the village market scene hanging above her bed?

"Sure I enjoy it. It's a challenge," she said. She settled him on the sofa and moved about the room, stacking papers, tidying, switching off the TV. "Right now we're investigating intelligent freeway systems and what they call 'smart' environment-friendly cars—electric or hybrid—that switch into traveling mode at various speeds in commuter lanes, then coordinate with on- and off-ramps to access roads and parking systems."

"Sounds complicated. And fascinating."

"It is. I'm also researching traffic flow in the larger cities and creating a computer model. Of course nothing will begin to happen until 2010, so you don't need to sell your gasoline-guzzling, polluting Porsche quite yet. If you still have a Porsche— you probably have an SUV by now. I can make some coffee if you like. It'll have to be instant."

"Wine's great," he said. He suddenly wondered whether he should have bought a corkscrew too; it would be like Micaela not to have one. When they'd been together there had been few gadgets in her immaculate kitchen, and the only food in the refrigerator the deli sandwiches or salads he'd bring over himself. On the few occasions he'd been able to spend the night, she'd run off early in the morning to buy croissants for which there'd be no honey or jam.

Tonight Micaela was better prepared. She came back from the kitchen carrying the opened bottle in one hand and two oversize glasses in the other. She poured, sat down facing him with cool self-possession, and asked, "What do you want?"

Ellen had used the same phrase just a few hours before. "Do I have to *want* anything?" Greg asked.

"Why else would you be here?"

"Couldn't I just be thinking of you, wanting to see you after all this time to make sure you're fine?"

"You could, but it's unlikely. Come on, Greg. We were together nine years. I know you."

"Can't I even say I'm sorry?"

"For using me all those years and dumping me when you were done?"

"It was never like that. You should know better. I had no choice. I'd have lost everything I'd ever fought for; my career, my family—"

"I see you still have your priorities straight," Micaela observed tartly. "And how *are* Jane and the kids?"

"I didn't come here to talk about them."

"Ah." She waited, inscrutable and dignified, giving him time to explain himself.

"All right," Greg admitted in the face of her silent scorn, "I was wrong, back then. I admit it—I was a lousy coward. I've thought of you ever since and wished I'd had the guts to do things differently—but sometimes you have no choice but to hurt the people you love." He was thinking about what he had done to Ellen as he said this, though fortunately Micaela, clever as she was, couldn't read minds and would assume he was talking about her. He wasn't lying—just knowingly misdirecting.

"So now I want to try and make it up to you, just a little," he went on, meeting her dark, unconvinced gaze. And, sternly, "If you weren't prepared to see me and listen to me, you should have hung up when I called. And you certainly shouldn't have let me in."

"You do this so well, you're so persuasive," Micaela said. "I could almost believe you. Though I *actually* think you just felt bored and lonely and decided my company would be better than none."

"That too—though never the last part. Never. See? I'm being honest."

She had to smile then, showing bright white teeth and sudden dimples, a smile made all the more enchanting for the unexpected mischief it suggested, like a ripple of sunlight on dark water. Greg rose and held out his arms. "Come here. Let me hold you just for a moment, then I promise I'll go, and you can get back to work or whatever you were doing."

Her thick hair was slightly damp from the shower and smelled of shampoo. He touched it, ran his fingers through it, so familiar, gathering it in a thick handful and pulling her head gently back so he could look into her eyes. He felt the exact moment when her body grew languid and heavy against his arm, when he could see the softening planes of her face and the slow droop of her eyelids. He leaned into her and kissed her on the mouth. Her breath came faster, and she didn't just permit his kiss, she returned it.

He moved apart from her, holding her loosely by the upper arms, looking at her intently, aware of how he must appear to her: disheveled, breathless, longing, and silently pleading.

Micaela glared. Then she sighed and said, "Oh hell, I was lonely too."

★ ★ ★

It was as if they'd never been apart. Their bodies remembered and anticipated each nuance of touch and feeling.

Greg ran his hand lightly over the contours of her body and curved his fingers to mold her hip. "We're so good together."

"I know," she said.

"Would it be too much to ask if we could start over? You and me?"

She sighed deeply. "Way too much. Anyway, we live a whole continent apart."

"It's only five hours from San Francisco."

"And you already have a family that you'll never leave. I dreamed once, but I don't dream anymore."

"Micaela, Jane and I don't—"

"Stop it. I don't care what you and Jane don't do. It's none of my business. What I do care about is that I *don't* have a family and you'll never give me one. Please, Greg, stop saying things you don't mean and making promises you won't keep. You don't really want me, you've never *really* loved me." She spoke matter-of-factly, without anger. "You've only ever really loved one person— and that's you."

"Not true."

"Okay. Maybe Ellen Fischer."

Greg rested his head on Micaela's chest. "I need you. And this is God's own truth—you're the only person in this world I really trust, who I can talk to. You and me—we were always such a great team. I've never been together with a woman the way I have with you; not just physically but mentally, with a true meshing of the minds." He could almost feel her smile, and knew he'd scored; Micaela was proud of her intellect. He felt her soft touch as she stroked his hair, and for a moment, just one flickering insane second, he yearned to bury his face in her soft flesh and weep.

After a moment she said, "I'm not one of those women who needs to be needed. I'd rather be loved."

"It's the same thing."

"Maybe to you. But I want the kinds of things that go with love, like someone to come home to, someone who cares for me *every* day, not just now and then when he feels bored. And I want a baby—"

"We've been through all this."

"I know. You've explained over and over how when you married beautiful Jane you also married her rich father, then found yourself in bed with his pal Carl Satcher, too. And that now you can't possibly get away because those two *own* you."

Greg said slowly, "At the beginning, I had no idea what I was getting into. Now I realize I'll always owe them. And I screwed up big time."

"On account of me?" she asked.

"In part, but mostly because of Josh and Ellen. I handled it all so badly. *But how could I have known Josh would wind up dead?*"

"You couldn't, so stop beating yourself up over it. It wasn't your fault."

"But what if I hadn't gone to him that night and told him about our investigation, yours and mine, and what we'd found out. What if I hadn't told him about that woman Bianca, and about the kid. Maybe Josh would still be alive." Greg added, "I'll never forget the expression on his face."

"There's nothing you can do about it now," Micaela said sensibly. Then, puzzled, "What kid?"

"Bianca's child."

"I don't remember anything about a child."

"You weren't there. I went down to see Bianca alone, remember? And I *met* the daughter."

"*Josh's* daughter?"

"Of course she turned out to be a year or so too young, only fourteen. But she looked older. Certainly old enough to make it plausible—and she already had a baby of her own."

"Wait, let me get this straight," Micaela said carefully. "You told Josh he had a daughter?"

"Not in so many words."

"But you *implied*. You knew just what he'd think. And you never made it clear the girl *wasn't* his daughter."

"For God's sake, Micaela, that's splitting hairs. I didn't know anything for certain, we hadn't seen a birth certificate or proof of anything, one way or the other."

"Convenient."

"And we had a job to do. We had to stop Josh running for the Senate, by any means we could find."

"That's horrible. Inexcusable. Him dying that way, thinking he had a child, when it was all a lie."

"It wasn't a lie, and it wasn't my fault. I made an assumption and he made an assumption, but it turned out not to be a correct one."

"Right. My God, you're unbelievable." With a tired sigh, "At least Ellen didn't know—did she?"

"No," said Greg. "I never told her—not about the child."

"Which means you told her the rest?" Micaela demanded, shocked. "*Why?*"

Righteously angry with Micaela for not understanding, Greg explained. "Because I had to. It was for her own good. She was going to run for the Senate. Suppose she'd never known about Josh and Bianca—obviously Josh had never told her—and read about it first in the papers or saw it on the news. I was doing all I could to keep it out of the headlines, but there's a limit!" Greg's indignation now was fueled by his attempts not to admit the deeper truth, that he'd *wanted* Ellen to know Josh had been unfaithful, that he'd been hoping he might win her back.

"Poor Ellen," Micaela said.

"If it's any comfort to you," Greg said, "I've hated myself ever since."

"Good. You should."

"Believe me, it turned out wrong, but I did it for the right reasons."

"I'm not the one you have to convince." Micaela pushed his hand away and rolled onto her stomach. "And that's enough show-and-tell for one night. I need to go to sleep."

He listened to her breathing grow slow and even, and wished she'd stay awake just a bit longer. There was more he needed to say, more guilt to unload. That was really why he had come, so somebody could tell him that he had no choice this time either, none at all. "Micaela?" he whispered, "I need you to listen. It gets worse."

After a long interval, wearily, she spoke from her pillow. "How can it get worse? And who for?"

"For Ellen. She wanted to block Frida Hernandez's confirmation to the Supreme Court but didn't know how she could do it."

"You saw Ellen?"

"Earlier tonight. And I gave her a way to stop Hernandez."

"That's good," Micaela murmured. "So what's the problem?"

"I gave Ellen proof that Hernandez used to abuse her daughter. Hospital records, school records, all showing that Hernandez beat her and burned her with cigarettes."

"*What?*" Micaela struggled up on one elbow, suddenly fully alert. "That's horrible! How could that woman do that! How did you find out?"

"You remember how we used to work. I can find out anything I want. I'm good at my job."

"True. But I don't understand. You said it gets worse *for Ellen*. That doesn't make sense. Ellen will be a hero, and Satcher and your father-in-law will be royally pissed off."

"No, they won't be," said Greg. "They'll be delighted."

"I don't get it. I assume they badly want her on the Supreme Court?"

"She will be."

"But if Ellen goes public—"

"Which she will—"

"Then Hernandez will be toast. No?"

Greg said with a sigh, "It's Ellen who'll be toast. She'll be discredited and ruined. Strictly a one-termer, assuming she can finish her term."

"But Greg——"

He didn't want to talk anymore after all, it wasn't making him feel any better. And maybe he should stop spelling it all out, even for Micaela. He slid down in the bed and pulled the sheet up to his chin. "Never mind," he said. "Go back to sleep."

Micaela persisted, "You still haven't told me. *Why* will she be ruined?"

Greg knew her well enough to know that she'd never leave the topic——or him——alone until she had all the answers. He should never have opened up the subject. "Because," he confessed, looking directly at her, though not able to make out all her features in the darkness, "those documents are fake!" He added softly, engulfed in a wave of guilt and self-pity, *"That was the whole goddam point!"*

★

1974

★

CHAPTER THREE

That January evening, Ellen Downey, as usual, grabbed her clipboard with its ruled pages ready for signatures, slung her satchel over her shoulder, and prepared to take on the shadowy vastness of the United States government.

Up and down driveways and flights of steps she would go, ringing bells, smiling and greeting, informing, cajoling, urging.

"Do you know how much it costs to produce one fighter jet? Or a tank? Or a missile? Hundreds of millions of dollars! Do you know how many kids live in poverty right here in the East Bay? Over seventy thousand. How many drop out of school and end up in the system, supported by your tax dollars? Thousands, every year. Do these numbers make sense to you? Will you add *your* name to my petition to the President to cut military spending and save the children instead? Ten thousand people have signed already. Won't you join us? Please, we need you! We need people with *hearts*!"

Few people refused her—this was Berkeley on the Left Coast, after all. Really, it was a no-brainer. How could anybody, any-where, no matter what their politics, fail to empathize with that shy smile, the friendly hazel eyes, and the sudden flooding blushes? Such a formidable little figure, too, in her patched denim jacket, the purple crocheted beret crushed down on her flame-colored hair, and the huge workman's boots with the red and yellow laces.

Ellen's sociology professor, who had organized the petition drive, had said, "I wish I could clone you, you're a natural. Just look at you. Nobody could refuse somebody so—" and Ellen braced herself, dark brows already drawing together, waiting for him to say she was *cute*. She'd been so branded all her life: *that cute little redhead, that pint-sized cutie*. But *"so determined,"* Professor Edwards had said, and Ellen reminded herself once again how much she liked and admired this man.

"In fact," he went on, "with ten thousand signatures already between us all, I'm thinking we could hit twenty-five thousand before Washington's Birthday. What do you think?"

"Easy," said Ellen with complete confidence.

Though sometimes she wished it was not so easy. Sometimes she longed to test herself against more opposition. She'd make anyone sit up and listen, she'd make them care, but there were few entrenched right-wingers in Berkeley in 1974; she knew she was preaching to the choir.

Still, right now she needed the numbers—and she would get them, too.

★ ★ ★

Ellen's roommate Gloria thought she was crazy.

"Not again! All work and no play? Can't you take one night off? It's Nixon's State of the Union address. We're all going to watch."

"What for? I know exactly what that creep's going to say."

"Do you really think what you're doing will make a difference?"

"You bet it will. We've got ten thousand signatures already. Ten thousand people who *vote*, Glo!"

"That's great. But listen—we're getting Chinese food."

"So you can throw egg rolls at him?"

Gloria looked shocked. "Who'd waste an egg roll?"

"Then save one for me."

"I still think you're out of your mind! And it's going to rain!"

"See you around eight." Ellen squeezed between her desk and their battered wooden table piled high with pamphlets, flyers, and binders, along with jars of peanut butter and Hi-C powdered juice for distribution to the Children's Alliance kids. Her stuff took up way too much room in here, but Gloria was a saint, truly.

Ellen headed out the door clutching her petition.

She would not be back by eight.

★ ★ ★

Ellen had worked out a grid pattern for her routes, different each night, looping out from the campus and returning two hours later within reach of her building. After three and a half years she knew these streets like the back of her hand. It was hard to remember that they'd seemed strange and even threatening when she first arrived, a wide-eyed, innocent freshman, from her quiet little town on the East Coast.

Back then, Berkeley had been terrifying in its hugeness, and so cold and impersonal. She was always getting lost, always late, miserably homesick on weekends wandering the streets among strangers, and the atmosphere so chaotic, fraught with argument and potential violence. There seemed to be no rules and no structure, people dressed and acted exactly how they liked, they said what they wanted. No matter how hurtful, they "let it all hang out." And there were the drugs—drugs everywhere. Ellen was scared of drugs, of losing control. She was disgusted by the blackened roaches she'd be offered, crimped in a paper clip and soggy with saliva. She would accept reluctantly so as not to seem too square, try not to touch them with her lips, and only pretend to inhale.

And the things she saw.

One of her first mornings in Berkeley, venturing along Telegraph Avenue in search of coffee, she'd turned a corner and walked directly and unwittingly into a scene from urban hell.

"Fucking pigs!" screamed the woman with the lank hair and stained gypsy dress, fighting with the police over the dirty bundle she carried in her arms. Her wispily bearded companion lunged into the fray, was cracked across the knees for his pains, and screamed like an animal. The woman yelled "Motherfuckers!" and the bundle dropped to the gum-splattered sidewalk, where the rags fell away to reveal a filthy, gray-faced baby, quite naked. A little girl.

Ellen stood rooted to the spot, hands clenched, a falling, liquid sensation in her stomach. Then she started to shake. She wanted to turn and run all the way back to the dorm, climb into her bunk, pull the covers over her head, and pretend it hadn't happened, but she didn't run, she didn't dare, they might think she was involved, an accomplice even, might chase after her and hit her, too.

So she backed slowly away, swallowing the rising bile in her throat, and watched among a little crowd of jeering onlookers as the police van came and the tattered woman, the still-shrieking man, and the silent baby were taken away.

But where to? And whatever happened to the baby?

Ellen had tried to follow up, calling the police and the local hospitals, but nobody would tell her anything. Perhaps they thought she was some nut who wanted to steal the child for herself. Perhaps—dreadful thought—the poor little baby was already dead when it hit the sidewalk and had been buried some-place in an unmarked grave.

Worst of all, however, was the disappointment and shame she felt for herself. She, Ellen Downey, had stood and watched that whole degrading scene and done nothing.

Gloria, sensible, had later asked, "What could you have done?"

"I don't know. Something."

"Forget it; these things happen."

Ellen set her small, pointed chin in what Gloria would come to recognize as intractable resolution. "Then they shouldn't. Ever."

★ ★ ★

That was a defining moment, when Ellen knew how she'd spend the rest of her life—that she'd been put here on earth to save its endangered children.

After this revelation, everything else seemed to fall into place.

She began to establish herself and find her way beyond her fear and uncertainty. She started to make friends. Professor Edwards took an interest in her and invited her to work on his mentoring project in the public schools, the Children's Alliance. Soon Ellen had invitations from Edwards and his wife, Patti, for informal meals at their home in the hills, which was reassuringly cluttered with small children, other students, animals, and the original artwork of friends.

Ellen developed her own particular style, shopped for cheap colorful clothes in the thrift shops, and watched her wardrobe grow increasingly eclectic. I'm adapting, she thought triumphantly. I'm a Californian!

She also made time to sing again. Back home in Albertson, Long Island, she'd sung with a small madrigal choir; here she joined the U.C. Berkeley Chorus. "Who'd have thought a tiny thing like you had such a big instrument inside?" the director had marveled when she successfully auditioned as a booming second alto. Her sophomore year at Berkeley, Ellen sang Mozart's *Requiem* in a redwood grove, and before the winter break there was Beethoven's "Ode to Joy" from the Ninth Symphony.

And always, there were the kids. She was mentoring three of them now, Talitha, Angela, and Ramón, needy children from backgrounds that, for sheltered Ellen, had until now been unthinkable.

"This is all quite wonderful," Gloria said at one point, "but can't you squeeze a bit of fun into your life?"

"You mean men."

Blonde, popular Gloria was always surrounded by men. "You might enjoy yourself."

"I do enjoy myself. You've known me for three years, Glo. I've not exactly lived like a nun—but guys are such a complication, aren't they?" Ellen added with a sigh, "And they take up so much *time!*"

★ ★ ★

Tonight certainly began well. She collected twenty-five signatures in the first two blocks. There were a lot of people still out, but the streets quickly emptied as darkness drew in and the drizzle began, and she was back to climbing steps and ringing doorbells. She knew that some people, warm and dry and eating dinner while waiting for Nixon's address, didn't even bother to answer.

Ellen had not brought an umbrella since she hadn't wanted to field that as well as her satchel and clipboard, and she grew damp and cold. Her boots began to leak. At least she'd had the foresight to bring a plastic bag to keep the clipboard dry. She thought how it wasn't supposed to be cold in California—she neither expected it nor dressed for it and was always taken by surprise. Her bag suddenly seemed incredibly heavy, and Ellen almost wished she had stayed home after all. Her stomach rumbled. They'd damn well better have saved her some egg rolls.

She decided to cut her circuit short right after this block of Eucalyptus Avenue, a narrow, leafy little street only two blocks long, and call it quits for the night. Just two houses to go, the first a neat bungalow with darkened windows—no one home, no point wasting time there—and a looming, turreted Victorian on the corner.

Ellen took in its features with a cursory glance: flaking paint, which in daylight might be dark green or faded black; missing shingles like gapped teeth; an ornate portico with the name EUCALYPTUS HOUSE 1889 etched into the stone lintel above. It was a depressing sight and she almost passed it by as well, but then she noticed the lights glowing inside, faint but warmly rosy, and the tangle of old bikes leaning against the wall. Student housing, then. A good prospect? Maybe. And positively her last call of the night.

Ellen tugged at the antique brass bellpull and wasn't surprised when it fell out loose on its wire. She rapped sharply on the panels but her cold wet knuckles made little sound. She knocked again, harder, the door gave under her hand, and she shoved it wider and stepped inside. "Hello? Anyone home?"

No response. She found herself standing in a vast, dank hallway, dimly lit by a lone lightbulb hanging from a cord, the walls papered in decaying crimson and gold flocked wallpaper, an elaborately carved staircase sweeping up into shadow. A creepy place. Ellen imagined the gaunt, white face of Morticia from the Addams Family parting swathes of cobwebs and descending that staircase in trailing black skirts. However, beneath the staircase, immediately facing her, stood a battered table heaped with books, sweatshirts, grimy tube socks, and crumpled newspapers, reassuring signs of student life, and from somewhere in the bowels of the mansion, she now heard the murmur of a radio or TV. A man's voice. A speech? Maybe *the* speech?

Ellen tried again, "Hello there?" Her boots squishing damply on the scarred floorboards, she followed the voice down a passage lined with rock concert posters, the voice growing steadily louder, distinct and familiarly abrasive, the voice of the President of the United States, Richard Milhous Nixon.

So she wouldn't miss the State of the Union address after all. However, the closer she got and the more clearly she could hear, the more bizarre his address seemed. Maybe he was actually cracking up on national television.

"… And you gotta admit," grated Nixon, "I've been a fucking good President! See how I scared the shit out of folks about Communism? See how hard I worked to get us even deeper into Vietnam so *I* could be the one to get us out?"

Has he really gone mad? Ellen wondered. Could he be drunk?

She reached the high, arched doorway at the end of the passage and peered cautiously into what must once have been a palatial dining room.

The room was sparsely furnished with junky furniture: a sprung couch, bookshelves thrown together from planks and breeze blocks, and a small television set that wasn't even switched on. What she noticed most clearly, though, were the two young men.

The tall blond one, center stage on the frayed rug, had adopted a classic Nixon pose with shoulders hunched to his ears, chin lowered and tucked. He was half turned away and didn't see her. He wore straight-legged Levis and a white T-shirt beneath which Ellen could see the sliding muscle when he raised his arms and punched Nixon's trademark V signs into the air. As he swiveled on his high-top sneakers she glimpsed high cheekbones, flared nostrils, and light eyes beneath heavy gold brows. He didn't bear the slightest physical resemblance to Richard Nixon, but with that posture and that voice he seemed older, chunkier, and really not unlike the beleaguered President.

The other young man, lean faced, his long black hair tied back in a ponytail, sat directly facing Ellen, hands linked behind his head, bare feet resting on the cluttered coffee table.

Their eyes met. Ellen opened her mouth to speak but he moved his head very slightly to one side. Don't move, that gesture implied, don't say anything. Wait.

Ellen clung to the door handle, obediently still as a mouse. Of course she knew exactly who these guys were, how could she not, now well into her senior year, even with Berkeley so huge. They were famous. The dark one was Josh Fischer the student activist, an upcoming liberal leader, some said, whose rich, deep voice could stir the vitals and the heart. The other was Greg Hunter, aspiring journalist, who worked for the *Daily Californian* and whose name was everywhere. Josh and Greg. The best of friends—brilliant, popular, and admired. They had their own table at the Sonnet, a coffee shop on Shattuck Avenue where aspiring writers spent whole afternoons pretending they were Hemingway in Paris and where, in the evenings, would-be actors and comics tried out their material on the open mike. Josh and Greg would hold court at their table, would argue into the night with their friends and hangers-on, and Greg, so said the gossip, would eventually go home with the best-looking girl in the room.

"... Not to mention saving all of you righteous folk from that left-wing radical Humphrey and that wacko George McGovern!" Greg lowered his voice to an insinuating hiss. "So I had to push the envelope a little with Watergate. So what? Listen up, fellow loyal Americans, it was for you! *And for your country!*" He paused to wipe imaginary spittle from his chin and sweat from his brow, then made a moody circuit of the coffee table, hands clasped behind his back.

So he was not merely a good writer but a pretty good actor too. Ellen had a vague notion he'd come to Berkeley on an athletic scholarship. How unfair that so many talents should be lodged in one person.

She was suddenly overcome by an urge to sneeze. She pressed her forefinger hard against her nose, but as she tried to slip silently back through the door she once again caught Josh Fischer's eyes. With another slight motion of his head he urged her, unmistakably, to stay.

She forgot the sneeze and studied him where he sat so quietly in the shadows. She found herself thinking of an Apache warrior. An image from a long-ago poetry class slid into her mind as if tailor-made for him: *bright darkness.*

She thought how she'd always wanted to meet him, but she was an English major with a minor in Psych, while he was Poli Sci. They'd never been in the same classes, and their paths had never crossed. Now, however, fate had delivered her onto his doorstep, into his very living room. And thrown Greg Hunter in, too, for good measure.

"And so I say to you war-protesting lefties—you, ma'am, yes, and you too, sir, you and all your radical Commie pinko friends— you'll remember when it's too late how I tried to protect the silent majority from the likes of you!" Greg spun around, arms raised, shoulders hunched up to his ears, again the double victory sign, and roared, "MAY GOD BLESS AMERICA!" He then lowered his arms, dropped his shoulders, and lifted his chin. "How about that?" he said to Josh. "Nailed him pretty good, don't you think?"

"We've got company," Josh Fischer said.

Greg turned and saw Ellen for the first time. "So we do."

"Hi, I'm Ellen Downey." She made a self-conscious little wave of her hand. "Sorry about just walking in, but nobody heard me knock and the door was open."

"So long as they're cute, anybody can walk in!" Greg was looking at her with practiced appraisal. As if I was a piece of steak, Ellen thought. Greg's head slightly tilted to one side, his full mouth curved in what seemed a patronizing smirk. She thought it too bad he was so good-looking. She was annoyed with herself for finding him attractive, and even more so to feel the red heat flood her neck all the way up to her ears and wash across her cheeks. To be called *cute.* And then blush! Damn and hell!

She drew a sharp breath and raised her chin in challenge but Josh stepped smoothly into the breach. "Hi, Ellen. I'm Josh Fischer, and this is Greg Hunter. Were you looking for someone?"

"No. I'm—"

"Selling something?" Greg took the petition from her hand and flicked his thumbnail at it dismissively. "What is this? Some kind of Jehovah's Witness stuff?"

"It certainly is not." Ellen explained with dignity, "It's a petition. I'm from the Children's Alliance." When neither Josh nor Greg reacted she added, "That's an outreach program my sociology professor started. Do you know Professor Edwards? It's designed to save at-risk kids *before* they get in trouble, pairing them with students as mentors."

"So there you are," Josh told Greg, "you should have more respect. She's out pounding the pavement doing good works while you just hang out at home dissing the President."

"I do it well though, don't I!" Greg turned to Ellen. "Did you catch the whole thing? What d'you think?"

He was so eager for approval, like a little boy, that she found herself smiling and nodding despite herself. "You got his voice, his mannerisms, everything. You really got into his head. I thought it *was* Nixon till I saw the TV wasn't on."

"He's practicing his act for the Sonnet," Josh explained.

"I thought he was a journalist," Ellen said, realizing too late that she was betraying how much she already knew about him.

"Of course he is; he'll be the biggest muckraker of all time one day. Woodward and Bernstein beware."

"And Josh here plans to be President and change the world," said Greg. "He'll banish corruption, and truth and justice will prevail."

"If he wants to be a politician," Ellen said, "shouldn't *he* be the one practicing his acting skills?"

"Good point, Miss Ellen, otherwise, how can he fool *all* the people *all* the time?"

Josh sighed with exasperation. "Hey! Nobody can do that, not even Nixon. He was digging his own grave perfectly well without Woodward and Bernstein."

"Anyway," said Greg, "Josh doesn't need to act. He'll make it all the way to the top with his platform of Mr. Really Nice

Guy. Mister Clean. No attacking. Makes you wonder what he's been smoking."

Josh reached for his cigarettes. "Parliaments. Just Parliaments."

"What did I tell you? He even smokes politics! It's pathetic—and he's the last person who should jump into the arena. No killer instinct."

Josh sprawled back in his battered armchair looking resigned and mildly amused. "Ignore him, Ellen. What does he know? Tell us more about your petition."

"My petition. Right. We're trying to stop the government from spending so much on the military and have them direct it to where it's needed, to the kids. We're giving the petition to Congressman Dellums to hand to Nixon personally."

Josh took a long drag and blew smoke. "Your timing isn't that great. Nixon has problems of his own. Better wait till the next administration."

"Do you *really* think he'll resign?" Ellen asked.

Josh checked his watch. "Maybe he already did."

Ellen glanced at the blank TV. "Shouldn't you be watching, then, to find out?"

"It's busted. Again," Greg said. He thumped a fist on the walnut veneer top. "But he better not have, not tonight, or I'll have to rewrite my skit."

Ellen pulled her clipboard from its plastic bag and stifled another sneeze.

Josh leaned forward to take the clipboard. "Hey—your fingers are cold!" He touched her sleeve. "And you're all wet."

"It's raining out."

"Then stay awhile," Josh said, "we'll light a fire. Stay for supper."

"We were planning on pizza," Greg said, pushing Josh's feet off the coffee table. He pawed through the clutter and dug up a take-out menu. "Listen, I'm hungry as hell. Where's the damn phone?"

Ellen felt a glow of pleasure thinking about eating pizza with these two. How impressed Gloria would be—"You sneaky devil!" she'd cry. "And me thinking you were just out there working your butt off for the cause!" Though of course Ellen shouldn't stay,

Josh was only asking her to be polite, and she really ought to go home and change her wet clothes. Her delayed sneeze finally escaped, a real honker, and Ellen groped for Kleenex in her bag. How could Greg walk around in just a T-shirt? Perhaps guys had naturally thicker blood.

"Thank you," she said, "but I have plans."

"What plans?" Greg demanded. "A hot date?"

"Dinner with my roommate. I'm not dating right now."

"Why not?"

"None of your business," snapped Josh. "She doesn't have to tell you anything and don't start practicing your investigative reporting techniques on her."

Ellen said, "It's okay, it's not exactly a secret. I just don't have time. I'm not planning on seeing anyone, like for a date, till I get all my signatures."

Greg looked up from the pizza menu and nodded understandingly. "We had the same kind of idea, no sex until Nixon resigns. But when we thought about it, it seemed like cutting off our noses to spite our face."

"And when you think about it," Ellen suggested pointedly, "a date and sex aren't necessarily synonymous."

"Of course they're not," Josh agreed. "But you're through with petitions for tonight, for sure. Look, Greg and I will both sign it for you. There—two more. So do us a favor now and eat with us. Think of it as business."

"Spoken like a true politician," Greg said.

"Take your coat off and I'll go find you a sweater. It's cold in here. Hunter, how about that fire? Start burning garbage."

"Yes, *sir*. Fire coming right up!" Greg bundled up a pile of papers and hurled them into the fireplace, tossing in old fast-food containers, paper cups, and crumpled copies of the *Berkeley Barb*. A wavering flame appeared, and prodigious amounts of smoke. Greg picked up the menu again and dialed the phone. "Olives, anchovies, fifty kinds of cheese, mushrooms, whatever you've got. Yeah, super deluxe sounds about right—and hurry! 197 Eucalyptus, don't bother ringing the bell, it's busted. Walk right on in." He turned to look directly at Ellen and said, "People do it all the time."

Josh returned with three cans of beer, a navy Cal sweatshirt, and a pair of clean white socks that reached to Ellen's knees.

She felt much better with warm, dry feet, and quite adventurous as she sipped her beer. Such cool guys, both of them. Josh so sensitive, intense, and caring; Greg so talented and good-looking. Of course he was also cocky, cynical, and far too used to women fawning over him—though she, Ellen, had no intention of joining their ranks.

She thought how Gloria would be proud of her. She could have run away from fun, but she hadn't!

CHAPTER FOUR

When the pizza was a memory and its box partly incinerated on their makeshift fire, which wasn't the greatest success though the burning wax on the box produced some cool blue and green flames, they took this Ellen Downey—strange, pixieish little thing, all hair and attitude—to the Sonnet with them.

The Sonnet was a good place with its hatch-cover tabletops and mismatched chairs, hubcaps for ashtrays—a lot of serious smokers here, the shoulder-high haze not just cigarette smoke and smelling quite fragrant. Weird paintings and psychedelic posters covered the walls, all for sale though nobody ever bought them, except maybe tourists.

Their favorite table was close enough to the mike so they could listen to the performers if they wanted, but not so close that they couldn't talk. Tonight they arrived late, and there was barely enough space left. Somebody passed an extra stool over the tops of heads, and Josh set it down for Ellen while Greg squeezed through the mob to grab three cappuccinos and give his name to the MC. He found out he'd be on about ten-thirty, number five, right after the wigged-out old hippie Avatar. That was great because Avatar's poetry truly sucked and he'd be an easy act to follow although, frankly, Greg knew his own Nixon imitation, the night of the State of the Union address, would bring down the house.

Returning to the table, he was snagged by a pretty, blonde drama major he'd been flirting with for over a week, who reached up to ruffle her hand across his crew cut: "Hey, dearheart! How's my Marine?" She was looking sensational tonight in a clinging black turtleneck and tight jeans, her long hair ironed straight, blue eyes huge behind round, tinted glasses. What was her name? Jan? Janet?

"Hey!" he said, flashing her a broad smile. "Later!"

She nodded. She tried to be cool about it but couldn't quite suppress her eagerness. She wasn't the only girl who approached him, either. The moment Greg sat down again Allie McLaren was leaning over his shoulder in a loamy waft of bodily odors mingled with patchouli oil. She, too, stroked his hair, as if it were cat's fur, then her hands were gripping his shoulders, thumbs familiarly kneading the muscles in his back.

Allie was a big girl, with a strong body and appetites to match. Not bad looking, either, though Greg knew without turning that her fingernails would be dirty, and her eyes fierce under her unplucked brows. She lowered her mouth level with his ear. "You said you'd call!" He reached up to pat her tousled head. "Sure I did, and I will too." Two tables away he watched as beautiful Jane—Jane *Hecht*—flipped her blonde bangs and pouted at him through the smoke.

Greg angled a quick glance at Ellen to see how much she had noticed and if she was impressed, but she was talking earnestly with Josh and wasn't watching. God, she was tiny. Josh was by no stretch of the imagination large, but his sweatshirt enveloped her like a tent.

Idly, Greg wondered what her body was like underneath.

★ ★ ★

The days and weeks went by, however, and Greg didn't attempt to try his luck with Ellen Downey.

She simply wasn't his type, too much the waif with her big eyes, Little Orphan Annie hair, and funky clothes—too serious, too principled, and too political.

If Greg tried to describe his own ideal woman, she would be a combination of Jacqueline Kennedy Onassis and Princess Grace with a dash of Farrah Fawcett. In other words, movie star looks, class, money (as much as possible), with a little spice and sex thrown in for good measure. Brains in a woman had never been a priority for Greg, nor had a passionate commitment to causes. He was bored by earnestness, eccentric clothes, hairy armpits, and natural body smells. At least Ellen always smelled like baby powder, shampoo, and good, plain animal warmth. Just as well, because she seemed to be around a great deal these days, when she wasn't pestering her young charges to get their asses to school and learn to read, or berating their deadbeat parents for not feeding them vegetables.

He had to admire her passion, he admitted to himself.

Ellen would perch on their worn sofa, eyes blazing, hair almost standing on end with frustration. "I checked out three stores in the neighborhood, and they *all* sold fruit! So what if it's a bit bruised, it's still cheap and nutritious." Pounding a small fist on her knee, "Why *not* give Angela a banana for breakfast instead of potato chips?" Or, "How can Ramón be expected to lead a successful adult life if he can't fill out an employment form, figure out prices in a store, or read a damn road sign?"

Josh's compassion and indignation would be immediate. Greg, however, couldn't help but consider young Angela or Ramón, most likely with a single mother on welfare and a father on drugs or in prison, and think of who was paying for all those social programs and safety nets. Greg's own dad and other hard-working people, that's who.

One night, at least, they'd been treated to a real success story. Eleven-year-old Talitha, Ellen's greatest challenge and admitted favorite, was finally learning to read. It wasn't so easy to find books with black children in them for her to relate to, but Ellen said she was having some luck with the Babar series. "*Everyone* can relate to little elephants, even if they *are* French!" she said. "Do you know, she's never even *seen* an elephant?"

Wasting no time, Ellen had taken Talitha to the zoo the next day to show her one. And a giraffe, too, a zebra, and polar bears because Talitha had never seen those, either. Isn't that just great, thought Greg. Lyndon Johnson's Great Society turns out to be all about a trip to the zoo.

He maintained his silence though, even if it sometimes meant biting his tongue. In Berkeley, just a hint of such subversive thoughts was an open invitation to contempt and social ostracism. Greg guessed that free speech was okay so long as it was Far Left and radical—in which case, how could it be free? He wrote an article to that effect for the *Daily Californian,* where he worked three afternoons and two evenings a week as an editorial assistant, but he didn't submit it. They wouldn't publish it anyway. Maybe he was a coward, but for now Greg couldn't allow himself to be perceived as sympathetic to the hated Establishment. He desperately needed his job. Although the money sucked, it was a whole lot better than washing dishes at a sorority house, and it would provide—at the very least—something relevant for his resume. Berkeley not only possessed a first-rate school of journalism but was the place where major news stories were continually breaking: the Black Panthers, the Symbionese Liberation Army, and now the kidnapping of Patty Hearst, with the eyes of the world witnessing live on-screen every night the mob hysteria, the floodlit trucks, and the forklifts unloading six million dollars worth of free food paid for by Patty's father.

No, he'd keep his mouth shut.

The only compromise he refused to make was in his personal hygiene and his style of dress. It was ironic how his plain T-shirts, clean jeans or chinos, and the buzz cut he insisted on sporting seemed to act as a magnet to women, though not necessarily the clean-cut beauties he admired.

Ellen seemed neither to notice nor to care.

Yes, back to Ellen. What was it about her anyway, he wondered. Her smile? Her fury at those involuntary and ludicrous blushes? That occasional, surprising laugh she sometimes let out, the wonderful belly rumble of a much larger woman?

Greg couldn't explain it but he liked having Ellen around. She wasn't only about preachiness and causes, she was a good listener and seemed genuinely to care about people, not just her welfare waifs but her friends, too. Even though she'd once accused Greg of being a male chauvinist pig, she'd also said she admired him, and for all the right reasons: for being the first person in his family to go to college, for earning a scholarship (even if it had been for swimming), for having ambition. She believed in him. "One of these days you'll be a household name," she'd said. "People will read the latest fast-breaking news over their morning coffee, scooped by Greg Hunter. You'll probably win the Pulitzer Prize! Why not?"

No, it wasn't so hard being around someone like that. He found himself increasingly warmed by Ellen, and for probably the first time in his life enjoying the company of a girl he didn't find particularly sexy and for whom he had no seduction plans—not, of course, that she'd put out even if he did, she just wasn't like that, and that was okay with him because he didn't want to find Ellen sexy. It was pleasant and restful having her just be a friend, someone he need not try to impress. Greg realized he had never had a girl *friend,* not since he was a little kid, unless you counted Ginny—but a sister was different.

Best of all he could talk to Ellen. *Really* talk.

Having barely noticed her for almost four years, now he'd find himself running into Ellen all around campus, in the library, in a bookstore, or a coffeehouse. In the evening she'd sometimes stop at their place on her way home. Josh was often out at night, busy with his student-faculty committees, seminars, and peace rallies. He volunteered for Congresswoman Shirley Lester, a major voice in the black community. He also attended study groups led by his mentor Professor Wolf, only fifty but stricken with cancer and looking much older, who still taught a handful of students at his home way up on Grizzly Peak Boulevard.

★　★　★

Josh was out one particularly dank, drizzling night in March when Greg was back early from the *Daily Cal* and Ellen dropped by after a Children's Alliance session. On impulse Greg suggested they go see *Young Frankenstein* on University Avenue.

"Great idea," Ellen responded. "It's supposed to be a riot. I love horror movies too."

"So do I. Always have. My brother used to sneak me in when I was a kid ..."

"I never knew you had a brother. You don't talk much about your family. What's his name?"

"Tim."

"Older? Younger?"

"Older."

"Tell me about him."

And that's when it began, in the privacy of the dark and the rain and the sheltered confines of a big black umbrella, when Greg found himself talking about his brother as he never had before, to anyone.

"The way I best remember him was maybe ten years ago, Halloween, on a night just like tonight. Not so wet, maybe ..."

Greg could see them now, the tall, rangy eighteen-year-old and the small figure at his side who sometimes broke ranks and gave an exuberant little skip before he remembered he was with his big brother and should act dignified. The streetlights glowed fuzzily through the mist, the air was tinged with wood smoke, and his young self walked proudly beside big Tim, blond and crew cut with the wide, bright smile, Tim who could have all the dates he wanted but had chosen instead to treat his little brother to a movie.

There they went, crossing the chilly park in the twilight toward the Alhambra Theater with its marquee proclaiming, in large black letters on glowing white, the special double bill:

IT ROSE FROM THE DEAD

THE THING

Ginny had said Greg was too young for that kind of stuff, he'd have nightmares, but Tim said baloney, the kid wasn't a baby. They stood in line for tickets, entered the red and gold lobby, got Cokes and a jumbo-size tub of popcorn. They found seats in the dark and swung backward to stare at the glittering stars on the ceiling while the credits unrolled against deliciously creepy music, the mist rose from the grave, and the mouldering undead *thing* clawed its way from the coffin—Yiiiii!

Young Greg knew that alone or with one of his own friends he would have been scared shitless, but he couldn't be afraid with Tim right there beside him, grinning and teasing, Hey, little bro, you scared yet? And him going, Nah! This is nothing! And Tim going, There's my man! But he'd taken Tim's hand anyway, such a hard, big, warm hand. Tim worked construction in the summers, and his shoulders bulked reassuringly wide under his new leather jacket. Big Tim could fight off any old vampire or monster. Timmy was indestructible. Timmy would keep him safe.

"When he graduated high school the next June," Greg told Ellen, "he enlisted and got sent right off to Vietnam. I hated him leaving, I knew how much I'd miss him. But Dad told me not to be selfish, he said the country needed Tim to keep us safe from the Commies. And Tim told me, 'Hey, it's not like it's forever!'"

Ellen said, "I've never known someone who actually volunteered."

"Well, see, Tim believed in the war. We'd been brought up that way, God and Country and Honor and all that. Dad was a Marine, Iwo Jima, Medal of Honor and Purple Heart, and Tim was a chip off the old block. He'd do his hitch in the military, marry his girlfriend, and go into the family business—Hunter's Hardware. Dad started it in 1946 on the GI bill, and Tim was planning on taking over when Dad retired."

Greg and Ellen had reached the theater, bought Cokes and popcorn, his treat, and now were squeezing past knees, searching for seats in the crowded dark while on-screen, lightning ripped the night sky behind the jagged castle battlements.

As with Timmy, Greg found himself reaching for Ellen's hand. It was small and warm and tender boned, and he'd have held it through the whole movie if she hadn't withdrawn it almost at once.

After *Young Frankenstein* they went to the Sonnet. The usual crowd was there, including Jane Hecht, the girl Greg had been seeing for a month and with whom, he suddenly remembered, he'd made a tentative date for tonight. Damn.

Avatar, in dirty smock and jangling necklaces, thrust his way to the podium, smoothed his smudgily mimeographed sheet of poetry, and launched into a crappy poem about mothers:

> In your eyes I see the love,
> The love I learned as I suckled
> On the breast of life,
> The sweetness of the milk
> A fond memory as I search my mind
> For those times and those days that I must replace. . . .
> Now that I have seen the ugliness—
> THE DARK AND PUTRID UGLINESS!

When he was done, the poet explained that the poem wasn't about mothers at all but the Pentagon Papers.

"Oh for crissakes!" Greg sighed and towed Ellen to a far corner and a tiny, secluded table under which their knees bumped together. "My mother died when I was six," he said. "I hardly remember her—at least, not holding me or anything. There were photos, but she didn't look real, all stiff and posed like a store-window mannequin."

Ellen said, "At least you had your dad and your sister. And Timmy."

"For a while."

"What happened?" She realized Greg had said, *The way I best remember him.* "He *did* come back from Vietnam, didn't he?"

"Sure. In a body bag."

Her eyes were wide with distress. "Oh, Greg. I'm so sorry."

"He had a great funeral, though, lots of flowers, the flag and his medals on top of the coffin, and a nice little piece in the paper." Greg heard his voice grow harsh and bitter as he remembered. "People came back to the house afterward. They brought so many casseroles Ginny didn't have to cook for a week." His eyes were burning now, goddam, after all these years he was going to cry. Real men didn't cry—he'd heard that often enough, for long enough—but he had the feeling it wouldn't be an embarrassment to cry in front of Ellen.

She asked, "Do you have a picture of him?"

"Sure." Greg certainly had a picture. Of course there were lots of photos of the adored older son, albums full of them. On Sundays after church the Old Marine would flip the pages and gaze at Tim stalwart in football jersey and helmet; Tim wearing shades and zinc oxide, perched on his lifeguard chair at the lake; Tim burr-headed in uniform the day he shipped out.

"This is the last picture ever taken of him, far as I know." Greg slid it carefully from his wallet: Tim in that place Greg could never follow—as much a state of mind, he thought sometimes, as a spot on a map—Vietnam.

Ellen gazed down at the picture of young Timothy Hunter, in jungle camouflage with cutoff sleeves, red bandanna knotted around his blond head, and his best bud Marco beside him, very dark and mustached.

"Dad hated that picture," said Greg. "He said Tim looked like some kind of sloppy hippie, not a soldier. And Dad didn't like the way he and Marco had their arms wrapped around each other, either. He said if he didn't know better he'd have thought they were drunk or stoned or sweet on each other. He didn't want to remember Tim that way."

"I think Tim's really handsome," said Ellen. She looked up. "You're a lot like him."

"Do you think so?" Personally, Greg thought that wild, dirty face in the picture bore scant resemblance to the brother he remembered and idolized, but if Ellen thought Tim was handsome, fine.

Before Ellen could reply, Jane was standing at his side. "Hey, don't forget we were supposed to get together tonight. You stand me up and you're out of my life," she said with a half-threatening smile.

Greg smiled back but sighed inwardly, finding himself, for one of the few times in his life, not so interested in sex. Even though the sex would be amazing. Jane, who had a rich and indulgent father, lived up the hill in a grand apartment furnished with family antiques rather than Salvation Army castoffs, including a canopied, king-size bed, upon which they'd cavort for hours. She was adventurous, very uninhibited in that bed.

Years ago, dragging young Greg to a children's party he didn't want to go to, Ginny would promise, "You'll enjoy it when you get there," and of course she'd be right. Tonight, he didn't want to party with Jane but would much prefer to stay here talking with Ellen. He wanted to explain how something inside his dad just seized up after Tim died, how instead of valuing Greg all the more he'd turned against him and didn't want him around anymore.

But Ellen, perfectly amenable to stepping aside, was already gathering up her stuff. "No problem," she told Jane cheerfully. "It's time I got home anyhow. I'd no idea it was so late. See you, Greg. Thanks for the movie!" And then she was out the door with a cheery wave and not a backward glance, a small sturdy figure in a bright yellow rain poncho and purple knitted cap.

Greg went home with Jane and, as in the old days with Ginny, enjoyed the party after all.

★ ★ ★

From that time on, he let his relationship with Jane dwindle. She wasn't happy about it, in fact she was furious, but he didn't feel guilty; a girl with her looks and wealth would hardly lack for consolation.

Greg, Josh, and Ellen became an established threesome, three friends, without a fourth because a fourth automatically meant two couples, complications, and a sexually charged atmosphere, which was not what they wanted. Why should he or Josh bring along a date when there was Ellen? Who needed Jane Hecht or, God forbid, Allie McLaren? Greg had never guessed one could have fun with a girl without sex, but it was so. Ellen Downey was their friend, *his* friend—he could be himself with no acting required; he could say anything, anything at all.

For probably the first time in his life, in those few weeks before finals and graduation, Greg was truly, innocently happy. It was a magical time when the three of them caught the rainbow, found the pot of gold beneath it, and managed to forget how easily and swiftly that fairy gold could slip away.

One glorious April Sunday they hiked the trails on Mount Tamalpais through drifts of purple lupine, the spring sun in their faces, and the Pacific Ocean stretching below them in a wrinkled sheet of silver blue. Greg declared that when he was a famous journalist with a Pulitzer under his belt he'd definitely have a house overlooking the water. Josh called derisively back over his shoulder to forget it, he might become famous but never rich, it was newspaper *owners* who got the ocean views.

Josh was in the lead, trail map in hand, their lunch sandwiches in his blue backpack; Ellen came next, wearing a yellow T-shirt and Levi cutoffs, her back ramrod straight and her freckled calves surprisingly muscular; Greg brought up the rear, happy to watch the lithe swing of her bottom and the sturdy pumping of her legs. She was humming, she hummed when she was happy, and snatches of song floated back to him on the breeze:

> I like to go a-wandering along the mountain track
> and as I go I like to sing, my knapsack on my back!

Then she switched to another of her favorites—about the trout and the angler—which she said was by an Austrian composer, Franz Schubert. It was classical, but it was catchy, and an easy walking tune.

Greg hummed along with her, and Ellen told him he had a good sense of rhythm and ought to learn more about music.

"Where I grew up it was all about Lawrence Welk, Liberace, and *American Bandstand*," he said. "We didn't trust culture."

"I bet you have a real good singing voice, too," she said, and hummed a snatch of something he actually recognized—*Dah—di dah—di dah di dah di DAH*—and told him to sing it back to her. He must have done an okay job because she told him he was a baritone and had perfect pitch—the piece was called *Eine Kleine Nachtmusik,* by Mozart.

He felt proud of himself. To think he'd sung Mozart!

Greg and Josh heard Ellen's choir perform something called *Carmina Burana* a few weeks later at the May Day celebration at the Greek Theater on campus, on a chilly and very un-May-like evening of swirling fog. They stamped their feet to try to keep warm, and shared a Coke laced with rum. Greg thought he'd die of cold long before the end, but it was great watching Ellen in the front row of the alto section, trying to catch her eye and make her laugh. All the girls wore long black skirts and white blouses. He had no idea she owned an outfit like that, sort of nun-like, dignified, and it sure set off her hair.

Carmina Burana was a very weird piece altogether, a collection of old songs about the wheel of fortune, drunken monks, and a swan getting roasted alive, though it was apparently really all about sex, Josh explained, and when the soprano voices soared up extra high toward the end, that was the climax.

Greg supposed there were all kinds of ways to get turned on.

★ ★ ★

Throughout that beautiful spring before graduation, in what was really one long, fragmented conversation, he and Ellen talked. Or, to be honest, he talked and she listened.

Sometimes she asked questions.

"Are you thinking of heading home this summer?" They were sitting together under the redwoods, beside the small creek that ran through the campus. Ellen was wearing a dress for a change, crinkly cotton with a design of rust-colored pagodas on midnight blue. It reached almost to her crimson ankle socks and husky workman's boots. On anyone but Ellen, Greg guessed the outfit would look bizarre.

He replied, "Not if I can help it."

"You don't go home much, do you?"

"I don't even have a room anymore. He turned it into a storeroom as soon as I left."

"He?"

"The Old Marine. My dad. Not Tim's room, though. That's not a storeroom, it's more like a shrine—hell, it *is* a shrine!"

He explained how Tim's room was unchanged since the day he had left for Vietnam—the same sporting trophies on the walls, the pennants, and the Raquel Welch poster over the bed. There weren't many books. Tim hadn't been a great reader. The posthumous medals were displayed in a glass-topped case in the front parlor.

"How do you deal with holidays, then?" Ellen asked.

"Summers I find work here, other times I go to Josh's house." Greg described his first Thanksgiving as a Berkeley student, a freshman barely eighteen years old, when Josh had invited him down to his home in Glendale. "I thought I'd died and gone to heaven. Can you imagine, turkey beside the pool in November. Sun and palm trees. Mom and Dad, Josh, and two cute little sisters, and all so goddam *nice* to each other, how a family ought to be, like Norman Rockwell in Southern Cal. I thought I'd kill to be Josh."

Ellen stretched her legs and considered the toes of her boots. "Nothing's perfect, you know. I love my parents to death and they love me but sometimes I wish they didn't love me so much. They're proud of me for being independent and going to school in California, but really they can't wait for me to come back home, settle down, and marry someone like the local dentist, like my sister Ruth did."

Suddenly anxious, Greg asked, "Is that what you'll do?"

"I couldn't. Not anymore." Then she mused, "I suppose people want their kids to be like them and live the same kind of lives. Our parents aren't so different; your father just doesn't understand how you feel. I'll bet secretly he's terribly proud of you for being the first in the family to go to college."

"Then you'd lose your bet. He doesn't trust college. College is for elitist jerks who don't know how to do an honest job, where they sit on their butts and talk too much. It's a waste of time and money. It's working stiffs like him, and his father before him who landed with just the shirt on his back, who are the salt of the earth and have made America great. He says what's good enough for him—and for Timmy—ought to be good enough for me. But it's not. No way! I don't want to be my father, living in the same crappy little house for thirty years, selling nails by the pound, paying my taxes, doing what I'm told because I have no choice."

"You wouldn't tell him that, though."

"Not in so many words. But I did try and tell him that if Tim had gone to college he'd have got a deferment and maybe wouldn't have gone to Vietnam in the first place and he'd be alive today."

"What did he say then?"

"Wouldn't listen. Just said how Tim had done his proper duty and died a hero and a real American, and for me to say he shouldn't have gone meant I was no better than those pinko radicals who're bleeding the country dry."

"Oh, Greg."

"I've tried to explain how I'm going to college for Tim, to make it up to him, to kick ass for him. I told him how I'm going to be a journalist because the press is knowledge and power, that you have even more power than the politicians, you can make or break them—look how Woodward and Bernstein just proved nobody's above the law! But Dad thinks of me as some kind of traitor, says how I'm scorning his values and everything he's ever stood for. He hates my guts."

"Don't give up on him. He's a sad, angry, lonely old man. And I bet deep down he's proud of you even if he can't admit it." Then she stood, moved behind him, and began to knead his back with small, strong fingers, massaging the tension from his shoulders and on down his back, so comforting. "Is he coming out for graduation?"

"Are you kidding?"

"Have you even asked him?"

When Greg didn't reply she abruptly stopped the massage, swatted him crossly on the head, and wheeled to face him again. She held him by the shoulders and glared fiercely into his eyes. "You are so stubborn, Hunter! Honest to God, I bet the two of you are exactly alike. Send him an invitation. You might be surprised."

"He won't come."

"You don't know that. Ask him. Do the right thing."

To his astonishment he heard himself agreeing that yes, he would invite the Old Marine to graduation. And not only agreeing but telling Ellen, with complete sincerity, "You know, being around you makes it a whole lot easier to do the right thing."

★ ★ ★

Greg's feelings toward Ellen underwent a drastic shift the day of the picnic at Stinson Beach.

The three of them found a good spot and spread out Josh's old Navajo blanket, the one he'd bought on a family trip to the

Grand Canyon ten years before. They unpacked the hamper, took their sneakers off, and dug their feet in the cool, damp sand. They popped the beer and passed around the squashed sandwiches and the potato chips, which were mashed to flakes—they would have eaten anything, however, they were happy and together and starving. They hiked along the beach halfway to Bolinas, past the homes of gated Seadrift with their ocean-facing plate-glass windows. "That one's mine," Greg said, pointing to the grandest. They went on as far as a beached rowboat turned into a planter filled with pink geraniums, then raced each other back to the picnic site, dodging in and out of the surf, the small, cold waves splashing up to their knees. Greg seized Ellen by the shoulders and whirled her into the air. Josh caught her ankles, and they swung her back and forth like a hammock.

"Let her go on a count of three," Greg cried. "One! Two—"

Squirming in feigned distress, Ellen screamed, "NOOO! Don't you dare! That water's freezing! Put me down! You *animals*! *I hate you!*"

But when Josh gently lowered her feet, Greg didn't release her. He held her above the waves in his arms, her eyes level with his.

"You heard the lady," Josh said, laughing. "Put her down."

"Now!" demanded Ellen, with a firm edge to her voice, and Greg slowly and deliberately lowered her, sliding her small body the full length of his and holding her against him until the cold water lapped her ankles.

He held her a moment longer before releasing her, still feeling, in intimate detail, how good her body had felt against his, how *perfect*.

His feelings shocked him. He'd never thought of Ellen that way.

It was like the pictures in his long-ago childhood coloring book where, once you filled in the outlines, you'd find the tiger's face peering through the jungle leaves and wonder why you hadn't seen it before, and he knew that from now on everything would be different. He couldn't help but feel sad that a very special—unique, for him—episode in their lives was over, nor could he wait to see what would happen next.

How did Ellen feel about him?

She seemed to care for him—but no more than she cared for Josh.

And what *about* Josh? Did Ellen's touch also turn him on?

Greg followed slowly behind the two of them, watching as Ellen now and then gave a small skip to catch up to Josh's longer stride.

He studied her small, square shoulders in the familiar yellow T-shirt, her firm body, her rounded calves and slender, bare feet. He imagined peeling her clothes off and taking her, naked, into his arms.

Just a few seconds, thought Greg, and everything had changed.

★ ★ ★

But after that day at the beach, Greg barely saw Ellen as their beautiful spring was overwhelmed in the final stretch to exams and graduation, and life was reduced to a cycle of panicked study, too little sleep, and too much coffee.

For Greg, time passed in a kind of fog, and he couldn't remember much of the exam process at all, as if he'd been functioning on autopilot. He hoped he'd done well.

Then it was graduation day, a hot Saturday in late May filled with flower scents and the drone of bees, a sea of black gowns and tasseled caps. Angela Davis gave the commencement speech— trust Berkeley to engage a radical, Greg thought—and Josh Fischer did a good job as valedictorian.

Parents, families, and friends from around the country if not the whole world milled about the plaza below the Campanile, and Greg found himself moving through a sea of hugs, kisses, tears, and sounds of laughter, and *Congratulations! You did it! We're so proud!*

Here was Ellen's family, the Downeys, from Albertson, Long Island: mother, father, sister Ruth, and brother-in-law Dwayne, the dentist. Ellen's mother was small and energetic with delicate features and a light, bubbling voice like Ellen's: "Please call me Rachel, Ellen's told me so much about you, I feel I've known you forever!" Rangy, redheaded Mr. Downey was also warm and easy, saying, "Tom, my boy, just call me Tom," as he pumped Greg's hand and slapped his shoulder.

Josh's family was there from Glendale: his parents, Hans and Judith, with wide-eyed teenagers Miriam and Susan. Hans Fischer clasped both of Greg's large hands within his smaller ones, saying, "You've worked so hard. You must be proud. We're all so proud!"

"But where's your father, dear?" Judith Fischer, sweet faced and cozily plump in maroon, was gazing expectantly into the crowd as if the Old Marine would materialize at any moment, all proud smiles. Not for the world, however, would Greg admit that he had no one of his own here to watch him walk up to the podium, shake hands with the chancellor, and accept his diploma. Ginny hadn't come; she'd said she couldn't get the fare together and anyway couldn't leave the children, which he knew really meant she was afraid to come all that way by herself, not knowing what to wear or what to do in a strange place among people she didn't know. As for the Old Marine, Greg had invited him just as Ellen had said he should, but he hadn't even acknowledged the invitation.

So much for doing the right thing.

"He's around," Greg shrugged. "Probably went to the bathroom."

Josh threw him a questioning look but said nothing.

Luckily Ellen wasn't paying attention. She was clinging to her father's arm, eyes glowing, talking a mile a minute. She loved her dad. He loved her. It hurt Greg to watch, and he felt a flash of jealousy toward his friends and their casual acceptance of their easy, loving lives. His envy, just for an instant, bordered on hatred.

Rachel Downey asked Greg to take a picture of them all while he waited for his father to return, so he snapped Ellen with her family first; next, one of Josh's family; finally, at Judith's insistence, Ellen took one of Greg with both families—so he wouldn't feel left out, he figured.

"What're you doing tonight, Greg?" Rachel asked. "Big plans?"

"Of course he has," said Judith. "He and his dad have a lot to celebrate, like we all do."

Greg lied, "We're going to Spenger's Grotto. Dad likes fish."

"I hear they have great lobster," Hans said, "though I don't eat shellfish myself."

"We're absolutely having lobster, putting on those huge, crazy bibs, and getting butter up to the elbows!" Greg said. Then he made his excuses: "We're eating early; Dad has to fly home early in the morning. I better go find him, he's probably gotten lost." Though old Mr. Hunter wasn't lost, he was back in Akron, Ohio, most likely watching sports on TV.

Ellen said, "Have fun," but with a doubtful, almost sad note in her voice so Greg guessed she wasn't deceived and she felt sorry for him, which he couldn't and *wouldn't* allow.

Feigning a light-hearted wave, Greg left the Fischers and the Downeys to their happy family evening and drove into San Francisco on his clattering, oil-guzzling Yamaha, found a bar in North Beach where nobody knew him, and got drunk all by himself.

CHAPTER FIVE

All three of them spent the summer in Berkeley: Josh as a volunteer for Congresswoman Shirley Lester, up for re-election in November; Greg as an intern at the *Oakland Tribune;* and Ellen, after a break in Albertson to celebrate her birthday with her family, back with the Children's Alliance.

Josh met Ellen at the San Francisco Airport on a hot, sticky, late-June afternoon. She was one of the first passengers through the gate. It had only been a few weeks, but seeing her again, her fiery hair hanging down her back in a braid thick as a hawser, he was struck by how much he'd missed her. He almost asked if she had missed him too but dared not. With a stirring of jealousy and unrest, he wondered how much she'd missed Greg.

"Was it good to be home?" he asked safely.

"Of course. But you can't *imagine* how good it feels to be back!"

"Glad to have you back," he said, a complete understatement. "And happy birthday, yesterday!" His gift, discovered in a Mexican craft shop, was a black taffeta vest embroidered with flowers and multi-hued, long-tailed birds.

Ellen eagerly unwrapped it in the parking garage and shrieked with pleasure. "Oh Josh, you're the greatest! Thank you, *thank you!*" She flung her arms around him and kissed him and put the vest on over the stylish silk blouse that her mother must have bought for her. Ellen still seemed to consider it a point of honor never to buy new clothes.

They pulled out of the airport and turned onto 101 heading north. Ellen swiveled to face Josh, curled in her seat with her legs tucked beneath her. "Don't get me wrong. It was wonderful to spend time with them all—they're sweet and generous and I love them—but two weeks was enough. This is home now."

Josh passed the off-ramp for the Bay Bridge and Berkeley, and drove all the way through San Francisco and across the Golden Gate Bridge while Ellen told him how the family pressured her to do her graduate studies at NYU, just a forty-minute train ride away from where she grew up. She could come home for weekends and bring her laundry. It would be like old times. They'd insisted it was much safer than Berkeley. "Just imagine, thinking New York's safer than here," Ellen said, "but everything's relative, I guess, and the things you know don't frighten you so much." They'd said nothing at graduation, she explained, but they were appalled by the whole Patty Hearst saga, the shootings, the murders. Had people all gone mad out here? They were also deeply concerned that her Children's Alliance work took her so frequently into the rougher parts of Oakland. "They were so hoping I'd stay back East, at least for the summer, but I couldn't waste my time lying on the beach knowing my kids were out there on the streets. Kids don't stop being needy just because it's summer. Summer can be a vacant, dangerous time."

They were about to plunge into the rainbow tunnel on the Waldo Grade when Ellen slowed her talking enough to notice where they were. "Josh, you took the wrong bridge! Where are we going?"

"To a funeral."

"Oh, no." Ellen raised startled eyes. "Who died?"

"Professor Wolf. It's very sad, Sam wasn't that old, but he'd been sick for a while so it was no surprise. I said I'd stop by the house afterwards to pay respects. I didn't think you'd mind."

"Of course I don't mind. Do you think I'm dressed okay for a funeral if I take my vest off?"

"Leave it on, this is California."

They passed the exits to Mill Valley and Tiburon, crested a rise, and dropped back down to sea level along the bay waters at Corte Madera, where the heat enveloped them like a thermal blanket.

Ellen rolled her window down and Josh yelled above the sudden rush of hot air, "Actually, I met Greg through Professor Wolf. We were both in his freshman class, Econ 101." He sneaked a glance at Ellen, but she didn't seem to react in any significant way to the mention of Greg's name. "We hit it off right away. Unlikely, huh? We had nothing in common and he seemed so weird at first, with his short hair and those clothes. So square, it made you want to laugh. To tell you the truth, I felt protective of him. I needn't have worried, though. He somehow managed to make himself seem kind of exotic, and not square at all. At least, women thought so." He risked another glance. "He helped me out, too. He was the one who found Euc House, with a bunch of his jock friends, and got me in there. It was terrific after the dorm. And when I got to know him better, and got used to that Mr. Clean image, I found out that we saw the world in the same way most of the time."

"Do you really think so?" Ellen asked.

"Don't you?"

"I'm not sure." Ellen wound her window up. The car got too hot again, but it was a lot quieter. "I've talked with Greg quite a lot, and I have the feeling he's coming from a very different place than you. It's not so much the things he says but the way he says them. You must have heard him, you were there some of the time. When we were hiking and all."

"And the other times?"

"We'd sit around and just talk. Him and me."

Josh didn't like the sound of that but there wasn't a lot he could do about it.

Ellen went on thoughtfully, her face pink and perspiring, "It may seem like you share a belief system, but I think in his heart he's a pretty conservative guy. Take your ideas for the future. You're going into politics for the right reasons, because you want to make the world a better place, but that's certainly not why Greg wants to be a journalist. He's going into it for what he thinks he'll get out of it, like personal power. Poor Greg. He has so much, so many gifts, but in some ways he's kind of empty." She added, "And he's very angry."

It seemed as if she'd spent a lot of time talking with Greg alone—and thinking about him. Josh figured he might as well be direct, though he tried to sound casual about it. "Do you like him?"

"Of course."

"I mean, *really* like him."

"As in, are we getting it on? No way! If you want to know the truth, I feel sorry for him." Ellen went on, "His father never did show up for graduation, you know; he was only pretending they were going to dinner at Spenger's. I don't know what he actually did that night. I didn't want to ask."

"How did you know?"

"I was watching his face."

"He seemed happy enough."

"He's a good actor."

"But why would he pretend?" Josh asked. "We're friends."

"He'd have been humiliated. He couldn't have taken that. He wasn't going to invite his father," Ellen admitted, "but I persuaded him to, which made Greg think his dad might show up after all. So in a way it was my fault. I felt bad about that."

"You shouldn't have. It wasn't your fault. And I'm sure he's over it."

"I hope so. And I hope he's forgiven me. At least he thinks he fooled everybody." Then Ellen rolled the window down to a roar of air and they didn't speak of Greg again.

★　★　★

In the cemetery, on a eucalyptus knoll overlooking rolling golden hills studded with dark clumps of live oaks, Josh greeted Mrs. Wolf, then took his place with Ellen in back among the professor's other students, behind the family and close friends and the four young children who gazed, subdued, at the shiny coffin, the deep, rectangular pit, and the pile of dirt waiting beneath its cloak of Astroturf.

The ceremony was sad, but moving. In due course the coffin was lowered, Mrs. Wolf tossed in the first handful of soil, and other family members rose in succession to approach the grave. As he listened to the repeated soft thud of dirt on the coffin lid, Josh found his thoughts veering from Sam Wolf to his own father and how the two men could have been brothers. They were so similar, in age and physique (small verging on frail), profession, faint but irradicable German accent, and searing childhood memories of Nazi Europe. How sadly ironic for Sam Wolf to die at just fifty. To make up for those early years he should have been allotted a rewarding middle age that would have shaded, finally, into a contented, scholarly twilight.

Suppose it was his own father, Hans Fischer, lying in that coffin? And suppose it was he, Josh, now tossing his handful of dirt into the grave? God, he found himself praying, please, give him the time he deserves.

Josh was silent on the drive back across the bay to Berkeley, consumed by thoughtful melancholy, still silent as he coaxed his laboring old Datsun up the precipitous heights of Marin Avenue. Ellen glanced at him from time to time but said nothing, for which he was grateful.

Soon they were at the professor's house on Grizzly Peak. Josh kissed Mrs. Wolf's wan cheek and Ellen gave her a hug. They walked into the living room, where platters of food were arranged on a long table and drinks set out, then through French doors onto a shaded patio with a view across San Pablo Bay to Angel Island and the skyline of San Francisco.

A stairway of railroad trestles led down into a steeply terraced garden. Ellen and Josh sat together on the top step and gazed out over the water. "You really liked him, didn't you?" Ellen said. "You'll miss him."

Josh nodded. "At the cemetery I was thinking how unfair it is for someone like him to die so young. Which got me going about my own father, and my grandfather—and what you said about me going into politics for the right reasons."

Ellen thought that over. "When exactly *did* you decide to go into politics?"

"When I was thirteen. My father told me about my family— the whole story—the night before my bar mitzvah. It was a shock, what you'd call a defining moment."

She nodded. "I've had some of those."

Josh's mind flashed on his childhood and the loving security of a family that he'd taken for granted, never wondering why his aunts, uncles, cousins, and grandparents were all on his mother's side, except for grandmother Miriam, who had come over from Europe in 1946. She had died when he was small, and all he remembered was a gaunt old woman who never smiled, whose hand felt like a loose skin bag with sticks inside, and who'd talked with a heavy accent.

Once, though it was hard to believe, his grandmother had been robust and pretty. In a photograph of his grandparents on the living room mantel, Grandpa was square and sandy haired in an old-fashioned black frock coat, and Grandma was smiling, in matching skirt and cardigan, a straw hat with a little veil, her hands resting on the shoulders of Josh's father, ten-year-old Hans. It was 1933, in Berlin.

Josh's attention returned to what he'd been saying to Ellen. "When I'd had a chance to sort out my feelings, I realized I really didn't have a choice."

Her hazel eyes were fixed on his face. "Can you tell me about it?"

"I've never talked about it with anybody outside the family. In a way I'd rather not."

"Which also means, in a way, that you would."

"It's not a comfortable story."

"We all have emotional baggage."

For a second, in his mind, Josh saw Greg's handsome face, his pale eyes righteously angry as he shared baggage of his own with Ellen. Did Greg easily bare his soul to Ellen? "It's painful," Josh said. "And way too heavy."

"So lighten the load. I have broad shoulders."

He glanced at the small body in the fanciful vest and he almost smiled. Then Josh found himself telling her the whole story, feeling the narrative take on such a life and weight of its own that as he spoke he almost forgot she was sitting there beside him.

"My grandfather owned a little shop in Berlin," Josh began. "He sold clocks, china, and fancy glass. My father remembers it as a good life, comfortable and cultured. He was a quiet child; he liked to read and play chess. When Jewish children were thrown out of the schools, he was tutored at home, which suited him just fine. The family kept their heads down, they kept a low profile, they got by. These things had happened over and over again, through centuries; times would get better, one day the Nazis would be gone, they'd be patient and sit it out—at least that's what they told themselves, right up until Kristallnacht."

"Nineteen thirty-eight," Ellen said. "Wasn't that when it happened?"

Josh nodded. "November ninth. The night the Nazi thugs burst into the Jewish districts."

From listening to his father Josh could picture it moment by moment as clearly as if he'd been there, his grandfather's shop the perfect target with its quaint bow-fronted windows, the displays of Dresden shepherds and shepherdesses, Steubenware, and blown Venetian crystal. He could hear the splintering crash of delicate antique clocks flung into the street and the crunch of alabaster chess pieces under iron boot heels. What a nightmarish racket it would have made, what an example, how they'd have laughed as they smashed Grandpa's glasses and thrown him down in the gutter. "My father, Hans, tried to run out after him," Josh told Ellen, "but his mother dragged him back. He felt so ashamed, he told me, sixteen years old, a man already, and he'd done nothing."

Ellen shifted her position to the step below him and leaned back against his knees, guessing he'd be more comfortable telling the story if he didn't look at her. Gratefully, he ran his hands lightly up and down her arms as he watched, far out in the bay, the raked prow of a white cruise ship nose slowly into sight, headed for the open ocean—and where then? Hawaii? Mexico? Alaska?

"But your family escaped," Ellen said.

"For a little while. They were among nearly a thousand Jews who sailed from Hamburg to Cuba on the *St. Louis* in May 1939."

"I think I heard of that. I know I should have—my mother's Jewish, after all—but nobody talked about it when Ruthie and I were growing up, and it all seemed so far away and long ago. What happened to the *St. Louis*?"

"It was a German luxury liner. Their fares cost everything they had. My grandmother didn't want to leave, she thought it couldn't get any worse. But my grandfather knew better. They had been comfortably well-off. They would be destitute—but there'd always be work for someone who could fix clocks. Can you imagine how they must have felt, standing at the stern, watching everything they'd ever known fade into the distance and then drop away below the horizon, gone forever? My father remembers it as a beautiful voyage—blue sky, warm sun, good food, and everyone slowly growing happy and well and learning how to smile again—until they got to Cuba and weren't allowed to dock."

Josh fell silent, watching the cruise ship, its decks a wedding cake of rising tiers, as it slid steadily from view behind Angel Island. In five more minutes it would pass beneath the Golden Gate Bridge and its carefree journey would begin.

"I don't understand," Ellen said. "Why couldn't they dock? I mean, they were *there*."

"Bureaucracy and corruption. The *St. Louis* could off-load Jews if the ship paid $500,000—like a ransom in reverse. The ship sat outside Havana harbor for almost a week while the officials negotiated. Permission was denied. So they sailed to Florida, but the United States wouldn't let them land either, because the quota for Jewish refugees was already filled."

Ellen turned to him, shocked. "I can't believe Americans—and *Roosevelt*—would turn back a shipload of helpless people. Didn't they realize it was a death sentence?"

"It was a political decision, pure and simple. There was protest—the *New York Times* wrote a scathing editorial—but whoever cared couldn't change things. By then the ship was low on fuel and supplies, so back it went—can you imagine what *that* journey was like? The British took some of the passengers, about two hundred and fifty, the lucky ones; the rest went to the Netherlands and France, which Germany swept over soon after."

"But your family survived. I mean, your father's here."

"Yes, he survived. My grandmother too, if you call it survival." Josh remembered his father's face, and the anguished rage in his voice as he told the awful story. "The family eventually ended up in a small town outside Amsterdam. The mayor was a decent man; he arranged false papers for them and passed them off as German-speaking relatives. He helped a lot of Jews, forging documents in the basement of city hall right under the nose of the Gestapo. My grandfather worked as a handyman during the day to earn a living and for the mayor at night. Eventually, they were caught. My grandfather was shot at once."

"Oh God." Ellen turned away, pulling her braid over her shoulder and twisting the end around her finger. Josh gazed at her bared neck and tender fair skin, and felt an ache throughout his body, that such atrocity happened in the world and that, even today, were she in the wrong place at the wrong time, it could happen to her.

"The mayor wasn't so lucky—they made him an example. They said he didn't have to die, not if he turned over all the Jews he'd helped or was planning to help. 'Which are the Jews?' they yelled at him, over and over. But they couldn't beat it out of him. Even when they'd smashed all his teeth, and much worse, he'd say nothing—except how he believed in human rights, and justice.

"'Justice,' they said, 'you stupid old man, we'll give you justice!'—and they murdered him in the main square, in front of the whole town, a firing squad of eleven, laughing while they did it. The whole town had to watch, including my father and grandmother. The mayor was a true hero. He couldn't save them all but he'd saved as many as he could."

"It's a dreadful story. I don't know what to say."

"Don't even try."

"But I don't understand why your father and grandmother still came to America after what happened with the *St. Louis*."

"They never blamed the American people. The *St. Louis* decision was immoral and unjust, but the people had no say and most of them weren't even aware. When I heard the story, that's when I decided I had to make a commitment. I remember telling Dad I'd make sure that kind of thing never happened again, and Dad saying I'd have to go into politics then and get to be President, and me saying, 'Well, why not?'"

Ellen reached up and kissed his cheek. "Of course you must. You have to fight for everyone with no voice and no rights. That's what you've been put in this world to do."

"So you understand."

"Of course I do. And I want to help you—if you'll let me." With a blinding smile that caught at his heart, she said, "Sign me on, Mr. President!"

Josh had been vaguely aware of the noise level rising in the house behind them as more people arrived and the comfort of good food and drink kicked in. The door onto the steps where they sat had been opening and closing, and now someone almost tripped over them but Josh didn't notice.

He held Ellen's face between his hands and said, "Oh, don't worry, I'll let you." Josh looked into her eyes in a way he never had before, then kissed her hard and long on the lips, an enormous joy swelling inside his chest. When they finally broke apart, he said, "I love you, Ellen. I'll never love anybody else. And I think we'd make a great team. So marry me! Please!"

CHAPTER SIX

Marry him! Simultaneously thrilled and dismayed, Ellen had blushed furiously and said how it was crazy, they were way too young.

"We're not too young," Josh had said firmly, "and it's not crazy."

She begged for time.

He said she could have some time, but not too much.

"Is a week too much? A month?"

"Oh, Ell. Take all the time you need." Josh sounded distressed. "I don't want to pressure you."

In a way, Ellen would have almost preferred to be pressured, even for Josh to rush her off to Las Vegas and marry her in one of those instant wedding chapels. It had seemed so simple at Professor Wolf's house, sitting outside on the step and everything so intense and emotional. With time to reflect, Ellen wasn't nearly so sure.

She did love Josh, of course she did, yet she was still only twenty-one, there were so many things she hadn't done, places she hadn't seen. But if she let Josh go, would she ever find anybody like him again?

Ellen withdrew into herself to sort out her feelings.

She stopped dropping by Eucalyptus House and rarely socialized at the Sonnet.

Josh understood her need and didn't press her.

Greg did not understand. He would call her on the phone and waylay her around the campus. "Where've you been? What's going on? What did I do?"

"Nothing," she'd insist. "You did nothing. I just need some space," and he'd retreat, grumbling, until the next time.

Independence Day came and went. Ellen did not celebrate with Josh and Greg but instead took Talitha and Ramón to watch the fireworks from the Berkeley Marina, buying them tacos and ice cream afterward.

The days and weeks went by. What was her problem? What was she waiting for?

Ellen knew she must tell Josh *yes*. That was what she wanted above all things, wasn't it? And certainly she should tell Greg that she and Josh had an understanding—though how primly Victorian that sounded. Surely people nowadays didn't have understandings.

Mid afternoon, one day in early August, Greg approached Ellen's desk at the Children's Alliance. He planted his hands on each side of her typewriter and leaned forward, looming over her, looking very large. "You and I are going to talk. No excuses."

"Not right now," Ellen said. "I'm busy."

"When are you through here?"

"Not till five. And then I have to take a book over to Talitha's house."

"How are you getting there?"

"Bus."

"I'll give you a ride." He checked his watch. "Exactly one and a half hours from now. Be here!"

★ ★ ★

Greg was an adventurous driver, which made for a possibly too exciting motorcycle ride through Oakland to the cottage Talitha shared with her grandmother and her two young uncles. Ellen clutched Greg tightly around the middle as they wove in and out of traffic, and at times even buried her face against his back until, to her great relief, they pulled up in a cloud of dust and a series of small, popping explosions.

Outwardly nothing had changed since Ellen's first visit six months ago. The small cottage was just as drab, with its peeling paint, small parched lawn, and barred windows, while in the street, the same pair of young men, Bobby and John-Jefferson, leaned against the flank of their modified Camaro, drinking beer.

By now, they were used to Ellen, and far from the brooding insolence with which they'd first confronted her, it was all smiles and welcome.

Bobby cried, "Hey, Red! What's in the bag?"

John-Jefferson—who'd invited Ellen to call him J-J—said, "Some of that peanut butter maybe? Oh man, how I dote on that Skippy!"

It was then that Ellen noticed Greg and J-J were wearing identical Oakland Raiders T-shirts. A coincidence? It must be— but Greg didn't like T-shirts with writing and pictures on them. Hadn't he been wearing a plain blue one earlier? Yes, he had. He must have gone home to change before picking her up. Could she have seen J-J's shirt on a previous visit and for some reason mentioned it to Greg, who had then borrowed or bought one in case Ellen took him along with her sometime, to score Brownie points?

Why hadn't she noticed the switch earlier? She thought of herself riding all the way across Berkeley into Oakland, her face pressed into Greg's warm back. Well, a good part of the time her eyes were closed.

It was all very mysterious. Whatever the real explanation, the T-shirt provided an instant bond—"Hey, man, go Raiders!"—and by the time Gran bustled out and said, "You again, mentor lady, you sure as hell don't give up, do you!" Greg was leaning against the hood of the Chevy sharing a beer and swapping tales about Kenny "The Snake" Stabler and Daryle Lamonica, and the chances for next season's Super Bowl.

Over the months, Gran's attitude toward Ellen had changed too. Initially, she had met Ellen with scowling suspicion. "Who are you, anyway? Some kind of nosy social worker? What is this mentor stuff?" When Ellen had explained that they were getting a reading program started at the university, that it was free, and would Gran let Talitha come because she was such a bright child and should be doing better, Gran had asked what was the point, she herself hadn't made it past sixth grade and never felt the lack.

But things were different now. Talitha's eyes were bright with the excitement of discovery, and today, eating coffee cake in the kitchen with a televised game show roaring along in the background, Gran displayed particular interest, even warmth, as she asked just who was that fine man Ellen had brought along.

Talitha giggled. "He's your boyfriend, huh?"

Ellen's hands still remembered the contours of Greg's hard waist and despite herself, she blushed.

"Well?" demanded the child. "Is he?"

"We're not here to talk about boyfriends but for you to show your Gran and me how well you're reading. I brought you a new book. It's called *Charlotte's Web*."

Then Greg came in, introduced himself, and plopped down at the table as though he'd sat there every day of his life.

"Mm *mmm!*" Gran surveyed him up and down and regarded Ellen with distinct respect.

"Just read, Talitha!" Ellen said.

By now the child had outgrown Babar. She was reading well up to grade level, and after a little fuss of sighs and eye-rolling, she settled down and showed them just how well.

" 'Chapter One, Before Breakfast,' " Talitha began. " 'Where's Papa going with that ax?' " enunciating calmly and precisely, face gravely concentrated, thick lashes lying over her cheeks like dark fans.

"Holy Jesus!" Gran exclaimed, "Will you listen to that child! And she never even saw that book before!" She turned down the TV. "Greg, honey, go get those boys in here! They gotta hear this!"

Bobby and J-J were hustled in and the family settled round the table. Talitha was up to page five when the silent TV screen caught Ellen's eye. The clapping, cheering game contestants had been replaced with the somber face of Richard Nixon.

Greg followed her glance. "What the hell—?" He reached forward to turn up the sound and Talitha's voice trailed to silence.

"—as I leave the presidency. To have served in this office is to have felt a very personal sense of kinship with each and every American.

"In leaving it I do so with this prayer: May God's grace be with you in all the days ahead."

"My God," Greg exclaimed. "He finally did it!"

Ellen asked, "You mean he's resigned?"

"Who cares?" Gran snorted. "Don't make no difference. Politicians are all the same. Now turn that darn thing off and let the kid read."

★   ★   ★

By the time Ellen and Greg got back to the campus it was growing dark and the fog had rolled in. Nixon was gone, and Sproul Plaza was a swirl of color and music like Mardi Gras, with beer and yelling and noisily revving motorbikes and the cops too smart not to turn a blind eye.

Greg grabbed Ellen with one hand and a shock-haired, tie-dyed stranger with the other, and the three of them pounded the air and howled like wolves, *whooo whooo*!

Then he held Ellen at arm's length and stared into her eyes. "This is a significant moment! We should celebrate!"

Well, of course they should—but she didn't want to do so alone with Greg, it just wasn't right. "We should all celebrate together," she insisted. "Let's find Josh; he'll probably be at the Sonnet," and suddenly all her reservations peeled away as she realized how much she'd been missing Josh, how incomplete she'd felt. She didn't want to waste any more time. All she'd needed, it seemed, was some kind of an outside jolt to bring her back to sanity. She thought, *Thank you,* Mr. Nixon!

★   ★   ★

The Sonnet was surprisingly full for an August night before the onset of fall classes, and their usual table was invaded by strangers. Ellen thought—more disappointed than she'd believed possible—that Josh wasn't there after all, until she saw him sitting in the back of the room talking intently with a stocky, brown-haired man in his middle thirties and an older woman, whom Ellen recognized as Congresswoman Shirley Lester.

Ellen hadn't seen Josh for weeks and he looked somehow different, more mature, and unusually elegant in black jeans and turtleneck, but the change was more than merely clothes.

His ponytail was gone. "You've cut your hair!" Ellen exclaimed.

He turned his newly shorn head and his face lit up with that wonderful, warm smile. "What do you think?"

"I like it. But it'll take some getting used to. Why did you do it?"

"I guess I decided it was time to grow up." Josh grabbed for a stool. "Here you go. And I'd like you to meet my friends."

Ellen smiled, shook hands across the table, and pulled the stool close enough to Josh's so they sat thigh to thigh. Yes, she had missed him badly. She wished they could be alone together now so she could tell him so, but Congresswoman Lester and the man— Will something, her executive aide—would no doubt leave soon, and inevitably Greg would be claimed by one of his women. Probably Allie McLaren, the girl with the killer body, sitting at a nearby table and preparing to pounce.

Ellen traced the seam of Josh's jeans with a fingertip but he didn't seem to notice. In fact, beyond that first smile, a quick kiss, and a handclasp, he seemed far more involved with his companions than with her and she wondered, with a flash of dismay, if she'd left him alone for too long.

Greg advised from her other side, "Now you're seeing the real Josh. Political Josh." In a tone which could almost have been a warning, he said, "He's in a whole different space."

Ellen understood that; she knew what drove Josh. And hadn't she let him know, just a few weeks ago, that she wanted to be in this space with him?

Allie McLaren approached Greg and leaned over his shoulder. "You going to do your Nixon thing tonight?" she asked.

"Not tonight," he said.

"Why not? It would be so cool!" She made a move to join their table and asked in a low pitched but quite audible voice, her hand on Greg's arm, "What's happening later? Want to get together?"

"I have plans for later," Greg said.

"Which I guess don't include me!" Allie flounced off with a frightening glare at Ellen, who edged her stool even closer to Josh. She had no wish to be involved in Greg's love life and far preferred to listen to Josh and his companions talk about where the country was headed now, after Nixon. At the same time, she couldn't help but feel increasingly neglected—couldn't Josh see how she longed to talk with him alone?

As the noise level rose and he glanced at her as if she was just anyone, not the girl he had so recently urged to marry him, Ellen's spirits began to flag and she felt a headache coming on. She willed Josh to call it a night—*Be with me! I want you! I love you!*—but he showed no sign of wanting to be anywhere but here.

Perhaps he'd changed his mind. Maybe he didn't want her after all.

Ellen was about to give up and leave when Josh, in response to a cue only he could have heard, rose and thrust his way between the tables to the podium, where he stood with dark head thrown back, hands raised, commanding silence.

"What's this all about?" Ellen asked Greg. "He never reads poetry on stage."

"Tonight's different," Greg said.

At first the unruly crowd took no notice; then, from one table to the next, the voices died away.

Shirley Lester leaned forward, tented her long fingers, and watched Josh with unblinking dark eyes.

"So it's over," declared Josh in a new, authoritative voice, lower and richer than Ellen had heard before. "It's over and about time, too. For people here who don't know me, I'm Joshua Fischer—and although I'm no poet, I'm going to offer some words from someone who is. His name is Josiah Gilbert Holland, and his words were read today on the floor of the Senate by a great man, Sam Ervin of North Carolina, Chairman of the Watergate Committee and one of the few people to come out of this sorry business with increased public respect."

Josh paused, and then began to recite the poem from memory.

His surprising new voice filled every corner and crevice of the Sonnet until even the espresso machine was silent and the aproned girl leaned forward to listen, elbows on the counter.

> God, give us men! A time like this demands
> Strong minds, great hearts, true faith and ready hands;
> Men whom the lust of office does not kill;
> Men whom the spoils of office cannot buy;
> Men who possess opinions and a will;
> Men who have honor; men who will not lie;
> Men who can stand before a demagogue
> And damn his treacherous flatteries without winking!
> Tall men, sun-crowned, who live above the fog
> In public duty and in private thinking. . .

Josh made eye contact with scattered members of the crowd, allowing a full thirty seconds to elapse before he spoke again. Nobody broke the silence. He'd always had presence, but on this night he ratcheted it up a full ten degrees. How had he learned to do this? Ellen wondered. Had he always had such instinctive timing?

" '*Men who have honor; men who will not lie'!*" Then, more softly, "Let's have no more lies! Not now that we have a chance for a new start and for some real changes."

His eyes lit on Ellen's, held them for a moment, and moved on.

Shirley Lester was watching him intently. Ellen could see that this was a pivotal moment—the word *audition* dropped into her mind—though surely Lester would not offer Josh a job with him starting law school in the fall.

"Something needs to be said tonight," Josh continued, "and I thought I'd be the one to say it. Yes, we're glad, we're celebrating, but we need to *mark* this moment. We'll remember this night for years to come, maybe for the rest of our lives—as *the night we got our country back!*"

A long-haired boy sprang to his feet and shouted, "Right on!"

He was joined by several others; before long, half the young people in the Sonnet were on their feet.

At Ellen's side Greg muttered, "Well, what d'you know…"

Josh signaled for silence and went on: "Any leader who would lie to us about a break-in that he ordered, and then lie about the lie, will lie to us about anything until lies become second nature and our country, the United States of America, will become one giant lie!"

Ellen grew aware of a soft but insistent chanting: "No more lies! No more lies!"

Josh raised his hands, palms forward, and the chanting faded to silence again. Ellen saw how he was playing the crowd like an orchestra conductor, as if he'd done it all his life—but he hadn't, so how did he know?

"And any leader who asks the people who believe in him to lie for him is a leader who cares nothing for them, who holds them in *contempt.*"

"NO MORE LIES!"

"At a time like this, with our world torn apart by war, brutality, and poverty, we need leaders who care about and respect the people—we *deserve* leaders who respect the people!"

Now he was asking, in soft tones: "So what do we take away from this sad, squalid episode? What have we learned? Of course"—voice hardening—"we've learned that power is sexy, power is addictive, power can be dangerously abused. But what else have we learned? I'll tell you.

"We've learned that we, the people, have not just the right but the responsibility and the means to stop the abusers. We can take the law into our hands because it's *our* law, written for *us!* So let us go on now, with the law on our side, and remake the world, with truth and justice for all! We need it. We've earned it!" The crowd rose up again and cheered because it was the end of an era, the dark times and dark deeds were over, and there'd be *no more lies.* Josh Fischer had said so and they trusted and believed him.

Someone roared, "Truth and justice!"

Another, "Josh Fischer for President!"

From behind her Ellen heard someone say with awe, "He's another Kennedy."

She had risen to her feet along with everyone else in the room, headache forgotten, face beaming like a flower turned toward the sun, clapping like mad, filled with joy because of course Josh could remake the world, there was no doubt at all.

Josh stepped away from the mike, himself again, but somehow much more than himself, laughing, slapping hands.

"Just like he's running for office," Greg murmured beside her.

Josh was back at their table. Shirley Lester grabbed his hand and pumped it. The man Will clapped him on the shoulder.

Greg cried, "Way to go! One hell of a performance—you're a natural!"

Josh caught Ellen up in his arms and kissed her. "This might take awhile," he told her. "I have to talk with some people. Maybe you better not wait." He let her go and put her from him as the crowd surged up to him. He turned to Greg. "Do me a favor and take Ellen home."

Ellen watched Josh lose himself among the press of bodies, the reaching hands, glowing eyes, and broad smiles. She wondered whether it would always be like this.

"Let's go," Greg said.

★   ★   ★

Greg hoisted Ellen onto the Yamaha but he didn't take her home, he took her back to Eucalyptus House, where he settled her on the sofa with a bottle of beer, then stretched out beside her, feet up on the coffee table. "Now you've seen Josh in action, what d'you think?" he asked.

"Terrific, like you said—a natural." Ellen's headache had slammed back again, along with a sense of distinct anticlimax. She couldn't help but feel resentful toward Josh, who had looked at her and seen just another unit of a crowd to be wooed and won, not Ellen Downey, life partner.

"When do you think Josh will be back?" she asked.

"Not for hours, not now that he's all caught up in politics. He might even pull an all-nighter."

An all-nighter, Ellen thought, great.

"Have another beer," Greg said.

She didn't want another beer, she felt bloated from the last one, and had a glass of white wine instead. And then another glass of wine because Greg hadn't finished his second beer yet.

Greg slipped his arm around her shoulders. Ellen felt a little woozy and more angry with Josh, who had courted her and then ignored her, who had told her he wanted her at his side all the way to the presidency but who had sent her home while he talked politics with the Congresswoman, as if Ellen was too young and insignificant to belong at the table. *Do me a favor and take Ellen home.*

Greg traced a light fingertip down her cheek, threaded his fingers through her thick tangle of hair, and pulled her face to his. He kissed her, long and deep, and she never tried to stop him.

She didn't want him to stop. Nobody had ever kissed her like that before. Ellen had never tasted such pent-up, aggressive determination and desire. She felt Greg's heart thundering against her ribs, and her body responding. She bit at his lips, heard her own gasping breath—and she knew she really must stop this, she was committed to Josh, and no matter what he had done or failed to do, this kind of revenge was wrong. But this wasn't about Josh, was it; this was something different altogether. Kissing Josh was like coming home, while kissing Greg was to venture out into a treacherous unknown that could damage and destroy her—and she absolutely did not care.

Greg pulled Ellen to her feet, led her down the passage, and shouldered open the door to his darkened room. She felt his competent hands undressing her, and they fell together through the darkness onto his bed.

Greg's naked body was long and elegant, his embrace enveloped her utterly, and they meshed with ease and grace. He smelled good too, faintly and astringently of aftershave. He was clinging to her as if he'd never let her go, and it was all so easy and right.

After a while she heard him get up and go to the door, open it, and close it almost at once. She wondered what he was doing, but then he came back to her through the dark, his hands were caressing her and awakening her all over—it was happening again until finally she found herself drifting down, down, deep into unconsciousness.

★ ★ ★

Ellen woke some time later to the sound of men's voices, running water, and the clink of cups or glasses. She stared around the dim room in bewilderment.

Where was she?

A window to her right showed a pattern of leaves against milky moonlight. A man lay beside her on his stomach; cool light outlined the curve of his shoulder, gleamed upon the musculature of his back and cast into relief the long shadow of his spine. It was Greg Hunter, fast asleep, snoring lightly.

He was stark naked. So was she.

She rose on one elbow and shook his shoulder, hard. He grunted in his sleep, rolled over like a sleepy lion, and reached for her. "Ell! Come here!"

She hissed, "Josh's in the kitchen. Right next door."

"So what? He won't come in."

"How do you know?"

"When we have someone over we hang a tie over the door-knob outside. He'll just think it's Allie or someone."

Allie or someone!

Ellen moved away from him to the far side of the bed, appalled to be so casually lumped in with all of Greg's girls. She felt cheap. She lay there rigid, furious, and still a bit drunk, while Josh and another man (Will the aide?) chatted and laughed just the other side of the wall.

Greg asked, dangerously loudly, "Ell? What's wrong?"

"Hush!"

After an eternity had passed, probably not more than ten minutes, she heard jovial sounds of departure and a slamming door, then Josh's footsteps, slightly unsteady, mounting the stairs. Moments later, the floorboards creaked right over her head and metal bedsprings clashed as Josh sat heavily down. There came the double thud of shoes flung about, more boards creaking, a toilet flushing, bedsprings again, then silence.

Time to go. To get away.

Ellen put her feet to the floor. Her head swam. She gathered up her clothes and clumsily dressed herself in the dark, aware of Greg watching her in brooding silence from the bed. As she buttoned her shirt a new worry surfaced. God! She'd been off the pill for six months. She'd never done well with birth control pills, her system didn't adjust and continuously rebelled. "Greg," she whispered urgently, "did you use anything?"

"Are you kidding? Aren't all girls on the pill these days?"

"Not me." She pressed her hands nervously across her flat stomach. Oh Lord, what now? Perhaps Gloria—yes, she'd know what to do. Thank God for Gloria. Ellen insisted, "I've got to get home."

Greg yawned and said, "In the morning."

"No. Now. I need to go. I can't let Josh find me here."

"What's the big deal? He must know we have something going on. He's not an idiot."

"What're you talking about?"

"And if we didn't before, we sure have something going on now."

"We do *not*!"

Greg sat up and stared at her, his pale eyes reflecting points of hard light. "What was all that about then, what we just did? I could feel your heart beating right through your skin. You wanted me like I wanted you and don't dare say you didn't!"

She hissed again, "Keep your voice down!"

"I'll say it as loud as I like. You wanted me too!"

"Yes, but—it wasn't real. You just caught me at a weak moment, when I was upset. It wasn't right."

"Wasn't real? Or right?"

Ellen's eyes filled with tears of rage and confusion. She brusquely wiped them away with the back of her hand. What had she been thinking, allowing Greg to sweep her off to bed? She couldn't wait to get away from him, though a small voice deep inside her pointed out that it wasn't all his fault, she hadn't exactly resisted. She pulled on her boots and struggled awkwardly with the laces. "Okay," she said. "I'm going now."

"You can't. I won't let you."

She crept shakily toward the door. "Try and stop me."

She heard him give a heavy sigh as he hauled himself out of bed and reached for his jeans. "You're not walking home by yourself at three in the morning."

"I don't need you. I'll be just fine."

"Don't be so dumb."

So, very reluctantly, she rode with him the few blocks back to her house. His back muscles were rigid under her hands as she tried not to hold on to him, tried not to touch him at all.

At her door she climbed off the bike with trembling legs and he took off with a roar, without saying another word.

She wouldn't see him again for eight years.

★

1982

★

CHAPTER SEVEN

The powder blue Mercedes sports convertible pulled up alongside where he stood at the corner of Van Ness and Franklin Street in San Francisco. "Hey, Greg Hunter! Where have you been all this time?"

He looked at the blonde hair, the silk scarf, the huge round sunglasses, and the dazzling car. He had no idea who she was. "Great to see you!" he called out. "You look sensational!"

"Like a ride?" She patted the navy leather seat beside her.

"Sure!" He placed one hand on the Mercedes door and vaulted nimbly inside.

"Do you always get into strange women's cars?"

"Never!"

"Liar! You really don't know who I am, do you?"

She took off her dark glasses to reveal a face he remembered well, though it was subtly altered now—the lips fuller, the cheekbones more prominent, framed with a tangled, pouffy mane rather than the signature, ironed-straight blonde fall. "Jane Hecht," he said as if never in doubt. "Last heard of going to Hollywood to make it big in movies. How could I forget you?"

"You managed to forget me before. And this time it's been eight years."

"You're crazy! You know that?" Greg said, a shade uncomfortably. "But what man in his right mind turns down a ride with a movie star?"

"Flattery will get you everywhere! Where do you want to go?"

"Wherever you're going."

"Are you hungry?"

"I could eat."

"How about lunch at the St. Francis Yacht Club?"

Greg—who'd been on his way to Safeway to buy a loaf of bread and cold cuts so he could picnic alone on the Marina Green—said, "That may be a bit over my budget."

"Lunch is on Daddy. You're not allowed to pay unless you're a member. He's vice commodore."

"In that case, what are we waiting for?"

Jane spun the sleek little car onto Marina Boulevard, the ends of her long scarf whipping in the breeze. "Where did you disappear to, anyway?" she asked.

"Nebraska."

"*Nebraska?* Didn't you have a job at the *Oakland Trib?*"

"Just an internship, it didn't lead to anything. The *Prairie Schooner* in Surprise Bend, Nebraska, actually paid money."

"And you've been there for eight years?"

"Not the last two. I was in Boise, Idaho. The *Herald.*"

"You've sure paid your dues."

"I'll say. But I'm back now. I start at the *Chronicle* next week. General assignment reporter."

"Hey! Great! We'll celebrate!"

Jane gunned past the hundreds of sailboats that bounced and tugged at their lines as if they were anxious to escape out to that blue water, and she turned a sharp right toward the most venerable yacht club in the West. Coasting into a reserved parking space just outside the massive double doors, Jane said, "I always think vice commodore sounds rather naughty, don't you?"

Greg wondered if this was a come-on, and whether they were going to pick up where they'd left off. He'd always liked Jane, and hadn't had a lot of company lately.

★ ★ ★

Jane was treated like royalty by the yacht club staff; Greg basked in her reflected glory and felt like a prince. It got even better: it was Friday, the "all you can eat" buffet day, so he piled his plate with shrimp and smoked salmon, returned for seconds, and later, for cheesecake, chocolate cake, and strawberries.

"I've always liked a man with a big appetite," Jane said.

Greg smiled and loaded his fork.

"Graduation seems eons ago," she said, sipping her coffee.

"I can hardly remember it," Greg said.

"Me either, though we must have been there. What a blast! We went to Trader Vic's afterward, didn't we, scads of us."

"Did we?"

"Didn't you come? I'm sure I invited you. I guess you had other plans."

"I must have," he said.

"Who were those people you used to hang out with? That dark guy who made political speeches?"

"Josh Fischer."

"Right. Whatever happened to him? He was kind of cute in a smoldering sort of way."

"He went on to law school at Boalt. Now he's a public defender in Oakland."

"Do you keep in touch?"

"More or less. He invited me to his wedding."

"Who did he marry? That itty-bitty, red-haired girl you dumped me for?"

"Ellen Downey. And I did not dump you for her."

"That's right, you dumped me for both of them. Was it a fun wedding?"

"I didn't go. It was a long way from Surprise Bend."

Ellen and Josh had been married the February after graduation, six months after Nixon resigned, in Professor Edwards's garden in the Berkeley hills.

Josh had sent Greg a full set of pictures: all the smiling faces, the Fischer family, the Downeys, Ellen's old roommate Gloria, Shirley Lester, Professor Edwards and his wife, a cluster of

Children's Alliance kids displaying a banner saying WE LOVE YOU JOSH AND ELLEN, Ellen with sprigs of apple blossom in her burnished hair—Mother Nature herself, if a mother could look so young—smiling shyly, blushing, holding hands with Josh, who wore a dark blue suit, silvery tie, and a dotingly idiotic grin.

Greg hated that picture of the two of them. They looked way too happy.

"I guessed they would get married. They always seemed like such a *couple*," Jane said. "Do they have any kids?"

"No." And thank goodness, thought Greg. He still couldn't get used to the fact that Ellen had married so soon after he and she had gotten together. But at least if she and Josh didn't have kids, he could pretend they weren't having sex. Or at least not very often.

"Have you seen them since you've been back?"

"Not yet." He'd called them; Ellen had answered him guardedly. Yes, of course they must all get together, she'd agreed—the emphasis on the "all"—but she and Josh were both so busy, he at the courthouse, she at the Children's Alliance, which, in case Greg did not already know, had officially been incorporated into the School of Social Studies, wasn't that wonderful?

He could take a hint: she didn't want to see him, then. But he didn't plan on giving up.

"It's nice to catch up with old friends," Jane said. "Have you had enough to eat?"

"Are you kidding? What a feast!"

"Then let's go. I'm sick of all these stuffy old people, we're the youngest by about forty years. Let's go play on Daddy's boat."

Greg was determined to set thoughts of Ellen aside—much easier to do when he saw Daddy's boat, a seventy-foot motor yacht called the *Freya III,* a stately vision of white paint, varnished mahogany, and dazzling polished brass.

"Take your shoes off or Roberto will kill you," Jane said. "He's a devil for his teak decks."

But Roberto the steward, stocky and taciturn in a white uniform, seemed a courteous enough soul. He welcomed them on board and settled them under an awning up in the bow with a bottle of chilled Roederer Cristal.

"Freya was my mother," Jane explained. "I never really knew her. She died when I was six. Dad always has a boat called *Freya;* this is the third. He was desperately in love with Mother—she was perfectly gorgeous. He met her at the boat show, she was working there as a model, in tiny shorts and striped sweater, handing out flyers and freebies. He bought the boat on the spot and married her the next month. It was all incredibly romantic. There's a picture of her in the saloon. We'll go below later and I'll show you."

Greg thought about going below with Jane. He vividly remembered her huge playpen of a bed in the Berkeley hills and the great times they'd had there together, but much had changed since then. If he got involved with her again, he knew it could get a lot more serious, and instinct warned him to play it slow, and carefully.

"My mother died when I was six, too," he said.

"Did your dad re-marry?"

"No."

"Why did I never know that? I should have known. We have a lot in common, don't we?"

But they didn't, not really. Mr. Hecht's little girl was clearly the apple of his eye, his fairy princess, and the object of his total devotion. "Your dad worships you," he said.

"It's tiresome, really," Jane said. "He wants to know everything I'm doing, where, and who with, even now I'm thirty—but that's okay, I guess. I'm seriously attached to my dad and he's entitled, especially since I'm living in his house."

If the man owns a boat like this, Greg thought immediately, what in the world must his house be like? "What does your father do, actually?" he asked.

Jane shrugged. "This and that. Development, mostly—industrial parks, shopping centers, that kind of thing. Pretty boring, but it pays the rent."

"I suspect it does."

"And he's into politics. Not that he'd ever run for office himself—he's strictly a power-behind-the-scenes kind of guy. He's a big Reagan supporter of course. 'Thank God we got those clowns out of the White House and the country back on the right track'—if I've heard that once, I've heard it a thousand times. Not that *you'd* agree with him."

"Why not?"

"Well, excuse me. But aren't you a die-hard Democrat?"

Slowly he shook his head. "Not anymore. I never really was."

"You're kidding! After your Nixon act? I remember that so well—you were great. You should have gone to Hollywood rather than me. And Josh Fischer, Mister Liberal, was your best friend."

"People can mature."

"Well good for you." Jane leaned back in her chair and stretched her arms languorously over her head. "Is champagne okay? We could have beer if you want."

"Champagne's fine. Absolutely. This is really good stuff!" Greg felt frankly dazzled, stuffed full of the best food he'd tasted in a long time, drinking champagne on a fantastic boat with this beautiful, forgiving woman who still seemed to like him despite having once been dumped, and whose father not only adored her but was loaded.

Jane was agreeing complacently. "Daddy always buys the best. Anyway, back to what we were talking about before—Berkeley, and what happened to us all."

"You went to Hollywood."

"But first I goofed around in Europe. Daddy knows lots of people. I got to stay in some really neat places in the south of France, and Italy, castles and palaces, you know—I was supposed to pick up French and Italian. I tried, but somehow I never managed it."

"I bet you picked up a slew of guys, though."

"I did, actually," she said, smiling, "including an Italian count. Perfectly gorgeous, with this huge palazzo in Tuscany and an apartment in Rome. We got married, as a matter of fact."

Greg sketched a mock bow. "What does that make you? A princess?"

"A contessa. Daddy was perfectly furious, of course. Said Luigi was Eurotrash just looking for a meal ticket and I'd marry him over his dead body. Not that I took any notice." Jane shrugged. "Too bad, because Daddy was quite right. The palazzo was mortgaged to the hilt and crumbling, the apartment in Rome belonged to Luigi's mistress, and there were about forty lawsuits pending against him he was expecting Daddy to pay. It was an awful, humiliating two years. I couldn't wait to divorce him and get home. That cost Daddy a packet too, bless his heart!" Jane reached for the bottle and refilled their glasses. "After that, he didn't want me to go to Hollywood. He said he couldn't trust me not to marry some other jerk—but I went anyway. At least Los Angeles is in the same state."

"But just as many jerks," Greg said. He lounged back in the white canvas deck chair, stretched out his long legs, and noticed his sock had a hole in it. Reaching forward, he took his socks off, rolled them in a ball, and stuffed them into his pocket, hoping she hadn't noticed.

Jane, in turn, stripped off her white linen jacket. Beneath it she was wearing a thin, peach-colored tank top. Greg tried not to stare—though perhaps she wanted him to because she said, "Why don't you take your shirt off? It's so hot! We don't get many days like this in San Francisco—we'd better make the most of it."

Greg stripped off his shirt. Even though he might be wanting in financial assets, and perhaps was no match for the gorgeous Luigi, his body was still something he didn't mind showing off.

From the way she eyed his broad, naked chest Jane obviously agreed. After a moment she continued, "So then, anyway, off I went to be a star. I guess I didn't have what it takes. I wasn't a total failure, I had a couple of parts in teenage flicks, I could still play eighteen. But they were tiny, just one line, maybe two. I got to scream a lot. I was up for a couple of shampoo commercials, and I was a dancing chocolate in a candy box. When I'd been there five years—time just drifts by in La-La Land, and I wasn't so young anymore—I began to wonder, who needs this? It's a horrible life. It's all about rejection. I started thinking, What am I doing here, with these awful people, when I could have such a wonderful time at home. I mean, let's get real, I'm never going to play Shakespeare. And Daddy was lonely and not getting any younger either, so I came back."

"I'm sure you made the right choice."

"I know I did. And now tell me about *you*. You just took off into the blue on your motorbike and never wrote me."

"I guess there just wasn't a whole hell of a lot to write about."

"I don't buy it. So make up for it now, we have lots of time, unless you have to be somewhere?"

He shook his head.

"I don't either. So tell me everything!"

"Well, for starters, I went back to Ohio and saw my family."

That visit had saddened and enraged him unbearably and stiffened his resolve never, *never* to become like them, but he didn't tell Jane. He would have told it all to Ellen, of course. He thought of the two of them sitting somewhere quiet and private, how he'd be spilling his guts after so long, and that she'd put her hand on his and tell him everything would work out all right and he'd believe her. But he wasn't with Ellen, was he. He smiled at Jane across the top of his champagne glass and said, "Then I spent a few years in Nebraska, a couple more in Idaho, and now, here I am, back in the Bay Area. Very dull story."

"Then tell me how you escaped being snapped up along the way by some farmer's daughter. You can't tell me there wasn't a farmer's daughter!"

"Of course there was a farmer's daughter!" And a doctor's daughter, and the high school football coach's daughter, and the Lutheran minister's daughter—but nobody for very long. Greg had quickly caught on to how cautious he had to be. Three dates got you invited to family Sunday dinner after church, and by evening everyone in town would know you were an item and within months you'd be walking down the aisle. "But that wasn't in my game plan."

"So just what is your game plan?"

"First, to work for a big city daily," Greg told her. "After that, we'll see."

★　★　★

The afternoon sun glanced blindingly off the paintwork and brass of the *Freya III,* and the deck felt almost too hot to touch with a bare foot. The water glittered, seagulls swooped and screamed. On the shore the passersby watched and envied him as he sat on this fabulous boat with this lovely girl, drinking champagne. Did they assume he was rich, too? Of course they did.

Jane pulled her knees up under her chin and circled them with her arms. Her skirt was so short she might as well not be wearing one. He guessed that soon she would suggest they go below to see her mother's picture in the saloon, where it would be cool and dim and where there would be staterooms with inviting beds. He still had enough sense to know he mustn't push his luck, he had to bide his time.

Jane drained her glass. "Shall we have Roberto bring up another bottle?"

"I guess not. I've had enough. I should really leave now."

"Don't go."

"I'm getting a sunburn. So are you."

"We just lost the shade." She leaned forward and tapped his knee. "Why don't we go below and get out of the heat, and I'll show you Mother's picture?"

Greg gazed at his twin reflections in her impenetrable sunglasses, then down to her pink, smiling mouth and the fine line of moisture above her upper lip. "Why not?" he said.

★ ★ ★

Jane's mother looked about the same age as Jane was now, with plucked eyebrows the way they did them back then, elaborately pouffed hair with turned-up ends, and a bright smile.

"You could almost be twins," Greg said.

"People say I'm like her."

He gazed from one face to the other. "No. You're prettier."

"Why, *thank* you, sir!" She took his hand and tugged him gently after her along a mahogany-paneled companionway.

The master cabin was a blur of opulence. Greg had an impression of soft blue carpeting, bright rectangles of light behind pale, silky curtains that rippled gently in the breeze, and a vase of irises—real ones. The bed was huge and soft with a blue and white comforter. He didn't notice Jane taking her clothes off but suddenly she was naked: long legged, lithe, and bronzed.

The sheets were cool, her body warm, her limbs strong and supple, and they meshed with his just as he remembered.

"Oh Greg, dearheart," she whispered in his ear, "I've missed you so. Welcome home."

★ ★ ★

Later he opened his eyes and found the cabin dim to near darkness. The curtains were still blowing softly and a shower was running a few feet away. Music played somewhere and Jane was humming along against the hiss of water. It was a song from *Hair*—"When the mooooon is in the second house…and Jupiterrr…aligns with Mars…"

She couldn't hold a tune to save her life, unlike Ellen, but she sounded happy. Well, Greg thought smugly, so she should be. He laced his arms behind his head and stared up at the shadowy ceiling. Did they call it a ceiling in boats? He wondered what would happen next. He imagined the two of them taking a walk on the beach, cool sand on bare feet, the ocean breeze, moon and stars. Was there a moon tonight?

They might find some little seafood place, eat cracked crab and sourdough bread, and hold hands across the tablecloth. The only problem: who would pay? Better to stay here. Roberto could whip them up something tasty for dinner, after which they could go back to bed.

The bathroom door opened and there stood Jane, wrapped in a fluffy blue towel, hair hanging in wet blonde strands over her shoulders, no makeup. She looked very young, almost the same as in the Sonnet days. She leaned over him to kiss his mouth. "That was the best day I've had in a very long time," she said.

"The day ain't over yet!"

"The best part is, though. I have to get on home. Daddy's expecting me for dinner." She touched his forehead, traced the line of his nose, his lips, his chin. "But I was thinking, maybe you'd like to come, too? I know Daddy would like to meet you. I actually think you two would get on quite well."

Greg's first impulse was to say no—*too much too soon*—but Jane knew he had no place else to go, no plans. He supposed she guessed he was flat broke, too. He'd forgotten how expensive rents were here, how he'd be expected to pay first and last month's rent and deposits on his utilities. "Are you sure that's a good idea?" he asked. Rich, protective Daddy would take one look at Greg and know not only that he was broke and had a hole in his sock, but had spent the whole afternoon in bed with his beloved little princess.

"You don't need to worry," Jane said tartly, "*I'm* not a farmer's daughter!"

He felt himself flush. "It's not that—"

"Good—then there's no problem. Daddy's always telling me to bring friends home, and you look reassuring. Frankly, he'd be relieved I was seeing someone like you. Especially since you're an old friend. He likes the idea of old friends."

"Well then," said Greg, "let's go."

★ ★ ★

Jane's home was on the same scale as the boat only more so, a pillared limestone mansion on Seacliff Avenue, with a wide view of the bay and the Golden Gate Bridge. Greg entered a grand hallway with a black-and-white marble checkerboard floor and paused in wonder, gazing at the sweeping staircase, the glittering chandelier with its myriad crystals, the huge porcelain urns filled with flowers.

What must it be like to call a place like this home?

Jane stood in the middle of the checkerboard and yelled up the stairs, "Daddy? Hey, Daddy, I brought a friend home for dinner!"

A foghorn of a voice boomed, "That's great, Janey!" and here was the king of the castle in person, beaming down on them from the landing and then ponderously descending the staircase: Gunther Hecht, a huge, craggy man with a shock of white hair, his red and gold paisley sports shirt billowing like a spinnaker across his substantial front.

He grabbed his daughter and planted a smacking kiss on her cheek. "Hi there, dearheart!" he cried. "Did you have a fun day?"

"I sure did. Daddy, this is my friend Greg Hunter. We were in school together."

Hecht's hand was enormous and enveloped Greg's completely. "Good to meet you, son!"

Jane was saying how they ran into each other completely by chance, after so long. "And I asked him back for dinner—that's okay, isn't it?"

Greg didn't hear her. He was looking at this enormous, ruddy man with the bright blue eyes who had immediately called him *son*. It had been tossed out so casually, more than likely he called any male of Greg's age *son,* but just the same, for a stabbing second, he'd felt a treacherous heat behind his eyes.

Jane's father laid a thick, jovial arm across Greg's shoulders. "Sure it is. Just perfect! C'mon through, we'll have us a cocktail and you can tell me all about yourself!" Greg was propelled through a doorway onto a tiled patio sheltered from the wind by walls of glass. This was how it ought to be, he thought, what I ought to be, a real son with a real father.

★ ★ ★

It was a fine dinner, filet mignon cooked to perfection, blackened on the outside, bright pink and juicy in the middle, tender enough to cut with your fork, and served with creamed potatoes, baby squash, and a romaine salad. The main course was followed by crème brûlée and fresh raspberries. Everything was washed down by a selection of private reserve Napa Valley wines, served by a quiet-footed Asian man so unobtrusive that the dishes seemed to come and go like magic. Greg had never eaten so well or so much in one day in his entire life. He knew he could get used to living like this very easily.

During the first part of the meal Jane insisted on reminiscing about their years at Berkeley, about the sit-ins and the be-ins, the outlandish clothes, the crazy parties, the bad poetry at the Sonnet, and what wild times those had been.

Hecht said it sure had changed since his day.

Jane said of course the Stone Age had been a long time ago. Her father told her, with a twinkle, to behave herself.

Greg listened to the fond banter and tried to fight off envy.

"Greg was quite the big man on campus," Jane said. "Quite an actor, too. He did this great Nixon imitation. It made us all howl!"

Greg shifted uneasily in his seat. The words he'd thought so clever and sophisticated at the time now seemed embarrassingly callow. "It wasn't exactly how I thought," he said. "Actually, I always rather admired him."

"Glad to hear you say that," Hecht rumbled. "Richard Nixon *was* a good man, and where foreign policy was concerned, he was one of the great statesmen."

"But I'd have been crucified if I'd said anything like that, at that time and that place."

"Berkeley is a land unto itself," Hecht agreed.

"Certainly a far cry from where I went next," Greg said. "Surprise Bend, Nebraska."

"Now there's an odd name. What's the surprise?" Hecht asked.

Greg had wondered that himself, riding into town for the first time on that hot August evening, as a crimson sun sank below the flat horizon. There, as with the Pacific Ocean, he could see forever—so where was the surprise? How *could* there be a surprise? Didn't this town look like any other along the brown, lazy loops of the Platte River?

"The surprise," he told Hecht now, "is that there *isn't* one. You can see it coming for miles. Local humor from the founding fathers."

"And they think that's funny?" Jane asked.

"They speak with their tongue in cheek," Hecht explained. "That's their way. It's a habit that comes with making the best of a tough situation and making do, and believe you me, the plains were tough living in the old days."

Greg said, "They were good people."

"Treated you well, did they?" Hecht asked.

"Made me real welcome. We got on well."

He'd gone beer drinking with his workmates, to football and baseball games, to hunt duck and deer. Parties, however, were dull and inclined to be segregated by sex, the women clustered together, talking gossip, clothes, and babies while the men discussed sports, guns, and politics, mostly local: "That was some piece of horse manure about the new zoning, that guy Sorenson should be run out of town on a rail."

"Backbone of the nation," Hecht said. "Sound family values."

After the meal, they were served coffee and cognac on the terrace by the same self-effacing steward. The night had turned cool but they were sheltered behind a heavy retractable glass screen and warmed by overhead heaters. Facing the featureless bulk of the Marin Headlands, the lights dimmed in the living room behind them, they might have been suspended in space high above the black, murmurous ocean.

Hecht returned to the subject of Richard Nixon. "Let me suggest something to you. Even though it's not part of the received wisdom—particularly," with a wry grimace, "the *Berkeley* received wisdom—Nixon actually *won* the Vietnam War!"

Jane yawned and sighed, "Politics! I'll let you boys get on with it. I'm going to bed. I can't imagine why, but I'm simply *exhausted!*" She lightly ruffled Greg's cropped hair, then planted a kiss on the top of her father's leonine head. "Don't keep him up all night, Daddy, he's had a tough day!"

Greg barely noticed her leave. "Want to explain how you come up with that?" he asked Hecht, honestly curious.

"It wasn't *me* came up with it; it's a fact. Nixon signed the Paris peace treaty in 1973 and the fighting stopped. Seems like winning to me."

"But a limited victory, like in Korea—the North was still Communist."

"Still a victory, not a mere holding action, like people said at the time." Hecht selected two cigars from the humidor that sat in front of him on the wrought iron and glass coffee table and passed one to Greg. "Nixon resigned in August '74, and because of the vacuum his resignation created in American power, the North Vietnamese re-opened the war. Saigon fell in 1975. And the rest is history." There was a pause while he clipped the end of his cigar and puffed. Greg followed suit, wondering whether he would ever look as imposing smoking a cigar as Gunther Hecht. "But suppose Nixon had remained in office, with that powerful mandate from the '72 election," Hecht said. "Do you think the North Vietnamese would have *dared* re-open the war, particularly with Nixon and Kissinger hobnobbing with the Chinese across their border? No goddam way! Here—let me freshen that drink up for you."

"Thanks." Greg leaned back among pillows, luxuriating in the fragrant smoke, and in the liquor that bloomed rich and warm inside him, quite content to listen.

Hecht splashed more cognac into his own snifter and continued, "Had there been no Watergate—forgive me for running on but I sure get riled here, Watergate was a fucking tragedy, pardon my French—Nixon's policies would have had a chance to mature and play out. Then, in my opinion, and that of certain other thinking men, various disasters wouldn't have happened." Hecht stabbed his cigar toward Greg in emphasis. "One—obviously no boat people. Two—the Khmer Rouge wouldn't have devastated Cambodia. But Nixon *was* discredited and forced to resign, and that power vacuum caused a ripple effect right across Asia, the dominoes falling one after the other, ending up with millions dead. And it needn't have happened at all."

Greg ventured, "But Nixon was tainted. No question."

Gunther Hecht snorted. "You want me to be honest? Okay, I'll talk to you straight and you can quote me in your damn paper anytime you want to. Nixon was a leader, a strong man when we needed strong men. He should have been left alone, with the support of the country behind him, to get things done instead of being hounded and disgraced."

"Even with all the lies and cover-ups? And the Pentagon Papers?"

"See here, son, it was war. Actions regularly get taken that the public never knows about, nor should they. How are they qualified to judge? With every little thing out there on the table in full view, everyone having an opinion, nothing gets done at all and it's only our enemies who benefit. Anyway, he got dumped. We got inflation, recession, our diplomats jailed in Iran, and the whole world laughing at us—*at the United States of America!*—and all because we then voted ourselves a weak president!"

Greg's eyes had adjusted to the night sky by now. He could see one very bright star above the black bulk of the Marin Headlands, casting a faint trail of light across the still, dark water. In the silence, he could hear the hiss and suck of the waves on the rocks below the house and the sharp bark of a sea lion. He watched Hecht's broad back as the big man paced across the terrace, leaned his hands against the glass and peered glumly into the night. Greg thought that with this kind of talk, he might be back in a bar in Nebraska or Idaho, or years earlier, listening to the Old Marine and Timmy venting across the kitchen table—and his young self eager to chip in.

Yes, they *had* all talked once. A long time ago.

The bright star expanded and contracted in front of his eyes and Greg felt a little fuzzy. Lethal stuff, that cognac.

Hecht had drunk a lot more but showed no effects at all. He mused, back still turned, voice hard and assured, "Of course, one thing that's evident these days, for good or bad, is the power of the press. If people don't recognize that, they're idiots. The press is a weapon, just like a gun—it all depends whose finger's on the trigger. And where it's pointing."

★   ★   ★

When it came time to leave, Hecht walked Greg across the courtyard with its lemon trees and koi pond and out to the street, giving him a warm handshake and a brief but generous hug. "You're a smart young man, Greg, and I'm glad Janey brought you home. You keep in touch now."

Oh, he would. He absolutely would. He thought it seemed a good omen, the two of them having the same initials.

CHAPTER EIGHT

The Children's Alliance had moved from the Berkeley campus in 1976, quickly outgrown its new storefront location in downtown Oakland, and now occupied an old meatpacking plant just off Highway 17, not far from Jack London Square.

The warehousemen, butchers, and packers would never recognize their old workspace. On the far wall, opposite the small door in the rolled steel entry, was a blazing Mexican tree-of-life mural with hot pink trunk and branches, its flowers and leaves picked out in orange, yellow, and deep violet. The children had painted it themselves under the eye of a professional mural-ist, and a photograph of the young artists standing in front of their creation—the kids proudly paint-daubed and brandishing brushes—was featured in all the Children's Alliance flyers and posters and had become their unofficial logo.

The other walls were painted sky blue, and the concrete floor was covered by dark blue carpeting, a castoff from the Holiday Inn at Emeryville. Heavy oak desks and chairs clustered in the corners of the big room, and an oval, blond wood boardroom table occupied the center (donated by the Bank of America fol-lowing an office remodel), around which Ellen organized writing workshops and editorial meetings for their newsletter, *AllianZ,* which was supplied free to high schools. There was a battered old upright piano where the children would gather for singalongs. An antique zinc counter, complete with etched-glass sneeze-shield (courtesy of Solano Joe's Finest Seafood) provided space for books, magazines, newspapers, college catalogues, scholarship information packets, and flyers for rock concerts, as well as for a commercial-size coffeepot and brightly colored mugs. There was a large bin into which the kids could delve for outfits—sweats, jeans, jackets, and caps—thanks to contributors like the Gap, J.C. Penney, and the Oakland A's.

It was amazing what you could pick up for free provided you asked, and Ellen was both a great asker and a determined persuader. People liked her and gave her stuff. "We get requests from nonprofits all the time," she'd been told, "but nobody else comes in with hair like a desert sunset and a smile that would light up a coal mine."

The place was kept well too. The kids tidied, dusted, and vacuumed it themselves; Ellen was tough about that. The Children's Alliance was their refuge from the streets and the gangs, a safe place in which to create, to learn, and to socialize. "This is your *own* place," she'd insist, "so treat it with respect."

Today was Ellen's morning for Juvenile Hall, where, six months earlier, she had initiated a creative writing workshop. It was a bold experiment, and the administration had been dubious at first, foreseeing all kinds of opportunities for mayhem, even though, as Ellen pointed out, at the very least the kids would learn some basic writing and communication skills. Why not give it a try—what did they have to lose?

This particular morning, Ellen had a more urgent claim on her time so the workshop would be led by Sue Polley, U.C. Berkeley junior, a doctor's daughter from the quiet, upscale community of Piedmont, for whom this expedition to Juvenile Hall was a venture to a new world. Sue anxiously followed Ellen's bright purple shirt across the parking lot—Ellen always wore vivid colors, to brighten up gloomy surroundings, and so the kids could find her. "They're going to be real disappointed to have me instead of you," Sue said.

"They'll enjoy having someone younger for a change."

Sue gave a wan smile, imagining herself all alone in a room full of delinquents. "Suppose they get out of control? What'll I do?"

"You holler for a guard. But it won't happen." Ellen spoke emphatically, comfortingly, and hoped she would be proven right. She had been warned by cops and caseworkers alike when she first started going: "Don't get any romantic ideas just because they're kids. Some of them would stick you as soon as look at you."

There were also the less dangerous but more gross practices. Passersby in the halls were occasionally pelted with baggies filled with urine, or worse, though Ellen had not dared mention such horrors to Sue.

The girl persisted, "Why won't it happen?"

"They're in this workshop because they *want* to be," Ellen said. "It's not like school, where they don't have a choice. It makes a big difference."

"You think so?"

"Of course. And if you do need me for any reason, I'm in the building and someone can come find me—but if I thought there'd be problems, I wouldn't have asked you to do this." Ellen opened the passenger door to her tomato red Chevy pickup and shoved Sue up into the seat. "You can drive us back afterward, if you want."

"I can? Hey, cool!" Sue cheered up at once. "I've never driven a truck!"

"Me neither till last year."

When Ellen's aged Taurus died of longevity and overwork the year before, Josh had persuaded her to buy the Chevy. After initial resistance—so big, so high up!—she was surprised at how much she liked it. She enjoyed its solid heft and loved its utility when picking up donations—odd pieces of furniture, rolls of carpet, light fixtures, and cartons of books.

Ellen smiled into the young, anxious face with the big gray eyes and curly reddish hair and inescapably saw herself ten years ago, determined to change the world in one day and sooner if possible.

She thought, That girl could almost be my daughter.

And the familiar pang sliced through her heart like an icy blade.

★ ★ ★

In late 1976, when Ellen and Josh had been married almost two years, Judith Fischer had demanded to know when would she get a grandbaby.

Josh had laughed. "Don't be so impatient, Mom."

"Just don't wait too long. Your father and I won't live forever."

Two years later Ellen decided they had waited long enough; their graduate degrees were behind them and they were both earning. Not a lot of money, but enough. Time to start a family. They'd found the perfect house for it, 33 Crescent Court in Oakland, a two-story brown shingle on a quiet cul-de-sac, with an oak tree outside the living room window and an ideally placed branch for a swing.

She and Josh noticed that branch at the same moment, and their eyes met meaningfully behind the back of the real estate agent as she fiddled with the lockbox and warned them how the house was a bit of a fixer-upper—an understatement—but would be perfect for a young family.

Two children, they'd agreed; the boy first, red-haired, freckled, and husky like his grandfather Downey, protective of his little sister, whom Ellen envisaged as dark and tomboyish in overalls, like Scout in *To Kill a Mockingbird*.

Josh had asked, "Suppose we have two boys?"

"Then we'll have to keep on trying, won't we?"

They worked on the house together every weekend for a year, stripped walls, sanded floors, repaired broken woodwork, and had the roof fixed. Ellen painted the kitchen bright yellow and the smallest of the three bedrooms yellow too, but lighter, more of a cream, gentle for the baby.

And the room waited. And waited.

She didn't understand why she didn't get pregnant, with both of them young and healthy and making love almost every night.

"Relax," advised the doctor. "It doesn't always happen to suit *your* convenience."

Another year went by.

Eventually, they had tests run.

Josh's lab results proved perfectly normal, which was a huge relief because Ellen was sure there was nothing to worry about on her own side. Her periods were regular enough to set a clock. The doctor had been right all along; their baby would arrive when it was ready and not before.

The day after they heard Josh's test results, the phone rang. "Mrs. Fischer? Can you come in this afternoon at two o'clock? Dr. Garner would like to see you."

It was a gorgeous, languorous day in late spring, the air heavy with the scent of blossom, warm with a gentle breeze, the birds singing, a perfect day, a *fertile* day. But somewhere deep inside Ellen, though she told herself there was nothing to worry about, *nothing at all,* an alarm sounded like a deep, cracked bell.

When she left the doctor's office she didn't return to the Children's Alliance. She went home, driving with mechanical competence through the familiar streets, stopping at red lights, signaling lane changes, an efficient other self taking over while her real self existed in a state of frozen suspension. She pulled into the driveway with no memory of how she'd gotten there, switched off the engine, and sat staring at the out-thrust limb of the oak tree, thinking that you never realize how badly you want something until you know you'll never have it.

Never.

Ellen sat there for an hour, cold hands still gripping the wheel, before she was able to make herself climb out and walk stiffly inside. She went to bed and lay down fully dressed under the covers, chilled to the bone, vaguely thinking she should make herself some hot tea with a lot of sugar in it.

The phone rang three different times and she didn't answer.

Josh came home around six. She heard his voice, "Honey? Ell? Where are you? Where've you *been?*" and his footsteps climbing the stairs and crossing the room toward her. "Ell? What's wrong?" His arms wrapped around her, hard and warm. "Ell, *please!* Look at me! Talk to me. What did Dr. Garner say?"

Eventually she heard her own voice reply, sounding strangely remote, "He said I have ovarian failure."

Josh sat back on his heels. "What does that mean?"

"Just what it sounds like."

"But you're not sick? You don't have—"

"No, I don't have cancer." Ellen heard Josh's sigh of pent-up breath.

"Oh, thank God!" He held her close again and buried his face in her hair. "For a moment there you really scared me."

After a pause, in that same distant voice, not her own, she said, "No, it's okay. Just that I can't have a baby, that's all." Then she dragged herself up from her pillow, eyes wide and hurt: "That word, *failure*—I can't believe he'd say that to me! I *never* use that word with the kids. I tell them there's always hope."

"It's only a medical term," Josh said. "Of course there's hope."

"There isn't. It means early menopause."

"But that's crazy. You're so young. And you've never had any weird symptoms. No hot flashes, or anything."

Drearily, Ellen shook her head from side to side. She felt tired and still so cold. "There don't have to be symptoms. He tried to explain but I couldn't take it in, didn't really listen, I couldn't believe he was talking about me. I thought there must have been a mix-up with the results. Mix-ups happen."

"Maybe there was."

"No."

"Then surely there's something you can do. Can't you take hormone supplements and get it fixed?"

"It's not like changing spark plugs on a car. It's irreversible. No, Josh; I can't have kids. Not ever. I'm a *failure*."

★ ★ ★

There were more tests, which confirmed the findings of the first, and courses of hormone therapy that were disastrous. Ellen's breasts swelled painfully; she suffered abdominal cramps and violent mood swings. She would wake up suddenly in the middle of the night and not be able to fall back to sleep. She yelled at her co-workers, was impatient with the Children's Alliance kids, couldn't stand Josh even to touch her, then she would sob, saying they'd never make a baby if they never made love. One evening, glaring sullenly at Josh across the kitchen, she flung a china pitcher of water onto the tile floor, burst into tears, and ran out of the room.

Josh patiently cleaned up the broken shards, went to her, and tried to take her in his arms but she pushed him away.

She stopped taking the hormone pills. Within a few weeks her system and her moods settled down again.

Josh suggested carefully, "We could always adopt."

But Ellen shook her head. Adopting would mean saving just one child, through working full-time at the Alliance she could save so many more.

★ ★ ★

They told their parents, of course.

It wasn't so bad telling the Downeys because Ruth and Dwayne had already provided grandchildren.

It was harder with Hans and Judith Fischer. Ellen confided to Josh, "After all they've been through, all that struggle to survive, the family line is dying out because of *me*." She felt she had let them down badly, and it did no good for Josh to remind her that Judith and Hans were fulfilled as grandparents by Miriam's little boy and Sarah's daughter—it was different. Josh was the only son, and Ellen knew in his heart, Josh agreed.

They didn't tell anybody else and shrugged off or ignored remarks about selfishness and putting career and convenience ahead of family commitments or, worst of all, reassurances that it could still happen, that after all, Ellen was only thirty.

Most of the time, she and Josh made every effort to avoid thinking about it.

They both kept terribly busy.

★ ★ ★

"Well," Ellen said to Sue, determinedly bright as she pulled up in front of Juvenile Hall, a fifties-style gray concrete box. "Here we are."

It wasn't so bad inside. The place was clean and in far better shape than some of the public schools she visited with her outreach program. The linoleum floors were polished to a slippery gloss and the walls painted teal blue. Unlike the schools, however, there were bars on the windows and locks on the doors. Always, upon entering those doors, Ellen had to fight the sadness that fell upon her like a weight as she thought of the young people locked up in here. She was unable to rid herself of the notion that the air smelled old and stale, as if the years of accumulated rage and frustration had mired themselves into the walls.

While Sue ran the workshop, Ellen was scheduled to meet with a multi-problem inmate, hostile and dangerous, picked up a week ago for systematically smashing windshields in a used-car lot. She was not more than twelve, maybe even younger, but a wild child and very strong; the cops had been afraid until they'd taken the crowbar away from her, and on the way in she'd punched a guard and broken his nose.

Derelle. Obstinately silent. No last name, no address, no possessions save a small spiral-bound notebook in her jacket pocket. Though the remaining pages were blank, some were torn out and the notebook obviously used. Perhaps it was the key to unlock this angry, closed young mind. It was all they had to work with anyway, and worth a try. If Derelle wouldn't talk, maybe she could be persuaded to write.

"And you're seeing her alone?" Sue said. "Aren't you afraid?"

"Sure I am—but there're different kinds of fear. There's the commonsense sort, which warns you to watch out and take care, the way I'm feeling right now, then there's the real, funky, gut-twisting fear."

If she ever did feel like that, Ellen knew it would be time for her to quit this work, because even if she had enough self-control not to show her fear overtly, she wouldn't fool the kids.

Actually, she guessed Josh was more afraid for her than she would ever be. Although immensely proud of her, he was appalled at the things she did, the places she went, marching the corridors of the worst schools in the Bay Area, braving crumbling housing projects on behalf of her endangered children.

Ellen hadn't told Josh about Derelle; there was a lot she didn't tell him.

★ ★ ★

The woman guard —counselor, rather; in the Alameda County Juvenile Detention Center, everyone was called a counselor— led Ellen and Sue through the central recreation room with its TV, ping-pong table, and desks where a few kids worked on homework assignments. They looked up warily as Ellen and Sue passed—parents, lawyers, or cops? Apart from the TV and the joyless *plock* of ping-pong paddles, the room held a strange quiet, pervaded with an edgy sense of limbo.

The writing workshop took place in a small, windowless room, where today six boys and four girls in their mid teens sat around three pushed-together card tables with a vacant seat by the door. Here, at least, was a throb of energy and expectation.

The kids greeted Ellen with very real pleasure, Sue with grumbles. A sub? You mean we got a *sub*? How could you *do* this to us?

Ellen explained how a little variety was good, they were getting in a rut. They'd better not give Sue a hard time or they'd sure hear about it later—she'd be close by and coming back in a half hour or so.

Then she gave Sue a grin and a thumbs-up sign, and followed the guard—*counselor*—out the door, along a corridor, through a locked gate, and halfway down a side passage.

"They tell you about Derelle?" the counselor asked Ellen.

Ellen nodded.

"Okay then." The woman unlocked the door. "I'll be waiting outside. You need anything, holler, and bang real loud."

★ ★ ★

The girl sat on the bed staring at her hands. She was wearing standard issue sweats in faded pink, a size too large, with the sleeves pushed to the elbows. She had light bronze skin, a splatter of freckles across her cheeks and the bridge of her nose, and a tangle of reddish-tinged dreadlocks. She didn't look up. Rage and suppressed violence emanated from every pore of her body.

"Hi, Derelle. I'm Ellen Fischer. I work with the Children's Alliance. They told you I was coming, right?"

No response.

Ellen laid the small notebook in the girl's lap. "I'm sure you'd like this back."

A shrug.

Ellen glanced around the cell but saw nowhere to sit.

The usual plastic chair had been taken away. Because they feared Derelle would use it as a weapon?

What was she supposed to do? Stand? Sit beside Derelle on the bed?

Ellen thought about calling the counselor and asking for a chair but decided against it.

She leaned her shoulders against the wall and allowed herself to slide down until braced in a squatting position, her face the same level as Derelle's. "Do you like to write?"

Silence.

"Keep a diary, maybe?"

Silence.

"See, we started a writing program here, with a workshop once a week. There's one going on today. There're usually about ten kids, with either me or a Berkeley student volunteer as a leader. You can write anything: poetry, a story, or your own thoughts and ideas. There're no grades. Everyone takes turns reading their work out loud, and then we talk about it together. Maybe you'd like to do that too?"

She might as well be talking to herself. Ellen studied the girl's closed face, the thick eyelashes lowered as a protective barrier—*if I can't see you, you can't see me. I'm not here.* She dropped her gaze to the small hands with their scarred knuckles and bitten-down nails, and wondered about this girl's life and what species of hell had brought her to a used-car lot in Oakland, with a crowbar, at 2 A.M.

Twelve years old. Ellen remembered being twelve quite well, remembered her frilly white bedroom and collection of teddy bears, and the framed poster of Ringo, her favorite Beatle. In bed by ten on school nights, eleven on weekends; good-night kisses every night. Had anybody, ever, held and kissed this child in the way a child should be held and kissed?

Ellen felt a flood of compassion. She yearned to take the girl in her arms, stroke that unkempt hair, and tell her that everything, eventually, would work out for her and be all right—but that would be against protocol and potentially disastrous. She must tread very lightly. She was not a social worker, a psychiatrist, or a drug counselor. She had no official status. She merely ran a volunteer writing program that gave a few kids something to do with their endless time and that perhaps, now and then, stimulated their minds. The Children's Alliance connection with Juvenile Hall could be terminated at the stroke of a pen—and that mustn't happen.

Ellen suggested, "You might enjoy it."

Derelle finally raised her head. "I don't have nothing to write about." Her eyes were large, a rich amber with a cluster of green and brown flecks around the pupil. Ellen looked into those beautiful eyes and thought, Talitha's eyes were just like that, though they'd been laughing eyes. Derelle's looked as if she might never have known what laughter was.

Few days went by without Ellen remembering Talitha. There was a picture of the child on her office wall, braids sticking out like a hedgehog's spines, grinning across the top of her favorite Babar book.

Ellen wished she had a photo of Talitha, serious and composed, sitting at the kitchen table that day reading from *Charlotte's Web*. That child should have gone on to lead a fine life, she certainly had the potential.

"Most people find it difficult at first, starting," Ellen told Derelle. "When that happens I tell them just to write about themselves. Half a page or a few lines, telling who they are, or who they'd like to be—"

The girl's mouth twisted. "I'm not into any of that psycho shit."

"That's okay; nor are we." Ellen regarded Derelle appraisingly. She was smart. "That's not what it's about, we're not trying to trick people into saying something they don't want. Like I said, this is just a writing program, once a week for people your age, telling stories. Most of them think it's fun, but you don't have to do it if you don't want."

Ellen knelt on the floor, opened her briefcase, and took out a package of crayons and laid them on the bed. "Here, perhaps you'll change your mind. I'd rather you had a pen or pencil, but they won't let you have anything sharp."

Derelle opened the package and took the purple one out, almost the same color as Ellen's shirt. She held it in her chewed-up fingers and inspected it. Then she turned her head and looked at Ellen square on for the first time, and the atmosphere changed as if the air was suddenly sucked from the room. Ellen was aware of real menace; she sensed the tightening muscles and the tension rippling up the girl's arm while those lovely eyes, hard and cold, flicked to her face, to the crayon, and back.

Ellen knew that Derelle couldn't do quite as much damage with a crayon as she could with a sharpened pencil or pen point, but she could still jam the thing in her eye, or use it as a distraction before slugging her.

Would she try?

Ellen braced herself. She had no idea what would happen, just knew she was down here on the floor at a huge physical disadvantage. She met Derelle's measuring stare and waited, every muscle tense.

After a moment the girl's eyes dropped, the crayon snapped in her fingers, and she laid both pieces down again, side by side on the bed cover.

Ellen exhaled silently; she didn't realize she'd been holding her breath. Although her knees trembled she felt euphoric, as if she'd won a contest, as if they had both won, the prize being that Derelle, out-stared, might actually write something out of sheer pride and cussedness.

"I'll be back in a few days and see what you come up with," Ellen said.

"What makes you think I'll come up with anything?"

"Why wouldn't you? What else do you have going on?"

The corners of Derelle's wide mouth turned up in a derisive grin. "Okay, lady, I'll write something for you. It'll be real good, too. You'll see."

★ ★ ★

Sue was proud of herself and her handling of the workshop. "Sure they acted up some," she told Ellen, "but nothing I couldn't deal with." Sue drove the Chevy with confidence all the way back to the Children's Alliance. She didn't ask about Derelle, and Ellen didn't want to talk yet about that strange encounter. She wanted to hug the memory of it around her while daring to hope she'd lit a fire where none had burned before.

She stepped through that little door in the roll-away wall into the clamor of her needful staff, and the dreaming, of necessity, was done.

"Ell? Richard's caseworker called and—"

"The Black Magic Bar says could we use—"

"—broken down again and can't be delivered till—"

It took Ellen half an hour to put out the fires and gain the relative peace of her own office, a small, wedge-shaped space partitioned into a back corner beside the mural. Her desk, reasonably clear when she left, was piled high again, and higher still as her assistant, following her through the door, dropped a grant proposal on top, which she begged Ellen to check at once.

Ellen dumped her briefcase on the floor but didn't immediately sit down. Instead, hands on hips and head tilted back, she confronted her portrait gallery of all the kids who'd passed through her life: Angela, Ramón, Talitha, Jocelyne, Inocente, Sandy, Laurel.

The successes and the lost ones, but all of them *her kids* and loved.

She thought how she'd save this girl Derelle if it killed her.

CHAPTER NINE

There were five courthouses in Alameda County and nearly one hundred public defenders. Josh spent most of his time based at Oakland Municipal, on Fallon between Thirteenth and Oak streets, close to Lake Merritt, where he'd scurry from his desk—one of many in the huge bullpen on the second floor—to the courtrooms.

He also spent time interviewing clients at dismal, teeming Santa Rita County Jail down in San Leandro. Josh loathed Santa Rita almost as much as the inmates did. The only marginal advantage about the place, at least for a not-so-well-paid young public defender, was the food. You could buy a fine lunch in the mess there for a buck, good filling stuff, too: chicken pie, hamburger, pot roast with all the trimmings—though it couldn't make up for the mantle of depression that dropped over Josh the moment he stepped through those steel gates.

By and large, however, the rewards of the job far outweighed the disadvantages and brought him closer to Ellen. Just as she was able to discuss her kids with him, so could he filter his cases by her. She was entirely supportive of what he was doing despite the nonstop pressure on him and the emotional wear and tear. By others, of course, he was routinely asked the same questions:

"How can you stand to do this work?"

"All they're doing is bilking the system."

"How can you bring yourself to defend someone who's so obviously guilty?"

Josh would try to be patient, though it angered him that a poor criminal should automatically be regarded as the scum of the earth, whereas a wealthy felon, who could afford a fancy lawyer, was frequently viewed as merely unlucky. "It doesn't matter what you think they might have done," he'd argue fiercely. "They have the right to a defense. They're innocent until proven guilty, remember?" Almost invariably his clients would plead guilty and be convicted, but still they were entitled to the full protection of the law, just like rich people. And sometimes, they really were innocent.

Usually, the best Josh could do for his clients was to make the best deal possible with the DA and soften the blow in the sentencing. When there were no extenuating circumstances whatsoever he would argue, eloquently, for judicious exercise of humanity—that the judge attempt to put him- or herself, for one minute, in the defendant's place, to walk in his shoes, to live his life.

Josh would demand, "Were *you* born in poverty and raised on the street? Do *you* live in an unrelenting atmosphere of violence, as likely to find a handgun on the kitchen counter as a saucepan? Do you go to bed hungry night after night? Does every cop and so-called upright citizen look at you like they fear and hate you? How many funerals do you go to every year, for a child, a family member, or a friend shot or knifed to death?"

He'd urge, "Think about living in constant fear, ever alert against the unsuspected blow, the shot from the passing car, the police breaking down the door in the night. You develop your own defenses because you must. You build a hard shell because you must, and you take what you can get—*because you've been given nothing, ever!*"

★ ★ ★

Josh was doing a gritty job in a tough part of the city. There were bad times, some dreadful, others downright gruesome, but in so many ways the public defender's office was also a heady place to be. He felt energized, a warrior of the people, glad to be part of this army of young, idealistic lawyers, crusaders for justice and human rights whose call to arms might as well be, "Bring me your poor, your downtrodden, your uneducated, and your under-represented, and let us show them that someone gives a shit!"

They would argue the injustices from desk to desk, in the street outside the courthouse, in the cafeteria, at one another's homes, and at the bottle parties (not as frequent as they would have wished) held to celebrate a winning case, when the success-ful lawyer was required to provide the booze.

Sometimes there were some welcome successes to celebrate.

Danny Tubman, charged with assaulting an officer and resist-ing arrest—which, on closer examination, proved to be a clear case of self-defense—with an investigation instigated against an overzealous cop.

Rose Gaines, charged with possession of a controlled substance—a first-time offender with desperate personal and family problems—diverted to a residential treatment program.

Taylor Scheer, charged with indecent exposure, which would have categorized him as a sex offender, a label to haunt him the rest of his life.

"Whatever happened with that one, that you'd come home laughing?" Ellen asked.

"Because he was not your basic pervert but a crusading naturist."

"Excuse me?"

"An ardent nudist!" Josh explained that Taylor, a muscular young man with rippling blond hair and beard who had taken off all his clothes in a place called Minky's Tavern, had no sexual motive whatsoever but merely wished to demonstrate the grandeur and wonder of the human body. "We got the charge reduced to dancing topless and bottomless against the Oakland city ordinance," Josh said, smiling. "He was fined and released."

Ellen laughed that wonderful rich laugh and said, "Only you would think of something like that!"

"Thank you!"

"Just so long as he doesn't get the urge to do it again."

"I think he learned a lesson."

* * *

Josh told Ellen almost everything, but he never told her about Hector Rivas.

If ever there was a man let down by the system, it was this man: born in a festering barrio in greater Los Angeles, poorly educated in a substandard school, then sent to fight in Vietnam, from which he returned with a metal plate in his skull, appalling dreams, and a drug habit, even less wanted by his country and now unemployable.

Josh faced Hector for the first time across a metal table in the interview room at Santa Rita, early on a Tuesday morning in late October. He saw a doleful young man with trembling, nicotine-stained fingers and several missing teeth, wearing orange prison coveralls at least two sizes too large.

Hector was charged with two counts of first-degree murder. It had been a corner grocery store robbery, the clerk and a young girl shopping for her baby (the blue basket beside her contained a package of disposable diapers and a can of Enfamil formula) both shot dead, the till emptied, and Hector witnessed fleeing the scene.

"It's all a big mistake," Hector explained to Josh. "I walk in, and there're these dead people on the floor. I don't know if the guy's still there, maybe in back. I'm out of there, man."

In the courthouse interview room, Josh met later with Hector's wife, Bianca. "He doesn't even *own* a gun," she maintained fiercely. "He was only guilty of trying to buy cigarettes. Goddam it"—with a wry twist of her mouth—"I *told* him smoking was bad for him!" She sat stiffly upright, her long fingers drumming furiously on the table. "My poor Hector! Things have never gone right for him, never. They send him to that hellhole Vietnam, use him up and cripple him, then toss him out like garbage."

Josh's first thought, upon seeing Bianca, was how in the world had she ended up married to someone like Hector. She was exotically beautiful, the result of a particularly fortunate blend of Pacific Rim ethnic mix, with dark, slightly tilted eyes, and thick, black hair springing from a deep widow's peak and rippling halfway down her back. Her skin was a warm olive, and Josh felt she glowed as if lit from within. She was fashionably dressed in a suit of crimson wool, her only jewelry a heavy chain around her neck and a gold watch on her slim wrist. Her skirt was very short, and Josh found himself mesmerized by her perfectly shaped, silken legs with kneecaps that reminded him of golden apples—he couldn't remember having been captivated by knees before—and her lustrous thighs. He tore his eyes away from Bianca's legs with the utmost effort.

Josh licked his dry lips. He asked, "Hector has full disability?"

Bianca pulled a disgusted face. "Oh *sure*. SSI—such a lot of money! They tell him, Hey, thanks, Hector, too bad your head's messed up and your teeth fell out but, hey, lucky you, we're going to give you all this money so if you're real careful you can afford to live in some cheap dump till you die of cancer." She glared at Josh. "If they don't commit suicide, the vets, it's the cancer that gets them, you know that? From the Agent Orange? You know, all Hector ever wanted, since he was a little kid, was to be a cop. He was going to apply to the police academy after the army, but they'd never take him like he is now."

Her eyes flashed with emotion. She was not merely beautiful but a force of nature and sensuous as Eve. Josh stared at her mouth, full lipped and painted dark red. He realized he hadn't taken in a word she'd said.

"Please!" She was begging him now, hands side by side on the tabletop, pressing so hard her fingers were bloodless and white. "Help us! They said you were the best. So, show me!"

★ ★ ★

For the rest of the day Josh tried to move Bianca safely to the sidelines of his mind and couldn't. He told himself this was bad, it was unprofessional, that he was in over his head and must transfer this case to another PD—but knew he wouldn't.

After a week of unsuccessfully trying to stay focused and get work done, but too often finding excuses to call Bianca, and with her calling him to ask questions and remind him that she was counting on him, he gave in just as he knew he would and picked her up on Friday after work. Bianca sold cosmetics at the Emporium department store, and as she got into his car, he was overwhelmed by the rush of sweet perfume and powder, and the gentle way she laid her hand on top of his.

He drove her to Pacifica across the bay, and down the coast, to the perfect hideaway where nobody would know him, the Moonglow, an old beachside motel where the waves pounded on the rocks outside the window and the fog wreathed ghostly spirals in the wind.

After that evening with Bianca, he walked in a dream.

★   ★   ★

"Josh? Are you in there someplace? You look at me like you don't see me," Ellen said, concerned. "Is something wrong?"

He shook his head, trying to force Bianca out of it, and failing. "I guess I'm just tired. There's a lot going on right now."

"Is it a really tough case?"

"Yes, murder one, with a lot of complications." His own insanity being complication number one. He'd thought he knew himself inside and out. What a joke.

"Do you want to talk about it?"

"Not this time. I'm sorry, Ell. It'll be over soon. Please bear with me."

"You shouldn't let yourself get torn up like this."

"I know. But this is one of those times it really gets to you."

Ellen said with innocent irony, "I guess you wouldn't be a good lawyer if that didn't happen."

Josh wasn't so sure he was such a good lawyer right now, as all he could think about was Bianca. Bianca, who hadn't had sex with her husband in so long. "Poor Hector has problems, after Vietnam," she'd confided—which he'd interpreted as an inability to function in bed. And just as Bianca was hungry for love, so did he, Josh, yearn for passion. Much of the spontaneity was gone from his marriage. During the years they were trying to conceive, despite his and Ellen's best efforts, lovemaking had almost become an anxious chore. After Ellen's final crushing disappointment, Josh suspected that for her, the sexual act was a sad reminder of what she could never have.

Or was that merely a convenient rationale to try to soothe his own conscience?

He didn't like to think about it. He didn't want to think about Ellen. He felt too ashamed. Too much the traitor.

★ ★ ★

Josh knew that Greg Hunter was back in town—at least, just across the bay in San Francisco—and here for good, it seemed. He was seeing Jane Hecht again and wanted to be in touch with his old friends. If the four of them couldn't get together right away—Greg said he realized that might be hard with their schedules—surely the guys could get together for a drink sometime soon.

Josh had forgotten just how persistent Greg could be. His answering machine was filled with Greg's messages. "Hey, old buddy"—had Greg ever called him *old buddy* in the past? Josh thought not—"I've been hearing great things about you but still no see. Got promoted, right? Chief assistant PD? That's great! If you don't make it in politics, you can be Clarence Darrow. Now how about that drink? We have a whole lot of catching up to do and time's going by. Next Monday's okay, or Tuesday? Wednesday or Thursday? Friday's good, too. Take your pick, Judge. If nothing works for you there's always next week. C'mon, pal, you don't have to hide from me."

What Josh had not forgotten were Greg's powers of perception when it came to sniffing out a good story. Josh knew he faced a distinct dilemma and, on balance, decided he was better off stalling. Face to face, Greg would see through him at once, and he pleaded total involvement with his ongoing homicide case. "Let's talk after Thanksgiving," he begged. "The case has to be over by then, and I'll be able to get my life back." Though secretly he had to wonder whether life, as he had known it, was already over.

★ ★ ★

"What happened to you? I waited till the last minute," Ellen said.

Josh looked at her with a blank stare. She lay in bed, dry eyed now but clearly she had been crying.

"I know you've been forgetful lately, that's why I called you at work, to remind you. You'd said you'd be there for sure."

And Ellen had called, he remembered now. He'd tried hard to concentrate on what she was telling him, something about a celebration at the Children's Alliance, about her winning some medal for community service and making a speech, and counting on him being there. But even as she was talking to him now, all he could focus on were Bianca's long legs and the feel of her delicate fingers twined in his hair.

★ ★ ★

"Josh? I'm back in town tomorrow, and we can talk at last." It was a call from Congresswoman Shirley Lester, whose staff he'd been invited to join and for whom he was supposed to be organizing a fund-raiser. "How about we meet on Friday evening to go over things," Lester asked, "seven o'clock, my office?" And here, at least, the bright shaft of ambition pierced cleanly through the turmoil in his head, and he found the means to postpone his meeting with Bianca.

Shirley Lester was about the only person who had the power to break the spell; otherwise, it was as if he'd become someone else, someone with no willpower at all, wracked alternately with guilt and helpless passion.

He tried his best to appear normal around the office. What a time to be promoted, he thought. Embarrassing, too; he was the youngest chief assistant in two decades, promoted ahead of people who'd worked there much longer. Lately, though, functioning reasonably successfully—at least he didn't make any serious mistakes or miss a court date—he was afraid everyone could tell he was out of his head.

What the hell did he think he was doing?

Away from Bianca, he'd shrink with dismay at his recklessness, his stupidity, the potential for disaster, the hurt to Ellen. He'd think of Shirley Lester, of his promising career just about to begin. Each day he determined to end it, to call Bianca—*this has to stop, it's horribly unethical, it's crazy, my marriage and my reputation could be ruined, it's over*—but each time he heard her voice he'd feel that surging, ravenous need to see her again, to touch her. He hadn't known there could be anything like this. He had always dismissed the legendary thunderbolt love as an excuse for guilt-free lust. But this was more than mere lust, way more; this was obsession.

And so he agreed to continuances of the trial date and made his own motions for delay, all to give himself more time.

★ ★ ★

The Monday after Josh met with Shirley Lester, he was back at the Moonglow with Bianca. As was her habit, she titillated Josh unbearably by taking off her clinging jersey dress slowly, exposing her radiant skin an inch at a time. Then she undressed him and pulled him down onto the bed and tied her long black hair around his neck like a noose. She turned his face to hers, kissed him long and deep.

He had planned to end this relationship tonight.

Now all he thought was, I love you. *Love you.*

Later, as they lay quietly on their backs, hip to hip, she said, "Joshua, my darling, I need to talk to you. I'm worried."

She sounded so forlorn Josh gathered her up at once into his arms. He stroked her hair away from her damp forehead and told her whatever it was he would take care of it.

"Do you really think Hector has a chance?" she asked.

"He's always had a chance."

"He'd never hurt anybody. He's the sweetest man. But he's sick in his head. He gets confused. He doesn't remember things."

"I'll do my best. I've promised you that."

She rose gracefully on one elbow and traced featherlight circles on his chest with a fingertip. "When Hector goes to trial, you'll put me on the stand, won't you?"

"I don't think so." Josh had already decided that Bianca on the stand would be counterproductive, and her glowing beauty a potentially negative factor that could turn female jurors against them. What could she do for Hector besides offer a character reference that, speaking as a wife, would have little or no weight? And she hadn't been at the scene. "I've told you all of this," Josh said gently. "There's nothing more you can do."

"But I *was* there," Bianca objected. "I was with Hector."

Josh started in surprise. "You never said that before."

"I must not have been clear. Or you misunderstood."

"Where were you?"

"Parked up the block, while Hector went in for his cigarettes."

"How far up the block?"

"Not far. At a hydrant on the corner. Just for a minute. And this kid came out of the store and ran right past me."

"You were watching the entrance of the store?"

"Of course. Waiting for Hector."

"What happened then?"

"Hector came out running right after. He looked real shocked. He got in the car and said to get out of there quick, something terrible had happened."

"That's what he said? 'Something terrible'?"

"That's right. But he wouldn't tell me what. Said he didn't want me involved. Just to drive him someplace, to this bar down on Fourth Street, he needed a beer."

"Tell me about the kid."

"What about him? He was just a kid."

"How old?"

"Maybe sixteen?" Bianca shrugged.

"Black, white, Hispanic, Asian?"

"I didn't really see. He was just a kid, running, wearing a hat and baggy pants. Maybe black."

"And you never thought of telling me this before?"

Bianca traced more circles on his chest. "Like I said, I thought I had."

Josh sighed. He didn't believe a word of it. Now, more than ever, he wanted to keep her off the stand. "It won't work, Bianca. I'm sorry."

"You believe me, right?" She leaned over him and kissed him on the earlobe, very fast, flick flick, like a cat. "I can be real persuasive."

"You won't be able to persuade the prosecution and jury. You'll get torn apart on cross-examination."

"But it's true."

"Stop, Bianca. Don't do this. It's great that you want to help Hector, but you wouldn't be helping him or yourself by testifying that you were there." Josh gazed at her smooth, rounded knees, at her delicate hands resting on his hip.

"It would get him a not guilty, if I said that."

"If they believed you, maybe. But I can't take that chance." And I can't knowingly put on perjured testimony, he thought, no matter how persuasive you are.

Bianca leaned forward, a hand on each side of his head, her body resting the length of his, her black hair tumbling across her shoulders and over his face, blocking out the light. "I know you'll do the best for Hector," she said. "You can do anything! I trust you." She brushed her lips against his. "And when you win, I'll make it all up to you. We'll be together like never before!"

★ ★ ★

"Has it occurred to you you're walking a real slippery slope?" said Jake Haywood, the PD at the neighboring desk, eyeing Josh with weary cynicism the next morning. "What do you really know about this woman?"

Josh said, "Can you do me a really huge favor and mind your own business?"

"Sure can. But a word to the wise: you're acting like an idiot. She's using you."

"What are you talking about?"

"I'm suggesting that, under the *circumstances,*" with a meaningful glance at Josh, "if Rivas loses he can appeal, claiming unethical behavior and ineffectiveness of counsel. It would be a slam dunk. You're not exactly acting solely in your client's best interests, are you—*Chief?*" Haywood added, "But I'm sure you know the circumstances better than I do."

The phone rang on Haywood's desk to Josh's relief. Haywood turned to answer it, but not before saying, "It would be on my conscience, though, if I didn't say, Watch it, pal."

★ ★ ★

As Josh rose to make his closing argument at the trial, Bianca sat expressionless in the first row of seats behind the defense table.

She wore a simple black linen dress, little makeup, and just the gold chain with a crucifix appended. Tone it down, he'd ordered, thinking yet again about the female jurors. Every day for ten days she'd been obediently demure, but no matter how she tried, Bianca could look nothing but beautiful and desirable.

"Most young men," said Josh, addressing the jury, "raised on the streets in poverty, with each day a struggle to survive and lacking job skills, hope, or opportunity, would have long ago given in to circumstances beyond their control and taken up a life of crime. Young Hector Rivas was different."

Josh had pulled out all the stops for Hector, had done his very best, as he promised Bianca, and the twelve assorted jurors gazed with increasing sympathy at the defendant, so small and beaten down in the neat gray suit, white shirt, and paisley tie Josh had bought for him at the Salvation Army thrift shop.

He hadn't put Hector on the witness stand, and he hadn't let Bianca testify, either. They generated plenty of sympathy sitting just where they were. The DA had made a few mistakes in putting on his case, which had some holes in it to start with, and Josh didn't want to risk cross-examination. If he won, Bianca would forget her resentment at not being allowed to testify.

"He dreamed of a better life, one of sanity and order," Josh continued. "He wanted to be a cop. He had a beautiful young wife and dreamed of starting a family. But before he could apply to the police academy, this great country—this United States of America, which has let him down all his life—sent him to Vietnam, a convenient dumping ground for its young male minority population with no money for college and no influential friends."

Josh lowered his voice, speaking with soft deliberation as he drew the jurors into the tragedy, watching them all unconsciously edge forward in their seats.

"Hector was badly wounded in Vietnam. He can never be a cop now, there's a metal plate in his head, holding his skull together, and his dreams and ambitions died with his health. The only thing that hasn't changed for Hector is his luck; it stays just as bad as ever."

Josh met the eyes of everyone on the jury in turn: the postal clerk, the hospital orderly, the antique store owner, the veterinarian. "The night in question Hector just happened to be in a good neighborhood. They call it a good neighborhood, you see, because mostly white people live there. It was the wrong neighborhood for Hector, though, and the wrong time. He enters a convenience store to buy a pack of cigarettes and walks in right after a robbery. A very bad scene, the clerk and a young mother dead and bleeding on the floor. Hector panics. Wouldn't you panic in his place? Especially when it's sometimes difficult to think too well? So he runs, he's spotted, and naturally, because he's running and his skin happens to be brown in a white neighborhood, this young man, this combat veteran, must automatically be a criminal.

"The prosecution has not shown us the weapon, has not shown Mr. Rivas with a weapon, has not shown us a surveillance camera video of him in the store. But it's true, Mr. Rivas did do something. What did he do? The act that got him into trouble was to run down the street wearing the wrong color skin."

He felt Bianca's eyes riveted on his back and forced his mind away from her, forced away thoughts of tonight at the Moonglow, clenched his hands on the edge of the jury box as if it was a lifeline, and begged, the emotion raw in his voice: "Don't do this to him, Ladies and Gentlemen. Look at the facts of his unlucky life, look at the lack of evidence in the prosecution's case, and look into your hearts. Hector Rivas did not commit this crime. You must find him not guilty."

★   ★   ★

In the hallway after the verdict came back, Bianca flung her arms about him, thanked him, and hugged him again. "What a gift," she said into Josh's ear. "Hector will be home for the holidays. And for you, I have a very special gift that I will give you very soon."

But Thanksgiving came and went without him seeing Bianca. She called him every day only to say that she had no time to talk, that she was busy at work, or that Hector was in the other room at home. "I can't wait for us to be together again, either," she said, "but not tonight."

Josh had convinced Ellen that they shouldn't go to see his family in Southern California for Thanksgiving, that he was too exhausted, but the real reason he didn't want to leave Oakland was that Bianca might call and say she could see him.

His parents were disappointed but understood that he was overworked and busy, and he felt worse than ever.

Greg called and Josh felt obligated to make a date for the four of them to go to dinner. He didn't want to go, but he had come to feel there was safety in numbers, and he'd deal with that night of socializing when it arrived.

By the second week in December a whole month had passed since the trial, and beyond that ecstatic courtroom embrace Josh hadn't seen Bianca, not once. After five days without a word, Josh called her at home. The number had been disconnected. With growing dismay, he called the Emporium cosmetics department.

"Bianca?" said a woman's voice on the phone. "No, she's gone. Hasn't worked here for weeks. Why don't you check with Christina? They were friends—she might know."

★ ★ ★

He stood at the sink in the men's room washing his face and hands when Jake Haywood appeared in the mirror behind him, the crude light shining through the thinning brown hair and exposing a pink scalp.

Josh wished Jake would leave him alone. He continued to soap and scrub.

"About to perform surgery?" Haywood said. "Or washing away the sins of the world?"

"What's that supposed to mean?"

"Nothing, I suppose." Haywood shrugged. Then he asked, "How's your wife? How's pretty Ellen?"

"Ellen's fine."

"That's good. But you, pal, I wouldn't say you're looking so hot."

Josh reached for a paper towel. "It's nothing—some kind of virus. It's the time of year."

"This virus got a name?" Haywood wondered. "Guilt, maybe? There's a lot of that going around."

★ ★ ★

It was five-thirty. Josh parked immediately outside the main entrance to the Emporium and leaped up the steps into the store. He strode up and down the aisles of lipsticks and fragrances and found Christina, but she was no help. She didn't know where Bianca was. He should talk to the supervisor.

Josh identified himself as Bianca Rivas's lawyer and said he had to get in touch with her right away. The harried supervisor said only that Bianca had left two weeks ago without giving notice and hadn't left a new address, though they thought she had gone back to Los Angeles.

Josh left the store in a daze.

He stood outside on the steps, in the rain, not knowing what to do next.

He stared unseeing at the Christmas window displays of reindeer, dancing snowmen, sleds filled with bright packages, and a super-sized mechanical Santa Claus who waved and boomed, "Ho ho *ho*! Ho ho *ho*!"

Beside Josh, beneath a wide striped beach umbrella, the Salvation Army woman relentlessly rang her little bell. "You just missed the tow truck," she said sympathetically between tinkles, "too bad."

That was when he noticed that his car was gone.

But what did a small thing like that matter now?

The festive lights swooped around him in blurry streaks and Josh realized he was crying.

CHAPTER TEN

In retrospect, Ellen didn't know how she'd have gotten through that awful fall season if it hadn't been for her growing friendship with Shirley Lester and for her involvement with Derelle.

Ellen confided to Lester the matters she used to discuss with Josh: her dream of building a hostel behind the Children's Alliance building, of opening a branch of the Alliance in San Francisco, and more immediately, her struggles to drag Derelle into at least the semblance of a normal life.

"It's clear she's been abused beyond belief and treated like an animal. She doesn't know how old she is. She doesn't know her own birthday. I have no idea where she came from and perhaps she doesn't know herself. Huge parts of her are locked away. She has lost the key and maybe will never find it. With all that, she's bright as hell. I told her to write something for me. Talk about creative writing…!"

Ellen recounted how on their second meeting Derelle, her expression frankly gloating, had handed over the notebook in which she'd filled each page with just one word—*shitfuck*—in alternating red, purple, and black. "I wore out those colors," the child had grinned. "Got none left."

Lester asked curiously, "What did you do?"

"Gave her more crayons and another book."

"And?"

"Same again, this time with twelve-letter embellishments. Not surprising, really; she saw herself as helpless, and writing filth was the only way of getting to me. But the moment I reacted the way she expected, I'd have lost her. At the same time, I couldn't help but feel what she was doing was a positive step, like putting the garbage out—and that when she'd done it long enough there'd be room inside for something new to grow. Anyway, I plan to keep the crayons and notebooks coming. And being such a bright kid, she'll get bored. I mean, how many thousands of times can you write just one word? Especially those?"

Derelle held out for longer than Ellen expected because she was stubborn and tough. Eventually, however, the satisfaction of writing *shitfuck* over and over ran down, as it had to without the encouragement of dismay or disgust, and she wrote instead, in alternating lines of black and blue, about a dream:

"Its dark and theres shooting and larfing loud loud and then the blue light getting bigger and the blue face over me and pointed teeth and white eyes and hes larfing at me I hate his larf and his hands tuching and I cant move or shout or nothing"

Ellen saved it to show Shirley Lester the next time the Congresswoman was back home in her district.

"What's your take on that?" Lester asked.

"That she's telling it the way it was. She's in bed with a TV playing in the next room—'shooting and laughing.' The door opens—'blue light getting bigger'—somebody comes into her room and the rest is unbearable."

★ ★ ★

Derelle's plight was clearly so much worse than her own that for hours at a time Ellen was able to set aside, and even sometimes to forget, her anxiety about Josh. Just as well, too, otherwise she thought she'd go mad wondering what had gone wrong between them.

Might it be something she, Ellen, had said or done? Some inadvertent act of unkindness or perceived insensitivity?

"It's nothing to do with you," Josh would insist. "Just bear with me."

So what was left?

Sometimes he looked at Ellen as if he didn't even remember who she was. Was this disaffection really, as he claimed, due to overwork on a particularly difficult case, this double homicide that went on and on in continuance after continuance and that he couldn't discuss?

No, Ellen couldn't buy that. Josh had all the energy in the world and even acknowledged an adrenaline rush when he was in trial. He invariably welcomed her input too: *Here's the situation, this is my strategy, and these are my tactics. How do you think they'll work?*

But not this time. What was it about this case that made it so hard to talk about? And why couldn't he even say up front that he didn't want to discuss it?

She'd obliquely raised the subject with Lester, that Josh was unusually preoccupied, but Lester, beyond a fast, sharp glance, seemed to have noticed nothing particularly amiss. Despite this endless trial, Josh had recently organized a fund-raiser for her that had been a great success. "He did a terrific job," said Lester. "He was totally focused. Well, you know all about it, you were there."

The event had taken place at the home of a well-known labor lawyer and his aristocratic and idiosyncratic English journalist wife, $50 per head, the guests including socialites, artists, writers, union leaders, and Black Panthers. A pretty good rock band had performed for free, there were clowns and a human statue wearing nothing but silver body paint. People had a blast; Josh had made a stirring, introductory speech, Lester made a ton of money, and the phone calls from donors and volunteers had poured in to her headquarters the next day.

Lester said Josh seemed to have enjoyed every minute of the preparation and the execution. But the Congresswoman didn't see Josh every day.

★ ★ ★

If it was nothing she'd done or said, Ellen thought, and it's not related to work, family problems, or Shirley Lester, what did that leave?

It had to be another woman.

Why else would Josh avoid her, not make love to her, rarely touch her, and generally behave with distant, dreadful politeness?

Ellen found herself doing things that at any other time she would consider despicable: checking the glove compartment of his car for scribbled notes, phone numbers, or condoms; sniffing his jackets for an alien perfume.

Once, on impulse, Ellen actually went to the courthouse unannounced, walking into that big room crammed with desks and all those earnest young men in their inexpensive suits and bright ties, already ashamed of herself and wishing herself anywhere but there. Fortunately Josh was out and she felt weak with relief.

"He's down at Santa Rita," said the older attorney at the desk next to Josh's, his eyes brightly curious behind horn-rimmed glasses. "I'm Jake Haywood. Can I help?"

Ellen introduced herself and shook her head. "Thanks anyway. I'll see him later." Then, knowing she shouldn't, but this man Jake seemed kind, she said, "You know, I'm worried about him. He seems to be under some kind of huge stress. Do you think he's all right?"

Jake said so far as he knew Josh was fine, but Ellen would realize later he hadn't looked her in the eye as he said it.

"Want to leave a message?" he asked.

"No message." She summoned a smile. "And could you do me a favor? Don't tell him I was here."

She clung to one small crumb of comfort. If there *was* another woman, she didn't seem to be making Josh happy.

★ ★ ★

In November, Ellen worked on finding a foster home for Derelle, a hard task that became a welcome diversion.

There weren't many families who'd take on somebody with her record. Even Oscarene Willis had to be persuaded.

Oscarene was a well-recognized port in many storms. She took in the worst of the worst, the toughest kids turned down or thrown out by every foster parent in town, and ran her place like a boot camp with zero tolerance for drugs, liquor, and trash talk.

You dressed decent, kept your room clean and tidy, did your share of chores without bellyaching, and went to church on Sunday. Oscarene took no b.s. from anyone, but in times of trouble—and there were plenty of those—she'd been known to sit up all night with a sobbing child enfolded in her massive arms.

"Sure I'd take her," she told Ellen, "but I don't have room."

Ellen wouldn't take no for an answer. It was Oscarene or back to the Children's Center—how Ellen longed for the Alliance to have its own hostel—and Derelle needed a real home so badly. "What about that little storeroom in back?"

"I got stuff there."

"Let's have a look."

So, during those long empty evenings while Josh worked late or did whatever he was doing, Ellen carted boxes of discarded clothing and broken appliances to the dump in her truck. The bundles of old magazines—Oscarene hoarded *National Geographics*—went to the Baptist Church basement where she sang in the choir. One Sunday, Ellen and two of Oscarene's teenagers scrubbed out the little room top to bottom and painted the walls yellow and the door white. The church donated some furniture: a bed, a little bureau, and a fluffy white rug.

Derelle, clutching a brown paper grocery bag containing all her worldly possessions, cast a cursory glance around the room and said she guessed it was okay.

Oscarene's nostrils flared with indignation. "This is your *own* room. All for *you*. You don't have to share like the other kids. And that's all you have to say? *Okay?*" But Ellen guessed that Derelle hadn't really noticed the room at all, that her focus was on the freshly painted door with the shiny new bolt—on the *inside*—and knowing she could lock herself in and be safe.

"I guess it'll work out," Oscarene told Ellen the next week, "she's getting adjusted. It takes time. She keeps herself to herself, just goes in back and locks the door. Won't talk to no one. Won't let anyone in. And another thing." Her voice sank and she leaned confidingly across the kitchen table. "That bag she brought, moving in? Just coloring crayons and books. That girl doesn't have more than the clothes she stands up in. I had to go buy her a toothbrush. She doesn't even have any underwear."

So Ellen packed Derelle into the pickup and drove her to the Emporium, riding up in the escalator with her to a whole floor of panties, bras, socks, and nightgowns, where Derelle stood rigid at Ellen's side, stunned and intimidated by the abundance.

Ellen gathered up two six-packs of panties, size medium, and said, "Now bras."

Derelle remained mute, folding her arms protectively over her chest.

"It's no big deal. You take them to a fitting room. You'll have a space to yourself, with a mirror. I'll wait outside."

A pair of teenage girls, probably younger than they looked, maybe even younger than Derelle, rolled their eyes and giggled. Derelle fixed them with a glare of enough potency to blister paint. The potential for violence flickered like summer lightning, and the girls exchanged a nervous glance and hurried away.

"Okay, no problem." Ellen quickly chose four bras, two white and two beige. "You can try them on at home and if they don't fit we can bring them back and change them, so don't cut any labels off." She added some brightly colored T-shirts, six pairs of tube socks with striped tops, and from the sports department a navy blue sweatsuit with white piping, Derelle walking stiffly alongside, uncooperative, eyes straight ahead. At the checkout, the garments laid out on the counter, she leveled a challenging glare at the sales clerk as if she expected to be accused of stealing them.

She was silent all the way home, seat belt dutifully fastened, the bag on her lap, untouched. She didn't look at her new clothes and made no attempt to thank Ellen. She didn't even say good-bye, but just marched into her room and bolted the door.

★　★　★

The piece began in angry purple; it ended in turquoise, yellow, and orange, the colors of daybreak:

> "The place is too big and there's so much stuff all over,
> miles of it so you dont know where to look. I dont no

how big I am how I should be and the girls laugh and I
could kill them for laughing nobody disses me or I beat
on them and the lady at the checkout she look at me
like Im shit but Ellen says how Im good as they and I
got a right to shop in a store like other people and we
drive back on the freeway right up high above the city
and I feel like some kind of queen or maybe an angel
flying like I could just stretch out my wings and fly
away over the roofs into the sun in my new yellow Tee
shirt she bought for me."

Ellen thought, This girl is the light in my darkness.

★ ★ ★

Before Christmas—in the middle of organizing the annual
Children's Alliance party and the toy drive, trying to persuade
various corporations to donate, and putting out a special holiday
newsletter featuring a fuller version of Derelle's visit to the
Emporium—came another flash of light, this time in the form of
a call from Greg.

He'd been back for months now, and she hadn't seen him. At
first she hadn't wanted to, then in the stress of the past weeks,
she'd forgotten all about him. Now, hearing his voice, she was
surprised by a rush of pleased anticipation.

"Josh and I were talking about all getting together sometime,
and we finally set a date. Next Friday look good to you? Jane and
I will pick you up," he said, "and go somewhere for a bite. Then
there's this old flick, the Invasion of the Body Snatchers. What do
you say?"

"A horror movie. Perfect!" Ellen said.

She hung up, feeling a lot more cheerful. The evening would
be fun and would be good for Josh. The case was over at last but
he still seemed quiet and distracted, and routinely after dinner,
during which he'd have little to say, he'd retire upstairs to his
office with a briefcase full of work and not emerge until she was
in bed. He had evinced none of his usual pleasure over winning a
case on which he'd worked so hard and for so long. Ellen hoped

that seeing his old friend and roommate would restore his spirits as she had been unable to do.

Ellen wondered how she would feel, seeing Greg again, but figured it would be just fine. After all, the night Nixon resigned, their night together in Greg's bed in Eucalyptus House, was a long time ago. The seventies had been a wild decade, but people grew up and times changed. Perhaps he's forgotten all about it, thought Ellen, though she had not. And anyway, Greg was seeing Jane Hecht again. Ellen had always thought the two of them suited each other.

★ ★ ★

On Friday, Josh was late coming home.

Ellen called his office at seven but there was no answer.

Greg arrived moments later in tan slacks, midnight blue turtleneck, and black leather jacket, without Jane. It seemed she had favored the opera with her father over the *Body Snatchers*.

"Can't imagine why," Greg said, "she has a tin ear."

It might have been awkward, just the two of them, but it wasn't.

Ellen fixed drinks, a beer for Greg and a glass of wine for herself. She found she had forgotten what very good company he could be. While they waited for Josh he entertained her with stories of Surprise Bend, Nebraska, where a stolen car, piece of vandalism, or Mrs. Jennifer Sonnenfeld giving birth to triplets was major, breaking news; where town meetings, Little League games, and the local cat show provoked howling mayhem; and where the local pastor admonished the tornado of 1976 with "Begone, you towering pillar from hell!"

He was as good an actor as he'd always been and had her in stitches of laughter. She decided she was not sorry Jane hadn't come. It would be so much better for the three of them to go out together when Josh got home, almost like old times.

Of course Greg had also been to Ohio, which was when the laughter ended.

Ellen asked, "How's your father?"

"The same, worshipping at Timmy's shrine. Let's not get into that."

"And your sister?"

"Fat, three kids." Then he asked, "Whatever happened to that child I met, the one whose house we went to the night Nixon resigned"—without a qualm in his voice—"Remember?"

"Of course I remember. That was Talitha."

"The one who liked elephants."

"Babar," Ellen said. And she related, with sadness, how the family had fallen apart and young Talitha, who'd have been nineteen by now, had succumbed to the lure of the streets and the boys with the flashy clothes and fancy cars, dropped out of school for good, moved in with a bad man, and three years ago caught a stray bullet during a drive-by shooting. Ellen described how she had never been able to banish a feeling of guilt that somehow she had failed the child, allowed her to fall by the wayside, and nobody else had cared enough.

"That's sad," Greg said.

"But at least she'd had those years with books," Ellen said, "and her world got bigger for a while."

"You don't get discouraged, do you?"

"No one said it would be easy."

Greg eyed her closely. "You know, sitting here with you, it seems as if I've never been away. You sound just the same. You look the same—no, even better."

"You haven't changed either. At least, not much."

He cocked an eyebrow. "No?"

"Just older." In fact, he was as attractive as ever, maybe more, but Ellen would be damned if she'd tell him so. She sensed that his conceit hadn't changed at all.

After a moment of silence, while part of Ellen wished Josh would come home right now and part of her wished he wouldn't, Greg said, "It's eight o'clock. Looks like it's just us chickens after all."

"I guess."

"So let's go."

"Where to?"

"We'll ride, and see where we end up!"

"It's raining."

"You won't get wet, Ellen. I brought a car this time, not a bike."

★ ★ ★

It was a Mercedes 240SL. Metallic blue.

"You've certainly moved up," Ellen said. "The *Chronicle* must pay well."

"It's Jane's."

"It *must* be love. I wouldn't lend mine—if I had one."

Ellen sank into the soft leather seat with a sigh. It was exactly what she needed, to go for a ride in a beautiful car with a handsome man. She decided she deserved it. For the first time in months, she felt young and carefree.

Greg gunned the car up the steep, steeper, and steepest blocks of Marin Avenue all the way to the top, and along Grizzly Peak Boulevard where Ellen had ridden with Josh after Professor Wolf's funeral, though she really didn't want to think about Josh right now. They looped along the ridge and down again, around the back of the Claremont Hotel, onto Highway 24, then roared through the Caldecott Tunnel and out to Walnut Creek where they searched in vain for a fifties-style drive-in place Greg had heard about with carhops on roller skates. They eventually settled for a steak house with dim lights, dark booths, and gigantic leather-bound menus with tassles on them.

When the waiter had lit a lotus-shaped candle in the middle of the table, served a London broil, medium, for Greg, poached Pacific salmon for Ellen, poured wine, and left them in gentle dimness, Greg said, "Do you want to tell me just what the hell is going on with old Josh?"

"It's a case. A bad one. It got to him more than it should."

"Just a case?"

"What else? Of course he shouldn't take it to heart, but Josh's like that. It's a good thing he's not going to make a career of the law."

"And he seriously believes politics is a warmer, fuzzier profession? Not to my recollection he doesn't."

"Sometimes depression can't help but come with the territory. The desperate lives these people lead—it's so sad. It's because, as a public defender, what he says and does has a direct bearing on those lives and he feels responsible. I know just how he feels."

"I don't buy it. Josh is a realist."

"You only lived with him four years. I've had twice that."

"Quite the old married couple." He shot her a contemplative look across the table, took a sip of wine, and asked gently, "Where d'you suppose he is tonight?"

"Working, like I said. He'll have forgotten to call."

"Everything all right with you guys?"

Ellen sensed that Greg had grown more acute, that he not only now saw beyond himself but had fully developed a keen reporter's mind. She thought that could be dangerous. I'm ending this conversation, she decided. And in a light, cheery voice, she said, "Never better. In spite of everything."

"Any little Joshes or Ellens in the works?"

"No. Now tell me about you and Jane. Is this serious?"

"Everything seems to point that way," and they were back on track again, talking of Greg's job at the *Chronicle,* how good it was to be home.

"Because this is home to me now, the same as for you," Greg said.

Such a lot to tell and to hear. By the time they got back to Berkeley, the last showing of *Body Snatchers* was well under way. Instead, they waited for the midnight showing of *The Rocky Horror Picture Show* at a funky little theater on Addison Street, standing in line in the drizzle among girls in wedding gowns or red wigs and strapping young men in garter belts or mummylike bandages, just like the characters in the movie. Greg dove into a nearby convenience store and returned with a small bag of rice. "Ammunition," he said.

Their seats were toward the back and to one side but it didn't matter. They flung rice during the wedding scene and chanted, along with the rest of the audience, "Don't go in there!" as virginal, saucer-eyed Susan Sarandon and buttoned-down Barry Bostwick approached the sinister mansion in the rain.

It felt so good to laugh again.

★   ★   ★

After the movie, Greg drove Ellen back to Crescent Court and parked at her gate, beneath a clump of trees. "Come here," he said.

"I don't think so," she said.

"Don't worry," he said, "I'm not going to maul you in a car like a teenager."

"I should hope not. Especially since it's Jane's car."

He pulled her gently against him and held her, smoothed back her tumbled hair, and kissed her, not a lover's kiss but more tender than that of a mere friend. "I've never forgotten that night."

"Me neither. But it's not going to happen again. Just so you know."

"I'd think about you, while I was away. How we were so good together. Did you ever think of me?"

"Sometimes. And of course Josh talked about you, wondering what you were up to. He'll be sorry he missed you tonight, he was looking forward to it." Ellen reached for the door handle.

Greg sighed and pulled away from her. "All right, you good girl! C'mon, I'll walk you to the door."

"You don't need to do that; I'll be fine."

"It's dark. There isn't even a porch light on."

"Josh'll be in bed."

"Maybe he'll be worried."

"No he won't. He'll know I was with you."

"And of course he trusts me."

"Of course."

Greg climbed out of the car, came around, and opened the passenger door. "Don't argue. Let me be a gentleman."

"All right." She let him walk her up the path beneath the oak tree. In her front porch lay a deeper puddle of darkness than the surroundings, and it wasn't until they got right up close that they saw the man slumped against the door.

Ellen heard Greg's sharp, indrawn breath; his arm stiffened around her, and he pulled her to a stop. "It's some homeless guy passed out. Get back in the car; I'll deal with this."

"No!"

"Ell, please—"

She pulled away from him and fell to her knees beside the huddled, soaking wet figure, who sighed and moaned when she touched him, then raised his head, coughed, and released a pungent waft of liquor fumes. "Ellen," he mumbled. "Ell? Is that you?"

"It's all right," Ellen said to Greg, who stood over them, ready to give the guy his marching orders, call 9 1 1, or do whatever else needed to be done. "It's only Josh."

Josh struggled, unsuccessfully, to sit up. "Whozit?" he demanded.

Ellen said, "It's me. And Greg."

Josh attempted a smile. "Just old Greg. That's all right, then."

★

1989

★

CHAPTER ELEVEN

It was 5:45 A.M., and the sky was beginning to lighten over the eastern hills. Josh had just climbed out of the shower when the phone rang—obviously Shirley Lester, in Washington, D.C., half an hour early with her daily call, important matters on her mind.

With wet hair and a damp towel sliding down his hips, Josh closed the door to the bedroom where Ellen was catching a last few minutes of sleep, hurried into his yellow-walled office—which he knew, in Ellen's mind, would forever be known as the baby's room—and picked up the phone.

The Congresswoman was exuberant. "He thinks it's a *great* idea, Josh!" She had been negotiating with Tony Cervetti, director of Veterans Affairs, about Josh's plan to use empty beds in VA hospitals as a resource for homeless veterans. "He'd actually thought of it himself, but knew he'd take too much heat from the bureaucracy at the VA for it to be a 'go.'"

"So now he can pin any problems on us," Josh said.

"Specifically, on you! It's your baby."

"At least it's still breathing."

"It actually looks hale and hearty. You'd better get started drafting a plan for Cervetti's people ASAP."

"I'll do that. First thing this afternoon."

"What's wrong with this morning?"

"I'm pitching your Town Hall for Kids at Central High."

"Right. Of course."

Josh could feel his boss shift mental gears. For Shirley Lester, Oakland born and bred, Town Hall for Kids was a project close to her heart, a planned forum in which young people might meet both with her and with selected public officials to discuss, in safe and neutral surroundings, not just the street problems confronting them every day, such as drugs, gangs, and the proliferation of guns, but ideas on how to make their town a better place to live. "Talk to us!" she'd urge. "Work with us and get involved. Let's find solutions together!"

"If anyone can convince them they can make a difference, that they *count,* it's you," Lester said to Josh. "You care and you show it. You can make them trust you."

★ ★ ★

"D'you want eggs? Scrambled? Over easy?" Ellen was fixing breakfast, still in her bathrobe, a black silk kimono with a dragon on the back, a treasure found years ago at a secondhand shop on Telegraph Avenue.

"Better not, just a muffin, I'm running late." Josh kissed the top of her head, put his arm around her waist, and gave a brief, close hug. She was not wearing anything underneath and his hand lingered a moment, only to feel her infinitesimal withdrawal. He touched his fingertips to the smooth hollow of her neck instead as she turned away from him, ripped open the package of English muffins, pried two of them apart with a fork, and dropped them in the toaster.

For the past seven years, Josh and Ellen had been very careful of each other, newly fragile-like disaster survivors, the old relationship ruptured and sloughed away to reveal the too-tender skin beneath.

He loved Ellen. He treasured her. The more so since the madness with Bianca, ending with that last night, the car towed, walking aimlessly in the rain with a hazy memory of drinking somewhere in a systematic obliteration of self until the bar closed, when somehow he'd found his way home because there was nowhere else to go, then discovering that somewhere along the way he'd lost his door keys. He'd been afraid to ring the bell and wake Ellen, so he'd crouched in the doorway, intermittently dozing, until he'd finally felt her light touch on his face and her small, strong hands under his armpits hauling him upright. "You're soaked," she'd chided, "and you're freezing. What are you *doing* out here? Let's get you to bed!" He'd hung on to her for dear life, overwhelmed with dismay at the damage he'd done to her, and for everything else he might have done if Bianca hadn't left. *I'm sorry,* he'd mumbled over and over, *I'm so sorry,* not sure if he spoke aloud, *forgive me,* while Ellen ran the shower steaming hot, pushed him under it, then toweled him dry and piled him into bed where he'd slept until noon the next day.

He'd known he should tell her about Bianca—*for a while there I went crazy; I made a terrible mistake; I wronged you*—but dreaded the hurt he'd see in her eyes. The anger. Suppose she left him? Tomorrow, he'd decide. I'll tell her tomorrow—but tomorrow came and slipped by and so did the tomorrow after that.

Later, his wits recovering, he'd wondered what Ellen had been doing up and out at three in the morning. She'd been fully dressed when she found him, hadn't she, not in bathrobe and slippers. Rather late to be coming home—but she'd been with Greg so that was okay. They'd been supposed to catch a movie with Greg and Jane, hadn't they, though he had forgotten all about it. Good old Greg, he'd tried to help. Josh was glad to know his old friend was still there for him.

Ever since, Josh and Ellen had both tried hard, but they hadn't made it all the way back.

He prayed they would.

In the meantime it helped that they were both so very busy.

★　★　★

Josh spread honey on his muffin, standing at the counter beside the buttercup yellow phone that would start to ring anytime now.

Ellen poured them both orange juice. The toaster popped again.

It was Wednesday, Ellen's designated morning of outreach in the schools. She had arranged to visit Central High this morning so that for an hour or two she and Josh could actually be in the same place at the same time. "Perhaps we could grab a coffee later?" she'd said. Josh quipped, *"Together?"* and she'd laughed. Not quite the old belly laugh—he hadn't heard that in a long while—but close enough.

Josh reached for the *Oakland Tribune* and scanned the front page: a double homicide in the Fruitvale district; half a ton of marijuana seized by the Port Authority; another savings and loan scandal. Could anybody do anything to combat such callous, monumental greed? Was there any point in trying? Then he read how the Hazlett Corporation, accused of dumping toxic waste, was being brought inch by inch but inexorably toward a settlement, and Josh reminded himself that one voice, or two, could indeed make a difference.

The phone rang. His aide, Vicente Aguilera, wanted to know what time he'd be in after the school gig, the janitors' union reps wanted to reschedule the meeting for eleven, and was that okay?

"I suppose." No coffee date after all, then. Josh stared regretfully at Ellen's back, upon which, at every movement, he fancied the dragon switched its tail and glared at him. "But don't arrange anything more for this afternoon," Josh said. "The boss called; she's got the ball into play with the homeless vets project."

Shirley Lester was fond of baseball imagery; she liked to think of herself doggedly running the bases in Washington while Josh slugged it out at the plate. "You and me between us," she'd say, "we're a great team. We get things done."

Vic was glad to hear about the developments in D.C. "Hey! That's great news!"

"It's terrific. I'll get going on the plan." Josh hung up and turned to Ellen. "You may have figured that coffee's out later this morning. Sorry."

She shrugged philosophically. "It was too good to be true."

The phone rang again. Carole Walker, principal of Central High School, was on the line. She planned to sit in on his talk, it was time she knew what he did for a living. Josh said he could use all the adult energy he could get in that classroom, especially hers, and she said they were a bunch of good kids—just one or two bad apples, but that was life.

He finished his juice, swallowed the last of his muffin, and dumped his coffee dregs in the sink. He made two more quick calls and received another. From upstairs he heard Ellen's swift feet rushing from bedroom to shower to closet and back again.

Then, briefcases packed, they were driving away in separate cars, Ellen leading in her scarlet Chevy, Josh following in the Toyota.

In the final rush out the door, they forgot to kiss.

He'd remember that later.

★ ★ ★

Josh thought the school looked like a prison.

He glanced at the gray slab of concrete, the asphalt, the chain-link fence, the graffiti, and the broken windows sheathed in plywood, all shown up so mercilessly by the bright early-March sunlight, and thought, What a disgrace. He wondered how young people, to say nothing of the teachers, could tolerate such a place day after day. How could anybody learn anything here except apathy, depression, and resentment? Ellen, however, didn't seem put off by her surroundings or even to be aware of them. Josh watched her, in today's shirt of hot fuchsia pink, vanish down the hallway, her elbow clasped by a girl in too-tight jeans whose sullen young face, on seeing Ellen, had grown suddenly radiant.

★ ★ ★

"Now, you've all heard of Congresswoman Shirley Lester. This is Joshua Fischer, her district director," said Carole Walker. She was a big woman, at least six foot, with strong facial bones and power-ful shoulders. She needed broad shoulders, she'd been principal at Central High for five years, a record, and was doing her best— which was considerable but, as she was dismally aware, not enough. Walker continued her introduction, "We've invited him here today to give you a hands-on talk about government, how you can get involved and work with Congresswoman Lester on the issues that affect you directly. You can ask him anything you want. Let's put our hands together for Mr. Josh Fischer!"

After desultory applause, Walker took a seat on one side of the teacher's desk and folded her arms across the thick tweed jacket that made her seem even bulkier. Surely, Josh thought, not even the rottenest apple would dare make trouble with Walker in the room.

He looked out at the forty or so young faces, their expressions ranging from cynicism to wary expectation except for the boy who wore a sweatshirt backward with the hood pulled over his face and another who seemed to be asleep on his desk. Josh wondered how best to conjure for them a world beyond that asphalt street, corner liquor store, and the dusty apology for a park full of dog shit with used needles in the sandbox. Could he ever make them believe there were options, that they had the ability to make changes, that their future belonged to them?

All he could do was try.

"I'll start by explaining how your Congresswoman's office works," he said, aware of a generalized rustle and shifting in the too-small seats, of the restless, lounging bodies and outstretched denim legs terminating in gigantic sneakers. He wondered how he and Lester had come up with the title for Town Hall for Kids in the first place. It seemed, with this crowd, not only misguided but quite ludicrous. That boy in the front row had forearms as large as most people's thighs; probably a football player, Josh thought, before remembering the sports program had been canceled for lack of funds, and physically he was no kid but a young man, maybe even a father.

Again Josh glanced around the room, wondering how many of this group had had a chance to be kids themselves. He recalled speaking on Lester's behalf to the ninth grade at another high school where there'd actually been a baby in the classroom, a cute bundle in little pink jumpsuit and matching bonnet, asleep in a basket beside her mother's desk. At the end of the period a huge boy had appeared, maybe seventeen years old, all bone and muscle like this one now, who had casually tucked the baby under one arm and taken it away while the child's mother prepared for her science lab.

Josh's eyes lit on the boy sleeping at the back. What was the story there? Zoned out on dope? Dead lazy? Developmentally challenged—or exhausted from working two jobs after school to support a family? He made a mental note to find out the student's name and alert Ellen. Maybe she could do something.

Josh continued, "We have about half a million people in our congressional district, which combines part of Oakland and part of Berkeley, and Shirley Lester is our representative in—" before his voice was drowned by sirens screeching along International Boulevard.

The kids nearest the windows leaped from their desks to look out. The others craned. You'd think they'd be used to sirens, but Josh supposed any diversion was better than none.

Walker ordered, "Okay, guys, butts back on those chairs!"

"—*Washington D.C.!*" Josh yelled. He drew a breath. "Now then, can someone tell me who else works in Washington?"

From a tawny-skinned child with a mop of straight black hair like the early Beatles, "The President."

"Right! Who else?"

Surprisingly, with a stirring from the backward-turned sweatshirt, came a muffled but stern pronouncement, "*Mis*ter Dan Quayle," which provoked proddings and back thumpings: "Hey, Ronnie!" "Way to go, Ronnie!"

"Great!" Josh beamed a smile toward Ronnie's hood, then he moved to the chalkboard and drew a slightly lopsided Capitol with a flag on top. "This is where Congresswoman Lester works most of the week while I run her office here. We have a staff of about ten people. Vicente is my special aide who makes sure I get to where I ought to be when I should be there. Loretta handles the phones and mail. There are three field staff: Leroy, Johanna, and Eric. They're our eyes and ears. They find out what's going on in the district, things Congresswoman Lester needs to know so she can do her job for you."

Josh waited for somebody to ask what kind of things Lester needed to know but nobody did.

"For instance," Josh said, "there're a lot of homeless people in Oakland. Some of them are vets—"

A girl asked, "You mean, like, dog and cat doctors?"

The general snort of laughter provoked a stern rumble from Principal Walker and Josh smothered a grin. "Not exactly." He explained that in this case vets were former soldiers, and as briefly as possible he described the plan: how homeless veterans, once identified, could be bused over to the VA Hospital, which would provide a one-stop shop for health and psychiatric care—and where they could remain safely until they were back on their feet.

Again, little response. He guessed he was being boring and had better hurry this part along. "We also have caseworkers who deal directly with people who have problems, like an old person who didn't get a social security check, or somebody with an immigration problem—"

A round-faced girl with a monumental hairdo spoke up, "My boyfriend's sister got deported. Even though she's married and the baby was born here and all. They called Ms. Lester. She got her let back in."

The principal rumbled, "Raise your hand, Beatriz. Mr. Fischer doesn't want you just cutting in."

"It's okay with me provided it's good news!" Josh said, smiling at Beatriz. "We also have an intern who works at the office, a student. She's called Amparo. Maybe you, Beatriz—or any of you— might think about doing that. We need all the help we can get, so we can help other people. *Our* people here in Oakland. What do you think? Why not come on down and check us out, you'd be welcome!"

He turned back to the board and wrote the words TOWN HALL. "Now then—what do you think when you hear those two words? *Town Hall?*"

Baffled silence.

"Maybe a building? Like this?" Josh drew an official-looking structure with pillars and pediment. A boy called, "Put a flag on." Obediently Josh did so, making it stand straight out as if in a stiff breeze. "And you'd be right, a big, fancy marble building where the town's business gets done, where the laws are made and issues discussed that affect everyone who lives there.

"This place, now"—pointing to his drawing of the Capitol with its proud but lopsided dome—"this is the Town Hall for the whole country—but it's very big and far away. That's why Congresswoman Lester likes to hold mini–Town Halls right here, in Oakland and Berkeley. She figures you don't need a big, fancy building; it's what happens inside that matters, that any place will do—a church, an office, or a storefront, where she can sit down with people, talk to them, and listen to their problems. And she especially wants to hear from young people like you because you guys are important—you're the future!" To one side and slightly below his drawing Josh wrote in large letters: INVOLVEMENT. SPEAKING OUT. "See," he went on, "she wants— she *needs* to know—"

And then, the gunshots.

Silence fell within the classroom and the air waited, dense with withheld breath while Josh tried to convince himself that the short, sharp volley had actually been a burst of firecrackers or a car backfiring outside in the street.

Of course the kids knew better and the dread and resignation were immediate: Here we go again, who's dead now?

Someone screamed outside in the passage.

Walker rose with surprising agility and lunged for the door, and at once, the spell broken, the class scrambled to follow in a confused, panicked melee.

"Let's get the hell out of here, man!"

"Outta my way!"

Somebody began to cry.

"Stop right there! Nobody's going anyplace!" Josh reached the door a split second before the principal, braced his back against it, and spread out his arms. "Get under your desks and stay quiet till we know what's going on!" He grabbed the huge boy from the front row and thrust him back in his seat with strength that surprised both of them, while the rest bunched uneasily in the aisles.

Walker, thank God, supported him. "You heard the man: DO IT!"

Josh turned, opened the door a crack, and peered out, aware of the principal's heavy hand on his shoulder and her breath stirring his hair. She hissed, "I can't see. Let me through! I gotta get out there—*this is my school!*" while all the way down the passage other doors opened, heads craned, teachers and yelling kids began to spill out into the hallway. Thirty feet away, the door to the principal's office swung open and crashed against the wall with enough force to knock out the inset panel, and a girl in a short plaid skirt and emerald sweater, her mouth a wide O of silent shock, shuffled through the tinkling hail of glass, staggered a few yards in Josh's direction, and crumpled to the ground on her face.

Josh stared at the dark pool spreading across the floor and began to run for the office, Walker lumbering at his heels. They found a middle-aged woman, blood in her gray hair, sprawled across the copy machine, two weeping girls crouching between the desks, and a skinny, brown-haired boy with a huge gun in his hand who smiled with concentrated intent as he aimed at the principal's wide, tweedy chest.

Carole Walker ignored the gun and surged determinedly forward, ordering *"Travis! Put that down right now!"*—for all the world, Josh thought, as if the kid had stolen some other kid's lunch or a toy that didn't belong to him. She did not seem aware of the vacancy in the youth's eyes or to understand that the real Travis was not at home behind that empty smirk but locked away in some bubble of his own creation upon which her voice would register as the merest scratch of a fingernail against glass.

Again acting on instinct, Josh grabbed Walker around her massive shoulders, pivoted her, and pushed her sideways against a bank of steel filing cabinets.

It was his turn to stare directly down the muzzle of the gun.

He said gently, "Better give that to me, Travis, you really don't want to do this," forcing himself to ignore that woman's still body, the whimpering girls, the shouting and chaos in the hallway, and now the approaching sirens—at least someone had had the sense to call 911. He didn't look at the gun either, but focused directly on the boy, talking to him, saying his name over and over like professional negotiators said you should at such times, when perhaps, identified with a name and thus as a human being, he'd think as one.

"Travis. Put the gun down. Put it down *now,* Travis." Josh took another step forward, ten feet away now, still too far away to jump the boy.

He licked his dry lips and knew by the instant gleam in those pale eyes that he'd made a mistake and looked vulnerable. For the first time real terror bloomed within Josh, his body felt watery and helpless, there was no way he could jump because his feet were lead, and he thought, This is crazy. I'm going to die here *and I never even kissed Ellen this morning. I should have kissed her. I'll never kiss her again.*

Then, as if the image of Ellen had actually summoned her into being, with a stab of horror he heard her voice from the doorway immediately behind him, gentle and calm, saying, "Hello, Travis. Remember me?"

And he'd thought it could get no worse. The dismay congealed in Josh's stomach.

From the side of the room Walker called, "*No,* honey!"

Ellen paid no attention. She asked Travis, "Do you remember when we talked? Right here, a couple of months ago?" She moved steadily forward, ignoring the gun as if it didn't even exist. She didn't reach out her hand for it, never said, *Give it to me,* and Josh watched the boy's mouth sag softly open as he turned his head toward her, sudden confusion in his eyes, the lines of his face softening into a different configuration altogether, the face of a lost child.

She's doing it, Josh thought in astonished wonder. She's really doing it; she's going to pull it off.

"We were going to work together, weren't we," Ellen said, moving between Josh and the boy as the room held its breath. "We can still do that."

Travis's lower lip began to tremble, the gun wavered in his hand, and for a moment it appeared Ellen had won—but then came the scream of sirens right up close, shouts and slammed doors, and the moment was lost.

Travis's mouth hardened, his hand tightened, the gun jerked toward Ellen, and Josh launched himself forward—never, not even with his high school track team all those years before had he leaped so far—and caught Travis around his skinny haunches and brought him down.

The gun went off, blasting a bullet across a desktop and through a shelf of books to crater the wall.

Afterward, after the police had arrived and Travis was taken away, with the plaster dust still sifting in the air, Josh gathered Ellen up in his arms and unashamedly cried.

★ ★ ★

Their bell rang and rang and an urgent fist pounded on the front door. "It's me," Greg was shouting. "Open up!"

"Get in here, quick," Ellen said. Josh saw Greg's shape momentarily silhouetted against a white barrage of camera flashes before Ellen pulled him inside and slammed and locked the door.

As Greg stood in the hallway of their house, winded, panting, and clutching a white paper parcel and a six-pack of beer, Josh warned, "I've absolutely nothing more to say. I said it all back at the school."

Talking to the press was the last thing he'd wanted to do, but Lester had advised on the phone, "There's no escape. Get it over with sooner rather than later." She herself was on all the news broadcasts this afternoon. With the debate on her new gun control measure coming up shortly in the House, the timing of this incident was viewed as particularly ironic: her own district director and his wife attacked by a crazy, gun-toting child. The timing was so providential, in fact, that Josh wouldn't even put it past some cynic to suggest the whole thing had been staged.

At the school, Josh had taken his turn in front of the cameras along with Carole Walker and Ellen.

"What does it feel like, looking down the barrel of a gun?"

"What did you think when Ellen came in?"

"How will this crime affect Congresswoman Lester's legislation for gun control?"

"Would you have shot him if you'd had a gun?"

"Did you want to kill him?"

Josh would have liked to yell back, in response to each and every damn fool question, *You idiots, how do you think it felt*—but he managed to hold on to his self-control, speak eloquently and sincerely, and like the skilled politician he was becoming, take full advantage of the situation. "The real crime is that a fourteen-year-old child, or *any* unstable individual, has such ready access to lethal weapons," Josh had said. "Now, two people have died. The pain and suffering resulting from these deaths is incalculable. Travis himself will be forever lost.

"With guns so easy to come by, this will happen over and over again until, as Congresswoman Lester fears most of all, we will all grow numb to the horror of it and accept such needless deaths as inescapable facts of life."

Josh had kept his poise and remained outwardly calm, even while he watched the swathed bodies being loaded into the back of the coroner's wagon. He thought how one of them might so easily have been Ellen—and felt himself tremble inside all the way down to the bone.

After the press conference they'd been driven home in a police car, two officers following with the Chevy and Toyota, and the still unsated members of the press falling in behind.

What more did those ghouls want? They had the facts, the body count, and the names; they'd taken the pictures (the coroner had actually posed beside a stretcher, straightened his jacket, run a comb through his hair, and assumed a stern, manly expression)—but of course that was just the official stuff. They wanted the juice, they wanted to see what happened when the heroes got home, they craved some emotional bloodletting.

The house on Crescent Court glowed in the afternoon sun, serenely and innocently welcoming as if they were returning from a picnic in the park.

"Hang on, ma'am, we'll soon have you inside." Their driver, six foot four and built like a tank, helped Ellen from the backseat as carefully as if she'd been made of glass and steadied her quite unnecessarily as she walked up the driveway. As Josh unlocked the front door with a suddenly shaking hand, the officer called out, "You folks take care now. Have a nice day!"

★ ★ ★

"I'm here because I'm a friend," Greg insisted. "This isn't an interview." He unpacked greaseproof packages of deli sandwiches— a roast beef on whole wheat and a turkey on rye. "I bet you two haven't eaten all day. You need something to eat. You're both in shock."

Josh looked queasily at the sandwiches. "Maybe later."

"A beer, then," Greg said. He pulled the tab and shoved a foaming can into Josh's hand.

"Thanks." What Josh would prefer was a stiff scotch. What he *craved* was a cigarette, and his fingers hooked automatically and vainly into his shirt pocket for the pack of Parliaments that hadn't been there for ten years.

But he'd hold himself together, he had to take care of Ellen— although she seemed to be bearing up better than he, a good hostess now, asking Greg did he want a glass for his beer, going to the kitchen and returning with a platter for the food.

Josh turned away and flicked the remote of the TV, catching Shirley Lester on CNN: "Josh Fischer is my strong right arm. And today, without question, he's a hero."

"You're both certified American heroes," Greg said. "I still can't quite get my mind around it. I think about what I'd do, supposing Jane walked right up to a gunman like Ellen. I'd like to think I'd do what you did—but I know I'd never be able to jump so far."

Josh smiled wearily. "Too much lard on you. You've gotten too used to the easy life."

"Hey, that's rude. You must be feeling better!" Greg went on, "Then I wonder if I'd have acted differently because of the boys. I mean, what about the boys if something happened to me *and* Jane?"

The thought spun out through the air.

After a silence just a heartbeat too long, Ellen said, "I guess, not having children, that's one thing we don't have to worry about."

CHAPTER TWELVE

Greg lay awake for hours after filing his story, staring at the ceiling, visualizing over and over again, in a nightmare loop, Ellen walking coolly up to that crazy kid and actually *chatting* with him.

It should never have come to that. Greg thought, Damn you, Josh Fischer, for your recklessness, for going in there unarmed! If you hadn't had the devil's own luck, that kid would have killed you both and giggled while he did it.

Turning his head, in the light of the half-moon slanting in through the shades, he could see that Jane was smiling in her sleep, perhaps dreaming of a winning set at the California Tennis Club. He wondered whether she'd have risked her life to save him. He thought she would. She loved him, and she would always defend those she loved like a tigress.

He reminded himself how lucky he was to be married to this beautiful, adoring woman who had not only given them two beautiful sons, but had brought him a surrogate father whose position could provide a strong boost to his career. No doubt Greg had gotten himself one hell of a deal—though it wasn't so much of a deal for Jane. "Do you love me?" she'd ask too often, with a hopeful smile and a swift kiss, and he'd reply sure he did, which seemed to satisfy her.

He sighed. He'd hoped he might grow to love Jane in time, but by now he guessed he never would.

He had a bad feeling that *he* would *not* throw himself in front of a bullet to save her. Though he would, anytime, to save Ellen.

Why did she choose Josh and not me?

Sometimes Greg hated Josh, sanctimonious prig, still sophomorishly saving the world. What world did he think he lived in, anyway?

★ ★ ★

Josh was on the phone first thing in the morning, his voice unnaturally cold. "You said you'd come as a friend, that everything was off the record, so what do you mean writing this *crap?*"

Patiently, Greg pointed out that he had in fact done Josh a favor. "What kind of a politician are you?" he demanded. "You need to come across as human, not some kind of machine. People don't give a shit for machines—they need emotion. You want my opinion, you should make me your press agent!"

Jane was filled with admiration for Greg's story. "Honestly, dearheart, you're such a star! How did you get them to say all that?"

"It only seems like they said a lot. Read it again; there's actually nothing more in there than Josh said already at the press conference. All I did was sit there and listen." And watch, thought Greg, aware that body language could tell you at least as much as words, often more. He'd learned that early, back in Surprise Bend, where words were used sparingly and sometimes grudgingly and the real telling was in the tightening of the jaw, the restless hands, or the sudden revealing silence.

Yesterday afternoon, clearly in delayed shock, Josh and Ellen had moved as if their bodies were strangers to them, and any normal action—standing, sitting, opening a beer—had to be carefully thought through in advance.

Greg had sought to convey this sense of dislocation in his article and, in conveying it, to punch up the noninterview by several emotional notches. The things he learned from how they held themselves and from what they didn't say! "A space is defined by its surroundings," he'd explained once to Jane. "If someone talks around it enough, it develops a shape."

Jane read aloud: "Ellen Fischer is immensely controlled, not by the flicker of an eye or a bodily tremor does she betray what she must be feeling until, 'Do you know what that police officer told me at the door?' she asks. 'Have a nice day!'—when the careful façade cracks into peals of laughter."

"*What* a clown," Jane sighed, "and a cop, too! He should know better."

"He was young and he'd have felt he ought to say something. What would you have said?"

"Certainly not 'Have a nice day.'" Jane was studying Ellen's picture now. "She's still pretty, isn't she? Awfully thin. Lucky girl. How does she do it? She must spend her whole life at the gym working out."

"I doubt she has time for the gym," Greg said drily.

"Then she must have a naturally high metabolism."

"That must be it—" though he suspected that saving the world's children was a more effective regime than aerobics.

"And Josh—you know, he's still kind of cute. He hasn't changed much since school. He reminds me of that movie star—what's his name—Daniel Day-Lewis! Those grooves in his cheeks, and those smoldering eyes, they bore right through you. Too bad they don't have any kids; they'd be good-looking."

"They would," Greg agreed, and asked, "What's on the agenda today, for you and *our* kids?"

"Taking them for shots, then to playgroup. Then I have a tennis lesson at the Cal Club. Hospital Ball meeting this afternoon to plan the dinner menu. Dress fitting—"

"Busy little bee." Greg leaned across Jane's breakfast tray to kiss her good-bye.

Still gazing down at the picture of Josh and Ellen Fischer, their faces pale and shocked, arms wrapped tightly around one another, Jane said, "The four of us really ought to get together some time. I haven't seen them since the wedding—and Josh was your best man. It's been years!"

It had been five years, and every time Greg thought of the wedding he was glad that Josh had been there to provide a ray of sanity.

Greg had known the wedding would be grand, but never in his wildest dreams could he have imagined such an event. The planning had taken almost a year, and in culmination there he'd stood up front in Grace Cathedral, so exposed, scrutinized by five hundred pairs of eyes, certain that everyone could see right through his outward composure and his fine clothes to the real Greg Hunter who certainly did not belong here among the rich and famous.

How grateful he'd been for Josh and Ellen's presence, and the comfort that flowed through them to him. Greg had thought, They're the only people here that really know me. My only real friends, who give a damn. I love both of them, yes I do.

Josh, stalwart at his side, had looked unusually distinguished in striped trousers and cutaway coat. Ellen, beautiful in something floaty and gray-green, sat beside Greg's sister, Ginny, in the front pew on the groom's side. Poor Ginny had worn a clunky, navy wool suit and a too-youthful white straw boater with a red ribbon, and clutched her purse as if she expected it to be stolen any minute. "I didn't realize Jane was quite so rich," she'd fretted at the rehearsal dinner. "All these fancy people. Jane's father is quite *somebody,* isn't he?" when Ellen had touched Ginny's hand, so kind, putting her at ease. "Don't even think about it," she'd said. "They're only people!" and Greg had felt ashamed of himself for being ashamed of his sister, who'd probably dreaded this day for months.

Now, moving toward the door, he said to Jane, "I'm not sure Josh and Ellen will be up for social engagements at the moment."

"No, you're right," Jane agreed at once, and Greg thought she actually sounded a bit relieved. "And on second thought, we don't really have much in common with them, do we. I mean, as a couple. They're kind of intense." She added, "And we'd probably have to go over to Oakland."

"That's probably true."

"We'll leave it as a Christmas card friendship then," Jane said, and turned to another page of the paper.

★　★　★

If Greg had been overawed then by his own wedding, he also knew that, thanks to his father-in-law's money, power, and connections, he had arrived socially. Nowadays, as Josh had pointed out, he was growing thoroughly used to the good life and was awed by very little.

Greg also tended to agree with his wife that, if not quite a star, he was doing very well in his chosen profession—though luck also had something to do with it, as well as being in the right place at the right time, and knowing the right people.

His article on the Central High shooting attracted attention. No doubt about it, he had a way with words as well as with people, and came across as natural, sincere, and warm—essential qualities in a top journalist. The very next week, however, when he was tapped for an investigative piece on the rising homeless crisis, Greg almost regretted his own talent.

"Hunter!" came the yell over the general buzz and racket in that long, smoky room, "Get yourself over here!"

Greg wended his way between desks to the east end of the city room, and the cluttered desk of Harvey Pilcher, city editor.

"Got something you might get your teeth into." Pilcher had a big head crowned with reddish hair fading to pink, curling insectile eyebrows, an implacable mouth, and a permanent, half-smoked unfiltered Camel held between his stained fingers. He tapped ash into an overflowing saucer before reaching for a pile of folders and loading them into Greg's arms. "Read up on all of that. Get out on the streets, spend time at the churches, food banks, and shelters, and find out just who these people are."

With deep dismay, Greg regarded his editor across the top of the files. "Are you sure I'm the right one for the job?" It might be a fertile assignment, but the thought of carrying it out appalled him. Greg loathed the homeless. He wanted them to go away, he didn't care where so long as he didn't have to see them. Returning from the Midwest after eight years, he'd been shocked by the state of the streets of San Francisco. WILL WORK FOR FOOD, DOWN ON MY LUCK, ANYTHING HELPS, GOD BLESS! clamored the signs on corners and median strips. In the years since, the homeless population had soared into a ragged army, clutching and importuning and sometimes abusive when their demands were not met. As darkness fell, more hunched figures emerged pushing their rusty carts from alleys and doorways like a scene from *Night of the Living Dead*.

"There're people who'd do a much better job," Greg assured his editor. Into a cold silence, he suggested Guillermo Gutierrez, with the battle-scarred face and street smarts, or Fay Young, the doe-eyed Asian whose gentle voice and manner belied a relentless tenacity for weaseling out a story. Greg said with certainty, "No homeless person's going to talk to *me*."

"Then make 'em talk to you, that's what you're paid for." Pilcher eyed him up and down, narrowing his hard, gray eyes against the smoke. "Got any old clothes? You're way too clean-cut." As Greg left, knowing it was useless to argue further, Pilcher called, "Grow a beard!"

★ ★ ★

It was an order, with no negotiation acceptable, so in due course Greg, wearing his ancient school sweatshirt with its worn-out elbows, and ten days of golden stubble on his chin, found himself hanging out at Glide Memorial Church, at the Salvation Army, and waiting in line for the free lunch at St. Anthony's dining room.

He wandered up and down Market Street and through the clusters of derelicts in United Nations Plaza, pausing in doorways, on the medians and street corners, acting his empathic heart out as he chatted with bag ladies and shuffling winos and surely no one, but *no one* could have guessed how he shrank from those filthy hands and reeking clothes.

How could they so degrade themselves, he'd wonder furiously. Had they no self-respect?

His own grandfather had been poor, but Greg knew old Mr. Hunter would rather starve than beg for money on the street.

Ditto the Old Marine.

And himself, too, damn it—he, Greg, had been working since he was ten years old, pushing a broom after school at Hunter's Hardware to earn his movies, ice cream, and candy. He'd earned his own way, he'd earned scholarships and never taken a dime from anyone.

★ ★ ★

"It's such a drag you have to work tonight." Jane was once again reclining against her lacy pillows, morning paper at her side, across her lap the low-cal breakfast tray (black coffee, slice of melon, two small triangles of toast with low-fat spread) prepared by Mrs. Hearn. Jane was still in training for tonight's Children's Hospital Ball at the Fairmont Hotel, for which she was chairman. "Try and make it later on," she begged. "We'll save you some dinner."

"I get dinner at the shelter."

"What a treat! What time do those people go to bed?"

"Nine o'clock."

"That's okay then. *Our* party isn't over till midnight."

"I'll be there." Greg pulled on his worn sweatshirt, an ancient pair of jeans, and shoved his feet into three-year-old sneakers.

"You'll finish with this homeless thing tonight, right?" Jane asked.

"Yes." Greg thought, *Thank God.*

"So you can shave."

"Finally, I can shave."

"Pity, in a way; designer stubble is 'in' these days," she said, running the tips of her fingers across his cheek. "It makes you look rather sexy."

★ ★ ★

At five-thirty, while Jane no doubt was home primping for her big event, Greg parked his borrowed, beat-up Volkswagen bug illegally in a side alley thick with garbage and sickening smells, the kind of place he could imagine bodies being dumped, confident that no beat cop or meter maid in their right mind would venture in here and give him a ticket.

The line already stretched around the block waiting for the shelter doors to open at six, when one hundred and fifty men and women, providing they were neither drunk nor stoned, would get a free dinner, a shower, and a night on a cot where they would snore, hack, and mumble, row upon row, until their rousting at six, free coffee, and a doughnut. They'd be back on the streets by eight because the premises double-dutied during the day as a senior day-care center.

Soon he, Greg, would be working the long tables with his little trolley of pitchers—"coffee, milk, or tea?"—smiling like some goddam airline stewardess.

And now here they came, shuffle shuffle and squeak of cart wheels, into the warm shelter where the cots were lined up in rows, each with its folded gray blanket and small pillow; the waiting toilets and showers; the dining room where volunteers were breaking out the TV dinner–style plastic plates and loading them with turkey slices—a supermarket had donated six fat, breasty gobblers—complete with mashed potato, carrots, gravy, and a chunk of cornbread.

Reverend Pat manned the doors, smiling welcome: "Hi, Susanna. Hey, Tony, how you doing? Good to see you, Tyler, Julie too—that's it, folks, come right on in now."

The clients, guests, or whatever they called themselves took their places on the benches on each side of the long tables. Many didn't seem particularly hungry, and leftover food was tossed into a black plastic-lined trash bin. Greg, in whom a few childhood exhortations still burned strong, thought that was wasteful. The leftovers could have been boiled up for soup. Ginny would have made soup.

Hey there, how you doing? Coffee, milk, or tea? I'm Greg.

The second time around, offering refills, there was a chance to chat, which was why he was here.

The old man, who'd been second through the door, had the sensitive face of a poet and a mane of silver hair. He claimed to be seventy-five but looked younger. "I prefer *Anthony.* Not Tony, if you don't mind. And you want to know my personal little piece of history? It's not so much, really." He told Greg that he'd been in the navy, and once, long ago, had taught college somewhere in the Midwest, though he couldn't remember the town. He'd been married, too; one son was a lawyer in Portland, Oregon. "I could go live with him if I wanted; he'd have me just like that!" A snap of the fingers and a gentle laugh. "Perhaps I'll do that someday. But probably not—I don't think his wife cares for me." Anthony had lived in San Francisco for thirty years and had been homeless for ten. He wasn't sure exactly how it came about, "But that's life. It's about change and drift. Not much of a story, no real meat in it—thank you, I'll take a little more tea if I may."

Tyler, middle-aged and black, showed Greg his crumpled right hand, where the index and middle finger were missing and the fourth a stump. "Sure I got workers' comp for what it was worth. My so-called lawyer should've gotten me more. For sure ain't no job for a machinist with only a thumb and pinkie and just *you* try shaving and dressing yourself or holding a goddam dinner fork."

Julie had a scrunched, marmoset face topped by a halo of gray hair and wore a drifty dark blue dress with little pieces of mirrorglass sewn all over it. "Hey, gorgeous," she said to Greg, "haven't seen you before! What're you doing, slumming? This place sucks. Of course it's not my scene at all, you can tell, can't you! Doing anything later?"

Greg smiled, said yes, he had plans, and surreptitiously checked his watch. Eight fifteen. By now dinner would be in full swing at the Fairmont, after which there'd be congratulatory speeches. Then the hospital spokesperson would introduce Jane, who'd stand at the podium blushing and glowing in her rose pink Valentino gown and tell everybody what a great time they were having and how wonderfully generous they'd all been, though how could they not be for such a good cause—while the waitstaff cleared the dessert plates and poured the coffee.

"Yeah, black, two sugars. And he'll have milk. No, man, I'm not telling you my name. What in hell you want my name for?"

They sat close together at the end of the table, both thin with grizzled beards, wearing military camouflage jackets with the name tags and insignia torn off. The speaker wore a black knitted watch cap pulled down low on his forehead, from beneath which he squinted up at Greg with dark, suspicious eyes; his companion sat with lowered head, compulsively crumbling his cornbread in his lap.

Watch Cap took the bread away and brushed off his friend's pants, "Leave that now, Bud," then turned defiantly back to Greg. "That's not *his* real name either, it's just what I call him. Because he's my bud, see?"

"Fine." Greg set a full cup on the table. "Here you go, Bud, here's the milk like you wanted."

Watch Cap said, "And you don't have to talk to him like he's some kind of *re*tard just 'cause he don't say nothing. He never talks. Not one word in twenty years."

Bud took the cup and drank, milk trickling over his shaking fingers.

Watch Cap complained, "You filled it too full."

"Sorry." Greg glanced from one wasted face to another, was reminded inescapably of Tim, and felt a sudden jarring dismay. Might Tim have ended up like this? On impulse he asked, "Were you guys in 'Nam?"

"What kind of a dumb-ass question's that?"

"My brother was in 'Nam."

"That so."

"Yeah. He didn't make it back." Greg was tempted to pull out Tim's photo. *This is him,* he'd say, *We're from Akron, Ohio. You didn't happen to know him, did you?* Then, perhaps, spurred by comradeship, Watch Cap would volunteer his own hometown, Springfield or Des Moines, after which he might relate war stories of booby-trapped jungle trails, burning villages, invisible foes, a mission gone horribly wrong, and carrying his wounded buddy away in his arms.

But instead of confiding, Watch Cap merely observed, "Then your brother's one lucky motherfucker. Now c'mon on, Bud, drink up like a good kid. You got cake for dessert."

"You ever talk about what happened?" Greg tried.

"With someone like you who wasn't there? What's wrong with you, you crazy?" Watch Cap's eyes were suddenly as menacing as twin bullet holes. "Get your ass out of here and leave us alone."

Greg had a vision of his brother and Marco wandering the cold city streets begging for quarters and people looking through them as if they were ragged ghosts or, worse, didn't even exist.

Marco had survived the war; he'd written once and sent a package of Tim's personal stuff, including the diary Tim had promised Greg he'd keep and in which, after the first few days in Saigon, he'd never written in again. What had happened to Marco? Greg had tried to find him, Marco Ascoli from Detroit. He'd called Information, found three M. Ascolis, tried them all but none was a Marco, a Marcus, or a Mark; none had heard of Tim's best buddy from Vietnam.

At nine Greg left the shelter with the other volunteers. Most of the inmates had showered by now and were setting up camp in their sex segregated dorms. A few were already asleep—and dreaming of what?

Greg's battered old car waited unmolested in the alley. A ragged man of indeterminate age lay asleep or passed out against the wall, knees drawn up and fists tucked under his chin. For a long moment Greg stood looking down at him. For all he knew that could be Marco Ascoli lying there at his feet, the buddy who had watched out for Tim's back, who'd cared for him. On impulse Greg pried the man's fingers apart and tucked the last of his money between them, a ten-dollar bill. He hoped nobody had seen him and would steal the money the moment he left. Nothing stirred and the alley seemed deserted, but there were always eyes watching.

He shivered.

God, was he ever glad to get out of there.

★ ★ ★

Greg could hear gunshots and shrieking tires from the little room off the kitchen where Jane's Irish "treasure" would be drinking her bedtime cup of cocoa and enjoying her favorite television show.

"That you, Greg, dear? Have a good evening?"

"Fine, thanks, Mrs. Hearn. How's *Miami Vice?*"

"Very good, dear. Detective Crockett's gone undercover to infiltrate this drug ring from Colombia. I could fix you a sandwich if you haven't eaten, a nice turkey on rye, the way you like it."

He thought of the grayish lump of meat congealing in its gravy on Bud's plate. "No thanks. I'm going to try and make the party. I'd better hurry."

"All right, dear, I won't pester you."

"Get back to your show. How are the boys?"

"Sleeping like little angels."

Upstairs, he peeked around the open door of his sons' room.

As usual Jeff had left his own bed and climbed into Doug's, and the two of them were tumbled together like puppies. He looked down on them, at their white blond hair, smooth skin, and soft mouths relaxed in sleep, and thought how beautiful they were. He yearned to take them in his arms and breathe in their warm, living scent. But not now, stinking like he must be.

Greg left the door ajar and entered his and Jane's sumptuous bedroom with the thick white rug, white bed, and the window looking into the magnolia tree.

Seeing all that pristine whiteness made him feel thoroughly filthy inside and out. He stripped off his clothes, flung them into the hamper, and turned the shower on full blast, leaning with closed eyes against the green and white tiles while hot water streamed onto his head and down his body.

He closed his eyes and instantly saw Watch Cap and Bud, those dead faces with their locked-in nightmares. He'd felt a sudden blast of eerie kinship with the two veterans and now yearned for someone to talk to. Jane wouldn't care. He thought of Ellen, and how, with her, he always found it easy to confide. Those two guys really got to me, he wanted to say now. They shook me up. What am I doing exploiting them for a story?

Out of the shower, he shaved and walked barefoot back into the bedroom. He stared at the tuxedo hanging on the back of the closet door waiting for him along with the white starched shirt with the pleated front, the black bow tie, the claret-colored satin cummerbund, and the pair of glistening, patent leather evening shoes.

"If you miss us at the Fairmont," Jane had instructed, "come on over to Stars. We're all going there for a nightcap."

He didn't want to dress and go to the ball, smile and make small talk and dance; all he longed to do was go downstairs again, pour himself a huge bourbon and soda, light on the soda, and bring it back up to bed. He was bone tired. But Mrs. Hearn would hear him and insist on preparing that sandwich, he worked so hard and needed taking care of, and he'd have to make small talk with her instead.

So, the lesser of two evils—put on the monkey suit, smoke a cigar with his father-in-law, and dance with his wife.

★ ★ ★

"Well, look who finally blew in!" Jane was flushed with triumph. It was a wonderful party, they'd sold out and made scads of money for the hospital.

The elegant white and gold room was hot and crowded, though the ranks had perceptibly thinned. Their table was still full, as it should be; nobody dared leave early with Jane Hecht Hunter being madame chairman.

Nice people, thought Greg, as he greeted them, all of them old friends.

Rich old friends—of Jane's.

You could tell old money, he had long ago decided, because everybody seemed to have interchangeable first and last names. Even the women, if they weren't addressed by some twinkly diminutive like Bitsy or Bunny, had names like Stewart, Courtney, or Morgan.

"Hello, Bunny," he smiled, still feeling unreal. "Hi there, Stewart!"

The band launched into a jazzed-up version of "Aquarius" from *Hair*.

Jane cried, "Perfect timing! Let's get out there, Greg!"

Gunther Hecht said, "The lad looks done in. Let him have a drink first."

"Dance first, drink later! I haven't danced with my husband all evening, and they're playing *our song*!"

His father-in-law, with a fond shrug, said he had better listen to the boss, and Greg and Jane danced. He owed her at least one. He knew she liked to show off to her friends—*see what a terrific couple we make, watch me dance with my handsome-as-hell husband who, unlike a great many husbands here tonight, is sober and actually loves me*—while she crooned untunefully with the music and he tried to will himself back into that reckless, sexy mood in the cabin of the *Freya III,* and failed.

Back at their table, an extra chair waited and, to Greg's immense relief, a double bourbon on the rocks.

He took a huge swallow and felt the spirit burn its comforting way down, spreading out like a smooth, warm blanket.

"There you go," Jane approved, "more color. You were looking quite pale." She stroked his smooth cheek. "I missed you, dearheart."

Morgan Davis told him how terrific his article had been about that young couple at the shooting, how she'd felt absolutely *there* in the room with them, that Jane had said they were old friends from Berkeley days and how frightening that must have been, and Jane agreed it was quite terrible, awful for poor Josh and Ellen, how it made violence so much more real when people you knew had been shot at and how, actually, she'd been thinking she might get a gun for herself.

It was then that Senator Carl Satcher strolled up to the table, whacked Gunther Hecht across the shoulders, demanded to meet the son-in-law he'd been hiding, and Greg found himself confronting a man who could be Hecht's clone, with the same broad, high-colored face, same waistline thickened by middle age and good living, the same sleekly muscular aura of power.

Gunther Hecht might tally his fortune in millions, but Carl Satcher's was greater by the power of ten. He was one of the two or three most influential men in Southern California, a close friend of the governor and a longtime pal of Western-movie star Thomas Turner, with whom he had frequently dined at the White House.

"Known Janey since she was knee-high to a grasshopper," Satcher told Greg cheerily. "I see she's found herself a keeper!"

"Glad to hear you say that, sir," Greg said.

"Heard a lot about you. All of it good"—with a bark of laughter—"not like the rubbish you'll have heard about me!"

"I guess," Greg said carefully, "that depends on who's doing the talking."

"True, son. Very true!" Satcher laid a heavy arm across his shoulders. "My friend Gunther thinks we have a few things in common and can work together. He may be right. Down the road aways—maybe not so far down—we'll spend some time together. I think we'll have a lot to talk about."

Greg said, "I'd like that, sir." He thought, *My first billionaire!*—and felt quite cold inside to remember his earlier spasms of doubt and sentimentality and how he'd almost not come here tonight.

CHAPTER THIRTEEN

Congresswoman Shirley Lester (D-Ca.) announced
today that Joshua Fischer of Oakland, California, has
been designated her new chief of staff, effective immediately. Fischer, 39, has worked with Lester since 1982
and as her district director since 1985. Lester said
Fischer would continue to be based in Oakland but
would fly back to Washington frequently.

"I have decided," said the congresswoman, "that
Josh's connection with my constituents back home
weighs in favor of his staying in the state."

Fischer said, "I am deeply honored that the congresswoman has put so much faith in me. I will serve her and
the people of the Fourth District with all my energy."

Fischer's wife, Ellen, is the well-respected director
of the Children's Alliance, a mentor organization for
at-risk youth in Alameda County.

The story had gone out over the wires on Friday. Late on Sunday,
Shirley Lester would be flying back to Washington, D.C., on the

red-eye. Sunday afternoon, she summoned Josh to her comfortable Victorian house near Oakland's Lake Merritt, where they shared a bottle of wine in the kitchen.

Lester said, "It was about time you stepped up to the plate."

Josh knew that, to many, he seemed to have held his old position forever. He was sure people wondered what was holding him back, was his career stalled, why hadn't he made a significant move before this? Of course he *could* have made a move, there'd been definite moments, and he'd not been without other flattering offers over the years. Why hadn't he? "Time flies," he'd say lightly, "when you're having fun." And he *was* having fun, he was learning so much, he and Lester worked so well together—but was that the entire reason he'd stayed so long?

Lester said, echoing his thought, "We've been together fifteen years, if you include when you were in school. In terms of a marriage, that's better than average."

"And no divorce in sight."

"Not yet, at least," said Lester, with a slight emphasis on the word *yet*. What did that imply? Was something else in the wind?

Josh had known for a while that Lester's longtime Chief of Staff, Will Blaine, was leaving, and Lester knew that he knew. Blaine had told Josh privately himself, months earlier, "It's been a great ride, but enough's enough. I'm tired. I'm getting out of here before they carry me out in a box."

The Blaines owned a place at Hilton Head, but Will seldom had a chance to visit. He wanted to spend a lot more time there, play golf, and maybe take up tennis again before he was too old. "I hardly ever get to see the kids, I still think of them being in high school but they're in college already and soon they'll be completely gone, out in the world, out of our lives."

Josh wondered what he, himself, would be doing at fifty-five. Would he also yearn for a life of retired ease? He doubted it. He hoped and expected, by then, that his career would be reaching its peak.

Lester said to Josh, "You never told me how Ellen feels about all this."

Lester had been married once to a fellow student from Howard University. The divorce had been amicable, there were no children, she never discussed that time of her life.

Josh could easily guess the reason for the breakup, the demands of a political career being tough on any marriage. "I'm not sure it'll make much difference to her," he said.

"Sure it will." Lester pointed out that inevitably there'd be more work, stress, and responsibility. "You won't see so much of each other."

"With our schedules, we already need to make appointments to get together, and we often have to cancel. Ellen's almost busier than I am," Josh said. "Her latest project is to open a hostel for homeless kids. She's out there every day pounding the pavements, looking for money."

"She'll get it. She always does."

"And then she'll move on to the next new thing."

Lester was eyeing him speculatively. "Everything's still okay between you two?"

"Fine."

"Good. Just checking. You acted like an idiot once, but I'm assuming it *was* only once," she said.

Josh had tried his utmost to conceal that crazy episode from Lester. It should have been easy—he'd only been a part-time worker in her office, and she was usually away anyway. He said, "I didn't think you knew."

"It's my business to know, though I never said anything. I thought you'd better work it out on your own. But there're no more skeletons in your closet, I hope?"

"None."

"I'm particularly glad to hear *that* because your license for idiocy just expired. I have something else I want to run by you, getting back to divorce—ours."

Yes, there was more coming, Josh thought, which was why Lester had wanted to talk here, at her home.

"Though I wouldn't really call it a divorce," she went on. "More of an amicable separation." She set her glass down on the green marble countertop and turned to him, her dark eyes gleaming with determination. "I'm planning to declare for the Senate in '92 and run against that bastard Carl Satcher."

So that was it. "Great news!" Josh declared. "You'll blow him away!"

"Somebody's got to stop him. He's sucking the juice right out of the state directly into his own and his cronies' bank accounts. He's a goddam octopus, with a tentacle in every pocket. It was a tragedy the governor saddled us with that crook after Janet Ehrenreich died, and we *cannot* allow him to be elected to a full Senate term. It makes my blood run cold thinking of six more years of that creature. For now, this is in absolute confidence. Any leaks and I'll know where they came from." The words were said lightly, but Lester's eyes held a core of steel.

"Understood. You know you can count on me." Josh refilled Lester's glass with her favorite Napa Valley Cabernet and topped up his own. "In the meantime, I think we should toast our new jobs." He clinked his glass against hers. *"Senator!"*

"Chief!"

"It'll be a tough race," Josh said. He considered Carl Satcher's deep pockets, his connections in transportation, construction, and the oil industry. "But if anyone can bring him down, you can!"

"At least I'll scratch him up some."

"And I'll be right there alongside you."

"Maybe not. You could be occupied on another front." Lester looked Josh square in the eye. "My congressional seat will be up for grabs. I'd sure like to see you fill it."

Congressman Joshua Fischer.

Josh recalled being thirteen and telling his father that he'd be President one day, and his father saying, "Well, why not?" He stared at Lester while the involuntary images tumbled through his head: the announcement of his candidacy in the papers; the campaign; the tension of election night; his acceptance speech, with Ellen smiling and proud at his side.

He drew a deep breath, took a gulp of wine. "Well," he said, "why not!"

Lester smiled. "Of course, first, you have to get yourself elected. That shouldn't be so hard, though—you already have terrific name ID over the way you handled that Central High shooting." She added, "And the Hazlett Corporation mess has given you a whole new platform. Those people out there love you, Josh. They'll do anything for you. Not just because of the money, but because you cared enough."

"I didn't do it alone," Josh said. "It was you who got the EPA to move. And the case is a long way from being over, it'll drag on in appeals forever. The families won't see a penny for years, if they see anything at all."

"You showed leadership," said Lester. "I tell you, Josh, you're already a local hero in Alameda County. Let's see you become a national one."

On hearing those words, Josh felt a power surge, like a live third rail, run clean through his body from his toes to the crown of his head.

★   ★   ★

Eighteen months earlier Josh had never heard of the Hazlett Corporation, and he was unfamiliar with the small, unincorporated bayside community between Oakland and Hayward known as Gettings Wharf until one of the field staff took a phone call from a Baptist pastor named Brother Washington. "We need your help, sir." The minister's polite tone had been unable to mask his despair. "Our children are getting sick."

The office often received calls for aid, but upon listening to Brother Washington, Josh thought the situation sounded particularly dire and decided to check it out for himself. It had taken him over an hour to get there, zigzagging from freeway to freeway, around abandoned navy yards, across railroad tracks, down narrow potholed lanes between chain-link fencing.

Bayside Baptist Church was a storefront in a street of dilapidated buildings. The few cars and pickup trucks lining the street were rusted and pocked, some sagging on their wheel rims. The street backed onto more chain-link fence topped with swathes of barbed wire, behind which sprawled an abandoned factory, its yards dotted with crumbling metal drums and piles of debris. The small park at the end of the street was a joyless place of weeds and leafless trees, a rusty slide, and a single swing set with a broken chain. Beyond the park on a silted-up waterway, stinking horribly now at low tide, a pair of decrepit dry docks tilted haphazardly on the mud.

The air smelled acrid. Josh's eyes itched.

"Mr. Joshua Fischer? Thank you for coming, sir. I sure appreciate it, a busy man like you." Brother Washington appeared to be around sixty though he might be younger, a once-vital man whose face drooped with weariness and whose clothes seemed too large for him.

He'd been born here, he told Josh, showing him around, back when Gettings Wharf was a fine place to live, bustling and prosperous, full of shipyard workers and their young families; his own father had been a master welder. Since the closure of the base and its supporting industries, the Wharf had declined into a forgotten wasteland wedged between Interstate 880, the railroad tracks, and a muddy slough.

"But you stayed on."

"Someone has to watch out for these folks. They don't have much." The pastor explained that there were few jobs here now. The young men were mostly gone, and the school had closed years before. A trip to the doctor was a long journey involving two bus changes—and the buses came less and less frequently.

"You were telling me the children are dying?"

Brother Washington nodded sadly. Three kids had died last year from leukemia, and more were diagnosed. He'd decided something was definitely wrong, and it was no big stretch to connect the outbreak of mortal illness with that old factory decaying in their backyard.

But who to call? The original owner had been out of business for years. The current owner, Hazlett Corporation, was owned by Tri-State Management, which was owned in turn by some shadowy entity called EastPac Development, and nobody returned the pastor's phone calls. The City of Oakland said they'd send a public health inspector but no one showed up, nor did the guy from the Water Department. Brother Washington said he'd watched his dwindling flock, seen their apathetic faces and the sunken eyes, and prayed for guidance.

He told Josh his prayers were answered in a double stroke. First his memory kicked in, and he recalled that the original factory had been engaged in government work. Then he'd thought of his representative in Congress, a sister, and by all accounts a fine lady.

"It was a wake-up call from the Lord," he told Josh solemnly, "and it came none too soon," though too late for three kids, perhaps for several more, and few of the adults looked particularly healthy.

Josh had looked into the records and found that the original company had manufactured medical diagnostic equipment for the military. They'd sold the land and plant to the Hazlett Corporation in 1975, presumably a sweet deal for Hazlett, which had hauled away any equipment of value and achieved a nice tax write-off by donating a chunk of land for a community park—where the soil turned out to be contaminated by strontium 90.

"In other words," Josh had fumed to Lester, "it's built on radioactive waste! Hazlett never bothered to clean up, just turned the dumping ground over to the kids. I can't believe these people! How can they ever face themselves in the mirror in the morning?"

He had stood tieless and rumpled at Brother Washington's pulpit, friend and champion of the entire population of Gettings Wharf, and the congregation ate up his words.

"A crime has been committed," Josh railed, "a crime against humanity. It's an outrage, and I can tell you that I'm speaking for your Congresswoman too. But you know how the Hazlett Corporation got away with it for so long? Because they *could*! There was nothing to stop them because nobody knew the facts, and even if they did, they figured nobody would care. But the whole world knows now, the world cares, and Hazlett will have to put it right."

In slow, emphatic tones, making sure his voice reached to the limits of the room, Josh said, "We're calling in the Environmental Protection Agency. Hazlett will be forced to clean up this place big time. Not only that, but every single one of you is entitled to compensation, which means money, lots of it, and by God we'll make them pay! Of course nobody can bring back Jamal, DeeAnn, and Jerry—no amount of money can make up for the loss of a beloved child. But what it can do is make sure anybody else who is sick gets the best treatment money can buy."

★ ★ ★

The morning after his talk with Shirley Lester, Josh studied his face in the bathroom mirror and said aloud, "Good morning, Congressman!" trying it on for size, and deciding it sounded good.

He was on the move.

They were all moving on up, he initially into the Chief of Staff slot, Lester beginning to plan her Senate campaign two years in the future, and Vic Aguilera moving into Josh's old position of district director. Right now everything hummed along so well in their district. The homeless veterans plan looked as if it would get off the ground. The Hazlett Corporation was on the run. Lester had recently infused the Port of Oakland with a large allocation of money, and the place was jumping day and night. And that was just for starters.

At eight-thirty in the morning Josh pulled into the parking area behind Lester's local office, in a sprawling industrial building at the intersection of Twelfth and Oak Streets, his good mood further enhanced at the sight of the mud-colored pickup with sagging tailpipe and headlights held together with duct tape, which meant Brother Washington was here.

The pastor of Bayside Baptist Church was a different man altogether from the troubled soul of eighteen months ago. He laughed, he sang, he looked ten years younger, and his clothes fit him again. "Chief Fischer!" Brother Washington, bald head glowing like polished ebony, grasped Josh by the hand and pumped it firmly, then reached inside his jacket for a paper scroll tied with a bright orange ribbon. "This is for you—the kids made it specially!"

Josh ceremoniously untied the bow and spread the scroll out on top of Loretta's desk.

A GATHERING
At the Bayside Baptist Church, Gettings Wharf
Sunday, April 24, following services at 10:30 A.M.
To Honor Congresswoman Shirley Lester and Mr. Joshua Fischer
And to express our deepest thanks and gratitude.

The story was illustrated, beginning with the gray sad monotone of Josh's arrival, moving on to the EPA inspectors in full biohazard gear looking like aliens from Mars, ending in glorious Technicolor with a cluster of smiling children picking flowers from an emerald lawn.

"It's beautiful!" Josh was more touched than he could say.

"And we've had a plaque made, something nice you can hang on your wall."

Josh tapped the scroll against his hand. "But I have something to hang on my wall *here*! I'll frame it this afternoon. Tell the kids thanks!"

"I sure will. And we'll see you Sunday?"

"You bet!"

Brother Washington departed wreathed in smiles, and Josh admired the invitation again. "Isn't this something!" He took a sip of coffee, hot, black, and sweet. Amparo, for whom coffee making was not a strong point, had got it right for a change. There was a brief, impassioned discussion about the frame, whether it should be red, green, black, or white. "Chrome," Loretta decreed, "to match your other picture."

"Chrome it'll be!" Josh said. "I'll take it to the frame shop this afternoon."

After its auspicious beginning, the day unwound as usual.

Walking down the hall to his office, Josh stopped by the fax machine to check on messages; most had to do with Lester's pet projects of education, health care, and gun control. The one about the closing of the old Metro Theater—"Please support us. The city *must* be prevented from destroying an art deco treasure"— was a local issue he left for Vic Aguilera to forward to a county supervisor.

Through his open door he heard Loretta carrying on with Aguilera the kind of conversation that, until recently, she used to engage in with Josh himself.

"The Mayor called," she was saying. "He was hoping the boss could stay over for his town hall meeting on Monday, about the development on Tenth Street."

"Where fifty families have to be evicted? Why should she get dropped into that can of worms?"

"I guess to take the heat off of him."

"Bingo! Remind them there's no federal connection, tell them we're way backed up, but we'll send a field worker to monitor...."

When Lester went to the Senate, Josh assumed she would take Aguilera with her. Vic would make a great Chief of Staff. Too bad, Josh thought; I'd sure like him to work for me.

He nudged the door closed with his toe and sat down beside his old oak desk. Lester herself had suggested he might upgrade his furniture now, but Josh didn't really see the point. He was not a man for fancy possessions, and he preferred his office the way it was: a no-frills work space with the big, plain, useful desk, the beige filing cabinets, and the six straight-backed wooden chairs for visitors, their spartan functionality discouraging any temptation to linger. The computer and two TVs were set up just how he wanted. The wall opposite the window was covered by the huge map of Lester's congressional district straddling Oakland and Berkeley, clusters of colored pins marking the locations where she'd held town meetings or press conferences. The only personal touches were two photographs, one on his desk of Ellen wearing a scarlet rain slicker and bright yellow rubber boots, and a photo enlarged almost to poster size on the wall of himself with Lester posing on the steps of the Capitol in Washington, D.C., following her latest swearing-in—January, the sky a dismal pewter, the steps a mush of dirty, trodden snow. Josh appeared as a monochrome bundle in his down parka and long brown scarf, Lester a blaze of color in a military-cut red overcoat and matching felt cowboy hat, looking dashing and elegant.

He thought if he moved this photo six inches or so to the right, then the kids' invitation, in its new, matching chrome frame, could comfortably fit alongside.

The day was cranking into full gear now; Josh could hear the muffled but incessant clamor of phones from the outer office.

He laid the scroll aside and sorted through the messages piled on his desk:

Could Lester make a Rotary Club lunch next week?

Write an op-ed piece for Mothers Against Gun Violence?

Open a day-care center?

His intercom buzzed. Shirley Lester, back in D.C., was on line one needing to talk with him, and Ellen was on line two.

Josh wondered why Ellen was calling him at the office. An emergency? No, she'd have said so; he'd have to get back to her later.

He picked up line one, and Shirley Lester's voice rang out loud and clear. "Good morning to you, Josh!" Fresh as a daisy after about four hours of sleep and a crowded morning, she was about to enter a meeting of the House Small Business Committee. "Any developments with the airport expansion since we talked?"

"Not yet," Josh replied. "People are being as cagey as we expected, but it smells bad."

"You can say that again."

"It shouldn't be hard to prove."

"I wouldn't be surprised if our friend Satcher's involved with this, like he's involved with everything else. Keep me posted. What else is going on?"

"Brother Washington was just in."

"Bless his heart. How's he doing?"

"How d'you think he's doing? He's celebrating."

"Fifty million dollars! Some reason to celebrate!"

"Premature. But they deserve a party. And we're invited." Josh described the invitation. Lester said she wouldn't miss it for the world and reminded him to arrange press coverage. "It's up to us to keep this thing alive."

When Lester hung up, Josh tried unsuccessfully to reach Ellen.

Then he moved the Hazlett files from the center of his desk and from his mind, and considered his course concerning the new Oakland Airport extension. To be eligible for federal money the main contractor was supposed to be minority owned. Although the contractor and his partners were black and most of the visible construction workers appeared to be either black or Hispanic, rumor had it that they fronted for a larger organization—white owned.

Josh sighed with disgust. When he was elected to Congress, he'd devote his career to flushing out these pockets of corruption and crony capitalism.

Today, however, there was work to do and calls to return.

Was Lester for or against the marshland development, which would need a permit from Fish and Wildlife?

Would Lester attend the ground-breaking ceremony for the new Native Californian Cultural Museum?

And then there was poor Mr. deCourcy ("I'm sorry, Josh," in Loretta's careful cursive script, "but he's absolutely determined to talk to you this time"), the retired mailman convinced that aliens were draining the calcium from his bones with some kind of death ray and if the Congresswoman didn't take care of it at once she'd regret it, he had friends in high places!

There was a new phrase entering the vernacular: multitasking. Josh figured if you couldn't balance at least ten things at once, you had no business in politics.

★ ★ ★

Josh reached Ellen at two o'clock when he finally got around to unwrapping the now tired-looking cream cheese and alfalfa sprout sandwich Loretta had picked up for him earlier, and before he had to leave for the meeting at City Hall to discuss the Department of Transportation grant for nonpolluting buses.

"Congratulations," she said. "It seems like you've won an award!"

"I know. Brother Washington brought the announcement over."

A pause. "Brother Washington?"

"It's beautiful. The Gettings Wharf kids made it." He described the invitation. "You'll be coming, too, right?"

Ellen said she wouldn't miss it for the world but she was talking about something else entirely, an award from the U.C. Alumni Association. "Very formal, embossed, with sealing wax."

Josh asked, puzzled, "What did I do?"

Ellen read, *"The Alumni Association of the University of California, Berkeley, requests the pleasure of your company on Thursday, June 2 5, to Honor Joshua Benjamin Fischer as U.C. Berkeley Alumnus of the Year—"*

"Alumnus of the Year?"

"—for his continued efforts to enrich the lives of the people of Berkeley and Oakland, and specifically for his courage in working against gun violence in the schools. I hope you're proud of yourself," Ellen said. "You should be!"

Josh still had nightmares from that day. Ellen was lying there on the floor in the principal's office, her pink shirt dyed crimson with blood, and he'd wake up sweating.

"Where's this great event taking place?" he asked.

"You won't believe it!" Ellen read on, barely containing her glee, *"Cocktails 6:30 P.M. at Eucalyptus House, followed by dinner and presentation ceremony at the Claremont Hotel. Black Tie."*

"At Euc House? You're kidding!"

"I'm serious." And then she remarked, with a new pragmatism, that bearing in mind his new appointment, this award could only be a heaven-sent piece of PR.

★ ★ ★

Josh returned from City Hall late for his meeting with the Hispanic Chamber of Commerce represented by—a fast scan of notes—Roberto Gonsalves, president, and Lidia Fuentes, secretary.

As he came in the door he could see them talking with Aguilera outside the conference room, Gonsalves short and muscular in a chocolate brown business suit, Lidia taller, slender with a long fall of straight black hair, a shockingly familiar back view—

Not Lidia at all.

It was Bianca Rivas.

Josh felt his stomach dip and fall away and his heart give one heavy, dangerous thud. He fought a wave of dizziness and clutched for the door frame.

As if it were only yesterday, that beautiful face looked up at him, dark eyes heavy with passion, mouth swollen from his kisses.

Josh tried to tell himself that woman was not and *could not* be Bianca.

Then she turned, smiling, and of course she was nothing like Bianca at all. Lidia had a broader forehead, a thinner nose, and glasses. And she was very young, she couldn't be much more than twenty.

With a feeling of shattering relief Josh smiled back and shook hands. He led them into his office, sat them down on his uncomfortable chairs, and asked Amparo to bring coffee. He affirmed to them that the encouragement of small businesses, especially those started by Latinos, was among Shirley Lester's top priorities, and he saw them to the door half an hour later, perfectly happy.

He still felt shaken, however. He told Loretta to hold calls and sat down abruptly at his desk telling himself to get a grip, that this was crazy. What could have triggered such a vivid flashback, after so long?

Because somewhere, deep inside, he still longed for her?

He wondered what he would have done if it *had* been Bianca.

Thank God nobody knew, and it was so long ago.

Just this morning, he had hailed his own reflection, *Good morning, Congressman!* But Josh knew that, in running for public office, no mistake could be too long ago. Fortunately, he thought, his secret was safe.

CHAPTER FOURTEEN

Gunther Hecht had been decidedly in favor of Jane buying a gun. He thought it a damn good idea that a woman learn to protect herself.

Jane thought it was a great idea, too. She was ready for anything these days, and invigorated by achievement. The Children's Hospital Ball had raised more than $100,000 for the new neonatal diagnostic clinic. The event had been written up in all the local papers and featured in *W* magazine with a picture of glamorous Mrs. Gregory Hunter, though unfortunately only in black-and-white. "And I was thinking," she told Greg, "you could write an article about me learning to shoot, for the paper. You could, couldn't you, dearheart—with pictures!"

Well, naturally with pictures, thought Greg wryly, and what a kick it would be for her, contrasting her glamorous society image with that of the woman warrior squinting down the barrel of a 9mm Magnum. It wasn't a bad idea, and Harvey Pilcher, when approached, turned out to be quite interested, provided it was written with the appropriate slant, along the lines of "Self-protection: Every woman's right!"

Jane was disappointed it would not specifically be about her. Did a tinge of jealousy enter the equation, Greg wondered, since he had written at some length and personally about Ellen? But Gunther Hecht agreed the paper had a point, the appeal should be universal rather than particular, and what better way of getting the message out there. "After all," he pointed out, seeing the business angle as always, "women are a growing market for guns."

★ ★ ★

Early one Tuesday morning, Greg, Jane, Gunther Hecht, and Bill the photographer pulled into the parking lot of the Marin Rifle and Pistol Club, regularly used as a practice venue by guards, police, forest rangers, and just about anybody else needing to keep up their skills.

From the outside, the place appeared disappointingly mundane, a long, low building with cinder block walls and a corrugated iron roof. "It looks like a chicken farm," Jane observed as she climbed out of the car.

The interior didn't impress her much either. With its burnt orange shag rug and teak veneer coffee table piled with magazines, the front office of the Marin Rifle and Pistol Club could have been a suburban living room from a tract house in the seventies. At least the magazines all related to firearms, hunting, or warfare—Greg noticed a copy of *Soldier of Fortune*—and instead of books or fine china in the glass-fronted cabinets, there were guns for purchase, from the snub-nosed, purse-sized Ladysmith ("Look at that. How *darling!*" Jane exclaimed) to the .686 combat Magnum with the seven-inch barrel. There was even an antique collector's item: a late-thirties Mauser with a well-preserved leather holster stamped with the insignia of the Third Reich for which Gunther Hecht wrote a check for $3,500 on the spot.

Greg had reserved an hour's lesson for Jane with the chief instructor, who turned out to be a short, stocky woman in her mid-thirties, wearing slacks and a rust-colored sweater, her ruddy face as wholesome as an apple farmer's wife. The name tag pinned to her bosom said LORAYNE. She asked, "See anything you like, hon?" as if Jane was shopping for a toaster oven or a new vacuum cleaner, then recommended the perfect tool for a beginner, a Colt .380 Detective Special—not too heavy, a nice rubber grip, and unremarkable recoil. "It's not too great on accuracy, but pretty damn good at stopping somebody. And that's the whole point, right?"

The real business went on behind a heavy, soundproofed door, in muffled bursts like popcorn in a microwave.

Lorayne opened the door and the sound was immediately deafening. It was much colder here in the lanes, and the wind whistled and hooted under the ill-fitting roof. Jane, in her canvas safari jacket, gave an exaggerated shiver. "Don't worry, hon," Lorayne assured her. "Once you get going, you'll warm up real quick!"

Bill took photos of Jane being kitted up with ear muffs and eye shield while Greg wondered precisely how to open the article.

Lorayne was saying, "You made the right decision learning how to protect yourself. My friend Myrna? I warned her she shouldn't have taken up with this guy, real possessive and abusive, wouldn't let up when she called it quits, threatened her and her kids." She clipped the target onto overhead wires, pressed a switch, and sent it whirling down the lane, then showed Jane how to revolve the chamber and load, snap it back into place, unload, reload. "So I told her, Myrna honey, you get yourself a gun and learn how to use it, and you're gonna sleep a whole lot better nights! I'm telling you, a gun can be a woman's best friend!"

How about *that* for a provocative lead sentence? Greg wondered.

Jane was ready. Lorayne encouraged her, "Let's go for it now, 5X—that big circle around the heart!"

Blam! Blam! Blam! Jane achieved two shots out of six onto the paper, none in 5X, and scowled with frustration.

Adjustments were made to the equipment and her posture: "Head more forward," Lorayne said, "point that toe. Let's not be so tense here!"

The next series was better. One shot actually made it inside 5X, four in outlying circles, one nicked the rim of the target.

"I felt more comfortable this time," Jane said.

"The secret of good shooting is being comfortable," Lorayne said—and Greg had another contender for his lead.

Half an hour later the silhouette had been moved back twice and was a mess of holes patched with black tape. Jane had graduated from the heart area and, flushed and excited, was consistently drilling into the more challenging target of the head. "Will you look at that!" Lorayne beamed. "You musta blown away three quarters of his brain!"

Gunther Hecht exulted, "That's my girl!"

He hadn't left Jane's side, a looming presence, indefatigably encouraging. Greg had let them get on with it and sought the warmth of the lobby where he browsed through literature and price lists and chatted with other clients putting in practice time. These included a high school math teacher—"you can't be too careful with students these days"; a middle-aged grocery store owner—"you never know who's going to walk in the door"; and a sixty-year-old widow—"I got some nice things in my home certain people might like to get their hands on!"

When father and daughter emerged in triumph from the lanes, Gunther poked his thick fingers through the clusters of holes on Jane's target and proudly wriggled them for Greg's inspection.

"Hey," Greg cried, "you're quite the pro! How'd you enjoy it?"

"It was great! Real fun!" She took the target back from her father and rolled it up carefully. "I'm taking this home and framing it."

"She has the makings of a fine shooter," Lorayne said. "She should maybe try an automatic next time."

Gunther Hecht glowed with pride.

Jane still clasped the .380 Special tightly in her hand, as if she would only relinquish it under force. Like a small girl choosing that special puppy—"I want this one!"—and her father reached once again for his wallet.

In the car going home Jane said seriously, "I can see how people get hooked on guns. I didn't understand before, but I do now. It's such a great feeling, knowing you have all that power! I felt so strong and it felt so *right* in my hand, like it was part of me!" She sucked at her trigger finger, which was red and raw though she hadn't complained about it. In fact, Greg suspected she considered it a badge of achievement.

"Strong," he agreed, still mentally writing. "How do you feel now?"

"Tired. *Exhausted*. All wrung out, like I've just played six sets of tennis."

Later, after Gunther dropped them off, Jane said, "And that wasn't *all* I felt!" She traced little circles down his arm with her sore finger and feather-stroked the sensitive inner skin of his wrist. "It actually felt pretty sexy. It's a *turn-on*. I guess a lot of people must feel that way. Don't you think?"

★　★　★

The article, with accompanying pictures, was published in the Sunday section of the *San Francisco Chronicle*. It could by no means be perceived as overt propaganda for the American Association of Gun Owners, but it wouldn't discourage gun ownership either, particularly for women who were—as Greg pointed out, though not crediting his father-in-law for the quote—a growing market.

No, it was all about empowerment. There was nothing wrong with learning to defend oneself in a safe, responsible environment with an experienced instructor, and nowadays it was a cliché to imagine a shooting range as the exclusive province of macho, beer-bellied, cussing yahoos.

Josh Fischer, predictably, was disgusted with Greg. "You're sending a message that guns are fun, empowering, and even sexy."

"You're reading a lot into it that isn't there. It's a perfectly objective piece."

"Bull*shit*! That's the whole point: one *can't* be objective. Writing an article like this doesn't just mean you condone it—you're actively encouraging people to buy guns."

Josh couldn't help but be biased, of course. He'd always had an aversion to firearms. And after the Central High episode, gun control was almost like a religion to him. However, his was a minority reaction (though Greg found it gratifying that Josh had read into the article precisely what he'd intended); most everybody else was impressed.

Certainly Harvey Pilcher was pleased. The piece generated a lot of attention, with a slew of phone calls and letters from both sides of the gun control divide, and controversy was always good for circulation. The Marin Rifle and Pistol Club folks were happy, too. Their phones were busy, they gained fifteen new customers overnight, ten of them women, and they were thinking of hiring another part-time instructor.

Gunther Hecht was delighted and promptly fired off a copy of the article to Carl Satcher in Southern California, who was glad Gunther's son-in-law seemed like such a well-grounded young fellow.

★ ★ ★

Two months later, in mid-May 1989, Greg found himself flying down to Ventura County in Senator Satcher's sleek little Lear jet, reclining alongside his father-in-law in luxurious, leather-upholstered seats, navy with scarlet piping, the same as Satcher's racing colors.

Although Greg had made several trips by private jet over the last few years, this statement of ultimate privilege—no waiting in line, a courteous escort to the plane, staff who knew your name—never failed to thrill him right down to the marrow. This is the life, he'd think, and this is me living it! Me, Greg Hunter! Oh boy, if the Old Marine could see me now—but suppressing the thought of how the old man would sneer, *So you married a girl with a rich daddy and you take what you can get! What does that make you? It's not a pretty word, boy.* Or worse—his father might shrug with indifference. But then, what did the opinion of one cantankerous old fart matter when he, Greg, was on his way to spend a weekend with one of the richest men in the country?

Greg had never been to Satcher's ranch, nor had he expected to be invited. As Gunther Hecht explained, it was Satcher's private retreat from the spotlight, a place both for relaxation and for high-level private conference, "kind of like his Camp David."

"So what's up now?" Greg had asked his father-in-law.

But Hecht was disinclined to tell him. All he'd say was, "You'll see soon enough," and Greg had to be patient.

"Something to drink, Mr. Hunter?" The suave steward could be a clone of Roberto, still employed as steward on *Freya III*.

Greg asked for club soda, which arrived in a heavy, cut-glass tumbler (Waterford, he assumed. He'd learned about such things now that he ran with the very rich), with a little midnight blue linen napkin, monogrammed CAS in scarlet. In the old days Greg might have slipped the napkin into his pocket as a souvenir, but he was beyond that sort of thing now.

Less than half an hour later they were touching down, feather-light, on the private airstrip to find Satcher himself, faded jeans tucked into well-worn boots, awaiting them beside a dusty Land Rover. Behind him a landscape of undulating green-gold hills rose to a rampart of indigo-shadowed mountains, their edges sharp as knives in the pure air.

Overwhelmed, Greg experienced that first afternoon and evening at the ranch only as a blur of overlapping images. First the horses, the soft green dazzle of pasture dotted with mares and foals, the private racetrack and the large, white-railed paddocks, one for each stallion, where Satcher dug into his pockets for treats, rubbed silken necks, fondled ears, and whispered endearments. The chestnut stallion was his pet, winner of the Derby and the Preakness, running second in the Belmont Stakes, Archangel by Heavenly Choir out of Last Trump, "but you better not touch him," Satcher warned Greg. "He's no angel, he'll take your fucking arm off, give him half a chance."

Then there was the house, plantation style with pillars and wraparound verandas like in *Gone with the Wind,* its lofty, high-beamed rooms filled with antique Mexican furniture, gold-framed paintings (Greg recognized a Diego Rivera), and Persian rugs in glowing colors laid down upon the shiny, beeswaxed floors.

The room-size freezer, its thick steel door fit for a bank vault, hissed open with a white gush of frigid air to reveal whole sides of beef and lamb swinging from hooks, where Greg watched Satcher and his chef choose steaks for tomorrow's barbecue.

Greg's brain was reeling by the time cocktails and dinner rolled around—huge highballs in more chunky crystal, followed by fine wines and a standing crown rib roast with the ends capped with little paper frills. There were no women present, the current

Mrs. Satcher remaining in the palace in Brentwood and Jane not invited. The only other guest was the horse vet (a private vet!), a laconic Texan who ate and drank very little and left early to tend two mares likely to foal during the night.

Afterward, Satcher, Hecht, and Greg watched a movie in the downstairs screening room, which seated twenty in swiveling buckets of black leather: *Border Feud,* starring Tom Turner. "A good buddy," said Satcher, "and a fine man! Friend of every real American."

★ ★ ★

Saturday found them all up early to admire the latest foal, a beautiful little filly with a fuzzy coat the color of coffee grounds, teetering amid the straw on the longest legs in the world while the new mother, a big bay, whickered warningly with laid-back ears and moved her body purposefully between her baby and the men.

With his carefully controlled voice masking obvious excitement, Satcher invited Hecht and Greg to watch Archangel earn his keep, "though I'd better warn you it's strong stuff!" He led them into a high-beamed barn, airy and smelling pleasantly of wood shavings, and up to a balcony at the back. Below, another mare, a beauty with a pale moleskin coat, shifted edgily from foot to foot and switched her tail. A very young foal nursed under her belly, and the vet stood at her head, holding her close by a double-roped halter while running his hand consolingly up and down her shiny neck.

"You mean they're going to breed her now?" Greg asked, surprised. "When she's just had a foal?"

"Of course. She's in foal heat," Satcher snapped, edgy. "Now *hush!*"

Greg felt the disturbance in the air and the tremble of the ground before he heard the thud of hoofbeats, the creak of leather, and soft oaths in Spanish. The mare emitted an alarmingly savage noise, and only the vet seemed relaxed as he continued his gentle stroking.

Then Archangel erupted into view through the big double doors, silhouetted darkly against the bright morning light, far more huge and powerful than on the previous afternoon when he'd placidly munched sugar lumps from Satcher's hand. Now, intensely aroused by the scent of the mare, he pranced and lunged with a sweating wrangler hanging on to him at each side.

Genuinely awed, Satcher demanded, "Will you look at that! Did you ever see anything so fine!"

"Jesus," Greg said. He had to agree Archangel was an incredible sight. A ton of finely tuned muscle, hide glistening, the crest of his mane risen in full sexual display, and his neck curved in an exaggerated arch that reminded Greg of a horse he'd seen in an old tapestry in some castle in Europe Jane had dragged him to.

The stallion approached, nostrils flared, hooves lifting with delicate precision, the wranglers hanging on grimly. Greg thought that, with the least of effort, Archangel could kick them clear into the next county, and they knew it.

Such an atmosphere of violence. He worried about the foal.

The vet relinquished the mare to two more wranglers who led her from her pen and up to her consort, her ears laid back flat, emitting a continuous rumble of threat, and to Greg's relief the cowering foal was taken away to a safe corner.

The stallion rubbed his nose against the mare's neck and nuzzled her withers. She promptly bit him on the shoulder and, when he attempted to mount, instantly became a plunging devil of teeth and hooves.

"She's from Argentina," Satcher remarked, as if to explain the bout of temperament.

Greg clutched the rail with white knuckles, wondering, as these two fierce animals were coerced into their majestic coupling by at least six people, how foals ever got born in the wild. But eventually the deed was accomplished, the wranglers led Archangel away, head lowered, mane no longer abristle, his job well and thoroughly done. "A hundred grand a pop," Satcher boasted, "not exactly chump change!" The foal was squealingly released to reclaim its mother, who welcomed it back with a gentle whinny.

Greg felt drained by the spectacle, but the day was only beginning.

Eleven o'clock that morning brought the arrival of three other men, pale and ill at ease in their country-casual uniform of creakingly new, pressed jeans and denim jackets. Men of a distinct breed, these three, the facilitators and strategists, the masters of the deal in the back room, desk warriors, armed with their law degrees and MBAs riding to the top on someone else's shoulders like remoras riding the really big fish. They'd be efficient, humorless, and ruthless, the kind of men, Greg thought, who would be unkind to their wives.

Noon found them all beside the ornamental lake for clay pigeon shooting with another quietly unobtrusive servant loading the guns and operating the machine.

PULL!

The crash of sound, without echo, hung oddly dead in the still air. Satcher, with narrowed eyes, aimed and fired in one fluid movement, and the disc exploded into flying fragments.

PULL!

Gunther Hecht's performance was equally proficient but the three desk jockeys—whose names Greg's trained ear had filed away safely but whom he privately labeled Baldy, Shorty, and Fatso—were, not surprisingly, poor.

When his own turn came Greg didn't do too badly. He hadn't forgotten everything he'd learned in Surprise Bend, although he didn't do well enough to outshoot either his father-in-law or his host. Under the circumstances, he thought it was just as well.

★ ★ ★

The morning ended with a lunch of chicken salad sandwiches and iced tea, after which Satcher retired to the library with Gunther Hecht and the remoras, and Greg was sent first on a jeep tour of the spread, driven by a genial young man called Pete, then into the air for a helicopter overflight.

At four o'clock Greg collapsed in his own quarters— canopied bed, Native American rugs, vast marble bathroom fit for an Arabian prince—and slept deeply for an hour. Afterward he showered, dressed in white linen slacks and a blue silk Armani shirt—no sycophant he with phony Western regalia.

Cocktails were served at five-thirty, the barbecue was at six (hunky rare steaks and enormous baked potatoes), and afterward they retired to the library, this time with Greg included.

He found himself seated facing an unnecessary but pleasantly crackling fire of sweet-scented apple wood, flanked by Carl Satcher on his left and Gunther Hecht on his right, while Baldy, Shorty, and Fatso clustered quietly behind them in the shadows.

Satcher made the first play. Leaning forward, big hands clasping his knees, he asked, "Want to know why I brought you down here, Greg?"

★ ★ ★

"We've been keeping track of you," Satcher said. "You're a pretty damn fine writer and building yourself up quite a following. That's good. Personally, too, you have solid opinions, the right ones, and that's even better. We'd like to have you on our team."

Greg glanced at Hecht, who had said nothing of any team, but his father-in-law's face offered no clues.

"Yes. Our team." Satcher himself was in no hurry. He reached for the humidor on the coffee table, chose a cigar, drilled the end, lit, sucked deeply, and blew smoke, explaining finally, "A group of us, influential people, are anxious to keep this country moving in the right direction. And we see you as a potential opinion shaper. Not for the lefty liberal loonies, you understand, there's no way anyone can shape *them* into seeing the light—but the folks in the middle, the moderates. You have credibility. That school shooting piece—I liked that, it made people think. The piece about Janey was terrific! And the homeless article—who are they, where did they come from, and why, all that crap—solid human interest stuff readers relate to. By now they trust and respect you, you grab their hearts. Best of all, you get into their heads. That guy Greg Hunter, they say, now *there's* someone got it all together, who knows what he's talking about, a family man with a beautiful wife and a fine pair of boys. Cigar? Help yourself.

"And with that in mind, I've—" with an inclusive gesture at the other four men—"we've *all* decided you deserve a wider readership than the *Chronicle*. You need a national readership—

and there's no reason this can't be arranged. In return, you can help us fight this insidious, liberal rot that's undermining our country." His voice deepened with passion. "There are dangerous people out there, son, who'll destroy everything you've ever worked for and hold dear and sacred, and we have to make sure our guys get elected. Do you want the government reaching into your pocketbook at every turn and pissing away your hard-earned money on cockamamie, bleeding-heart schemes that might sound good on paper but don't have a chance in hell of working in the real world? Don't you want to hang on to real values and freedoms?"

A national readership. What could that mean! Inwardly, Greg pulsed with excitement. Instinctively knowing the risk of appearing too eager at this stage, he schooled his face to stillness like a good poker player.

"Of course you do," Satcher said brusquely. "And we propose to build you up, make sure your name's known and your words are heard, every one of them. We'll help you with resources and researchers. Incidentally, we have a great gal in mind, young and bright as hell, works as a researcher for the *Wall Street Journal* in Palo Alto. Micaela something—we'll get you two together, you'll hit it off, and pretty soon a word from you, a question here and there in the right quarter, is going to make one hell of a difference. Good for our side, not so good for theirs. You'll be forcing people to ask what they really want for this great country of ours. We're going to clean house, cut away all that faulty lefty logic, and keep a strong, right-thinking leader in the White House.

"And *that's* why we need you on our team, as a stealth weapon against the enemies of our party who happen to be the enemies of the United States of America." Satcher fell silent at last and puffed contemplatively at his cigar. In conversational tones he added, "By the way, Greg, that friend of yours, Joshua Fischer, the best man at your wedding—you fellows still close? No? Then make sure you stay in touch. We're hearing rumors in that quarter, and they're troubling."

Greg thought, mildly startled, *Josh an enemy of the people?* Misguided, maybe, but surely no enemy—and, *does this mean they expect me to spy on him?* His eyes must have displayed a flash of doubt because before he could even draw a breath, Satcher moved smoothly in and sweetened the deal.

Flashing a confident grin that exposed large white teeth, he said, "There's a commission coming your way, too. You'll like it. I've always had a yen to write a book about my old pal Tommy Turner, but I don't have the time or the know-how. Nothing heavy or political, light reading, lots of pictures, the story of a friend, written by a friend. How about you take a crack at it? Co-authorship, split fifty-fifty?"

★ ★ ★

Later, Greg lay beneath his canopy, spread-eagled under his down duvet, his head a teeming jumble of private jets and racetracks, Thoroughbred mares and stallions, armies of servants, and mile upon mile of lush green land, stretching from the mountains almost to the ocean. They'd known he would be impressed. Showing him all that, they'd known he'd never be able to resist.

They *want* me, he exulted.

He thought of his father's dingy little house in Akron, of lost hopes, dead-end jobs, and second-rate lives.

Then he thought of Tim dying in Vietnam, of Marco, perhaps homeless and drunk in an alley, of Josh standing up for the forlorn and voiceless, of Ellen battling for her army of ragged-assed children. How far away they suddenly seemed, how faint and faded, a gallant but irrelevant dream.

Greg knew he stood at one of life's crossroads: he could continue the way he was going—or turn right. He could be part of all of this, with a vital role as a maker or breaker. He wouldn't end up like one of those remora men, he'd be a big fish in his own right, powerful, respected, *feared*. A stealth weapon. Of course there'd be a price, Greg knew. But it would be worth it.

CHAPTER FIFTEEN

They drove to Eucalyptus House in Josh's Toyota—he was earning more money now but had not upgraded his ride. Josh was at the wheel, Ellen at his side, Judith and Hans Fischer in the back, all of them dressed to the nines.

Josh had always found something too elitist about a tuxedo. Now, as Chief of Staff, there would doubtless be formal events in his future, and Ellen had persuaded him to buy a tux, along with two dress shirts with pleating down the front, a set of collar studs, a cummerbund, and several bow ties including one in plaid. She thought he looked great in his new clothes, and she'd fussed over him tonight, making sure his shoes were shined, straightening his tie, and helping with the cufflinks, the heavy gold ones she'd given him when he graduated from law school. "When will I ever wear these?" he'd wondered then with a smile. "Don't you think they're a bit fancy for a public defender's office?"

"You'll wear them," Ellen insisted. "You won't be a public defender forever."

Ellen also wore a new outfit, a forest green tunic and slim matching skirt from Second Chances on Shattuck Avenue, vintage Oleg Cassini, 1963. She still haunted thrift shops; there would be time enough to seriously upgrade her wardrobe if and when Josh was elected to Congress. While absently listening to her in-laws in the backseat—Hans fretting that the sleeves of his rented tux were too short and Judith, resplendent in lavender silk, saying it didn't matter, nobody would be looking at him anyway—Ellen couldn't help but wonder what other, far more serious changes would take place for her and Josh, what living adjustments would need to be made, and exactly what would be her new role. Of course Josh would never expect Ellen to play the part of Political Wife, standing perpetually misty-eyed in his shadow and smiling till her teeth ached, but long ago she had pledged her absolute support for his political career, and she intended to honor that promise. On the other hand, she had no intention of setting aside her work with the Children's Alliance.

They would just have to see how it all played out.

★ ★ ★

Ellen and Josh had driven down Eucalyptus Avenue many times since the restoration of the Victorian mansion on the corner. They had contributed to the "Save Eucalyptus House" fund. Now, instead of being torn down to make way for a tall block of student housing, the decrepit old building had a new lease on life as residence of the assistant chancellor of the university. Its outside was glorified with a four-color paint job. The carved oak door on which Ellen had pounded in vain all those years ago had been stripped, stained, and oiled. The dank straggles of ivy and pile of old bikes had given way to a freshly laid brick driveway bordered with multicolored petunias. The plaque above the lintel, EUCALYPTUS HOUSE 1889, was now picked out in elegant white on black. Ellen couldn't wait to see what it looked like inside. However magnificent the transformation, to Ellen it would always remain Euc House, a transforming part of her life and Josh's— and of Greg's, who would be here tonight too.

"Won't it be nice to see Greg again?" Judith said. "I've always had a soft spot for that boy, ever since he first came to visit!"

Josh gave a noncommittal grunt that could have been agreement, though Ellen guessed it probably was not. Josh no longer trusted Greg, especially since his recent close involvement with Carl Satcher.

His parents, however, remembered Greg as a charming, golden-haired eighteen-year-old. "We'd worry, you know," Judith had told Ellen long ago at graduation. "Josh up here in Berkeley, all alone, and the place so big, so different from what he was used to. He was such a shy boy then, so quiet. It was good to know Greg was there taking care of him, and always so neat and clean, not like some. 'Don't you worry, Mrs. Fischer,' he'd say; 'Your boy's doing just fine. I'll make sure he calls.'"

"I didn't need a babysitter," Josh had objected. "He didn't 'take care' of me."

"Well, no. He was more of a big brother," Judith had said.

"I'm older than he is!"

"Yes, dear, but he *seems* older—except when he jumped in the pool with all his clothes on. Those were such good times," Judith recalled now, "even with all the goings-on, that crazy political stuff and the arguing. We miss Greg. And we've never even seen those babies."

"They're not babies anymore," Ellen said. "They must be almost four years old, but we haven't seen them since they were born. We hardly ever see Jane—there never seems to be time for socializing."

"Because you're all far too busy," Judith said. "That's wrong. You should keep up with your friends. Make an effort."

"Time moves on," Josh said. "People change. Friendships aren't necessarily forever."

"How can you say that with Greg coming tonight specially to see you get your award?" Judith said. "He's an important part of your life—your roommate for three whole years. Old friends should be cherished!"

For his part, Greg seemed to want to stay close, and he was usually the one to call about getting together; now, perhaps to make it up to Josh for those articles over which he'd taken offense, Greg had proposed writing a series about the Children's Alliance.

The *Chronicle* was running an education issue later in the summer with a special feature on problems of literacy, delinquency, truancy, "all the -cy words," Greg told Ellen. "The Children's Alliance would fit right in there."

"I'm not sure," she'd said. "Let me think about it, okay?"

"What's to think about? Just go for it!"

And why, indeed, did she even hesitate? Was she concerned about the inevitable close proximity with Greg? Surely not anymore. And anyway, they were both married, Greg with those two gorgeous little boys.

Ellen turned in her seat to tell Judith, "You'll be glad to hear Jane's coming tonight."

"That's more good news," Judith said.

"And bringing her father," Josh said. "Maybe to check out potential political opposition for his pal Carl Satcher."

Hans Fischer wondered mildly, "Couldn't he just be showing support for his son-in-law's friend?"

"I'd say the chances of that were slim to none," Ellen said.

She thought of the speech Josh would give tonight, upon which he'd worked long and hard. It was a fine speech, reflecting all his principles, and she knew Gunther Hecht would hate it. She wondered whether, knowing Hecht was in the audience, Josh would amp it up somewhat. She wouldn't be surprised. She thought again about the offer of the Children's Alliance article and whether Greg's timing in proposing it, following so soon after his induction into the Satcher camp, was of any significance. Then she wondered why she was even thinking this way. Is this what it was like in the world of politics? It was a depressing thought. In fact, she rejected it totally. Josh was going to give a great speech, and Greg, a good friend, had made a generous offer that she was going to accept.

As they drove across University Avenue and turned right, Josh told Ellen, "Stop worrying! Gunther Hecht's not going to hear me say anything he hasn't heard before."

"I suppose what's more important is the way you say it."

"Then I'll do my best to knock his socks off. I'll make sure it's a memorable evening. Now let's lighten up." He smiled at her. "Did I tell you that you look terrific?"

"You can say it again, I won't mind."

"Like a movie star!" Judith said. "Hans, doesn't Ellen look like a movie star?"

Hans agreed. "Like Rita Hayworth."

"You only say that because of the red hair," said Judith. "Didn't you know Rita's color was straight out of the bottle?"

A brief and amicable argument followed about which actresses were natural redheads, or blondes for that matter, unresolved because Hans and Judith seldom went to the movies these days. "Too much violence and swearing," Hans said. "Who needs it?"

"Anyway, you look very lovely, dear," Judith concluded firmly.

And then Josh was rounding the corner into Eucalyptus Avenue, joining the steady stream of cars inching their way toward the end of the block. "Are we ready for this?" he said.

★ ★ ★

If it hadn't been for the familiar staircase with its elaborately carved banister, Ellen wouldn't have believed that this was their old Eucalyptus House.

The floors were refinished to a golden gloss, the walls painted a rich terra-cotta with white trim, the coffered ceiling cunningly spotlit. What a grand ceiling. She'd never noticed it before.

She was still marveling when they were fallen upon by Mrs. Barnett of the Alumni Association: "Joshua Fischer! So good to have you with us, such a thrilling occasion—and Ellen! What a pleasure! What great things I hear about you, too!"

Josh introduced his parents, and Mrs. Barnett, still gushing, led the way down the passage, past oiled wood paneling and original paintings, where, years before, those rock concert posters had been thumbtacked to the wall.

Ellen thought back to that first night, hearing Greg perform his Nixon imitation and mistaking it for the man himself; opening that door, seeing Josh lounging on that ratty old sofa and his eyes meeting hers as if he'd been waiting for her.

Now, in their old living room, she gazed, disoriented, at twin loveseats that faced each other across a cherrywood coffee table (no overflowing ashtrays and old pizza boxes on *that* satin surface);

crystal vases filled with summer flowers; cream and gold oriental rugs; a marble mantel and brass grate behind which crackled a small, ornamental fire.

She remembered Greg burning garbage to keep her warm, Josh lending her his sweater and socks, and found herself thinking this was all too much, it was no longer Euc House but a decorator's showcase, and glared with downright resentment at the nearest loveseat and the well-dressed couple sitting on it who were not the young Josh Fischer and Ellen Downey.

Mrs. Barnett was saying, "Such a lovely old house. I hope you approve!"

Ellen, nostalgic for the past, said carefully, "It's a miracle."

"You must have so many memories. Nineteen seventy-four— what a time that was. You and Josh probably watched the Watergate hearings in this very room."

People were crowding in now, a procession of well-wishers from the Poli Sci department clustering around Josh. The vice chancellor, a billowing, white-haired presence in peacock blue, parted the throng, crying, "*Mister* Fischer! I don't need to tell you how pleased we are about tonight!"

Josh towed Ellen into the center of the circle from which, with another influx of more hellos, handshakes, and congratulations, she found herself being edged to the periphery, but not before Jane Hunter joined the group. Jane was wearing a short black dress that Ellen guessed would have cost a month or two of her own salary. She was with a younger, dark-haired woman in mushroom-colored satin.

Ellen watched Jane bestow an air kiss on Josh's cheek. "Isn't this all quite wonderful!" In her elegant black strappy sandals Jane was as tall as he was. "And Ellen—*there* you are! I didn't see you hiding back there. You look marvelous, where *did* you find that dress?"— though the warmth of her smile didn't quite reach her eyes.

"Remember my parents?" Josh was asking Jane, "Hans and Judith Fischer?"

"Of course! You came to our wedding!"

"Where's your handsome husband?" Judith asked.

"Right here somewhere. Have you met my father?" And there was that large, florid man Ellen had not seen since that afternoon in Grace Cathedral, his left arm reaching loosely but possessively around his daughter's waist.

"Mr. Hecht! Good to see you again," Josh said.

"Gunther, son. Gunther! And this is Micaela Calder—she'll be doing some work with Greg." He checked around the room. "Where *is* Greg?"

Ellen edged herself around an approaching waiter and backed away toward the door.

"If you're looking for the powder room, Ellen, take a right and it's the second door on the left," Mrs. Barnett said with a toothy smile, showing lots of gum. "And *do* take a peek at the library. We're particularly proud of it. It's our little museum."

Ellen smiled in acquiescence, squeezed her way back into the passage, waved to Shirley Lester, who was entering with Carole Walker, the principal at Central High, and turned left toward the kitchen. Ellen visualized the peeling linoleum, the ancient rust-streaked refrigerator, the sink piled with dirty dishes, and the stove that squealed like a wounded animal each time the door was opened. She would have liked to see what they'd done with it, something fancy in granite and tile she'd bet, but waiters and servers were scurrying in and out with trays and glasses.

Besides, here was the famous library, empty and peaceful, with a cozy fire.

The little museum, at one time Greg's bedroom, was transformed with comfortable maroon leather chairs, more Persian rugs, and shelves of perfectly matched leather-bound books. Ellen crossed over to the central table with its display of historic yearbooks opened to illustrated spreads of bygone campus life, and idly leafed through pages of straw-hatted, striped-blazered young men, one clowning with a ukulele, and shingle-haired co-eds in middy blouses and Mary Janes.

A voice from behind her asked, "Visiting old haunts?"

"They said I shouldn't miss the library."

"Where's the guest of honor?"

"With the vice chancellor and your wife."

"Then I guess I'll have to stand in line," Greg said.

"Hans and Judith are here. They're looking forward to seeing you."

"Hans and Judith! Bless them! I saw them at the other end of the room. They haven't changed much, just a little grayer."

"They're very fond of you," Ellen said.

"I'm fond of them. They were good to me. Don't you have a drink?"

"Not yet."

Greg offered his glass of champagne. "Here, have mine."

"No thanks. I——"

"Take it. I'll get myself another one."

Ellen just had time for one sip before he returned, a waiter at his heels, carrying glasses and a bottle on a silver tray. She found herself thinking that Greg was now someone who would never be neglected by a waiter or have to wait for a cab.

"Here's to us!" he said. He clinked his glass to hers.

"To all of us. Particularly Josh."

"To Josh." They stood on the rug facing each other, and he looked her over slowly from head to toe. "I've never seen you look so lovely. The little flower child, all dressed up!"

Ellen strove for a lighthearted but deflecting reply. She managed, "You look okay, too, but men always do in a tux," thinking actually how very much more than okay Greg looked. Confident, sleek, and well brushed in his custom-tailored outfit—no off-the-rack alterations for *him*. "And anyway, it's Jane who's beautiful, not me."

"Jane works at it very very hard." He cocked his head quizzically toward her. "To others it comes more easily."

"Be serious now, Greg. I wanted to find you. We need to talk about the Children's Alliance article."

"Of course we do."

Greg took a step toward her as Ellen took a step back, wishing they weren't standing in his old bedroom, feeling that sudden, unwelcome blush heat her face. Damn Greg Hunter! Just when she had comfortably slotted him in the friend and colleague category, he managed to disrupt her all over again. She wished someone else would come into the room.

"Can you tell me what you have in mind?" she asked.

"Yes," Greg said, "but this isn't the time or the place. I'll call you—" and just then, in the doorway, Jane appeared and said, "There you are, Greg—and Ellen too. I hope we're not interrupting anything."

Ellen amended her wish, *Anybody but Jane,* wondering what interpretation Greg's wife would give to those innocent words— "This isn't the time or the place. I'll call you"—and to Ellen's own flushed face.

Micaela was standing beside Jane, surveying the scene. Ellen caught her coolly speculative eye and guessed that the woman didn't miss a thing.

"Of course you're not interrupting," Ellen said firmly.

Jane slipped a graceful arm around her husband's waist. "Come on, darling, everyone's looking for you. The vice chancellor particularly wants a word."

Ellen watched them leave the room, the back of Greg's hand momentarily brushing Micaela's bare shoulder. To her surprise, she found herself suddenly feeling sorry for Jane. She guessed she was not a happy woman.

★ ★ ★

The Claremont Hotel, high on a hillside with a commanding view of San Francisco Bay, was a white, crenellated confection of a hotel set among lawns, flowers, and trees like a seated dowager with billowing green skirts. It looked, thought Ellen, exactly how a grand hotel should look.

The ballroom was quite magical—a candlelit landscape of gold and blue (the U.C. Berkeley colors), with a centerpiece of creamy magnolias on each table.

"Who's paying for all this?" Judith wondered.

"Not us," replied Josh, "that's all you need worry about."

They took their places at the table on the raised dais, below a huge, blank movie screen: Judith to the extreme left; Carole

Walker; the vice chancellor; Josh; Judge Beth Wedley, president of the Alumni Association; Shirley Lester; Ellen; and Hans on the far right. For Ellen the night was turning out to be rather more stressful than she'd expected, and she was grateful to be sitting between Hans (how hard to relate this man, with his warm eyes and gentle smile, with that terror-stricken boy in Berlin) and Shirley Lester, elegant as usual in a gray caftan edged in silver.

Over the shrimp and arugula salad Lester said, "I hear your creative writing program is going really well." She leaned across to Hans. "It developed out of their writing workshops in Juvenile Hall."

"Wonderful how you got those kids motivated," Hans said.

"A lot of them have real talent," Ellen said. "Like this boy Davey who's writing poetry now. Not quite *New Yorker* material yet, but who knows?"

"You should be proud," said Hans.

"And so should Davey be proud. He's off drugs, spends time in the library, he's even thinking about college later on—but our real star is this girl Derelle. She starts at Berkeley in the fall."

"It's a great program," Lester said. "Ought to go national."

"That's the plan, someday," said Ellen.

Lester said, "When Josh goes to Congress—which he will—you'll be wanting to spend more time in D.C. That could be the right time. But the Children's Alliance still needs to build more of a presence, so we can promote it."

"Greg wants to do an article for a special education edition of the *Chronicle*. That would certainly help get national attention. What do you think?"

Lester looked dubious. "I'd say, absolutely, go for it—if it was anyone but Greg Hunter."

Ellen glanced involuntarily at Greg's table, up front below the dais, found him gazing right back at her across the magnolias, and quickly looked away. "He did a good job with that homeless piece with those vets," she said.

"I agree," Lester said. "He surprised me. I didn't know he had that much compassion. But is it smart to get involved with him,

Ellen? He runs with the wrong crowd, and now he's doing this Turner book with Satcher—I'm sure you read about it in the *Chronicle,* if he didn't tell you himself. And what about that piece about his wife learning to shoot? I saw that as an outright endorsement of the AAGO." When Ellen didn't immediately respond, Lester added, "Didn't *you?*"

"I'm not saying I liked it or approved of it. But couldn't it have been a regular assignment?"

"Given the subject matter? Unlikely. I saw the hand of Satcher behind that. Are you committed?"

"Not yet."

"Think carefully about this."

"Trust me, I already am."

"But I'm obviously prejudiced, and to do him justice, Greg Hunter's a good writer, he has quite a following, and provided he gets it right, the exposure would be useful. The donations would pour in, too." The Congresswoman speared a shrimp and ate it contemplatively. She turned to Ellen and said, "If you go ahead with it, have him do a story on you."

"On me? I've done nothing special—it's all about the kids."

"Nothing special?" Lester chuckled. "Well, I guess not—all you did was start that organization up when you were still a teenager—"

"It wasn't *my* idea. It was—"

"—and build it into an important entity. Your professor got to first base but you brought it home. And don't think I don't know the work and energy that goes into *keeping* an organization like the Children's Alliance going." With emphasis, Lester said, "I could sure use you if you wanted to work for me."

"Thank you!" Ellen said, both pleased and startled. "I appreciate that so much—but one politician in the family's enough."

"In fact, I could definitely see you running for office yourself." Lester regarded Ellen thoughtfully. "The superintendent of schools slot will be open in the next two years. Seems to me you're a natural. Why not consider it?"

"Are you trying to keep me busy while Josh is in Washington?"

"You keep yourself busy enough without help from me."

"The answer's no, anyway. It would mean endless adminis-tration, and there's way too much of that in my life already," Ellen said.

"Ah, administration. The curse of success!"

The main course arrived, breast of chicken in some kind of creamy sauce. The Congresswoman surveyed the edge of Ellen's cuff and pushed back her full silk sleeves. "Take my advice, girl: wear short sleeves or no sleeves and you won't get some smart-ass photographer showing the world how you messed up your outfit." She sighed and dabbed with a napkin. "Anyway, it's not you on the receiving end of the cameras tonight but your man. I admire the hell out of him. I think he has a big future and I'm proud to be a part of it." Then Shirley Lester turned shrewd eyes on Ellen. "But you know something? I have this gut feeling that sooner or later the world's going to hear a whole lot more from you."

★ ★ ★

Lester turned to talk to the judge, and Ellen to her father-in-law. She heard him tell about that other time Josh was honored, at his bar mitzvah at the Biltmore Hotel, how hard he had worked on his Hebrew, what a fine speech he had made, and how proud they had all been. "That was when we realized he had a real gift."

Hans talked all the way through dessert—he seemed to have memorized every word of Josh's bar mitzvah speech—and Ellen found her eyes drawn back to Greg's table. Their involvement over the article need not be an issue, she knew he'd do a good job, and the publicity might give the Children's Alliance a huge boost. Did she have any right to pass up such an opportunity?

But she'd think about it all later, tonight was for Josh.

As the waiters collected plates, Judge Wedley, in black beaded jersey that glinted like armored plating, rose majestically to her feet and took her position behind a podium to one side of the dais. The theme from *The Way We Were* swelled from the speaker system. The lights dimmed and an image flashed on-screen of the great seal of the University of California, which then dissolved to a shot of the famous Campanile with its four corner spires.

"On behalf of the Alumni Association, I want to welcome all of you on this very special occasion and introduce you to our distinguished guests." While the judge introduced, welcomed, and praised, a rapid photo montage unfolded: Berkeley scenes starting from the turn of the century, including that ukulele-playing fellow Ellen had glimpsed in the old yearbook in the library.

It was like riding a time machine. Ellen watched the pants widths, hemlines, and lapels variously widen, narrow, drop, and rise again; buildings appear where none had been before; bushes and trees rise and fall or become parking lots, then the sudden explosion into color and the Free Speech Movement, the hippie revolution, and the rainbow throngs of protesters on the steps of Sproul Hall.

And finally, the seventies.

The camera held on a panoramic view of the Berkeley campus, still watched over by the Campanile.

"There's an ancient Chinese curse," the judge declared, "which says, 'May you live in interesting times.' And by any definition, the sixties and seventies fulfill that saying—times of conflict, of idealism, of searching, and of sweeping change, a time when Joshua Fischer's generation came of age. But if it was a curse, it was also a thrilling period to be young here at the University of California, Berkeley, one of the foremost institutions in the country to provide a forum for the ultimate questions and their often surprising answers. It was a time that can surely never be repeated and certainly never surpassed."

Her gaze swept the room during the dramatic silence that followed.

"This evening's honored alumnus combines the very best of that time! He has fearlessly declared his life's work as a fight for justice, wherever that fight may lead him and whatever it may cost. And whatever influenced his life's choice, we are proud that U.C. Berkeley surely played a role!"

Josh's face now filled the screen, his yearbook photo face, the ponytail gone but still, compared with the return of more conservative styles, such an extravagance of hair and sideburns.

"Joshua Benjamin Fischer, we salute you as Alumnus of the Year, 1989!"

Judge Wedley allowed the applause to swell, then commandingly raised her hands for silence.

"Now, you all know the story of this man's exceptional courage, but I'll tell it again. It happened last fall, on a morning that began like any other."

The judge took the story right up to the confrontation in the principal's office, when she called upon Carole Walker to carry on, and then the principal took the mike, her resonant voice carrying effortlessly to the farthest recesses of the room.

"This nice-spoken, gentle young man had the guts to do what he did, to put his body in harm's way, and not once but twice—the first time was when he threw me aside, yes, *me* [a pause for a ripple of welcome laughter]—and most definitely saved my life. *Oh* yes! He dove and grabbed the gun from that deranged boy just as it went off, again saving my life, and his wife's, and the lives of others. Then when the officers came he told them the child was off his head, that he needed help not a bullet. I never saw anything like it," boomed Walker, "and every night I pray that I won't get to see it again."

She leaned forward, scooped up the award in one hand, and presented it to Josh. "On behalf of the Alumni Association of the University of California, Berkeley, thank you for your brave heart, and for inspiring our students by your courage and by your example. Let me thank you and Congresswoman Lester for continuing to fight for sensible gun laws. And, on a personal note, you may be Berkeley's Alumnus of the Year, but you're my hero for life!"

The spotlight beamed onto Josh as he planted a kiss on the principal's cheek, accepted the award—a crystal replica of the Campanile, eighteen inches high on a brushed steel base—and raised it over his head in both hands like a winning athlete holding up a trophy.

When the room was quiet again, he declared in a soft but carrying voice, "I'm not a hero. I'm an ordinary person who, on one particular day, found himself in an extraordinary situation. I didn't think, I acted on instinct, and there may well have been a worse outcome if my wife, Ellen, hadn't come to my side and almost pulled off a miracle. It's people like her who are the real heroes, with her never-ending and often heartbreaking work at the Children's Alliance. People like Ms. Walker, on the front lines day after day, year after year, who never give up on our kids. Like my boss, Congresswoman Shirley Lester, who has never stopped fighting for gun control legislation so that neither criminals nor troubled individuals nor children have ready access to deadly weapons, and ordinary people can take back the streets; and she continues to oppose that powerful gun lobby, those people who capitalize on violence, the American Association of Gun Owners—"

Enthusiastic applause.

Ellen risked a glance at Greg and saw that he wasn't looking at her this time but at his father-in-law, that ruddy, smiling man who was not smiling any longer.

Josh went on, "But our fight is not only against the prolifera-tion of guns—and remember that, to a doctor, the word *prolif-eration* has a decidedly negative aspect, as in 'proliferation' of cancer cells—it's against all social injustice. Tonight, the Alumni Association"—a dip of his dark head toward Judge Wedley—"has also seen fit to honor me 'for continued efforts to enrich the lives of the people of Berkeley and Oakland.'" Josh paused and once more surveyed the room. As usual he was speaking without notes, fluidly, without a stumble or a single hesitation that was not purposeful, never once taking his eyes from his audience.

"But you cannot enrich a life when there *is* no life, and there're too many who turn their eyes away from disaster if it means cash out of their own pockets. We're not only seeing the rise of the special-interest gun lobby, but the rise of the moneyed special interests that use the lure of jobs to blind poor people to the environmental dangers and the degradation of their commu-nities. It takes time to reap the bitter fruits from this despoilment, with its harvest of disease and death; it can take years, so that the

profits have been made, the moneymakers are gone and their corporations dismantled long before the people get sick and the
funerals start. A year or so ago this man came to me . . ." and Josh
related the tale of Brother Washington and Gettings Wharf, the
poisoned children, the corporate indifference, Lester's intervention, and the hope now dawning for that blighted little town.

"So here's the good news," he concluded. "We're vigilant.
We're beaming the light of truth into dark corners, and with your
help and with the help of all people of honor, we'll roust this corruption and bring truth, justice, and health to the community."

More applause.

"And why stop there?" With a challenge to the once-more
silent audience, Josh demanded, "Why not fight the good fight for
the entire nation?"

Then he ducked his head and smiled tiredly. "I've said enough."
He held out the trophy again. "Thank you for this, thank you all
for being here, and from the bottom of my heart, thank you for
listening!"

The room roared its approval.

People leaped to their feet.

Ellen saw Greg look across at his father-in-law and, following
his lead, remain seated.

Ellen watched Gunther Hecht watching Josh and was
reminded, by the forward slope of his heavy shoulders and the
angle of his leonine head, of a large predator calculating the
length and force of his spring. If he were a cougar, thought Ellen,
his tail would be switching from side to side. She watched his big
hands as they clapped, so slowly and so deliberately as to be derisive: One. Two. Three.

Josh had given no quarter in his speech to men like Gunther
Hecht, and Ellen knew, with a touch of chill, that Josh now had a
dangerous enemy.

CHAPTER SIXTEEN

On a Wednesday in early July, a typical San Francisco summer evening, cool and windy with swirling fog, Greg met Ellen for dinner at Mel's Drive-In on Lombard Street to discuss his plans for the Children's Alliance article.

He guessed he'd picked an unusual, even whimsical, venue, but it was certainly convenient, both for Ellen—who had been a featured speaker at a seminar on truancy, attended by teachers and social workers, at the conference center at the decommissioned Presidio army base just blocks away—and for Greg, whose house was directly up the hill in Pacific Heights.

It could also be fun. He'd reminded her of the time they'd driven all the way out to Walnut Creek to search for just such a place as this, retro fifties with glass and chrome, a real soda fountain, and jukeboxes.

"Of course I remember," Ellen said, with perhaps a fractional beat of hesitation and a faintly guarded tone to her voice; she hadn't really wanted to remember that particular evening that had ended with finding Josh passed out on the doorstep.

Now, from his booth facing the parking lot, Greg watched the red Chevy pickup pull in and the slender, auburn-haired woman in the charcoal business suit and sensible shoes climb out of it. Ellen's skirt rode up above her knees, those strong, rounded hiker's legs—in a flash from a simpler time he smelled the wild lupine on that mountain across the bay—and he watched as she tugged the skirt un-self-consciously down again, disappeared momentarily around the side of the building, then reappeared in shifting fragments beyond the beveled glass doors.

In she came, scanning the tables, finding him, and sliding into her seat.

"Good to see you at last!" he said smiling into her eyes, and then they went through all the meeting and greeting circus: *"Hey there, how are you? I'm fine, how's Jane? Fine and how's Josh? Josh's fine. How was your event tonight? Pretty good, useful. Great!"*

"And the boys?" asked Ellen. "Do you have pictures?"

"It just so happens I do." Greg reached for his wallet and extracted a picture: Jeff and Doug, with springy yellow hair and identical grins, both wearing striped rugby shirts, Jeff's red and blue, Doug's blue and white.

"They're lovely. They already look like you." Perhaps only he, who knew her so well, would have noticed the sad sheen of longing in her eyes.

A year or so ago Jane had told him, "I like to think of them growing up the way you should have, and turning out the way you might have." Greg had said nothing at the time, it was an uncomfortable observation; Jane was more perceptive than he thought.

He said now, sincerely, "My boys are two of the few things I've ever done that I'm totally proud of." He tucked his wallet away again. "Let's order."

He went for the cheeseburger, medium rare, fries, and a glass of white wine. Ellen ordered the tuna melt, coleslaw, and a diet Coke. He fed a quarter into the jukebox: Mama Cass's cello of a voice, sang about California dreaming.

"This'll have to do," he apologized. "They don't have *Carmina Burana* or *The Trout* on this thing. Doing much singing these days?"

"Who has the time?"

The food arrived. Way too much of it. Ellen looked at her plate and sighed. Greg said she should take a doggie bag home. "You could probably use it with Josh gone. I'll bet you forget to shop for yourself."

She regarded him with a quizzical expression. "How do you know Josh's away?"

"You told me on the phone."

"Did I?" After a moment, she said, "Perhaps I did. How else would you know?"

"Ell, it doesn't really matter. Josh's movements aren't a state secret."

"Of course not. Sorry. And anyway, you're a reporter. It's your job to know things."

"Exactly. So let's cut to the chase." Greg reached into his briefcase for his notepad and made a place for it beside his overloaded plate.

"I never told you how much I appreciate this," she said. "I'm still not sure why you're doing it and how you talked the *Chronicle* into going for it."

"Because it's a story that needs to be told. It has huge human interest—and will sell a ton of papers." He smiled. "And of course it gives me a chance to see you, which these days ain't so easy!"

She blushed, almost like the old Ellen, and smiled back.

"So, okay. We're on track," he said. "I've roughed out a plan. I'll walk you through it, and you tell me what you think."

The article would have four main components, the first of which would focus on Ellen herself, how she worked with the schools, with the social services, and with the cops.

The second would be about the volunteers: college students, local residents, merchants, grannies and grandpas. "Like, how do they contribute?" explained Greg. "Do they bring food? Teach a skill like word processing or computer? Do office work? Let's see the community involvement spreading like ripples on a pond."

The kids themselves would be featured next, as ethnically mixed as Ellen could manage. "What are their stories? How about that little boy—what was he, eleven?—who was living in a transient hotel room, sharing a bed with a terminally ill grandmother?"

"That's Richard," said Ellen. "He was skipping school to shop for her, buy her medicine, care for her as best he could. He's one of our big success stories, placed in a good foster home, back in school, and getting straight As."

"And what about the granny?"

"Comfortably woozy in a hospice."

"Can we get ahold of Richard?"

"I'll ask him."

The final and most prominent segment would be Ellen's writing program, featuring brief samples of the kids' work. "I can particularly use that child from hell you found in Juvie."

"Derelle? Yep, she's from hell all right, but she got away. If she hadn't, she'd probably be dead by now."

"Abused?"

"Undoubtedly."

"She hasn't talked about it?"

"She writes about it. Obliquely, as a dream, or as if it happened to someone else. She writes well, too; she has a strong, natural voice."

"And all because you handed her a pencil and said, 'Write something.'"

Ellen picked up one of his french fries, dipped it in ketchup, and leveled it at him. "A wax crayon. I thought she'd jab it in my eye."

"Aha." Greg made a note.

"But you can't use that."

"Why not? Readers like a bit of drama."

"I don't care about the readers."

"I'll pretend you didn't say that."

"And it might not be true. I don't *know* what she was thinking and it was a while ago. Don't use it, Greg. Please."

"I think you can assume it *was* true." He sighed. "Okay, I won't run it if that's what you want. But stop trying to do my job! I don't try to do yours. Not that I could."

"Damn right!"

"And don't jump on me for every little thing. All I want to do is turn out a good story. It's my last big assignment for the *Chronicle,* and trust me, I'll make it good. It'll get you some great publicity and hopefully a few bucks for your kids. Then I'm taking a leave of absence to work on my book."

"Ah, yes. That Turner book, with Carl Satcher. I heard about that. I guess I should congratulate you."

"That would be nice."

"It must be quite a coup."

"It is. I'm sorry if it offends you."

"I wouldn't go so far as to use the word *offends.* If it's what you want—"

"The advance isn't so bad either."

"So you've sold your soul to the devil!"

"Oh, come on! Satcher's not the evil bogeyman you people paint him. In his own way, he's no different from Josh. He wants to do good the way he sees it."

"Josh would take exception to that."

"Well, fine. There are always two sides to a question. That's what makes this country great, that we recognize that. Carl and I were talking one time"—what immense satisfaction to drop that so casually—"about the protests in the sixties and seventies, how in a lot of countries protesters would have been shot or locked up and the key thrown away—but not here."

"Of course. But why should that even be a question? This is America—the land of the free, for God's sake. And Satcher has always been a supporter of the haves and the have-alots. When's publication of this famous book, anyway?"

"Fall 1992. In time for the President's re-election."

Ellen regarded him over her glass of Coke. "Strategically timed for Satcher's re-election campaign," she said, "provided he decides to run."

"Oh, he'll run."

"With Tom Turner's influential friends endorsing him."

"Naturally. Though Turner's own endorsement should be enough; people have begged Tom to run for President for years.

The strong, silent, compassionate cowboy. He'd have won in a heartbeat, too. And speaking of running," Greg added casually, just throwing it out there, "is it possible that Josh's on the move himself and won't be playing second fiddle much longer to Lester's first violin? That was the impression he made, anyway, with his speech at the Claremont."

"Which your father-in-law didn't appreciate."

"An anti-business tirade? Is that surprising?" Greg swirled the last of his wine in his glass and finished it off. "I'd say Josh has plans. What do you suppose he'll do next?"

Ellen smiled. "Whatever he thinks is right. As always."

"Spoken like a true political wife." Greg went on, "You want my prediction?"

"Do I have a choice?"

Greg said, repackaging Satcher's thoughts and passing them off as his own, "It seems almost a no-brainer. Lester will run for the Senate in '92. I can hear her mantra now: 'Let's get that special-interest Senator Satcher out'—which will leave her congressional seat open for Josh, who'll be a shoe-in, especially since the shooting. He has Alameda County in his pocket. And after that?"

Ellen shrugged. "Ask him, not me."

"I can see him making his own Senate run. Will he run in '94 when Sunny Williams is up for re-election, or since Williams is a popular Democrat, will he wait until '98 and go after Satcher himself?"

"Supposing it's Lester, not Satcher?"

"It won't be. She'll lose in '92."

"Provided, of course, that she runs."

"She'll run."

"Then she'll win. Shirley Lester is a wise woman with talent and experience, and a base that's deep and loyal."

"She'll still lose."

Satcher himself had asked Greg, sitting on the veranda in the blue dusk, his sweat-stained cowboy hat shoved to the back of his head, and a curl of fragrant smoke rising from his cigar, "Who would you vote for if you were the average working stiff in the Valley? Carl Satcher or some granny from the ghetto?"

Greg said to Ellen, "Let me tell you why she'll lose. It's very simple. Lester's too old—she's already over seventy—and she has no real money. She might look pretty good in Oakland, and she'd do well in the inner cities, but Satcher has credibility where it counts. People see stature, security, and progress. He has statewide recognition and important endorsements, like the President himself."

Ellen said drily, "He also has a hand in every pocket. What about his corporate shenanigans? They won't stand up to much scrutiny. I'm thinking in particular of EastPac Development. And the Hazlett Corporation."

"Even with the closest scrutiny, I doubt you'd find any evidence of wrongdoing."

"You mean he's bought the lawyers and destroyed the evidence."

"Evidence! Oh, Ellen, please. You're talking as if he's accused of murder."

She looked him in the eye. "He's not?"

"By whom? By Josh? Or by Brother Whatsit from Sludge City?"

"And by lots of others who see the slow poisoning of a neighborhood as slow, painful murder."

"Really, Ell, don't put people you don't like into boxes marked *evil*. It's so—" he searched for a word.

"Berkeley?" she offered, smiling.

"There you go. But we got ourselves sidetracked." He determinedly shifted the conversation back to where he wanted it to be. "We were talking about your husband, about Josh, not Satcher. How it's a foregone conclusion Josh will be elected to Congress, and how, in all likelihood, he'll end up running for the Senate. The only question is when."

Again, she evaded. "That's your take. Like I said, you'll have to ask him yourself."

"But he's thought about it."

"You seem to know more than I do."

Greg watched her closely but her eyes gave nothing away. She hadn't quite learned to mask her emotions, she protested a little too much, but she was learning. He thought how much and how fast she was catching on to the ways of the world and how, in so many ways, he wished she would not.

"Whatever happens," she said with emphasis, "it's Josh's life and Josh's choice. It's out of my hands."

"Which will be full enough anyway, even more when the article's published," Greg said and watched Ellen's clear relief when he returned the subject to her own home ground of the Children's Alliance.

She said, smiling, "That article will open a lot of doors."

"Just as well. With Josh in D.C. so much, you'll need to keep especially busy." Abruptly, he asked, "Don't you ever get lonely, Ellen?"

"Are you kidding? I'm with people all the time. Being alone is a luxury."

"I'm not talking about being alone, I'm talking about being lonely."

"Josh and I talk to each other every day on the phone."

"Is that enough for you, Ell?"

"It has to be. And I think I'd better go now." Ellen rose and glanced with a surprised expression at her empty plate. "Thanks for dinner. Tuna melts never disappoint."

"Never have," he said. "I'll walk you to your car."

The pickup stood out among the family sedans in the parking lot. Greg looked at its bulk and back to Ellen, slender and elegant in her suit, and couldn't help but grin.

Suddenly and impulsively the old Ellen again, she grinned back and playfully slapped a bright red fender. "You know, I love this thing! I feel so powerful and tall, for a change! And it's so practical for work."

He opened the door for her. "Listen," he said, wanting to hold this moment of camaraderie, "I didn't mean to insult Shirley Lester. I do sincerely believe she's a great woman."

"I know. Though I can't say the same about Carl Satcher."

"I know. Satcher's not a woman."

"You know what I mean. I still think you've sold out to the dark side."

"You're entitled."

"Though I'm sure you'll produce a fine book. Forgive me if I don't buy it. I'm not interested in contributing to Satcher's royalties."

"I'll give you a copy. Autographed."

"Then, thank you. And thanks again, really, for writing about the Children's Alliance. And for dinner."

"My pleasure. Let me give you a boost." But Ellen was already propelling herself into the driver's seat. She sat there looking down at him for a moment, as if there was something she still wanted to say to him. He waited, but she didn't say anything after all and started the engine. He reached through the window and touched her arm. He wanted to do so much more. "Take care. I'll call you. Drive safely."

★   ★   ★

In so many ways, Greg thought, he'd blown it. Of course the evening hadn't been wasted. It had actually been quite a success. Ellen had given him the final go-ahead for the article, which he'd make sure was a terrific, feel-good story, featuring all those cute, deprived graduates of Juvie Hall who were proving to be such talented writers (and of course he was going to use the crayon incident; how could she imagine he'd pass up a juicy detail like that?). Greg was already considering potential follow-ups to the article: an internship at the paper, for instance, for the best and the brightest, or even the funding of a college scholarship, with the winner's progress followed step-by-step. That would hook the readers all right, it was great stuff—and naturally he'd have to be in close touch with Ellen every inch of the way.

While Ellen had refused to discuss her husband's future plans, she had denied nothing—which, to Greg's thinking, might as well be confirmation.

But between himself and Ellen personally? Nothing. Not a thing! She'd been wary, at times almost adversarial. Only at the

last moment had the old, affectionate, joyous Ellen surfaced—
and then she had gone. And left him.

Greg leaned against the shiny black flank of his Porsche
Targa, a gift from Jane on his last birthday, and watched as Ellen
pulled into traffic, the Chevy's taillights merging with all the
other lights so that very soon he could no longer pick out which
were hers. He imagined her turning right onto Van Ness and heading toward downtown, for the Bay Bridge and Oakland, and the
little house she shared with Josh.

Two weeks earlier at the ranch, Satcher had wondered, "This
friend of yours, Josh Fischer. Kind of a hotheaded guy, I guess."

"He's an idealist," Greg had responded.

"And that cute little redheaded gal, his wife—she an old
flame of yours?"

In no way had he wanted to discuss Ellen with Satcher. "She's
a friend. We go back a long way."

"So you and she did have a thing going."

Greg had neither agreed nor denied, and Satcher approved.
"Never could respect a man who bragged about his women."

She was never *my* woman, Greg thought in a flash of honesty,
though she could have been. *Should* have been.

"I won't ask you if there's any kind of spark still there," Satcher
said, "but it's always good to keep in touch with a friend."

The Porsche's windshield was thick with condensation, the
wind had died but the air was damp and chill, the fog heavier than
ever. Greg shivered, climbed inside, switched on the heat and the
windshield wipers. Then he placed his hands on the leather-
covered steering wheel and rested his forehead on his knuckles.
Ellen could hardly be described as an *old* flame, and her attitude
tonight, so cool and professional, had discouraged him pro-
foundly—but what had he expected? That she'd fall into his arms?
Go to a motel with him?

Suddenly, though he was loath even to articulate the thought,
he wondered whether the real reason he had chosen this place
on Lombard Street for their meeting was not for convenience but
for the proliferation of anonymous tourist motels—he could see

at least four of them within two blocks, all displaying vacancy signs.

But that was a crazy idea—he'd never take Ellen to a motel. Nor would she have considered it, even for a moment. She'd have laughed at him.

There was one consolation. At least he hadn't confided in her about his failing marriage. No, he had his pride. And there'd be other meetings with Ellen about the article, and after a while she might not find it quite such a luxury to be alone.

Greg guessed Ellen would be on the Bay Bridge by now. The traffic wouldn't be bad, this time of night. She'd be making good time.

He switched on the engine and slipped an old tape into his player, Glen Campbell on the road to Phoenix, having finally left the girl he'd tried to leave so many times before. It was a song that always made Greg feel nostalgic and sad.

Where am *I* going tonight? he wondered.

He thought reluctantly of returning to his fancy house on Pacific Avenue, where Jane would be asleep between the Porthault sheets with the hundreds of threads per inch that she seemed to think so important.

Or he could find some bar and make arid conversation with a bored bartender and all the other losers. There were lots of bars here too, among the motels. Bars and motels and gas stations like any other strip in any other town all the way across America.

Greg drummed his fingers on the steering wheel. *He wasn't a goddam loser.*

In his mind's eye he saw Ellen turn into her driveway, open her front door, and walk inside. Perhaps she'd make herself a cup of tea in her yellow kitchen. Then she'd go to bed, alone.

Damn you to hell, Josh Fischer, for taking the only woman I've ever really cared about.

Greg pulled out his cell phone and punched in a number.

It rang five times before she answered; she had probably gone to bed, though her voice sounded as alert and business-like as ever. "This is Micaela."

"Can I come over?"

"Right now?"

"Yes."

He waited for her to ask why, and what couldn't possibly wait until the morning, but she didn't. All she said was, "Do you know where I live?"

★ ★ ★

Greg swung onto Doyle Drive toward the Golden Gate Bridge, powered through the toll plaza barely slackening speed, his headlights glaring on dense, white sheets of fog while sprays of moisture slapped at the windshield, and every few seconds, beneath him, boomed the deep, mournful cry of a foghorn.

Micaela had given up her condo in Menlo Park south of the city and lived in Tiburon now, in a waterside development whose inhabitants always seemed to be in transition. Corporate gypsies lived there and the newly divorced, mostly men because the wives got the house and kids. Each unit had a deck, a water view, and a place to moor a boat. Micaela's one-bedroom apartment was on the third floor at the end of the walkway, no neighbors above or to her right. As private, in that complex, as it was possible to be.

Greg eased the Porsche into a guest parking slot under a eucalyptus tree, whose trunk gleamed eerily in the lights from the management office and the gym, in which a lone male figure sweated on the treadmill, left right, left right, left right. Greg switched the engine off, and suddenly it was deathly quiet. The slam of the car door sounded loud as a gunshot. He approached Micaela's building, hearing the sound of his footsteps, the water slapping around the pilings, the foghorns, and, out in the bay, the bark of a sea lion. Moisture dripped from the trees, and he wondered what in hell he thought he was doing.

Though of course he knew. He was unbearably lonely and had to be with someone, and if he couldn't be with Ellen, then it would have to be Micaela.

It was wrong of course, and selfish. But, he reasoned, Micaela was not exactly inexperienced, and her origins a lot more sophisticated than his own, with a filmmaker father and a scholarly mother who had published erudite articles on pre-Columbian art. Micaela had a master's degree from the Columbia School of Journalism, had lived alone and successfully in Manhattan. She'd survived more than one intense relationship upon which, now, she felt secure enough to look back and laugh.

No, he didn't have to worry about her. Micaela could take care of herself.

★ ★ ★

The porch light was on. He reached for the bell but the door opened before he could touch it.

A tall, thin, barefoot waif stood in the doorway, wearing white sweatpants and a blue T-shirt with a yellow smiley face on it.

Greg felt a small pang beneath his breastbone. Micaela looked so young, though she must be at least twenty-seven. He realized he had never before seen her without makeup.

"Hi." He kissed her cheek. She smelled of soap. She stood aside to let him through and closed the door behind him. He said, suddenly awkward, "I hope I didn't wake you."

"I was watching TV." She led the way into her living room, tidy and neutral with a wall-to-wall beige rug, a sofa and matching armchair upholstered in oatmeal tweed, and a glass-topped dining table flanked by chrome-framed chairs with white leather seats. Micaela could move out anytime, thought Greg, and not leave a trace of herself behind. The self-discipline and containment that showed was another consoling thought. She could walk away from anything, including him.

The only personal notes were the shelves of books which he'd inspect another time (yes, of course there'd be another time), a muted television set tuned to CNN, a computer in one corner, and on the spotless table, a large ceramic vase decorated with brightly colored mystical birds and animals that appeared, to Greg's untutored eye, to be of museum quality.

He chose the armchair beside the TV and sat down.

Micaela picked up the remote and clicked CNN away. "Can I get you something? I don't have much in the way of liquor, but I could boil some water. Instant coffee, maybe? Or tea? I only have Lipton's."

"Lipton's would be great. Nothing in it."

Her kitchen opened off the living room—he could see stain-
less steel and immaculate gray-flecked Corian counters. He heard
water running, a minute later a high-pitched whistle, and she
returned with a tray bearing a mug glazed with a red and yellow
rooster, a matching plate, and a glass of milk.

He said impulsively, "You look twelve."

"Thanks. I guess. Like a cookie?" She dug around in the jar
and arranged chocolate chip cookies on the plate, placed it on
a small table beside his chair, then took her glass of milk to the
sofa, where she perched cross-legged, watching him. "Okay then,
so tell me why you're here and what couldn't wait."

Greg gazed at her slim ankles, the narrow bare feet, and
sipped his too-hot tea. He set it down and instantly forgot it. He
didn't want a cookie either. She waited quietly. He thought that
she always knew when to be silent, a great quality in a woman. "I
guess I wanted to be with someone," he said. "With you. I've been
thinking about you."

"About me?" Micaela looked at him with such open intensity
he at once realized she felt more for him than as a mere colleague
for whom she researched documents, checked facts, and bur-
rowed through archives. Well, he thought, who'd have guessed it.
How gratifying—and how very useful this relationship would be
down the road if he played it right. But he must be careful.

"I've been thinking about you too," she said. "About us. But I
never thought we'd—I mean—what about Jane?"

"Jane would be a wonderful wife—for somebody else."

"But you're still together."

He sought for exactly the right words; he needed her to
empathize. "As a marriage, it's empty. There's nothing there,
never has been. I guess I married Jane for all the wrong reasons.
It was a mistake from the beginning, my fault of course. I was
so insecure, coming from a background like mine. I couldn't
believe somebody like her would choose me when she could have
anyone."

"That's honest, anyway."

"I owe you honesty." And the appearance of it could go a long way, he knew.

"But you and Jane looked so happy together that night at the Claremont."

"We know how to put on a good face, but that's all it is. Apart from the kids, we have nothing. Nothing in common, nothing to say to each other."

"So what happens now? Are you splitting up?"

He thought about all the divorced men living in this complex, coming home alone to an empty apartment with a nice sparkly view of the bay, and walking the treadmill into the night. Not now, he thought. Not ever, not if I want to keep my life. "We're quite civilized about it. We lead our own lives in different rooms, but we're friendly when we meet."

"Different rooms?"

"Bedrooms. That part of our marriage has been over quite a while. Her choice."

"I see."

A silence hung between them. Greg knew he should be ashamed of himself for lying. Of course he and Jane had sex, and pretty good sex, too—but that was all it was, sex, not love-making, so perhaps it wasn't a lie after all.

What was Micaela thinking? What would she do?

After a full minute during which she did and said nothing, he put his hands on his knees as if to rise. "I'm sorry. I shouldn't dump this on you. It's not fair, it's my problem not yours. I'd better be getting back."

Just as he had hoped she might, Micaela cried, "No, don't go yet. I'm glad you came." She rose and held out her hands, such delicate hands with their mother-of-pearled nails. "Come out on the deck and see my view."

Greg took her hand and let her lead him out into the darkness that wasn't so dark after all. The fog still slid over the Headlands and the Golden Gate Bridge, but here in this Tiburon inlet it was clear. A three-quarter moon spilled a bright path across the black water while across the bay the towers of San

Francisco twinkled like a city of stars. "Beautiful," said Greg. "I can see why you live here." He pulled her against him, ran his fingers through her hair—strong hair, blue black, dead straight, so different from Jane's blonde, baby soft hair, and from Ellen's coppery wire.

Safe hair.

He gripped Micaela by the shoulders, held her at arm's length, and asked, of himself rather than her, "What am I going to do?"

"What do you want to do?"

"I want to go to bed with you. But it's not fair."

"Isn't that for me to decide?" and she led him back through the stark living room into just as stark a bedroom, same pale wall-to-wall, and another row of glass doors onto another deck, this side looking out onto the dark flank of the Headlands. There was one painting—a gaudy market scene, brilliant colors of fruit and spices and women's bundled skirts—which he forgot upon seeing her bed with the rumpled sheet and the thrust-aside white comforter. So she had been in bed, maybe asleep, and CNN in the living room had just been for show.

She turned to Greg in silence, pulled him down beside her, raised her arms so he could take her T-shirt off. She was naked under it. He ran his hands over her silky, olive skin, held her slender wrists in his hands, and bent to kiss her throat. "I thought I knew you," he said, "but you're a total surprise."

"It's not so difficult to know me."

Greg was aware of nothing but the feel of her skin against his and the scent and strength of her body.

Micaela, he said. Oh, Micaela—not even sure if he spoke her name out loud.

★ ★ ★

They lay quietly together on their backs, hips touching, her leg hooked over his. Greg felt her fingertips trace down the inside of his arm to his wrist, then to the palm of his hand.

She shifted onto her side. "Confession time," she said. "I've dreamed of this happening for months. I never thought it would."

He kissed the corner of her mouth.

"But Greg, listen, I know you're here tonight because things were going wrong and you were hurting. I'm glad I made you feel better, but please don't think you have to take this any further if you don't want to."

What a noble girl. And smart. He kissed her again. "How could I not want to take it further?"

★ ★ ★

Greg crossed the Golden Gate Bridge again, this time north to south, at three o'clock in the morning.

"You could spend the night," Micaela had offered. "It's so late now. It'll be dawn soon. I'll make you breakfast."

"What with?"

"I have instant coffee. Remember? There're cookies. And the bakery opens early; I can buy croissants. We can eat on the deck and watch the pelicans and see the sun come up."

How tempting that sounded and how incredibly tired he felt. It had been a long, stressful day. How badly he wanted to burrow back under Micaela's soft comforter, hold her in his arms, fall back to sleep, wake up in a few hours, and make love to her again. But Jane knew he'd been meeting with Ellen tonight. What would he say when he returned to the house at nine o'clock in the morning? Sorry, dear, it all took a bit longer than I expected?

Sure. And how long before she told her father?

Greg thought about the wrath of Gunther Hecht, and of his cozy berth being yanked from under him. He visualized himself back in Surprise Bend, covering weddings and 4-H club shows. Strapping teenage girls in overalls. Calves batting their deeply lashed eyes at him. He vowed, Never again. Not now he'd tasted the good stuff.

He thought of Micaela lying as he had left her, arms and legs flung out across the bed, and felt deeply depressed. He fumbled for his money at the toll plaza and let a five-dollar bill blow away. Well, somebody would find it, maybe someone who really needed it.

Five minutes later Greg pulled up to the garage, knocked his elbow against the steering wheel, and dropped the door opener. It slid so far under the passenger seat he couldn't reach it. He felt too tired to get out of the car, unlock the garage door, get back in the car, drive inside, and get out again. He just left the Porsche outside in the driveway blocking the sidewalk—if he got a ticket, to hell with it.

The burglar alarm beeped shrilly as he let himself into the house. He punched in the code—*damn* that alarm, no chance now of not waking Jane, to say nothing of Mrs. Hearn—but luckily no one called out or came to greet him.

He tiptoed upstairs, as softly as he could, along the passage to the master suite and through to the bathroom.

Greg dropped his clothes on the floor for the second time that night. Then, dragging himself together—at least he was capable of some residual rational thought—he bundled up socks, shirt, and underwear and tossed them into the hamper for Mrs. Hearn to deal with in the morning, and flung a towel on top.

He crept into the bedroom, consumed by a relentless need to sleep, to forget, to leave everything for the morning. Longing only to fall into that huge, waiting bed.

That *empty* waiting bed.

Where was Jane?

Then he remembered she had left that afternoon—yesterday afternoon now—to play in a tennis match at the Burlingame Country Club. She was staying down the Peninsula, had taken the boys with her, and given Mrs. Hearn the night off.

He could have stayed with Micaela. Jane would never have known.

Or he could have taken Ellen to a motel after all, and he needn't have started this thing with Micaela in the first place.

★

1998

★

CHAPTER SEVENTEEN

The kickoff for Josh's campaign for the United States Senate, with a tour of the five biggest media markets in the state, began at eleven o'clock on a wet Tuesday morning in January in Gettings Wharf.

Nobody had yet received money from the lawsuits. "Don't hold your breath," Josh had advised from the start, and Brother Washington agreed ruefully somewhat later, "Folks would've died of asphyxiation." Gettings Wharf had nonetheless undergone a transformation during the past several years. It was amazing what goodwill could achieve, coupled with federal funds matched with tax breaks for new businesses. After the clean-up, Gettings Wharf was firmly re-established as the thriving community it once had been. Bus service was restored. Gus's Café opened, and Feleesha's Market, even a gas station to service the increasing number of cars. The desolate ruin of the old Hazlett factory was now a busy lumberyard with an adjoining farmers' market, where yuppies had begun to shop on Saturday mornings, after which they'd enjoy a brew and a searing chili dog at Gus's.

Under the spotlight of publicity, Tri-State Management, with its dubious parent EastPac Development, somehow managed to disappear like mist. The 1940s frame cottages were being refurbished inside and out, brightened with new paint and flower boxes, and young families were moving in. The location was really pretty good, and it was only a short commute to the airport, where there were plenty of new construction jobs.

The original Bayside Baptist Church building, long abandoned in its disrepair, was renovated and shining with white paint, and the extra collections from its more prosperous congregation had enabled the pastor to buy the brand-new brass weathercock, glittering bravely from the spire, which Orvis Hancock, new resident and a machinist at Oakland International Airport, had installed for free.

Now the grass actually grew in the little park, except where it was stomped away beneath the cleats of the kids' soccer shoes. In the center of the park, once the ground zero of foulness, stood the brand-new Lester Community Center, a simple structure, basically four cinder block walls and a roof, but embellished by the local kids who had created a wraparound mural inside depicting the travails of Gettings Wharf and its miraculous renaissance. The story began with haggard faces, gray skies, the wide mouth of a pipe dripping brown sludge, and a row of tombstones: R.I.P. Jamal, DeeAnn, Jerry. But then came the arrival of Josh himself, shown shaking Brother Washington's hand outside Bayside Baptist Church, and the cautious advent of color. Congresswoman Shirley Lester appeared in a smart pink hat, and the EPA inspectors in space suits laid out their Day-Glo yellow caution tape. Next came the Capitol dome decorated with red, white, and blue dollar signs, and from then on the walls positively blazed. Children played on the greenest of green grass, golden birds flew in an azure sky, and youthful faces grinned from each window of a fat, yellow school bus.

Gettings Wharf had come alive again.

This morning Josh waited in the doorway of the Lester Center while the rain drummed on rooftops, clattered from the roofs of parked cars, and swirled down the street in muddy streams.

"Nobody'll come," he'd told Lester earlier, for this was no day for venturing outside, certainly not one in which to crowd into a small concrete building on an East Bay slough.

Lester, however, had assured him with quiet certainty, "They'll come."

And she was right. The hall was already full, humming with energy and the expectant clamor of voices, smelling of warm bodies and damp wool. Looking down the aisle toward the small stage at the other end of the hall, he could see Shirley Lester standing with Brother Washington and a cluster of elected officials including the local Democratic Party chair, the city attorney of Oakland, and two Alameda County supervisors. Lester looked much the same as ever except for a powdering of white at her temples. She caught Josh's eye and smiled. *What did I tell you, that smile said. Of course they came! Trust me!*

The white-robed adult members of the Bayside Baptist gospel choir were packed tightly into the space to the left of the stage, while twenty excited children giggled and fidgeted in front. Crews from local television stations KTVU, KRON, and KCBS and the political reporters from the *Oakland Tribune, San Francisco Chronicle,* and *San Jose Mercury News* crammed two tiers of hastily erected risers.

Ellen, wearing a flame-colored pantsuit, stood on Josh's left, tightly clasping his hand. Derelle stood to his right. Brother Washington approached the podium and stretched his arms wide as if to embrace the whole world, and the buzz of voices stopped. "Brothers and sisters," he boomed, "welcome to the community of Gettings Wharf on one of the happiest and most triumphant days of our lives!"

★ ★ ★

The success of this event was, Josh was sure, mostly due to Ellen. She had ridden herd on his campaign staff, headed now by Vicente Aguilera, who had taken a leave of absence from his regular duties as chief of Josh's congressional staff. Ellen had helped raise the seed money (though happily much had remained in his congressional campaign war chest), she oversaw the drafting of the press releases and followed up in her usual ebullient form. When he'd voiced his admiration and surprise at the results of her fund-raising, she'd merely laughed, "Haven't I been doing this half my life?"

Brother Washington introduced Democratic Party Chair Roger Wu, Supervisor Sandra Leigh, and Assemblyman Pete Sanchez until finally, his face glowing with pleasure, he beckoned Shirley Lester to the podium. "And let's now welcome *our* former Congresswoman, who believed our community counted, who made sure our children were saved, Shirley Lester, who was our voice in Washington for so long!" The whole crowd rose to its feet, applause rang out, and voices called, "Shir-LEE! Shir-LEE! Shir-LEE!"

"Gettings Wharf is an important place for me," Shirley Lester's voice came low, soft, and intimate, and Josh knew each and every person in the room felt personally addressed. It was a gift to be able to reach out and touch with one's voice; Josh wished he could do it half as well as Lester. Perhaps one day he would. She went on, "Today is one of huge importance and expectations for all of us, and it's only right that it should take place here. I know that this community center, which I'm proud to have named for me, represents something special to you. For the rest of the Bay Area as well, this center represents the victory of hope over callousness and greed. The real credit, however, doesn't lie at my door but with the young man I'm about to introduce."

Josh automatically moved forward; Ellen and Derelle caught his arms. *Not yet.*

"He's the one who helped bring the disgrace and tragedy of Gettings Wharf to my attention," Lester said, "so I could make it known to the outside world. He's the one who did battle against the corporate elements who were destroying this town.

"During my years as your representative to Congress, this young man, Joshua Fischer, California born and bred, worked diligently at my side as my district director and later as my chief of staff. He also did everything he could to get me to the Senate, which didn't work out exactly as we hoped. He has since served as your Congressman for almost six years. It was he who raised his voice against the Airport Authority so that small and even smaller minority-owned contracting companies from Alameda County were not shut out of the bidding on construction jobs.

Also thanks largely to Josh, the Authority, in conjunction with the primary construction company, set up local training programs to sharpen the skills of the long-term unemployed. No longer have minority workers been so cavalierly passed over at union hiring halls.

"I have total admiration for his courage and confidence in his integrity. I have direct experience of his caring and energy, as indeed have you.

"Ladies and Gentlemen, for most of you he needs no introduction: Congressman Joshua Benjamin Fischer, the man who I'm most proud to support in his bid for the United States Senate!"

On cue, a bright banner dropped down the wall behind the stage, sky blue with letters in white:

JOSH FISCHER FOR SENATE, FIGHTING THE BATTLES FOR YOU!

A happy shout issued from four hundred throats: "JOSH! JOSHUA!"

The gospel choir burst into his campaign song:

Joshua fought the battle of Jericho, Jericho, Jericho,
Joshua fought the battle of Jericho,
And the walls came tumbling down!

"Okay," Ellen said in his ear, "go *now*," and pushed Josh gently between the shoulder blades, out into an explosion of flashbulbs.

He ventured slowly down the narrow aisle, half blinded, only dimly seeing the hands reaching out for him, reaching out himself, feeling his hands caught and held, his back and shoulders patted, until he confronted his own poster-size face on the front of the podium, FISCHER for SENATE, and sturdy Brother Washington hauled him up on stage.

Josh clung to the podium's sides like a shipwrecked mariner in a wild sea, vaguely aware of a husky teenage boy emerging from the ranks of the choir holding a glittering trumpet, toylike in his giant hands, and raising it to his lips, and a tiny old man, looking well over eighty, bald but for a white fuzz behind his ears, wearing a black suit that might have fit him once but now hung around him in folds. He was blinking in the light like a tortoise and raising a gigantic trumpet made of horn, curved and fluted, almost bigger than himself.

The choir swung into the final verse, "Then the ram's horn began to play"—and the massive bray of that horn issued with unimaginable force from those wizened old lungs, enough to wake the dead.

"And the trumpet began to sound"—and it did, clear and golden.

"Old Joshua commanded the children to shout"—and twenty young voices yelled "JOSHUA!" while light exploded from a hundred cameras, the walls and floor trembled—

"And the walls came a-tumbling down!"

Josh felt blasted quite out of himself. He couldn't feel the floor beneath his feet, might not be standing on the floor at all but flying through outer space between brilliant waves of sound—and what sound! It reverberated through his skull and rang in his ears. He recalled Brother Washington telling him the old man's name was Sonny Marsh, that he had played with the greatest, that there was no horn on earth he couldn't blow—or in the universe, thought Josh—and the boy was Lionel Rose, leader of the local high school marching band. Well, bless their hearts.

And now, dazed but once again in command, he saw how everybody was smiling up at him, a vista of faces and hats and waving hands, family, friends, and supporters, and in the very back, standing, conspicuous by nature of his height and his bright blond hair, Josh's old best friend and new worst enemy, Greg Hunter.

"JOSH! JOSH! JOSHUA!"

"BLOW DOWN THOSE WALLS!"

As the choir's voices faded to a vibrating silence, Josh held up his hands to settle the crowd.

His ears still hummed. He counted to ten, pushed the hair from his hot forehead, and when he finally spoke couldn't be sure if he whispered or shouted.

"Now I know," he said, "what it truly means to be blown away! I want to thank the singers and musicians, especially Lionel Rose and the great Sonny Marsh, for an unbelievably awesome performance and for making me feel like such a winner already! I want to thank my dear friend the Reverend Washington, and the community of Gettings Wharf, for opening their doors to us—I can't imagine better company or a finer venue for what I'm about to say. I also want to thank my wife and partner, Ellen, back by the door there, first for her talent for organization—this event has her sure touch—and, most important, for her love and support. I wouldn't be here without it. Finally, I want to thank my great friend, mentor, and hero, Shirley Lester. Boy, is she a hard act to follow! As I was walking up to the stage, I promised myself I'd never follow her onto a podium again!" He paused for the ripple of appreciative laughter, then raised his head and sharpened his voice. "You can't imagine how badly I wanted Shirley Lester to win her Senate seat five years ago, but it wasn't to be. However, I, Josh Fischer, have the privilege of declaring my candidacy for the United States Senate, to carry our battle to the walls of Washington, D.C."

★　★　★

Later, on the campaign bus, Lester said quietly, "I'd say you've achieved liftoff. Let His Mightiness Carl Satcher try and top that!"

It was noontime, though it might as well be dusk. Josh sat beside Ellen, his head resting against the cold window as the bus hauled onto Highway 80, frantic windshield wipers barely able to keep up with the flooding streams of water. Lester was across the aisle beside Brother Washington. Sonny Marsh snoozed in the seat immediately behind them, the ram's horn cradled in his lap. The choir kids rode in an excited babble behind. They'd spend the night with local families organized by the church. Most of them had never been out of Oakland, and this was a big adventure.

"You were good," Ellen agreed. "Really, really good."

Lester warned, "Of course the easy one came first. They love you there already in the East Bay. Once you get into the Valley, and the southland, you'll be moving onto Satcher turf. But you'll be okay. You have what it takes."

But would he be okay? Josh wondered. Fortunately, he had no significant opposition in the Democratic primary, and he could focus on Satcher right from the start. But did he have what it took to beat him?

He had once been confident that Shirley Lester would have done so handily—but she had not.

Even with enormous appeal in the big cities, she had never achieved enough statewide traction and had been unable to compete, in the end, with Satcher's money, the television time it could buy, and his sleekly scripted speeches that sounded so good but cunningly managed to say nothing at all. The conservative press labeled Lester as old, and Satcher painted her as a remnant of the ideological revolution of the sixties, stuck in the politics of the past, irrelevant in an age of high technology—and people bought it. Then there'd been Satcher's book *Tom Turner, Friend and Neighbor,* co-authored with Greg Hunter. It was an instant best seller, humorous and upbeat, and with photographs involving favorite dogs, horses, and intimate family occasions, with a grinning, vigorous Satcher in all of them. What a good fellow he must be, those pictures declared, to have a best friend like Tom Turner.

But now Carl Satcher had Josh Fischer to contend with—young, strong, and determined. *I'll match his energy pound for pound, and then some,* Josh vowed.

★ ★ ★

Sacramento was sodden and gray, melting into its river and floodplain, the venue a union hall this time, but otherwise the same pattern as for Gettings Wharf with the TV news vans, newspaper reporters, local elected officials, the crowd of expectant people.

Shirley Lester once more swung into her introductory speech.

Josh grasped instinctively for Ellen's hand, but she was out front playing conductor for the kids this time because the gospel choir was not traveling with them, and it was Derelle now, controlling the timing through her walkie-talkie, who told him, *"Go, go!"*

Once again Josh stepped forward into a strobe-like barrage of light, smiling, upbeat, shaking hands, touching, and being touched.

At the podium again, he looked out at the sea of waiting faces, then smiled as Ellen, so vivid among the little group of kids in their white shorts and blue shirts, raised her hands and led them into the rafter-rocking siege of the walls of Jericho.

"Just like the song," Josh said when the music finished, "my mission is to tear down those walls that divide us one from the other, because this is our state and everyone deserves a seat at the table. As a Congressman from the San Francisco Bay Area, I have shown that if we work together we can bring positive change for all the people. Now, with your support, I'll extend my efforts to the rest of California. Stand at my side when we give our state a giant wake-up call."

"Josh—Josh—Josh," the crowd chanted.

★ ★ ★

The new intern Isobel came up to him with the box of freebies, and Josh took out the bright blue T-shirts, each rolled into a tight bundle, and flung them into the audience. Right, left, center, up close, far back.

Then a detour into a small room on the way out, five minutes with the reporters, fielding questions—*Where are you going now, what're your plans, how do you defeat Carl Satcher in the face of his money, his traction, his influence?*

And back to the bus in the rain and another two hours on the freeway, this time to the Valley city of Fresno.

Another town. Another hall. Another speech. The same questions from the reporters.

CHAPTER EIGHTEEN

The rally at the Fresno Hilton had garnered a smaller and less enthusiastic audience; people were there more from curiosity than fervor. The kids, battle-fatigued and far from home, sounded less emphatic with their rallying cry of "JOSHUA!" and Lionel's trumpet call was not so precisely on the money. Only Sonny Marsh, ancient and oblivious, had blasted his ram's horn with enough verve to rattle the windows.

After the speech, Brother Washington took the Greyhound back to Oakland, and Josh retired to their room in the Best Western. Derelle, armed with a pile of blue and white flyers, had found a student hangout where people were still up and had gone there to spread the word and down a couple of beers.

Ellen and Lester sat together in the hotel coffee shop. It was nine o'clock, and they were alone but for a yawning waitress. People rose early in Fresno and went early to bed.

Lester asked, "So what's it like, having your husband around?"

"I'm not sure this counts as having him around," Ellen said. "I don't see much more of him. He's always with other people."

It had been a strange five years, with Josh gone so much. Earlier, there'd been a break-in period while Josh was Lester's

Chief of Staff, theoretically headquartered in Oakland but actually spending more than half of his time in D.C. Then, with Josh a member of Congress, it was suddenly a whole new ballgame, as Lester would say, and he was gone even more—except now, during the campaign in his home state.

Home for Josh in D.C. was a small, furnished apartment in the old Methodist Building, right across from the Capitol itself. It might as well be a hotel room, Ellen had thought on her first visit, looking at the bland and inoffensive furniture and wall-to-wall carpeting. Josh's living environment didn't much matter to him. He only returned to the apartment to sleep. His real life was spent in his congressional office, in the Capitol, in corridors and restaurants, or in the House gym, where a surprising amount of business got done.

Of course it would be different if she moved there, Josh had assured Ellen. They would find a nicer place, Georgetown maybe, old, mellowed brick and trees. One look at Georgetown prices, however, had been enough to shoot that idea dead. And even if they could swing it, Josh was going home to Oakland most weekends and Ellen would have to stay in D.C. alone since there was no money for a spouse's travel. What was the *point?*

So she had sat on Josh's oatmeal sofa staring at a blank white wall upon which Josh hadn't gotten around to hanging a single picture or photograph, looked at his luggage, at that big red wheeled suitcase that seemed to be permanently half packed or half unpacked, and decided that she wasn't intended to be a political wife.

Then she had thought of the house in Oakland, the yellow kitchen, the oak tree, their peaceful little cul-de-sac, the mural at the Children's Alliance building, and finally, most important, of all the kids who depended on her. Two years before, at the awards dinner at the Claremont Hotel, Shirley Lester had suggested Ellen take the organization national and open a branch in the nation's capital, which made a lot of sense with Josh in D.C. But it was not her path, at least not yet. She stayed in Oakland—the right decision, she knew—because suddenly everything was falling into place.

Ellen had been approached by the State Senate president to head the newly formed Commission on Children, Youth, and Families, a complicated network involving health officials, educators, law enforcement, social services, and religious groups. Their aim was to reach out and better the lives of thousands, maybe millions, through improved health care, pre-school and after-school programs, counseling for at-risk families, drug and alcohol rehabilitation programs, and intervention in cases of family violence and child abuse.

Between weekly trips to Sacramento, overseeing her core staff of ten, making herself available to Sue Polley, who was now running the Children's Alliance in Berkeley, and constant fund-raising, Ellen found herself with barely enough hours in the day. Josh's weekend appearances often caught her by surprise. Good God, she'd think, is it Friday already?

Josh would complain, "I don't think you miss me at all."

Ellen would give him a kiss. "And the same to you," she'd say. They were both doing what they loved and did best—though both had to wonder what toll it was taking on their relationship.

After years of dual careers on different coasts, Ellen took a leave of absence to jump-start Josh's Senate campaign. "You could organize this thing with your hands tied behind your back," Lester had said. And then she'd asked curiously, "What will you do when it's over and you get him elected? It's addicting, this game we play."

"Go back to work for the CCYF."

"You think so?" Lester had wondered. *"Really?"*

★ ★ ★

Now, in Fresno, Lester asked Ellen, "More coffee? Or bed?"

The waitress, middle-aged, wearing an inappropriately girlish pink uniform, was ostentatiously wiping off the counter and setting up for tomorrow.

"I think she'd kill us if we ordered more coffee," Ellen said.

"Poor thing," Lester said. "I know how she feels. I waitressed all through school."

"I didn't know that."

"And even worse for her, having to wear that uniform."

"I can't somehow see you in a pink ruffly miniskirt."

"You betcha. With a neckline down to *here*." Lester gestured toward her waist. "That was when I was hustling cocktails, of course. Whoever designs waitress outfits should be forced to wear them themselves. That was when I decided, no matter what the cost, only to buy good clothes for the rest of my life."

"Hey, guys." Derelle moved sleekly into their booth. "I got the kids all fired up."

"Good for you," said Ellen. "Want a coffee?"

Behind the counter the waitress looked up with murder in her eyes.

Lester said, "I have a better idea. There's a bottle of California wine in my room. I wouldn't mind a chance to open it."

★ ★ ★

Derelle was now twenty-eight, a tall, striking young woman, though not a classic beauty. One eye was slightly higher than the other, and her nose had a slight slant to the left. She had always been matter-of-fact about her misaligned features, and silent about the violence in her past. Not once had she confided about what she had gone through. "Why talk about that time? It's over. I got born again when you walked in through that door with those dumb coloring books," she would say to Ellen.

But Ellen felt Derelle still retained a feral quality. There was something anxious in the way she held herself and moved, something wrong about the way she could look at you if she suspected you meant harm. She feared nothing and nobody—and why should I? she might have asked. Seen the worst already.

To those she loved, such as Ellen and to a slightly lesser degree Josh and Shirley Lester (although love was a difficult, almost abstract concept to Derelle and she had never been able to express it), she would be loyal to the death.

Upon entering high school, Derelle had given herself a new last name. She became Derelle Simba. "You say I walk like a lion," she had told Ellen. "Well, *Simba* means *lion* in Swahili." She would have preferred to call herself Derelle Downey, Ellen's maiden name. Once she'd announced forcefully to Ellen, "You should adopt me! If you'd had yourself a black soul mate, with your hair and all, you'd have got a baby looking a lot like me!"

Ellen said, sincerely, "I'd love to adopt you."

For a moment Derelle had looked at her with a hazy, almost soft expression. "You mean that! You really do."

★ ★ ★

In Lester's hotel room, Derelle kicked off her black boots with the thick soles that made her look even taller and curled her legs under her on the bed.

Shirley Lester poured a generous glass of wine into their bathroom tumblers, raised hers, and announced, "To Josh. Off and running!"

Ellen took a warming sip and thought how this time of night it was a lot better than coffee.

"We all set up for tomorrow?" Lester asked.

"Ready to go," Ellen said.

Lester asked Derelle, "Advance team covering their bases?"

"Check."

"Sound systems?"

"Check."

"Security? Press kits? Flyers? Posters?"

"All set." Then Derelle asked, "How come Greg Hunter showed up today? Not just in Oakland but Sacramento too. He stalking us?"

"He'll be checking us out," Lester said. "Watching what's going on and reporting back to his boss, Satcher."

"He doesn't need to do that. He can read about it."

"Not as good. He's a journalist. He wants a sense of the atmosphere, to feel it and smell it."

Derelle said, with a touch of menace, "If he shows up in L.A., maybe I should talk to him."

"Best leave him alone," Ellen said.

"You still burning a candle for him?" Derelle asked suspiciously.

Ellen felt herself flush. Would she ever grow out of this disastrous, ridiculous, giveaway, childish tendency? "I don't hold any candle. Never have."

"Yeah, *right.*"

Ellen sighed. She'd never be able to fool Derelle, whose inner eye saw beneath the skin.

Derelle added, "You better take care. That man's bad news."

Her mistrust of Greg was frank and basic and went back a long way, to the Children's Alliance article he'd written for the *San Francisco Chronicle.* "He wouldn't leave it alone, on and on about that lousy crayon. 'You wanted to stick it in her eye, didn't you! C'mon, Derelle, you can 'fess up. Nobody's out to get you now.' Oh, he was nice, awfully awful nice. He's one fine-looking dude, and he was smiling like he really liked me and wanted to get to know me, but it was only his mouth smiling, know what I mean? He didn't give a damn; all he wanted was to juice up his story, and I wasn't about to give him that. 'Come on,' he said, 'you can tell *me!*' I said, 'You mean it's just between us two? Gimme a break.' Anyway, I didn't stick Ellen in the eye, did I? So what's the story? Only that I was *thinking* about it? I told him, 'What I do or don't do is one thing, but what I feel and think is something else again. Private. Not for anybody's reading pleasure.'" Derelle crossed her arms protectively against her chest. "So of course he went and wrote it anyway."

Ellen said, "He made a big mistake."

"What goes around, comes around. And I don't like his friends. You and Josh better watch your backs. Especially watch that Micaela who works for him—aide, researcher, girlfriend, whatever."

Ellen remembered Lester's advice to Josh: if there's anything that could zap you from left field, be sure it will. She wondered if Derelle was sure about the girlfriend bit.

"If you say so. I haven't noticed anything myself," Ellen said.

Derelle gave her a stony glance. "Because your eyes have blinders on. That Micaela's smart, tough, and dedicated, and more than anything she wants to get Greg away from that rich lady he's married to. She's a straight shooter but she needs to make a move, and she knows it. She has to do it quick."

"What d'you mean?"

Emphatically, "Cause her clock's ticking. She's thirty-three. She wants a kid."

"How in the world d'you know all this? Did you ever talk to her?"

"Some things are clear without talk."

Ellen said, "Greg will never leave Jane for Micaela. His whole career's tied up with Hecht and Satcher."

"Don't be too sure. She's one determined lady. She could put him places maybe even Carl Satcher can't. Don't forget, Greg didn't win his Pulitzer yet and he's ambitious as hell."

Ellen thought how, in comparison to most, Josh had led an almost exemplary life. There was probably that one affair she had suspected when he was a public defender, but that was a long time ago. These days, it took a lot more to derail a political career. Was there something else from his past that could really hurt him, and would Micaela find it? Ellen had heard she was an investigatory wizard, a fantastic researcher able to track anything and anyone.

Sometimes—perhaps too often—Ellen looked far back to that perfect spring of their senior year, she, Josh, and Greg hanging out together, those carefree hikes and beach picnics, concerts and café gab sessions when they were so happy and life seemed simple.

Until the night Nixon resigned.

She'd never told Josh about her night with Greg, about having sex with his then best friend. Sometimes, her conscience tugging, she would wonder whether she ought to tell him—before reasoning, why cause unnecessary pain? It had only been once. And she and Josh hadn't been married at the time, they hadn't even been engaged. She would keep her secret just as Josh had been keeping his.

She remembered Greg being so vulnerable back then, the tears he tried so hard not to shed when talking of Tim and the Old Marine, of a family destroyed by war, of an inarticulate father living in a new time he didn't understand, unable to love or appreciate the son who was left to him.

Now Greg had everything he'd always wanted. *Tom Turner, Friend and Neighbor* had made him a lot of money of his own. He wrote regularly for right-wing journals, and his articles appeared on the op-ed pages of newspapers around the country.

Was he any happier?

Ellen doubted it. When you craved riches, celebrity, and power as Greg did, you would never have enough.

Once, long ago, he'd told her, "Being around you makes it a whole lot easier to do the right thing."

What would have happened if she'd stayed with Greg after that night at Eucalyptus House? Given up Josh and been Greg's partner? And married him? What would her life be like now? And his? Would Greg still have his Allie McLarens and his Micaelas—to prove to himself that he *could*?

But it hadn't happened and never would, and it was all so long ago.

★ ★ ★

Los Angeles, 2:00 P.M., thirty minutes from showtime, Derelle was up front beside the driver, cell phone to her ear, coordinating their arrival with ground staff at the Democratic Party Headquarters, the biggest in the state. The kids didn't need much psyching up today, they were in "El Lay," they were going to be movie stars, they'd sing their guts out and get a contract, tomorrow, next week at the latest, Oprah would be calling. "Just don't overdo it," warned Lester. "No hamming it up for the crowd. Don't forget what we're here for; this is the Josh Fischer show!"

★ ★ ★

"So when you elect me as your Senator," Josh said to the crowd, wrapping up his speech, "education will be a top priority, as will sensible gun laws. The American Association of Gun Owners, and our esteemed gun lobby, seem to see nothing wrong with lethal weapons being as easy to buy as a pack of cigarettes or that a young child, even a small child, can lay hands on a gun." With a grimace, "Anybody can tell you I've been personally involved in such a tragedy, and if it hadn't been for my wife, Ellen, I wouldn't be standing in front of you today. I'd be history, like the two people who died that day; like that disturbed fourteen-year-old who found his mother's boyfriend's gun on the kitchen counter, who will never be able to undo or forget the terrible acts he committed—but could not have committed without the gun."

The crowd was hushed now; Ellen noticed the sheen of tears on a few cheeks.

It was the first time Josh had told the story of the shooting, and she was glad he had saved it for this afternoon, here in Los Angeles; it felt right. He always had an instinct for what would be right, and when. He worked the crowd into a frenzy one more time, the kids sang their hearts out, and Josh left the stage smiling and happy.

The Los Angeles stop was definitely the best and the most rewarding so far. At an informal press conference after the speech, Ellen was interviewed too.

"What's your role in this?" she was asked. "Are you Josh's campaign manager? Fund-raiser? Speech writer?" When she admitted only to being part of the organization, Josh smiled and said, "She's the inspiration for this campaign!"

"And Derelle Simba?" the interviewer asked.

"Our ear to the ground."

Then it was back on the bus, twenty minutes behind schedule, Lester hushing the kids, who were hyped up and bopping in the aisles all the way down the 405, chanting they were on TV, they were celebrities, and the driver, phlegmatic, saying he'd make up the time some, but he wasn't about to be pulled over for speeding, no way.

★ ★ ★

That night in San Diego, Ellen and Josh sat on the tenth-floor balcony of their hotel, a Spanish-style room behind them with red-tiled floor and white stucco walls. They watched the lights and the palm trees reflected in the pool, and shared a bottle of Piper Sonoma champagne. It was balmy and very late. Ellen wore one of her mid-thigh bedtime T-shirts; Josh was in his blue-and-white striped boxer shorts. It was the first time they'd sat like this together for far too long, and they knew they should make the most of it. Tomorrow morning early, they'd fly back to the Bay Area and the organization of Josh's campaign office on Van Ness in San Francisco. They might not get to spend another evening together like this for a while.

"You ought to sleep well tonight," said Ellen. "You deserve to. You were good. You've been good everywhere."

"There's a point where you get too tired to sleep," Josh said. "My brain won't shut down, just keeps circling and circling. What I should have said; what I could have said; who I forgot to introduce. I guess I've just gotten used to not sleeping."

"Try another glass of champagne. It won't keep; it'll be flat in the morning." Ellen topped up his glass. "And surely it's the very best kind of exhaustion."

"Not really. I should think it's like postpartum depression—" Josh trailed off into appalled silence.

She moved her chair against his and touched his arm. "It's okay. Don't worry about it." References to pregnancy and parenting hardly made her flinch anymore.

He rested his hand on hers and pressed it. "I'm sorry. I'm not thinking straight. I guess I'm even more tired than I thought."

Ellen wanted to hold him close. She needed the feel of his skin, his hands, his lips. Even now that they were together more, their lovemaking was rare and rushed. There ought to be time for love. Once this was all over and Josh was elected to the Senate, Ellen was determined there'd be changes made. "Come on, Josh," she urged. "Let's go to bed."

But he made no move, didn't even seem to have heard her, just sat there staring down at the shifting reflections of the palm fronds on the pool where, now, a tall, pale-skinned girl in a black one-piece bathing suit was swimming laps, almost silently, mostly underwater. Josh said, "I can never see a pool without thinking of Greg."

"Let's not think about Greg."

"He didn't show up today."

"He must have decided he'd seen enough."

"Did you talk to him at all?"

"I tried in Oakland but he slipped away. I didn't see him in Sacramento and Fresno. Derelle said he was standing in back of the hall each time, but I was up front with the kids."

Josh leaned back in his chair and stretched out his bare feet. She wanted to touch his knee, run her fingers along the long muscle of his thigh, feel his response, but this was obviously not the time. "Are you worried about Greg? Is that why you can't sleep?"

"If he tries to talk to you, Ell, or if he calls, don't. Okay?"

"You're afraid I might say something indiscreet? You don't have to be."

"Greg can spin anything."

"I know that."

Ellen suddenly knew this was the moment when she should ask Josh what he was afraid she might say to Greg. Is there something I should know? She remembered the dreadful fall of 1982. What had Josh done then, and what did he fear now? Whatever had happened, it had left an indelible shadow from which he had never fully escaped, and it had never been the same between them since.

Not even after the high school shooting, Ellen thought, when she realized she'd want to die too if she lost Josh, and would do anything, anything at all to save him—after all of that there had still been some vital element missing.

I wish you'd tell me, she thought now, so we could put it behind us and get on with loving each other properly again.

She began, "Josh, do you think—"

But all at once he was on his feet, turned toward her, two fingers under her chin raising her face to his. Kissing her mouth. "It's late," he said. "We can finish the champagne in bed."

And she knew talking would have to wait for another time.

CHAPTER NINETEEN

Senator Carl Satcher stretched his burly frame and settled his shoulders back into the comfort of his maroon leather recliner. "There was that English king once, long ago," he said to nobody in particular, "who told his go-to people something like, 'Won't anybody rid me of this accursed priest?'"

It was mid-May, and they sat together in the den of the big ranch house, the venue for countless late-night conferences: Satcher, Gunther Hecht, Greg, and a new addition to what Greg had come to think of as the Cabal: Professor Frida Hernandez, dean of Boalt Hall School of Law at Berkeley, commandingly tall, dark-haired with a wing of white at either temple, piercing black eyes, and a wide, thin-lipped mouth. She looked every inch the law professor. She'd look even better robed, on the bench of the Supreme Court. Carl Satcher planned to get her there, and aware that she was boundlessly ambitious, Greg knew that was where Frida Hernandez could best picture herself.

Dinner was over. Outside it was cool and clear, the only sounds the chomp of horses' teeth tearing at the grass and the occasional whiffling equine snort.

It was the time for reflection over single-malt scotch and cigars, with the exception of Hernandez, who preferred soda water with a twist of lemon and who didn't smoke. In the shadowed background, a ring of outer planets in a solar system where Satcher reigned as the sun, the remora men sat quiet and attentive.

Hecht said, "Thomas à Becket. And they killed him. In Canterbury Cathedral, as I recall."

Satcher mused, "Of course we can't go that far but it's a good thought, specially after what the little bastard's done in the East Bay. Josh Fischer has cost us a packet with his meddling. Save me from these bleeding-heart liberals; they make me puke."

"Something needs to be done," Hecht agreed.

Both men looked at Greg.

"So you want me to do the deed?" Greg asked.

"Only with some well-placed words," Satcher said. "You have a way with them, son." He picked up the copy of *Tom Turner, Friend and Neighbor* from the coffee table, telling Hernandez, "Couldn't have written this thing without him. You should have seen him take my words and finesse them so they sounded just right."

Frida Hernandez pulled the book toward her and leafed through the pages. She asked Greg, "Did you spend much time with Tom Turner?"

"Sure. I even went horseback riding with him. He was a nice guy, wanted me to have a good time, showed me all the landmarks, told me about the native plants and animals. Not at all the way you think of a movie star. Very down-to-earth and unaffected."

Satcher picked up the book and opened it to a picture of himself and Thomas Turner, wearing matching Western shirts and bolo ties, standing in front of a gigantic Christmas tree, handing out gaily wrapped gifts to a gaggle of towheaded grandchildren. "That's one terrific guy," Satcher said, sounding emotional. "Wouldn't have trusted just anyone with this material."

"Guess you got yourself a fine partner," Hecht said. "And you got yourselves a bestseller to prove it!"

The book not only earned a lot of money for Greg, but it had also opened many doors. In addition to his position as outside consultant to Senator Carl Satcher, on Satcher's private payroll, Greg produced a syndicated weekly column, "The Right View." He was a respected conservative pundit. He also happened to be terrific on television.

"If anyone can stop Josh Fischer in his tracks," Satcher added, "it's you. He's far enough to the left to scare the shit out of the voters."

"Easy," Greg said. "I'll just lay it out for them." He held up fingers, one by one, listing: "There's tax and spend. Jobs leaving the state. Tree huggers and enviros killing the forestry, oil drilling, and construction industries. Homeless and illegal immigrants flooding in from all over, straining our services to the breaking point. Failure of all those social services that Fischer loves so much leading to meltdown and rioting in the inner cities...."

Greg ran out of fingers.

"Good, good," Satcher nodded. To Hernandez, he said complacently, "What did I tell you?"

The dean smiled grimly. "It's a good start."

Greg went on, "We'll follow up with mailing pieces and radio and TV spots. We'll have the guy looking like some lunatic hippie who's completely out of touch with reality. Though I don't think you need worry—Josh Fischer will run out of steam soon enough. He has a lot of support right now. He's a fresh face, he has fire in his belly, talks up a storm, and makes the average little guy think he matters. But there's a long way to go until November. Can he sustain? Come election day, will enough tree huggers, farm laborers, and homeless actually get out there and vote for him? They never vote. And then, of course, there's the money. What is it they say? There are two aspects to every campaign: money, and everything else. His pockets are shallow. He's going to need millions, and he doesn't have the base."

Satcher shifted in his seat. "Let's not underestimate him."

"He's got the black vote in his pocket," Hecht offered.

"That's not near enough votes to swing it," Greg said.

"Still," said Satcher, "Fischer is dangerous and let's not forget it. He's going to pick up a lot more money and more endorsements.

The Dems already see him as a rising star. We're going to have to hit him hard where it does most damage."

Hernandez said, "And don't underestimate his wife either. She probably has more recognition around the state than he does. People like and respect her, and that rubs off on him."

"Cute little gal," put in Satcher. "Children's issues, right?"

Hernandez corrected, "Children, youth, and families. But don't forget that goes hand in hand with health, education, welfare, and crime prevention. She was making quite a success of her Family Commission before she started working on his campaign, and the word is she gets things done. She's a great fund-raiser too." After a reflective pause for a sip of water, "If you're thinking of floating some scandal on them, you have a problem. They're both squeaky-clean. I'd be surprised if they had one outstanding parking ticket between them."

"Nobody's squeaky-clean," Satcher declared. "And never trust someone without an outstanding parking ticket; you can bet they're hiding something. You don't get that far without screwing up big time somewhere along the line." He crossed his ankles on the ottoman and gazed at his feet in their scuffed Frye boots. "Josh Fischer is no saint." With a humorless chuckle, "Or rabbi for that matter. He has his weaknesses, just like everybody else."

"The problem," Hernandez said, "is finding them."

"You've known Josh the longest," Hecht said to Greg. "Any thoughts?"

"Nothing comes to mind as yet. Josh planned to run for office since he was thirteen years old and has never done anything to hurt his chances. He smoked, but only the legal, nicotine kind of cigarettes, and he gave it up twenty years ago. He didn't get drunk or screw around. He's always been totally *visible,* no secrets, what you see is what you get, married to the same woman since 1975, no kids with drug problems, impeccable career, an unimpeachable straight arrow."

"Sounds boring," Hecht said.

Satcher grumbled, "Too good to be true. There's always something. And I trust you to find it, Greg. You and Micaela."

"We'll find it if it's there," said Greg.

Satcher added, "Or even if it isn't."

★ ★ ★

By July, Josh Fischer's campaign was picking up momentum.

He was everywhere, tireless, seeming to be in several places at once as well as holding down his congressional seat in D.C. He talked on college campuses, at labor union halls, and in senior centers. He was jeered by loggers in Humboldt County, and cheered by environmentalists in Mendocino County and gays in San Francisco.

The money and endorsements poured in.

Satcher went into full attack mode, and it was ugly. Josh responded with his own more moderated assault: "My opponent accuses me of losing touch with reality; but consider how out of touch he is with the people he's supposed to represent. What does he know about normal people's lives? Has he ever worried about choosing between prescription drugs and eating dinner? About balancing his checkbook? About losing his health insurance? His kids getting sick because of contamination in the water they drink and the air they breathe, or being caught in crossfire on their way to school? Why should he? He owns the bank and the insurance company. He owns the shopping center, he owns the hospital, and his kids went to boarding school in Montana. I tell you, Carl Satcher lives in his own world—and it's not yours or mine. Isn't it time you had a Senator who is on your side because he *understands* your side?"

★ ★ ★

On a warm, late-July afternoon in Tiburon, Micaela lay on her back, one knee drawn up, her arm flung across her eyes against the sun, and complained, "I'm hungry."

"So you should be," Greg said. "You've exercised to the max."

"Can I have my sandwich now?" They'd made love outside, on the white foam pad that she'd taken off her chaise and laid down on the narrow deck outside her living room. Nobody could look down on them except from an airplane, and they were shielded from curious eyes on passing boats by the elaborate wrought iron railing. It was perfectly private.

"Sure thing; you deserve it. And you need feeding." Greg rose, not bothering to cover himself, and slid open the screen door. He had stopped at the deli on the way over for a six-pack of imported beer and two sandwiches: chicken salad on whole wheat and pastrami on rye, two fat pickles, and a small container of stuffed olives. If he wanted to eat, he had to bring food; Micaela never bothered to shop. She didn't seem to think about food if it wasn't there. When it appeared, however, she fell on it like a starving beast.

Returning, he laid the paper plate with the chicken sandwich in the middle of her bare stomach, and she pulled herself into a sitting position with one fluid motion and dug in.

Greg sprawled in a canvas deck chair, pressed the sweating beer bottle against his hot cheek, and thought yet again how lucky he was. He was married to a beautiful, rich, loving, complaisant wife who accepted the fact that when duty called Greg would be leaving for Sacramento, Los Angeles, New York, or D.C. and got on with her life without protest. And he also had a beautiful, smart, adoring mistress—though *mistress* was hardly the right description of Micaela. She was no piece of fluff to be enjoyed upon a whim. She was strong and independent and insisted on paying her own way. Greg had offered to pay her rent, or at least contribute, but she'd indignantly refused. Nor would she accept gifts other than flowers or books.

He respected her for it, though he would have at least liked to buy her a nice string of pearls or even a sports car. Why shouldn't he? He would not be spending Jane's money, which he was sure was at the base of Micaela's objections; he'd be spending his own. He could afford it.

Best of all, she was Greg's intellectual equal, her mind meshing with his like cog wheels in a well-tuned watch. He never had to explain things to Micaela as he often had to with Jane. She was always right on the money. Alert and interested, up to his speed— hell, she was often way ahead of him. Their relationship was perfect. Unfortunately, he suspected, too perfect to last.

"Does it bother you at all, spying on your best friend?" she asked between mouthfuls. Micaela had the annoying habit of raising issues of conscience from time to time, but at the moment she didn't seem too concerned about Greg's faithfulness to Jane, and she'd surely get over his investigation of Josh.

Of course it still gave him an uneasy feeling, that digging into Josh's past could be perceived as spying, even treachery, but when push came to shove, he didn't really have much choice, did he, and anyway, it was just a political reality. He pointed out, "Josh knows perfectly well Satcher will bring him down if he possibly can. Josh would do the same to Satcher—is doing it. He's gone negative too. Anyway, I owe Carl Satcher one hell of a lot. For one thing, if I hadn't met him, I'd never have known you."

"That's true." Micaela caressed the arch of his foot, and he felt a tingle run all the way up his thigh. "But what happens if you *can't* get anything on Josh Fischer?"

This was an eventuality Greg hadn't yet wished to contemplate, hoping that Josh's momentum would burn out for lack of funds. So far, that hope was unfulfilled. And it was true what Professor Hernandez had said—Ellen was a phenomenal asset. She was not merely inspirational, but had a genius for fundraising and damage control.

Odd that Jane had seemed to care far less about Micaela—for surely she must know—than about Ellen, whom he very seldom saw and who was married anyway. But maybe it wasn't so odd because he loved Ellen and didn't love Micaela. Jane might not be the brightest, but her instincts were usually right-on.

Greg dragged his mind back to the matter at hand. "I assume Satcher would be truly pissed if we came up empty."

"He could hire a private investigator," Micaela suggested.

"Who'd have to start from square one, with no more resources than we have. And I'm supposed to be an investigative reporter. I'd like to think if I can't turn something up, then nobody could. And right now Josh Fischer does seem to be pure as the driven snow. There's only one possibility I can see."

Greg told Micaela about the night he and Ellen had dinner together back in the fall of 1982. "She wasn't happy. She looked pale and stressed. Josh was working such long hours she never saw him anymore. He was forgetting things, plans they'd made, that kind of thing." Greg described dropping Ellen off at her house, watching her open the gate and walk up the path under the oak tree, and discovering the dark shape sprawled on the front porch. "I got out of the car and followed her, I thought it was some drunk or a druggie, passed out, but it turned out it was Josh, and he'd lost his key."

Micaela looked dubious. "So what's the big deal about that?"

"Exactly. With most people, so what? The guy gets home late, can't get in, assumes the wife will be home any minute, and decides to wait for her rather than trying to break in or call a locksmith. But in the normal course of events, even if he *was* drunk, Josh would *never* lose or forget his key—he doesn't do that kind of thing." Greg mused, "I'd been gone eight years, just come back to the Bay Area, and he kept making excuses not to get together."

"So? Maybe he didn't want to see you and didn't like to tell you outright. And he probably *was* working really hard."

"It was more than that. There was something going on. I could feel it. Smell it."

"Your nose for news."

"Exactly. And it's usually right."

"Then don't ignore it."

★ ★ ★

Two weeks later, on a Friday afternoon, Micaela waved a file in front of his face. "Here it is," she said. "You owe me for days of dust and grime."

Greg read it over, smiled, and rewarded her with dinner at Ondine in Sausalito.

They sat at a corner table overlooking the water, which glowed bloodred in the sunset, Greg in his yacht club blazer and white slacks, Micaela wearing black. He ordered the petrale sole; Micaela ordered the sand dabs, which she tackled with gusto.

"How come you never have any food at home?" Greg asked.

She shrugged. "I forget. Anyway," she said, with a panoramic sweep of her fork, "this is better."

"It's good to see a girl who enjoys her food."

"I need feeding. I lost at least five pounds hauling those filthy files around."

"So let's discuss what we can do with the results of your hard work."

"Later. I don't want to talk business just yet. It's too pretty out there."

Greg had a feeling he knew where she wanted to take the conversation.

"Tell me, Greg, just where are we headed? You and me?" She was on her second glass of wine and sounding serious.

"Where we are right now seems pretty good."

"Not to me. I want more."

Greg braced himself.

"I don't expect you to marry me," she said, "but we've been together nine years now. And I'm not getting any younger."

"You don't look a day older than when we first met."

"Looks deceive. I want to have a baby while I still can."

"For God's sake, Micaela. You're only in your thirties. Women are having babies well into their forties now. Time is nowhere near your enemy."

"You're supposed to have them while you're young enough to enjoy them. You've got your boys. I want mine."

The last thing he wanted was to start a second family with Micaela Calder. Greg laid a hand gently on her arm. "I understand. I've been unbelievably selfish. I never thought beyond just us. But please, darling Micaela, can it wait until after the campaign? Then we'll talk again. We'll do more than talk."

"Is that a promise? A real promise?"

"As real as it gets."

Micaela looked at him, doubtfully he thought, and probably figured she'd gone as far as she could go at this time. "Okay then," she sighed, "let's talk about your goddam list."

★　★　★

It was a list of every case Josh Fischer had handled between August and December 1982, along with names and ultimate sentences.

The first page was all the plea bargains, and the second page a shorter group of cases that had gone to trial. There was only one acquittal: Hector Rivas.

The name seemed to tremble before Greg's eyes as if lit by red neon.

★   ★   ★

They were in luck. One of the Oakland public defenders from 1982 was still there, a cheerful redheaded fellow called Chuck Davis, who seemed to live without a shred of personal ambition and still clung to outdated happy hippie idealism. Greg thought that Chuck actually believed he was doing good in the world by defending the worst bottom-feeders the county could provide.

"You're doing a story about Josh? Great. I'll help you all I can," enthused Davis, only too happy to tell how Josh Fischer had always been first out of the gate, sought after, promoted. No, of course he, Davis, hadn't been resentful, it seemed only right and natural. Davis didn't remember much about the fall of 1982. The years kind of blended into each other, but he definitely remembered Josh. You could tell Josh was going places. He was head-hunted right and left by the big law firms but that wasn't what he wanted. No one was surprised when he went into politics.

Had Josh ever seemed particularly stressed? Maybe. Sure. He tended to take things personally, get steamed when he perceived an injustice—though the whole system was unjust, how could you expect anyone but a saint to live the lives of some of those people and *not* commit crimes?

"I've got a list of cases," Greg said. "Maybe some memories or incidents will come back to you."

"Let's give it a look," Davis said. "You never know."

Greg watched the lawyer scan the list of names, his lips moving slightly at each one as if sounding them out in his memory, then regretfully shake his head. "Sorry, nothing comes to mind. Though that acquittal, Rivas—you'd think I'd remember that one; an acquittal was a rare, triumphant thing, 'specially a murder. We'd celebrate afterward, the winner got to buy the drinks—but it was right around the holidays and we were all in and out a lot."

"Do you remember if Josh hung out with anyone in particular? Another PD?"

"Not really. We all basically chummed around together. Met for a beer or a baseball game sometimes." He reeled off some names. "You could check with them. Jake Haywood had the desk next to Josh. But he got divorced and left the area. We lost touch. Sorry, man. I guess I haven't been much help. Hey, look. When you see Josh, give him a big hello from me, okay?"

★ ★ ★

Jake Haywood, bald and pallid with a face set in lines of perpetual discontent, lived in bachelor squalor in an icily air-conditioned house in Tempe, Arizona. He swept the empty fast-food cartons and pizza boxes off the kitchen counter and offered Greg and Micaela beer or iced tea. They both accepted iced tea and carried their glasses to a cluttered living room, dark with closed drapes. Jake muted the baseball game on TV with the remote.

"Josh running for the Senate!" he exclaimed. "Well, what do you know."

"That's what we're asking you," Greg said.

★ ★ ★

After some preliminary questions about Jake's experiences and career, Greg turned the focus back to the Alameda County Public Defender's office. To Greg's huge satisfaction, rancorous memories began to surface.

"That whole scene was something else," Jake said. "There was something really sleazy about it, and I'm glad to finally get it off my chest to tell the truth, though I'd like some kind of reassurance this isn't going to come back at me. I don't want to be involved. I mean, I can point the direction, and you can find your own way, right? You could have found it out for yourselves eventually."

"Of course," Greg said.

"You have to protect your source, right?"

"Exactly. You have our word. Now, tell me about Josh Fischer. How was he acting?"

"Like a fool and a jerk. It was like nobody existed in the world for him except that woman. I felt real sorry for his wife; she must've been going through hell. She came into the office once, asking questions, real sad face. I didn't tell her anything, of course. I covered for Josh. Didn't want to make things worse. Anyway, I didn't know anything for sure."

"But it seemed to you that Josh and the defendant's wife were having sexual relations."

"Are you kidding? The guy was getting it up, down, and sideways."

"You ever see them together?"

"Only when she'd come in to talk about her husband. Josh wasn't a total idiot."

"You have any idea where they went to have sex?"

"Nowhere he'd be recognized, that's for sure. He'd have been careful. Some out-of-the-way place."

"You ever hear him talk to her on the phone? Personal stuff?"

"Like I said, he was careful. If and when he called her, he'd have used the public phone in the hall. When she called, he'd leave to call her back."

"What was your own feeling about Josh Fischer? Did you like him?"

With bitterness now, "No, I can't say I did. He was one of those people who knew exactly where he was going. Even the Senate's just a stop along the way. Wanted it all, and got it. Promoted ahead of others who'd been doing the job longer and who had more experience. Not to say he wasn't good at what he did, he was—put up one hell of a show in court—and he got results."

"You say a 'show.' You didn't believe he was sincere?"

"Nobody could be that sincere and live in this world."

There was more, but it wasn't relevant. It had to do with Jake's divorce, his general sense of injustice, how some people were givers and others takers. On and on.

It was hard to get away; clearly the man was lonely. Lonely and bitter.

Greg held out his hand. "Thank you, Jake," he said, "you've been very helpful. If you remember anything else, anything at *all,* I'd appreciate it if you'd be in touch."

"Wait—let me think." A pause, then, "You know, something about that woman didn't quite fit, something of the player about her."

"A hooker?"

"Not the impression I got. But she seemed too savvy about the system, and she dressed too well for what she was supposed to be. I wouldn't be surprised if she didn't have a sheet someplace."

* * *

On the plane back to San Francisco, Greg said, "They say flattery gets you everywhere, but me, I'd rather bet on jealousy."

"He hates Josh," Micaela said.

"It's the nature of mediocrity, and knowing it, to hate."

"It can also be hell on a person's judgment."

"We don't care about Jake Haywood's judgment or lack of it. That's all shading; it doesn't impact the facts. We need to find this woman, Bianca Rivas."

"'A babe,'" quoted Micaela. "'A knockout. Dressed to kill.'"

"And all of it for Josh, nothing for poor old Jake." Greg leaned his head against the window of the 737, gazing at the ripples of ochre- and rust-colored desert far below, at the dark threads of roads and the occasional sprawl of dusty little towns. They were fast approaching the eastern wall of the Sierra Nevada, where blue-glinting patches of snow still lay in the hollows between the highest peaks.

"She shouldn't be too hard to find," Micaela said.

"You think? It's been almost twenty years. We don't have a hell of a lot to go on, and it could be a wild goose chase anyway."

He hated the image of Ellen going down to the courthouse, to a roomful of young lawyers, her face sad. He hated Josh for doing that to her.

The captain's voice on the intercom announced that they were beginning their descent to San Francisco. Micaela sighed, "So it looks like it's back to the files."

"But now," Greg said, "you have a name. And she might have a sheet. Check out police records."

"For the whole of the State of California, going back fifteen years or more. Thanks."

"You're not alone, Micaela. You have Carl Satcher at your back. Hire yourself as many helpers as it takes."

"Right." Then she asked, "What happens when we do turn up the goods and have Josh Fischer nailed?"

"He'll drop out of the race in a nanosecond. He'll have no choice."

"I was talking about us. You and me."

"We'll do whatever you want."

★ ★ ★

"How much money?" Bianca Rivas asked Greg with a sudden gleam in her dark eyes, all that was left of what must at one time have been a striking beauty.

"We'll make it worth your while." Greg had not brought Micaela with him; instinct argued that a woman like Bianca Rivas was more likely to confide in a man alone.

"I can make it worth your while too," she said. "Imagine, Josh Fischer running for the goddam Senate. And God only knows I need the money."

Greg glanced around the narrow living area of the trailer, in a run-down park in Simi Valley beside a bottling plant. She could use some help, that was for sure. Everything he saw was old and tired and cheap—the table and countertops scarred with cigarette burns, the floor littered with bright plastic children's toys, most broken. The only new, expensive item was the twenty-seven-inch TV in the corner on which a handsome young man and a beautiful young woman argued with silent vehemence. The air conditioner pumped around stale air smelling of disinfectant and cigarette smoke.

"So. How much?" Bianca massaged her fleshy forearms and considered, the tip of her tongue touching the corner of her over-lipsticked mouth. Greg wondered whether, long ago, that little mannerism would have driven Josh crazy. "I'd guess the *Daily Sun* or the *Flash* would go for a couple of hundred grand."

"We're not dummies. We're not about to pay out till we know what we're looking at."

Bianca insisted, "Believe me, it's good. Cash. Up front. No pay, no play."

Greg gave her the $500 he'd brought as seed money, and they bartered back and forth, eventually agreeing upon $125,000. It seemed like a large sum to Greg, but he was authorized to go to a quarter million; still petty cash to Satcher.

He managed to say, with an appropriate amount of admiration, "I'll bet you knocked his socks off. I'll bet you blew him away."

"I blew him every which way from Christmas," Bianca said with a short bark of laughter, which turned into a deep, phlegmy cough and finished as an angry sigh. "Shit. I didn't even smoke till I got to Chowchilla."

Micaela's research had turned up all sorts of things about Bianca Rivas, including her five-year stint in the women's state correctional facility for grand theft. It hadn't been her first incarceration, either. Greg almost, but not quite, felt sorry for Bianca. He thought of Josh's appalled face, seeing her now, and she could be made to look like an old, beaten hag through the wizardry of photography, plastered right across the front of the tabloids with a juicy 8-point headline: JOSH FISCHER'S SECRET LOVER.

"So," Greg opened, "you were saying you and Josh Fischer made some kind of a deal."

Bianca shrugged. "He had me where he wanted me. First time I met with him, with poor Hector in Santa Rita looking at a murder rap and not knowing what time of day it was, all on account of doing his duty for his country, Josh Fischer said sure he could get him off, or at least make a real good deal with the DA, but it would take cooperation from me."

"Which meant sex."

"Of course sex."

"Doesn't sound like the Josh Fischer I know."

She gazed at him scornfully. "You think I'm lying?"

Of course you're lying, Greg thought, you're a mercenary bitch. He made a negating gesture.

"I looked like something then, you know," she said.

"I heard you were a knockout," he agreed.

Bianca lit another cigarette from the smoldering butt of the last. "Yeah, well..."

"You're not so bad now."

She bridled a little bit. It was pathetic. "Ah, come on. All I need to do is look in the mirror."

"Beautiful, and helpless," he pressed. "Josh Fischer did a bad thing to you. It's been a long time, but we can still do something right. Tell me about it."

Which she did, in graphic detail. If a fraction of it was true, Greg thought, then his admiration for Josh would soar. "He'd take me down to this motel in Pacifica, can't remember the name, something with *moon* in it, right on the water, then he'd go at me till I was crying, and then he'd make me do these *things.*"

She described what Josh would make her do. Greg stared at her as his tape recorder captured every word.

"But I have to give him credit," Bianca concluded. "He delivered. Made good on his promise, and Hector walked. And so did I, the minute the jury came in with that not guilty verdict. I told Hector, we're getting out of here and going back to L.A. That man's a maniac. I sure feel sorry for that wife of his."

JOSH FISCHER'S SEX SLAVE.

HOW I PAID FOR MY HUSBAND'S LIFE.

Greg thought how this was worth every penny of $125,000. They'd even have the name of the motel. No matter what Josh did or didn't do, no matter who abandoned whom, enough of the basics was true to do real damage.

"Where's Hector now?" he asked.

Bianca sighed. "Lompoc. Poor Hector never got any breaks. They had it in for him all along."

The door to the trailer opened and a teenage girl walked in carrying a struggling infant in one arm and a bag of groceries in the other.

"My daughter, Brenda," said Bianca, "and her kid, Joey."

"Hi," greeted Brenda. "God it's hot!" She had a pretty, round face with abundant, curly black hair and bold eyes, and wore a cropped top and too-tight denim cutoffs. In almost the same motion she planted Joey in his grandmother's lap, the groceries on the table, tore open a package of potato chips, and switched on the sound on the TV. She asked Greg, munching, "Who're you?"

Without answering, Greg demanded, "How old are you?"

"Fourteen. Why? You going to give me some shit about having a kid?"

★ ★ ★

Greg didn't rush back to Tiburon that evening, he dined one-on-one with his father-in-law at the venerable Pacific Union Club on Nob Hill opposite Grace Cathedral, with its mahogany, leaded glass, hushed carpeting, and the ancient smell of money.

"We've got him cold," Greg said. He told the story over a dozen Pacific oysters and a bottle of Taittinger champagne, a magnificent juicy filet mignon, and a bottle of Beringer private reserve. "Of course that girl isn't Josh's child—she wasn't born for another two years—but it doesn't matter. All we need to do is say there's a kid and he'll freak out. If Josh decides to tough it out and we go public, just the insinuation, on top of all the other stuff, is enough to sink him."

"Slam dunk," smiled Gunther Hecht. "Very well done, Greg. Fischer is history, whichever way you slice the pie. Carl's going to love this."

And then, with a sudden shift in tone, his words as hard-edged as icicles, Hecht continued, "You know, son, Micaela's done well by you, hasn't she?"

"Couldn't have done it without her," Greg said warily.

"Nonsense. Good researchers grow on every tree."

"Not in her class."

"Let's not argue the point, son. You know perfectly well what I'm saying."

"I don't th—"

"Sure you do." Hecht summoned the aging waiter. "Two Napoleons, George."

They sat in silence, watching the old man walk away. When the brandy arrived, Hecht swirled it slowly around the glass, inhaled, drank, and sighed, "Nectar of the gods." Then, "Micaela

Calder has run her course. She ran it very successfully, but it's time for her to move on."

Greg nodded. "I expect you're right."

"Of course with a generous severance package and the very best of credentials. She's a sensible girl; she'll understand." He regarded Greg across the table. "And you had better understand, too. From now on, I expect you to pay a great deal more attention to my daughter. For some reason Janey still seems to love you, even though you're a cheating, double-dealing bastard. Stabbing your best friend in the back is business, but my daughter is not. Bear in mind, son, that I'll be watching you very closely from now on."

Greg had no idea those blue eyes, which until now had regarded him with approval, with liking, and even—he'd thought once or twice—with love, could look so cold.

Nor that the beautiful word *son,* said in that particular tone, could sound like an insult.

But at least, for sure, Micaela would be out of his life.

CHAPTER TWENTY

Labor Day Saturday was a scorcher, the air resting heavily over Sacramento like a thermal blanket, the sunlight brassy with pollution and glinting in oil-slick colors from the roofs of the crawling traffic.

The park wilted in the heat, the trees exhausted, leaves limp and dirty after a long dry summer, the grass brown despite the nightly sprinkling and balding in ever-widening patches. The crowd, however, was huge and cheerful: a lot of young working families, perspiring fathers in short-sleeved sport shirts and baseball caps, mothers in shorts, sunburned teenagers, kids, bounding dogs. The lawn was a mess of blankets and coolers; sizzling hamburgers and hot dogs added their greasy smoke to the already overburdened air. The racket of howling babies, salsa, rap, and rock and roll mingled with the broadcast of the Giants' game from Candlestick Park.

Josh witnessed all of this from his high perch at the front of the parked bus, experiencing it as if he shared the collective emotions of the crowd. Feeling it. Seeing it through their eyes.

As the minutes ticked by and the people kept pouring in, he watched the personal territories reduce, the food put away, the blankets retracted then pulled in yet again, the crowd thickening in front of the platform with its skirt of blue and white folds and the enormous banner—FISCHER FOR SENATE—because they knew if they got lucky they might catch a flung T-shirt at the end of the candidate's speech.

It was clear to the crowd that something was about to happen.

The sound technicians had been busy, and rousing music suddenly poured from the speakers—the themes from *Star Wars* and *Rocky*.

A truck disgorged a mess of helium-filled balloons that billowed up in a glorious blue and white cloud.

The TV people, the cameras sprouting from their shoulders giving them the silhouettes of space aliens, began to muscle for footing on their platform, and now a bunch of children were climbing onto the stage, in their white shorts and bright blue T-shirts with "JOSH!" on the front in big black letters and on the back "FIGHTING THE BATTLES FOR YOU!"

Josh watched Lionel and old Sonny take up their positions, and the usual gathering of officials filed onstage.

He heard the music die and the noises of the huge gathering fade to an expectant murmur.

He wished Ellen was up there on stage with the kids where he could see her and feel the support flowing out of her, but she was in San Francisco, at a meeting with the Hotel and Restaurant Workers Union. He thought how, increasingly, she was shouldering his burdens and how amazingly lucky he was to have her on his team. He wished there hadn't been a scheduling conflict, and she could be here with him today, at the start of this final stretch, the insane sixty-day sprint from Labor Day to the finish line.

In the future, he thought, one way or another we're going to be together a lot more. I'm going to make certain of that.

★ ★ ★

"... And now, it's my great pleasure to introduce a young man who has spent the last six years in Congress making sure people like us get a square deal, a guy who fights our battles for us—"

And Josh was off again, striding across the dusty grass with the crowd parting for him, clasping hands, smiling into numerous sets of friendly, wary, or just plain curious eyes, touching, embracing, ruffling the hair of small children. *Thank you for coming; it means so much. Thank you, thank you. And to you, too. Hey, love you, too!*

He arrived at the podium panting and sweaty, his body thudding with adrenaline. The crowd was his, he felt it, and he rode that feeling, knowing that today he'd speak as never before, that he'd easily win these thousand people, and later, on the TV news, he'd win over a lot more.

★ ★ ★

"How many of you here are with organized labor? Let's see hands! And veterans! How many veterans...."

A forest of waving arms.

"Now listen up, my friends," Josh said, drawing them in. "My opponent voted against raising the minimum wage, against the law requiring notice to workers before a plant shuts down, and against ergonomic standards to avoid repetitive stress injuries"— the crowd hissed and booed—"He's reducing benefits to veterans. He's also voted to contract out about 50,000 federal government jobs without any rules about the new employers having to pay health care or retirement benefits. He won't debate me on these issues, has refused to debate me at all, so I say he's afraid to be exposed in all his right-wing glory."

Josh's blood was up now. He was going after Satcher with a new intensity. Then he laid out his ideas to lift workers and help small businesses and honor California families.

"Help me win this, folks. We don't need six more years of a well-orchestrated attack on the people of our state."

The cheers now were out of control. "Josh. Josh. Josh," over and over.

Top that, Carl Satcher, just try!

★ ★ ★

Josh was wearing just a towel, combing his damp hair, when Derelle pounded on the bathroom door. "You better come out here."

"What is it?"

"Somebody to see you."

"They'll have to wait."

"Says he can't."

Although not personally a respecter of privacy—she would cheerfully barge into the men's room to find him if she had to—Derelle was an implacable gatekeeper against everyday low-level intrusions, so this must be important.

Josh sighed, shrugged into the white terry robe on the back of the door provided for hotel guests, and opened the door.

Greg Hunter stood in the middle of the room, waiting.

One look at Greg's face, set and somehow pitying, told Josh that Greg was not bringing news he wanted to hear.

Derelle looked from one to the other then moved to Josh's side, reminding him unmistakably of a lioness guarding its cub.

Greg said, "We have to talk. Now." To Derelle, "Leave us, please."

"I'm not leaving till Congressman Fischer tells me to leave."

Josh said gently, "We need to be alone. Fifteen minutes, Derelle."

"No more. You're running late. You have the trial lawyers' reception at seven."

Greg said, "It won't take that long."

★   ★   ★

"Do you want to sit down," Greg asked, "or hear this standing up?"

"I'd rather stand. Thanks."

They faced each other six feet apart, like duelists. Greg tall and imposing in beige slacks and well-cut navy blazer with brass buttons; Josh barefoot in his bathrobe.

Greg said, "I felt I owed it to you to come in person. I'm here to ask you, to *beg* you, to drop out of the race. Now."

So here it was, coming at him from left field, as Lester had warned him.

He supposed he'd always known it would.

Josh listened to Greg tell him why he must drop out, watched his eyes, seemingly so sorry and kind but suffused with a kind of triumphant glow, while everything in the room except Greg's eyes darkened and shimmered with unreality.

"—Moonglow Motel in Pacifica, eleven times between October 15 and December 12, 1982, dates on record, I have them here if you want to see, always 225 except for November 21 when it was 237—"

Number 225 had been their lucky room. Josh curled his hands into fists. *Lucky.*

"—that you promised to use your influence with the DA on behalf of her husband provided that she—"

He couldn't believe it. Bianca would never have said that. It was a lie. It was sick.

"—that you were violent and that the moment Hector was free she quit her job and left the Bay Area to get away from you—"

"Because I was *violent?* She was *afraid* of me?" Now, Josh thought he would actually vomit. His head felt hot, his stomach cold. "It's lies, it's *outrageous* lies. You have to believe me."

"Of course I believe you. But other people won't."

No, Josh guessed not. It could only be her word against his, there was no proof, but he'd still be labeled a predator. And she was his client's wife. Dazed, he said, "You actually *spoke* to Bianca?"

"Of course."

"Where is she?"

"I don't know where she is now, Josh. They have her in a safe place. Her and the child. That was a condition of hers—that you not be able to find her."

It took a second or two for those three words to sink in. *And the child*—"What child?"

"Bianca's kid. Actually, she's not a child; fifteen or so—single mom with a baby boy."

"Are you're saying the child's mine?"

Greg shrugged. "Do the math." Then, "I've done my best for you; so far, we've kept all of it out of the papers."

"Noble of you."

"But if you stay in the race, I can't do the impossible. I can't hold back the tide. You're a candidate for the United States Senate; you're front-page news." And, "Josh, for God's sake think of Ellen."

★ ★ ★

Derelle scowled after Greg, who walked past her and out the door without a word, then she whipped around to Josh. "What's going on? What did he say?"

"I'm giving my speech to the lawyers, then I'm going home."

"You mean back to Oakland? Tonight? There's the Davis Democratic Club coffee at ten-thirty tomorrow up here, then the Young Farmers' Club. You'll be coming back for—"

"Have Vic cancel them."

She stared at him, aghast. "You can't do that! We can't just up and leave. The kids have gone to their host families. Someone'll have to round 'em all up. It'll take forever. And the bus—"

"The bus can go back tomorrow as planned. I'm getting a rental car."

"You can't drive tonight. You're already wiped. And you look weird—you feeling all right, boss?"

"I'm okay."

"If you want to get home that badly, let someone drive you."

"I told you, *I'm* driving."

"No way. I won't let you."

"Derelle, you're terrific and I appreciate what you're trying to do, but *leave me the hell alone.* Okay?"

★ ★ ★

Josh's speech to the trial lawyers was competent but uninspired, just his usual stump speech, delivered on autopilot. They were polite enough and no doubt attributed his lackluster performance to exhaustion. He answered a couple of questions in mechanical fashion, then left.

Josh claimed his rental car from the concierge. It was a black Nissan Maxima, light and frisky. He pulled onto the freeway a little after nine o'clock, driving into a cool clear night, with no moon. The straight highway crossed rice fields, darkness to either side and a blanket of stars above. He flicked through radio channels: cheesy music stations, talk shows, and news he couldn't bear to listen to. He switched the radio off altogether. Once, he had listened to Ellen's choral group singing Mozart's *Requiem*. He would love to hear that right now. He thought of her in her black skirt and little white blouse, singing her heart out. Those long-ago days, lost.

Josh opened the window wide, glad of the rush of air on his hot face. In not much more than an hour he'd be home, when at last he'd tell her everything.

He couldn't rely on Greg's promise not to publish.

Josh saw himself sitting Ellen down in the yellow kitchen—not the bedroom, this was not a story to be told in a bedroom—and saying, My darling, I have to pull out of the race because a long time ago I made a terrible mistake and Satcher has found out. Ellen, I was unfaithful to you. It makes me feel sick now, remembering, but I was obsessed, I couldn't help myself. I know there's no excuse. There can *be* no excuse. All I can do is ask you to forgive me. You're the only woman I love and will ever love.

And then of course, Josh thought with dread, there was worse—how to break it to her that he had a child? How could he bear to tell her? That might hurt her more than anything. The affair was one thing, but there was a child, his child.

The freeway lay in front of him in a ruby necklace that blurred up ahead in a patch of fog. An overpass swept up on him and fell behind. He passed a slow-moving sedan on the right, cut in too close ahead of a truck, and earned an angry blare of horn and flash of headlights. He was driving too fast. He eased his foot off the gas pedal and watched his speed fall to seventy. He decided to remain in the middle lane. Derelle was right—he should not be driving. Oh poor Derelle, he shouldn't have spoken to her like that. He felt bad about it, and he'd apologize tomorrow; she was only doing her job. Doing her best, as always.

Then he realized he had no idea where he was. Had he passed through Davis already? Was he approaching Vacaville? There seemed to be no signs or landmarks. There should be a big complex coming up soon on his right, with gas stations and fast-food places. He should stop and have a coffee. Strong and black.

Josh thought numbly, I'm a grandfather. His heart felt like lead.

His eyes blurred with tears and he wiped his arm across his face. He didn't see the blank white wall of fog rushing up toward him or the dull crimson glare of the truck taillights until he was almost on top of them, and then it was too late.

CHAPTER TWENTY-ONE

Ellen sat on a folding chair in the front row facing the freshly dug grave. Josh was down there, lying in the coffin with the white rose that she'd placed on the lid. Her mother sat on her left, her father on her right. They'd been holding her hands, but now she sat very straight in her pink shirt, the color she wore to the schools or to Juvenile Hall, her battle color, Josh called it. Her fingers twisted together in her lap, and she stared at the steep, golden flanks of Mount Tamalpais, where she and Josh had walked long ago through the flowers in the spring. They should have taken more walks there. Well, surely they would again.

Josh wasn't really dead, it was all a terrible mistake.

The call had come on her cell phone at nine-thirty Saturday night while Ellen drove home after the hotel workers' function. "There's been an accident," Derelle had said. "It's bad; I'm so sorry." Nothing Derelle said made any sense. It couldn't be Josh who had crashed into a truck in the Valley—he was spending the night in Sacramento and he didn't even own a Nissan Maxima.

Even when she got home and found Shirley Lester waiting at the door, and the cop, and the bunch of news photographers, she still hadn't believed it. Nobody so young, strong, and vital as Josh could be dead. She'd said, "But I saw him just this morning and he was fine."

Shirley Lester had taken Ellen's purse from her, found the door key, and shoved her into the house, then cried, "Honey, oh honey—" and held her in her arms.

Now, she sat there in the rippling heat of this September afternoon remembering that twenty-five years ago she and Josh had gone to the funeral of poor Professor Wolf, under this same grove of eucalyptus, surrounded by the golden hills. Josh had said to her, "Suppose it was my own father lying in that coffin? And suppose it was me tossing dirt into his grave? I begged God to give him the time he deserves."

Well, God had given Hans Fischer the time, he sat just on the other side of the aisle, he and Judith, gray haired and shocked. Soon they too would be tossing dirt into the grave of their only son.

A child wasn't supposed to die before the parent. It was a mistake of nature.

It was so wrong. So unfair.

What was she going to do now?

★ ★ ★

A sad procession drove across the Richmond Bridge, back to the little house in Oakland. The small living room and the kitchen were packed with friends and family and too much food—coolers of beer, wine, and soft drinks waited on the back porch—and flowers were everywhere, many of the bouquets homemade.

They were all here, everyone who loved Josh. The entire Fischer family. The Downey clan, with Ellen's latest niece, one-year-old Rebecca. Gloria and her husband, Paul, had flown in from New York; she hadn't seen them in years, just cards at the holidays.

"But we couldn't not come," insisted Gloria. "God, I remember the night you met him!"

Shirley Lester and Carole Walker, Brother Washington, Derelle, Vic Aguilera with all the campaign staff, many of the Children's Alliance staff and kids, and even, briefly, Greg Hunter with Jane. It was good of them to come. Greg held her and kissed her hair, whispering, "Ellen, Ell, I'm so very sorry."

Everybody else was sorry too. *I loved him...A terrible loss...It's like a light went out...I brought this, hope you can find room for it...I'll call you...So very sorry!*

Once or twice Ellen grew confused and began to think it was a great party. How nice to see everybody! What was the occasion and where was Josh? He was missing it all, it was too bad—then she'd remember again and be enveloped in dull grayness.

Josh wouldn't be back. He was dead.

★ ★ ★

Ellen coasted through the week of shiva in a kind of fog, sitting in the living room while the people came through. She listened to stories and memories, she was shown pictures of her husband: Josh as a toddler, grinning in a pointy paper hat at a children's party, very serious as he lit menorah candles. He was such a pretty baby. *Lovely boy!* people said, *wonderful man,* while the tears remained somewhere inside her unshed, the world held at bay by a rampart of family and friends.

Occasionally she'd vaguely wonder what would happen with the Senate race now that Josh had gone, but it didn't seem to affect her much; she was no longer involved, and Al Perez, the California Democratic Committee chair, would have to deal with it. Al had left the kindest messages and sent a beautiful bouquet of yellow roses for remembrance. She'd thought, *I'll never forget you, my darling!* That was the only time, so far, that she nearly completely lost it. Greg and Jane sent a huge pot of white cymbidiums. The kids at the Bayside Baptist Church delivered a painting of a rainbow with Josh floating above it wearing big white wings and an expression of mild surprise. Flowers kept coming and a deluge of letters and cards, endless phone messages. What a shame Josh couldn't enjoy all this outpouring of love. Yes, Lester said, he was loved all right, but this is for you! Don't forget you are loved too, Ellen.

The newspapers feasted on Josh's death. Ellen didn't read them, though the obituaries were apparently very flattering. Nor did she pay attention to the endless conjecture on his spur-of-the-moment, tragic dash for home. Why? Had he received sudden bad news? Was he ill? There'd been horrendous photos of the flattened Nissan wedged underneath the truck with Josh's crushed body still inside. She didn't see the pictures. Someone was compiling the material, she could have it all later if she wanted; right now, she couldn't bear it.

Vic Aguilera dealt with the reporters while Derelle, brusque and efficient, ran errands, drove loads of leftover food down to the Children's Alliance, and dropped off flowers at a convalescent home. Ellen spent a last evening with Hans and Judith before their flight out, hugging them close. "Oh my dear," Judith said, "whatever we can do, just let us know." They were so kind and loving, she could only guess what they must be feeling. As she held each of them in her arms, she found them smaller than she remembered and realized they were getting old. Her heart ached for them.

And then, at last, after a week, she was alone. The house sparkled clean from top to bottom, the fridge was full of food she'd never eat. The pills kind Dr. Bernstein had prescribed for her, which had allowed her to sleep, were finished. Ellen lay in the big bed she'd shared with Josh, her head clear, gazed out at the oak tree with its perfect branch, and knew she must soon begin patching together her broken life.

And why not start now?

She reached for the phone and switched the ringer back on. It seemed like a symbolic act. She dialed a number. "Can you come over? We need to talk."

★　★　★

Derelle arrived within half an hour.

Having been well dressed and soft-spoken all week, she now appeared in jeans, clunky boots, and leather jacket, dragging a heavy briefcase. "You back with us now? Good. There's a lotta stuff you better know about—I've got it all in here for you—and about a million e-mails, and it won't wait much longer." Sounding almost truculent, "Things go on happening, you know."

Still wearing her bathrobe over wrinkled pajamas, Ellen climbed weakly onto a kitchen stool. She felt as if she was taking her first steps after a month in a hospital bed. "Can you fix us some coffee? I could use about a gallon."

"Sure thing."

Derelle fixed a brew you could stand a spoon up in, and they sat side by side at the counter drinking it. She said, "There's a whole lot of people want to talk with you."

Ellen dumped more sugar into her cup. She never used to take sugar; now she needed it. She guessed she was still in shock. "I'm not talking to the press," she said.

"Not the press. To Vic. To Lester. Al Perez wants to fly up and see you."

"What about?"

"You'll find out. You gotta call them ASAP, now you're out of the fog you've been—Oh *shit!*" Derelle clapped her hand over her mouth and stared at Ellen, stricken. "Pretend I didn't say that."

"It's all right. It's okay. Please don't try and monitor every-thing you say. Just talk to me. Who else?"

"Greg Hunter's been calling every day. Wants to see you." Now her voice sounded ominous. "Which I have something to say about."

"I know you never liked him. But he's still my friend."

"You won't say that when you hear what happened that night. Got any cookies? You better have a cookie. You need a sugar fix."

"Of course there're cookies somewhere; there's everything. Go take a look."

Derelle delved into the cabinet and found a tin: homemade chocolate chip. They both took one and munched.

"All right," Ellen said. "What about Greg? Fill in the blanks for me. I still don't understand what happened in Sacramento and if you do, just tell me. Right from the beginning."

Derelle related the events of the day, beginning with the rally. "It was great. A fantastic turnout. Josh kept saying he wished you were there. I've never seen him so pumped. I tell you, the adrenaline was pouring off of him in sheets. But then that son of a bitch Greg Hunter showed up afterward at the hotel room. Told me to get out of there like I was a servant. Said he had something to say to Josh alone, and I could feel this kind of *current* running between them, like Josh knew just what it was. Afterward Greg leaves and Josh is all quiet and I can feel it's all gone bad, like *really* bad, and Josh tells me he's decided to go home right away. Won't wait for the morning, needs a rental car right after the lawyers' talk, which he walks through sort of like he's not even there, and won't have anybody drive him. I tell him forget it, he's tired and acting weird, and he tells me to get the hell out of there." Her hurt was still vividly real. "That man *never* sounded off like that to me before. He was always a gentleman, no matter what."

"You couldn't hear what Greg said?"

"I tried. But that was one solid door, and he made sure it was closed tight. But whatever it was Greg said to Josh, it was enough to drive him out there and kill himself."

Ellen felt a cold stab of horror. "Come *on,* Derelle! You don't mean that."

The girl's face froze in shock. "Oh God! I don't mean Josh committed suicide. Oh, Ell, me and my dumb mouth!"

"It's okay. It's okay. But what could it have been that set him off like that? What couldn't wait till the morning? I still don't understand."

"Me neither. But it was something Greg Hunter said, and he's bad news, Ell. No matter how you felt about him in the past, he's out to bushwhack you now and don't trust him further than you can throw him. Not even that far. However, there's other stuff going on front and center in your life and you've got some decisions to make. Go get yourself together, Ell, while I make a call."

★ ★ ★

Half an hour later Shirley Lester and Vicente Aguilera drove up in Lester's bright red Buick. From the bedroom window, Ellen watched them walk up the path side by side, faces grave. Both were dressed soberly and almost formally in dark gray suits. Ellen was reminded of door-to-door evangelicals.

Or process servers.

They sat in the living room, Ellen and Lester on the sofa, Aguilera in the leather recliner. Derelle leaned in the doorway.

Lester asked, sounding almost apologetic, "Can you guess what this is all about?"

Ellen sat in silence, drinking yet more of Derelle's coffee, which made her feel as if windows were flying open in her skull to admit shafts of jittery white light, while Lester, every inch the lawyer now, explained what happens to the Senate race with Josh gone.

"If a candidate for statewide office dies after they've won the party primary but more than thirty days before the November election, the state Democratic Party gets to choose a replacement whose name will appear on the ballot. Since Josh has died sixty days before the election, this law applies. The executive committee of the party now has two weeks to name the replacement."

Ellen said, "If an endorsement from me will help—"

"They need more from you than that."

Ellen ran her fingers through her hair. She still felt a bit fuddled. Perhaps she'd drunk too much coffee after all. She was sure she ought to understand why they'd come to her without having it all explained by chapter and verse. "What, then?"

"They want you to run in Josh's place," Lester said.

Ellen almost laughed because it was ridiculous. More than that: it was *crazy*. How could they expect such a thing of her at such a time? She said so. She demanded, "Who and what do they think I am?"

"They think you're the only candidate who has more than a snowball's chance in hell of unseating Carl Satcher." Shirley Lester set down her cup, leaned forward, and took both of Ellen's cold hands in hers. "Look at me, Ell. Listen. The executive committee met in Los Angeles yesterday. Forty of them. They took a secret ballot. Seventy percent—that's twenty-eight out of forty—want you to run."

Ellen shook her head. "Nobody should expect it of me. I just can't do it. And even if I could, I'm not qualified."

"Sure you are. More than qualified. Certainly more so than a lot of those businessmen senators like Satcher who've never held public office before. You've run the Children's Alliance for years and built it to national stature. You've made a huge success of the Commission for Children, Youth, and Families. You're a known quantity throughout the state. You're respected and loved. Most important of all, when it comes to mudslinging, you're bulletproof."

Aguilera said, very seriously, "Josh would want you to carry on for him."

Lester said, "He's right. You, and especially you, remember Josh's commitment to the people. Would you undo everything he's done by staying on the sidelines? Would you destroy the hopes of everyone who counted on him? Because Josh was going to pull it off, you know. He was already running three points ahead, *over an incumbent!* The Satcher camp was terrified of him. Just imagine how they must be whooping it up right now! You're the only one who has a chance to beat him, Ellen."

"You're making me feel guilty. Please don't do that. I told you, I can't."

"At least promise us you'll think about it." Lester drew a deep breath. "Remember telling me how you first met Josh? You were going door-to-door with a petition for kids. Well, when you make it to the Senate, you can hand-deliver those petitions yourself, in the form of your own bills. You can pass those bills and send them to the Oval Office with your name on them. On behalf of the children."

Ellen tried to look into the future but only saw darkness and doubt. She felt very weak, very sad, and very tired. She shook her head. "I'm sorry to disappoint the party—Al is so wonderful. Please thank them for their faith in me. But I can't run. Nobody can expect this of me, not right now. This is not the time."

Lester said softly, "I know. It's very hard on you, harder than I can imagine. But if ever there was a time to run, it's now."

Yes, thought Ellen, I want to run and run, far away, to some-where safe and warm where I can curl up and not have to think or feel and where nobody can find me.

★ ★ ★

"No," Ellen told Al Perez and Becky Kennedy, vice chair of the California Democratic Party, during the afternoon conference call. "No, no, and no."

Al urged, "We know it's tough, that we're asking more than anyone has a right to ask, but nobody else has a chance. We've had another meeting. Ninety-six percent of the executive committee want you now. By tomorrow it'll be unanimous."

"I'm sorry," Ellen said.

"Josh would want you to. You owe it to him," Becky said.

"That's blackmail."

"As long as it works. We'll use any leverage on you we can," Al said.

"I can't."

"Then sleep on it," Al said. "Think about it. You don't have to make a decision today. Here's my cell phone number. Call me anytime, day or night."

She knew she wouldn't call him.

But she would call Greg.

★ ★ ★

Ellen looked inside the refrigerator at all that food—why did it seem so necessary to overfeed the bereaved? She took out the fixings for an omelet.

She wasn't hungry. She hadn't been hungry for a week, but she supposed she should eat something. She cracked two eggs into a bowl and whisked them. Sliced cheese and chopped parsley. She made herself a small tomato salad and sprinkled dill on it.

She found a half bottle of leftover white wine and poured herself a glass, switched on a CD of the San Francisco Symphony playing Mozart's *Requiem,* and settled on the sofa, half wrapped in Josh's Navajo blanket. She imagined it captured his body warmth and unique personal smell, that he was all around her, holding her, and she didn't feel quite so bereft.

Half an hour later the doorbell rang and there Greg stood, exactly on time, the porch light glinting on his gold hair. He was holding a small bunch of purple lupines.

"They're from New Zealand," Greg said, arranging them in a small vase. "It's spring down there right now."

"They're pretty."

"They reminded me of—"

"I know. Thank you." Ellen saw herself sitting in the front row at Josh's funeral, looking across to Mount Tamalpais, imagining the mountain's spring meadows all drifted with blue. She wished Greg hadn't brought the flowers.

He tried to embrace her, but she didn't want to be comforted. Not by him. "Sit down," she said, indicating the recliner. "We need to talk."

"I've been trying to reach you."

"I know. Like a drink?"

"Whatever you're having. White wine. Fine."

She poured him the rest of the bottle. "Did you eat?"

"I grabbed a bite."

She sat back down on the sofa.

He said, "I assume Derelle told you I dropped by Josh's hotel room that night."

She pushed aside her plate with its half-eaten omelet, cooling now and looking increasingly unappetizing. "Of course she did. And I'd like to know what you said to him to make him drop everything and take off like that."

Greg set his wine down on the table and gazed at her full on, impelling her attention. "I went to his room to warn him. Somebody had to."

She met his eyes. "Warn him? About what?"

"About what would happen if he didn't drop out of the Senate race."

"Why should he have dropped out?"

"Forgive me, Ellen." He leaned forward and reached for her hand, but she pulled away from him and folded her arms tightly across her chest. "I'd give anything in the world not to have to tell you, but I don't have a choice. The story could still be leaked, and if you have to know, I'd so much rather you heard it from me."

She made a huge effort to control her face and her posture. Whatever she was going to hear, she must not react. Stay cool, she told herself. Stay aloof.

Greg lowered his voice as if they could be overheard, and Ellen resisted the temptation to look over her shoulder. "It was something that happened to Josh long ago, a mistake he made, normally something that would be covered over in time and forgotten—but when you're running for high office you're transparent, time doesn't matter, and there's no such thing as too long ago."

"Sadly, that's politics today."

"Exactly. And as you must assume, the Satcher group has been digging hard for anything that'll discredit Josh; it's the name of the game."

"And you found something."

He ignored the accusation implicit in the *you*. "They did. Something Josh did long ago that, if it had come out, would have not only destroyed Josh's career but hurt you badly. And it could hurt your future."

Ellen raised her chin. "I don't understand. *My* future?"

"There's an insane rumor going around that you're going to run in Josh's place."

She stared at him. "How did you hear that?"

"There're no secrets. Are you denying it?"

"For God's sake, Greg, how could I think of something like that right now?"

"But you're not denying the offer's on the table."

"You're twisting everything I say."

"Listen to me." Greg made space for himself beside her on the sofa, determinedly unlocked her hands, and held them in his large, warm clasp. For a fraction of a second she fought the impulse to fling herself into his arms and be held and comforted—but no, of course not—what was she thinking? She tried to pull her hands away, but Greg held her firm.

"So far I've made them keep this out of the media," he said, "and when Josh died it seemed like the end of it. But the knowledge is out there; if you decide to run, it'll be dug up again, and there'll be nothing I can do to protect you."

"So," Ellen said, feeling chilled despite the warm house and the closeness of Greg's body, "go ahead."

She heard him give a heavy sigh. "All right, then," Greg said. "I'd give anything for it to be otherwise, but it seems like you have to know. It happened back when Josh was a public defender. He had an affair with a client's wife while the guy was on trial for murder. She was young and beautiful. It was a bad mistake."

Well, she guessed she had always known. It didn't hurt so much as she had expected. Ellen heard herself say, slowly and logically, "We all know by now it takes more than an affair to kill a political career."

"But when sex is used as coercion in a capital case?" Then he told her exactly what Bianca Rivas had said, sparing her only the more lurid details.

Ellen listened, her face stony.

"It was a betrayal, both personal and professional," Greg concluded. "And absolutely unethical. Josh would have been disbarred. You must understand that disclosing that information now would undermine all the trust he asked for from the voters."

"I don't believe it," Ellen said. "That woman's lying. Josh would *never*—"

"I'm so sorry, Ellen."

She met his eyes. They were inscrutable, but she sensed a small avid flicker deep down as he watched her. She wrenched her hands from his. "And you're telling me now because—?"

"You can save his reputation by not running. Then he can stay a loved and respected hero."

Greg finished his drink and took the glass to the kitchen. She heard him rinse it. He returned and stood immediately before her. "Like I said, I'm more sorry than I can say, being the one to tell you, especially at a time like this, so soon; it was unforgivable, but I had no choice. You're more than welcome to shoot the messenger."

"I'll bear that in mind."

"Politics is not for the likes of you. It's dirty."

"I think you'd better go now, Greg."

He stood there, still so handsome, once such a good friend, saying he only wanted the best for her. Only the messenger. Not so long ago, or she might have believed that. "I'll call you," he said. "When this is all over, we'll get together. Good times will come again, I promise. And in the meantime, forget about running. Please. Because I won't be able to protect you."

Then he was out the door. Ellen double-locked it behind him and leaned her back against it.

Well, now she finally knew why Josh had been rushing home—to tell her. Silently she accused Greg, You as good as killed him yourself, didn't you.

She felt nauseated.

How could he? she thought. How dare he come here and tell me those things? I hate him, *hate him*!

Ellen returned to the sofa, wrapped herself in the blanket again, and sat, cocooned, while toxic thoughts and images tumbled around in her mind.

Josh, you betrayed me. How could you do it? I always loved you.

Then she thought of her own act of perfidy; how, that time, loving Josh hadn't stopped her from making love to Greg. And she'd never told Josh, had she?

So don't judge *him,* Ellen told herself. He made a mistake— he's human. It was just once, a long time ago, and he made up for it a thousand times since.

She unwrapped herself, got up, and threw Greg's specially ordered, out-of-season, horrible New Zealand lupines in the trash. Then she walked upstairs to the small room that would have been the baby's room but instead had become Josh's office. There was still a pile of flyers on his desk beside the phone with its four incoming lines, silent for seven days now. On the wall behind it, a framed poster. She studied it carefully and Josh gazed back at her:

JOSH FISCHER FOR SENATE, WINNING THE BATTLES FOR YOU!

Life-size, eyes so warm and so deep, mouth firm but smiling, a face of love, a face you could trust.

A man you could follow to the ends of the earth.

She leaned forward across the desk, touched her forehead to his, and could almost persuade herself his skin felt warm. She closed her eyes, emptied her mind, and felt his voice deep inside her saying, *I love you. Trust me.*

Trust me. That was the sum of it, really.

Ellen sat down in his black leather office chair, leaned back, and looked into his eyes. Suddenly she felt very calm.

She told herself to grow up. To think it through.

She remembered Josh's devastated face the night she'd found him collapsed on the doorstep. Was that the face of a man who used coercion and threats for sex? He'd been half incoherent with misery and shame.

Somebody was lying.

Josh Fischer was an honorable man, a man who believed the world could be a better place and was not afraid to do something about it.

He would have won the election, but Satcher and Greg dug up the worst dirt and invented the worse lies with which to force him out of the race.

Now they were threatening her, Ellen, with public exposure of the same lies. They'd do anything to win.

She couldn't, and wouldn't, just stand aside; she had to fight back. And the very fact that they were threatening her meant that they were afraid—afraid of her!

Ellen thought, They brought this on themselves. She remembered how Lester had said, "You're the only one who has a chance to beat him." And Aguilera, "Josh would want you to carry on for him."

Lester had said, "If ever there was a time to run, it's now!"

She remembered Al Perez saying, "Call me anytime, day or night."

★ ★ ★

Ellen called him at midnight, sitting at Josh's desk. "Okay," she said. "Count me in. I'll do it."

After hanging up she lowered her head onto the pile of flyers with Josh's face on them and at last allowed herself to cry. She cried, all alone, for more than half an hour.

Then she stood up, feeling very weak and beyond exhausted, stumbled to the bathroom, took a long hot shower, and went to bed.

Tomorrow, all hell would break loose.

CHAPTER TWENTY-TWO

Ellen held a press conference upon acceptance of the Democratic nomination for Senate, standing on the steps of the state Capitol in Sacramento, in front of more than forty television cameras.

It was unseasonably hot, a little too late to call Indian summer, the air so crackling dry it seared the lungs. Ellen felt drained and fragile. The rage of two weeks ago had carried her just so far, and now had dissipated.

There hadn't even been time to mourn. She'd had no chance to return alone to the cemetery, to take flowers and sit quietly with Josh for a bit. Instead, not yet a month after his death, here she stood beside the governor of California, the focus of a thousand pairs of eyes.

Ellen's gaze took in the reporters in an all-encompassing sweep—was Greg among them?—and she guessed that many of them waited with avid curiosity to see whether she would get through her speech without breaking down in tears. Ellen thought in horror of people watching her cry on-screen, in a million living rooms coast to coast. She clenched her hands in the pockets of her jacket and vowed, No way! For now, she must stay cool. She was a public person, and private grief must wait.

The governor came to the end of his peroration, and Ellen realized she hadn't heard a word of it. She smiled up at him and mechanically shook his hand.

She looked out beyond those threatening cameras to all the faces watching her—friendly faces, she hoped—then focused on the cluster of young people in the front row, standing behind a long banner whose blue letters on white read: !!GO, ELLEN, GO!!

The Children's Alliance kids!

Derelle had organized a busload to follow Ellen to Sacramento, where some would display their banner and others deploy through the crowd, one here, one there, and when in doubt, cheer their butts off. Many were grown now, but all of them were still Ellen's kids, who had each sought sanctuary, over the years, in that old warehouse beneath the freeway.

Ellen smiled at them and murmured a silent, Thanks, guys! Then she squared her shoulders and began.

"Thank you all so much for being here today! A lot of you were the heart and soul of my husband Josh's campaign. I want you to know that Josh was the love of my life. Josh *was* my life. But I can't *be* Josh. Nobody could be Josh Fischer.

"But I can fight for the things Josh believed in—things that brought you to him—like dignity for all people, a chance at the American Dream, and the preservation of our environment, which we both believe is a gift from God."

The Children's Alliance kids let go with their first cheer.

Ellen pressed on too fast, "At the time of his death—" She started over, louder. "*At the time of his death* Josh was winning the race—because Josh Fischer was a winner."

She told herself not to rush. She drew a breath and waited out the next burst of applause, again led by the children, but a deeper sound as more people joined in.

"Josh Fischer dreamed of public service. He learned very young, from his own family, that one person *can* make a difference, even though he knew it wasn't always easy. And Josh wasn't afraid to speak out and fight for what was right—if he was in the majority, or in the minority—even if his was the *only* voice!

"At first I said no to running for the Senate. But I know Josh would want me to do it, not only to carry his issues, but to carry to the Senate an issue that has defined me since before I even met him—our children."

The Children's Alliance kids began to chant now, "EL-*LEN*, EL-*LEN*, EL-*LEN!*"

"Yes, our children! Their well-being: their health, their dreams, their education, their economic well-being, their protection. Because let us not forget, our children are not just our own future, but the future of the whole human race!

"And so, to the people of California, I say this: You were getting to know my husband, and I believe you would have sent him to the Senate. Tragically, you lost that chance on a highway on a dark night. But you now have the opportunity to elect the person who knew Josh Fischer the best and shared his victories, his battles, his hopes, and his dreams.

"I ask you to vote for me on Tuesday, November 3.

"Not because of your pity, but because of your hopes.

"Not because of your sympathy, but because of your own dreams, and the dreams of your children.

"Because, after all is said and done, this race is not about me, nor is it about Josh. It is about *you*. And I promise you that if you elect me your United States Senator, I will fight for you every day that I have breath in my body."

★ ★ ★

Ellen and her campaign team were visiting the major media markets just as they had nine months ago with Josh, driving down Highway 5 to Fresno again, the peaks of the Sierra Nevada barely visible to the east, trembling above a line of brownish murk.

Steve, the taciturn driver, had been sent up from Los Angeles by Al Perez. He drove with calm, professional skill and always, regardless of distance covered and the vagaries of traffic, managed to pull up at the next stop within minutes of the scheduled arrival time. He was short and muscular with dark hair cut very short, and he seemed unaffected by temperature, always wearing a short-sleeved sport shirt while in the frigidly air-conditioned van, always donning his black blazer with the emblem on the pocket (a crown and anchor in gold thread) before stepping out into the heat.

Ellen's college rommate Gloria had returned to California for the duration. She and Ellen sat immediately behind Steve, a large satchel between them containing power bars, fruit, bags of nuts, six-packs of Gatorade and spring water, and a giant bottle of vitamins and minerals. Gloria, consultant to a chain of health clinics, had assembled the contents personally. "You don't eat, you don't sleep, and you drink too much coffee!" she'd chided. "You have to watch it. You absolutely *can't* get sick."

Vic Aguilera sat beside Derelle in back, laptop open on his knees. They mostly conversed in low tones among their maps and schedules and constantly ringing cell phones while they organized the ground troops. There was so much to do, details Ellen knew well, she'd done it all herself for Josh not nine months ago: the rental of halls and sound systems, volunteers to coordinate at every stop, flyers and posters to be delivered with boxes of hastily produced new T-shirts: ELLEN FISCHER: KEEPING OUR DREAMS ALIVE.

"That was a good beginning," Aguilera had said on leaving Sacramento. "You did well, but don't make it too much about Josh from now on."

"Why should it not be about Josh?" Ellen had asked.

"Because his race is over. This is about you—and about them, the voters. Why they should vote for you and not for Satcher. Of course, just at first, you still need to orient yourself as Josh's successor, but move quickly on after that to yourself."

Steve donned his blazer once he'd pulled up outside the Hilton in Fresno and stepped out into heat solid enough to cut with a knife. He walked around the van to the passenger side, rolled back the door, positioned the blue milk crate he kept under the dash for Ellen to step out onto, and held her arm while the cameras flashed.

She moved through the lobby, smiling and shaking hands, to the packed dining room, where she mounted the podium. She began her speech by expressing her intention of carrying

Josh's torch, then stated her own goals and how she would address local issues.

"I was talking with a plum farmer last week, on the edge of town," she said. "His family has owned their farm for two generations. It was a prosperous business. But for the past five years the leaves are withering on his trees, the fruit is small and coated with filth from the air itself. He is growing instant dried prunes. This is happening in the Central Valley of California, some of the richest farmland on earth. That's why my husband—*why I*—will take such a firm stand against polluters who refuse to pay for their own cleanup and pump their toxins into the ground. Who burn their chemicals into the air at night when nobody can see the emissions.

"Ladies and Gentlemen, when I'm elected to the Senate, I commit to you that I will make sure that the polluters pay! It's only fair. Will you help me?"

★ ★ ★

In Los Angeles they drove down a wide avenue of mixed high-rises and low-slung office buildings beside a line of palms that rattled in the hot Santa Ana wind. People went a bit crazy when the Santa Ana was blowing. Ellen hoped that things didn't get too crazy.

The county labor council was in an unassuming two-story building. TV vans were drawn up outside and a couple of a police cars idled at the curb. Across the street a cluster of people chanted and held signs aloft:

SATCHER FOR SENATE.
HE'S OUR MAN!

★ ★ ★

"Some think of Los Angeles as my opponent's home turf," Ellen began, "but it's Fischer country too. My husband grew up in Los Angeles, he went to public school here, he thought of it as home." *Move on from Josh. Get personal and local.* "His family always made me so welcome that I think of it as my home too, even though I grew up on the other side of the country.

"My family is ordinary. We're not rich. My father was manager of a trucking company, and my mom was a grade-school teacher."

Ellen drew a breath, picturing Satcher's supporters out there, waving their placards, trying to negate her visit. She felt the steel creep down her spine. "My opponent is insulated from the world by a veil of privilege and billions of dollars," she said. "How many truckers does *he* know personally? How many teachers, nurses, waitresses, mechanics, or welfare mothers? Does he have any idea what it must be like to be a first-generation American struggling to just get by? Or to be old or disabled or sick, living in a dingy, single-occupancy hotel room, hoping the Social Security money will last till the end of the month?"

A voice cried, "Tell it to us, Ellen!"

"Do you think he cares?"

A rumble from the crowd: *"NOOOO . . ."*

"Well, *I* care, and I understand the challenges facing so many families in Southern California. I know how hard you work and how tough it can be to pay the rent each month. I know how we all want the best for our children, to live in safe streets so they're able to walk to the corner store without fear, and sleep at night without listening to sirens and gunfire."

She paused, not smiling, hearing the murmurous groundswell of anger and frustration, watching as people rose to their feet, arms raised, hands clapping above their heads.

"I know, and I understand! I've worked in our public schools for over twenty years, I can see firsthand how inadequate they are and how they're getting worse. Don't our kids deserve the best? How can they learn anything, forty to a classroom, without books? Why should they be deprived of art, music, and sports programs because there's no money?

"The system needs fixing—let's work together to do it. There are answers. There's always hope!"

The applause was prolonged and genuine.

She thought, If only Josh were here.

★ ★ ★

With two and a half hours to San Diego, Ellen lay stretched in the backseat, her hands aching from the constant grabbing and shaking, wearing the cotton gloves Derelle kept on ice in the cooler.

Why did some people have to grasp your hand so hard the bones grated together?

At the Hyatt Regency, she hit all the issues San Diegans care about, with an emotional visit to a very successful after-school program for at-risk kids. The photographers had a field day.

"That's great," Aguilera said afterward. "Now you're humming!"

★　★　★

Ellen had taken over Josh's campaign office in San Francisco. Located on Van Ness close to its intersection with Market Street, it had once been an automobile showroom. The front space, formerly showcasing gleaming new automobiles in paint-box colors, was now filled with long trestle tables at which volunteers, most of them young, manned the computers and phones, stuffed envelopes, and coordinated precinct walkers.

They worked eighteen hours a day under fluorescent strip lighting. There was little natural light, for the huge plate-glass windows were plastered with FISCHER FOR SENATE posters, a hasty print run with Josh's face replaced by Ellen's. She had felt uncomfortable at first, conscious of a feeling of usurpation. Nor had she cared for the picture that Vic Aguilera had chosen, shot the year before at an unusually contentious meeting of the CCYF. She'd been at the podium making a speech, caught at a declarative moment, head back, her hand raised, palm outward.

Aguilera thought Ellen's face, with the firm mouth and focused eyes, conveyed action and authority. "You have to get beyond the helpful wife image," he insisted. "This is the new you, a strong, feisty contender. Trust me."

Now, she approved of her poster. Strong, she thought with awed surprise, and indeed feisty.

Ellen's office, in back where the sales offices used to be, was the hub of the organization, a small island of relative calm amid the chaos of phones, faxes, and television screens. She had installed a conference table and chairs, several comfortable armchairs upholstered in blue and gold, and on the wall her gallery of photographs from the Children's Alliance.

Ellen, Aguilera, and Derelle sat with David Makins, communications director, and Mike Spellman, pollster.

David Makins was tall and balding with a reddish beard, Mike Spellman was the same height, with a grizzled brown beard, and they both had twinkly hazel eyes. The pair of them reminded Ellen of a brace of bears. She usually found them sturdily comforting—but not today.

The issue was television. And money. Or lack of it.

Josh's TV spots had all been in the can, expensively produced and carefully tested before focus groups during the summer. Now they were useless.

Ellen might have come out of the gate fast, but if she couldn't sustain on TV, she'd be history.

"This is what we're up against. It starts to run today." Makins shoved a tape into the VCR, and they all watched as Carl Satcher's image filled the screen.

He sat in his Senate office in Washington, D.C., an image of the Capitol dome behind him, U.S. and California flags to either side of his desk. He was wearing a dark blue suit, light blue shirt with a crimson-and-navy-striped power tie, lamplight gleaming on his helmet of white hair, the picture-perfect Senator.

"Good-looking son of a bitch," Makins said, irritated.

In mellow tones redolent of sympathy Satcher said, "For the past two weeks I've suspended my campaign in honor of my opponent Joshua Fischer, who was so tragically taken from us. We all know politics is tough, but there are times for us to come together, to pull together. Now, it's time to go back to work." The camera zoomed in for a close-up. "I know how to lead in hard times. I did it in the navy. I've done it as a husband and a father. I've done it as a businessman and a Senator. I've done it all my life."

The screen faded to black, with the words:

KEEP CARL SATCHER IN THE UNITED STATES SENATE.

SOLID LEADERSHIP IN ROUGH SEAS.

Triumphal music swelled, lush and grand, played by a full symphony orchestra.

"Noble," Spellman noted wryly. "A calculated class act."

"Class act," Derelle said scornfully. "Ha!"

"And a tough one to follow," Spellman said. "He's the incumbent, he's telegenic, and he's rich. He's holding all the aces."

"He's missing the last one," Derelle said. "He's a crook. Ellen's honest *and* she's telegenic. She's holding aces too. And we're up five points."

"A sympathy bump," Spellman said. "It'll adjust down."

They're talking about me as if I'm not even here, like I'm not a real person but a product—even Derelle—thought Ellen, disconcerted to hear her staff discuss a sympathy bump as just another item to be factored into the campaign and not as a validation of Josh's death. She bit her lip. Well, she supposed she'd have to get past her feelings for the duration.

Spellman ejected the tape and replaced it with one of Ellen's three spots, all using different sound bites culled from her Sacramento speech.

They watched as white letters typed themselves silently onto a dark screen:

MOST CANDIDATES SEEK PUBLIC OFFICE.

SOME HAVE IT SEEK THEM.

Then there was Ellen, standing beside her red truck, her bright hair whipping in the wind. She was surrounded by children, who leaned into her, touching her, seeming simultaneously to be protective of her and to seek comfort in her presence.

Ellen said into the camera, "I ask you for your vote not because of your sympathy, but because of your dreams and the dreams of your children. [A boy, maybe twelve, serious and big eyed, with a mop of thick dark hair, slipped his hand into Ellen's.] When I get to the Senate I'll fight for you every day I have a breath. And that's a promise."

The image dissolved.

ELLEN FISCHER FOR UNITED STATES SENATE.

KEEPING OUR DREAMS ALIVE.

There was no music. "We thought it best to keep it simple," Spellman explained. "More powerful."

"It makes Satcher's spot look way overblown," Makins said loyally.

Aguilera agreed, "She comes across dignified, but warm and emotional too. And the kids are terrific."

"The other two spots are okay too," Spellman said. "But they're not *great*. They strike the same note."

"We didn't have much choice, or time," Makins said.

"We need a new spot, something different. But we're already bleeding a million five a week putting those three out there," Spellman said.

Aguilera said, "We can't outspend Satcher, and we'd better not try. What we have going for us is Ellen's basic talent and charisma—we need to dream up a way to properly harness them."

Derelle picked up Makins's video camera from its customary spot in the center of the conference table, trained it on Ellen's face, and zoomed in and out. "That shouldn't be so hard. She looks great. Why can't she just talk?"

"So write her a script," Spellman said.

★ ★ ★

New Satcher spots aired constantly, and Ellen's team reviewed them in her back office: Satcher, casual and chummy in V-neck sweater, hugging a frail, elderly woman in a convalescent home: "Did you remember your medicine today, Mrs. Houlihan?" "Why thank you, Mr. Satcher," the quavering response, "I surely did this time!" The deeply mellow and instantly recognizable voice of Tom Turner then insisted, "When it comes to health care, Carl Satcher is on top of things. And remember, Carl Satcher *cares!*"

"Oh *God*," David Makins exclaimed in disgust. "Has that man no shame?"

Next, Satcher was striding across a construction site, rugged in a hard hat, then consulting with workers on a factory floor, and finally overlooking white-coated workers in a research lab while Tom Turner trumpeted: "Carl Satcher knows how the world works. He'll keep the jobs in California. Doesn't California need a *real* professional?"

"We're down," Mike Spellman said gloomily. "Five points. He's blanketing the damn screen."

"He has the resources to throw it all at us," Aguilera said, "and his pal Tom Turner's worth another three points right there."

★ ★ ★

With two weeks to go until the election, Ellen went on the road in a last-ditch effort to get out the vote, covering the state, up, down, and across, her days a succession of hotels and highways, union halls, schools, old folks' homes, community centers, and auditoriums, punctuated by fund-raisers in the living rooms of wealthy supporters, always standing on her by now well-known milk crate. She could no longer easily keep track of the faces and names, where she was going, or what she would say when she got there. "Brief me," she'd demand of Aguilera. "Walk me through it." She felt like a wind-up toy: take her somewhere, then set her loose to do her thing and make her speech.

"*Please,*" she'd conclude each time, "if you need a ride on election day, let us know and we'll send a driver. But *get out there and vote!* I need you, each and every one of you!"

Then it would be back to the van, to be fed fruit and granola bars by Gloria, and to stretch out, cool gloves on her inflamed hands, until the next time.

★ ★ ★

She spent an afternoon performing damage control with the loggers in Humboldt County, reached via a long winding drive north up Highway 101.

"But they hated Josh," she'd objected when Aguilera planned the trip. "They called him a tree hugger and a freaky environmentalist—"

"Then you try to turn that around," Aguilera said. "It's about respect. You can't give them a chance to say you ignored them. Or didn't care. Worst of all—were afraid of them."

So Ellen stood on her crate wearing jeans and a bright purple, snap-fastened shirt, her surprisingly far-reaching contralto voice rising over the sullen murmur.

"They say I'm feisty," she said, "and I guess I need to be, standing in front of you guys, saying what I'm going to say!"

Someone yelled something unprintable, then something about fruits and nuts and how she should get her ass back to San Francisco if she knew what was good for her.

"But there're things that need to be said," Ellen pursued steadily. "You can't turn back the clock! Times have changed, and no matter who you decide to send to the Senate, me or my opponent, your industries will never be what they once were. My husband knew the issue here was about jobs, first, second, and third. He felt strongly about preservation"—she raised her voice against an instant angry howl—"not just of trees, but of the *people* who make their living in these forests. And when I go to the Senate, I hope with your help, one of my first priorities will be to focus on areas like this one, where there's hardship, and help you to find good workable solutions."

The same voice, or perhaps another voice, was raised again in expletive-laden jeers, but this time he was ordered, just as colorfully, to shut his mouth.

"I'm not promising any easy fixes," Ellen went on. "It'll be tough sledding. It'll mean a lot of energy and determination not to give up. But if we all pull together, it can—and will—be done! For instance, did you know that the biggest industry in the state of California is not lumber, agriculture, oil, or even Hollywood, but tourism? Now then, think what you can bring to the party. Think of these forests and mountains, the coast, the rivers and streams—and your wonderful clean air. Think what can be done. I'm telling you, I'm planning to give you all the support I can once I get to the Senate. This was a boomtown once—let's make it a boomtown again!"

★　★　★

On the phone late one night to Shirley Lester, Ellen said, "So I guess Satcher's not going to release those foul stories about Josh after all."

"He doesn't need to when he's ahead," Lester said. "Though frankly, there's no way even Satcher would have dared pull a stunt like that. He's no fool. Can you imagine how it would have backfired? Think of the reaction to such an attack on a grieving widow!"

"Greg said he was trying to protect me," Ellen said.

"A convenient concept," Lester dismissed. "And you notice our boy's lying low these days."

★ ★ ★

Ten days before the election Ellen was trailing Carl Satcher by four points—then he made a serious mistake.

For his latest and final ad, wearing a blue work shirt open at the neck to show a tuft of grizzled, masculine chest hair, he was accompanied by a rainbow of kids, from Nordic blonde to ebony black, all looking up at him with glowing eyes and trustful smiles. "Too many of our kids are falling behind," Satcher declared directly into the camera. "That's why I decided to go to the Senate, to make sure that young folks like these get the education and the chance I did. They deserve it. That's what you pay your taxes for. We need results *now,* not just empty words from a well-meaning bleeding heart."

"What did he just say?"

Ellen froze the on-screen image and whirled to face Derelle, Aguilera, and Spellman, hands on her hips, her mouth hard, eyes flashing fire. "How *dare* he! Who does Carl Satcher think he is? I've spent my *whole life* fighting for kids and their families."

"Hold it!" Derelle snatched up the video camera and trained it on Ellen's face. "Okay, keep it coming!"

And Ellen did, for ten full, angry minutes. Carl Satcher had just made a mockery of her entire life. She didn't know it was possible to be so furious.

"Carl Satcher has a lot to say, but he has *no idea* what he's talking about. Has he spent one minute, or one *second,* more than absolutely necessary in a public school or in public housing? *I have.* Has he tried to comfort a mother whose son was killed in a gang shooting? *I've done that too!"* Ellen roared. "I've worked with desperate parents doing their best to raise their kids, struggling against odds you couldn't believe, too many of them failing because they're human and they're driven beyond human limits. I've worked with teachers, truant officers, police officers, and foster parents. I've worked with thousands of kids."

She strode to her wall of photographs, with outflung hand. "That's Talitha"—pointing to a particularly vivid little face with the hedgehog braids—"She loved to read. She might have had a great life, she had the talent, but she was gunned down in broad daylight on a street corner. This is fourteen-year-old Davey, homeless, sleeping under the freeway at night, chaining himself to the stolen bike he called his only friend, and dealing drugs to exist because that was all he knew."

Ellen turned, and Derelle moved in for a close-up. "That story, at least, has a happy ending!" Ellen said vehemently, oblivious to the camera. "Davey's in college now and working three jobs to stay there, he has a chance—because *I cared,* and made sure others cared too."

She pointed to a serious little face in thick, round glasses. "That's Richard. He was living in a transient hotel room with his terminally ill grandmother, sharing the only bed, missing school to shop and care for her. We found her a hospice, where she died with dignity, and a foster home for Richard, who's doing real well and plans to be an engineer."

Ellen swung to face the camera directly, visibly trembling with rage. "Does Carl Satcher have any idea how these children live? Does he know how *anybody* lives, outside of his own tiny world of supreme privilege? He does not." In a voice of utter scorn, "And then he *dares* to call me a well-meaning bleeding heart! Well, you listen up, Carl Satcher. I'm calling you on that one, and I'm telling you it's *your* words that are empty! And come election day, you'll find a lot of other people think so, too!"

★ ★ ★

"Well!" Derelle cried when Ellen collapsed, panting, in her seat, "I guess we got our spot."

"Quick thinking!" Spellman told Derelle. "That's winning footage! Now we have to cut it to sixty seconds and a thirty-second version."

"Totally goddam awesome," Aguilera said. "Authentic as it gets."

"Best of all," Makins said, "no candidate's ever done that before—nobody's ever sounded off into the camera so spontaneously—and have most of it usable!"

Making it even better was Satcher's face, frozen on the TV screen in the background, his mouth half open.

"This will be our turnaround moment," Spellman predicted. "And not a second too soon."

"You'll win this thing now," Derelle told Ellen. "I can feel it. You've nailed him."

Ellen said fiercely, "I'd better."

This time she didn't think about Josh at all.

★ ★ ★

Election day dawned cool and damp in Northern California.

Ellen had gone to bed knowing that, thanks to her new, judiciously edited TV spot, she'd pulled up almost level with Satcher, and that with one more week she might have drawn ahead. Now, however, she'd done all she could and it was up to the voters. She slept well for the first time in months, and woke feeling calm and rested.

The day began prosaically with an early-morning hair appointment, after which, attended by press, she ceremoniously drove to the polls and punched out her choices, staring in disbelief at her own name.

Early in the afternoon she relocated to the Marriott Hotel in downtown San Francisco, where, from six o'clock, she would hold three parties: a private affair for family, staff, and close friends in her suite; the major donors' party in the select, wood-paneled Club Room; and later, win or lose, the big bash for all the hardworking volunteers in the ballroom downstairs.

In Los Angeles, Carl Satcher would confidently be presiding over parties of his own.

But let him *not* be victorious, Ellen prayed. Let me win!

She felt there was one good omen. The janitors' union was demonstrating outside every hotel in San Francisco, shouting and chanting and banging the wood staves of their picket signs on the sidewalk, but as an unsolicited gift to Ellen they suspended activities outside the Marriott until the following morning.

★ ★ ★

By six o'clock, all her special people were assembled in Ellen's suite. Her parents, with Ruthie and Dwayne and their children; Josh's parents, Hans and Judith; Gloria and her handsome husband, Paul; Shirley Lester; Carole Walker; Sue Polley; Ellen's whole faithful staff; and a contingent of Children's Alliance kids.

The atmosphere was hushed, exit polls coming in from precincts up and down the state, veering this way and that, hard to read, slightly in Satcher's favor. "But don't trust them," Spellman warned, "it's too early. Anything can happen."

He and David Makins had installed a table in front of the largest of the six television sets and sat there with their charts and statistics, watching while the talking heads and pundits prognosticated and the numbers for the various precincts flashed up on the screen. Gloria and Paul sat in front of another set; Aguilera paced restlessly in front of a third. The tension was palpable, and nobody spoke much. "It's awful quiet in here," a young voice complained—Ruthie's daughter—"it's not much of a party if everyone's watching TV!"

Ellen hoped the party would improve and had the waiters push the hors d'oeuvres and drinks.

Her father, white knuckled, was already on his third beer.

A young waiter, circulating with a tray of champagne flutes, was sent trembling back to the bar with a thunderous rebuke by Aguilera: "*Never* serve champagne till the votes are all in—it's seriously bad luck!"

★ ★ ★

By 8:00 P.M. Carl Satcher was ahead in the absentees, winning big-time in the Republican strongholds of Orange and Ventura Counties and in certain precincts in the Central Valley—though in Humboldt County he was losing by a very narrow margin to Ellen. On one screen, a broad-shouldered, bearded man in a plaid shirt, interviewed outside a diner in Eureka, offered one reason why: "Senator Satcher never bothered to come up here and talk with us. Guess folks just don't like being taken for granted."

"*See?*" Aguilera told Ellen. "It's all about respect."

"I'm not sure I can stand this much longer!" Rachel Downey said, snagging a waiter and downing a glass of wine in one gulp.

Ellen's father sat hunched in his seat, hands clasped loosely between his spread knees, his shoulders stiff with tension.

Picking up on the suspense, the children were quiet.

Then, at nine o'clock, the cities, precinct by precinct, began reporting a record turnout of minority voters heavily in favor of Ellen Fischer, and the tide began to turn.

A Hayward family was interviewed leaving the polling station, a stocky, dark-haired man with his young wife, and their baby beautifully outfitted in an embroidered dress and tiny pink shoes. "Maybe the Senator got the jobs," Emilio Chavez shrugged while his wife smiled shyly and the baby kicked in her arms, "and maybe he don't. But he never came around asking what we needed and what he could do for us, not like Miz Fischer did."

"Oh my dear," Judith Fischer said, giving Ellen a tight hug, "Josh would have been so proud."

★   ★   ★

At ten-thirty Ellen rode the elevator down to the Club Room, where she was vociferously greeted by the Democratic office holders and her major donors and supporters. She gave a brief, rallying speech, upbeat and hopeful, then moved about the room welcoming, hugging, and shaking hands. Either her hands no longer hurt or the surging adrenaline kept the pain at bay.

Onstage, flanked by Derelle and Vic Aguilera in front of the huge TV screen, she said, "Thank you from the bottom of my heart for your support. It's still too early to call, and I'm not going to try—but I have to say we're looking good!"

Upstairs again, Ellen found herself two points ahead, with Los Angeles, San Francisco, and Alameda Counties still to report. Los Angeles was a possible win, but San Francisco and Alameda were certainties, and by a wide margin, too.

"When can we break out the bubbly?" Gloria asked.

"Check with my pollster," Ellen said.

"Any minute now," Mike Spellman said.

★   ★   ★

Carl Satcher officially conceded at 11:45 P.M. Ellen took the call upstairs, away from the parties, in her thirty-sixth-floor room overlooking the lights of San Francisco, Berkeley, Oakland, and on south toward the glow of San Jose.

"My pollsters tell me you've won," Satcher said in a tone of faint amusement.

Ellen thought, I suppose it's too much simply to say, Congratulations. "Mine have, too," she agreed.

"A potent force, sympathy!"

"Indeed." Ellen felt the hot fury rise in her throat. She knew the moment called for a temporary truce between honorable adversaries, but Satcher wasn't playing the game. "I appreciate your call, Senator," she said coldly. "Now I must go. Good-bye."

She hung up and stood there a second, feeling a bit sick, leaning hard on the receiver as if to prevent Satcher's vitriol from escaping.

I'm not going to let him ruin this evening for me! she thought.

Ellen walked down the stairs with a smile on her face, her head held high. She paused three steps from the bottom.

"Well," she announced, "the opposition says we won!"

★ ★ ★

Pounding music was playing, Aretha Franklin demanding a little respect:

"R - E - S - P - E - C - T!"

As the music faded, Ellen moved center stage in the enormous ballroom, beneath a hugely blown-up image of her own face.

"Ladies and Gentlemen, and all of my friends in California," she cried, her voice hoarse but still strong, "I just received a call from Senator Carl Satcher. It's now official. *We did it!*"—to have her words drowned out in the cheers and chants of "EL-*LEN!* EL-*LEN!* EL-*LEN!* EL-*LEN!*"

My God, she thought. Oh my God.

She'd had no real idea of what it could be like and how it could feel. How could she? I'd never give up this moment, Ellen thought, never in a million years.

After a solid minute of joyful uproar, she held up her hands.

"Thank you, thank you, all of you! *Thank you!*" She beamed an endless smile. "We finished a campaign that was started by a great man who brought his talent and his energy and his love of California to the people. I was proud and honored to pick up that banner and run with it as hard as I could, to bring those walls down, for our children, for our families, for our workers, for our environment, for our *world*.

"I'll never forget how hard you all worked in this race, and I'll do everything in my power as your United States Senator to honor the faith and the trust you've placed in me today.

"Each time I walk onto the Senate floor you'll be at my side. Thank you for giving my life meaning, and for giving me this chance to fight for you!

"And now, let's get it on! Let's all celebrate together!"

At Ellen's signal, amid roars of delight, thousands of blue and white balloons were released from their net under the high ceiling and came drifting downward. Ellen listened to the cheers and the laughter, and watched her people wade waist deep in balloons, toss them about, and whack each other over the head with them while the balloons bounced and flew and burst, rat-a-tat.

"Guess it doesn't get much better than this, Senator," Derelle said at her side.

Ellen shook her head. "No," she replied very seriously. "It very truly doesn't."

★

2001

★

CHAPTER TWENTY-THREE

May 22

TUESDAY

6:00 A.M.

Greg woke in a strange bed. Of course he had expected to find himself in a strange bed, he had checked into a hotel. This, however, was not a hotel room—and yet it was familiar. Of course! He was in Tiburon, in Micaela's condo. He recognized the pale carpeting, the neutral walls and drapes, and there above the bed, as he cautiously raised his aching head, was that Central American market scene with its colorful piles of fruit, the striped awnings, the blue-purple sky. He could smell her perfume too, faint but distinctive, and stirring.

Greg smiled sleepily. He reached out for Micaela, all warm and drowsy and tousled beside him—but not only was she not there, it looked like she hadn't been there for a while. Her side of the bed was cool. And then Greg's mind cleared with a rush and he remembered.

He was not in Tiburon but in Micaela's apartment at the Watergate in D.C. He recalled tossing an empty bottle of wine in the trash and then convincing Micaela to open a bottle of expensive tequila, a gift she'd been saving, the only liquor she had in her apartment. It had never been his drink of choice, and right now his pounding head reminded him why. He also had a hazy recollection of becoming quite garrulous at some part of the evening, but no matter, Micaela had been drinking too. In any event, he could count on her discretion.

How good it was to be together again, with no complications, the way he had always wanted.

Now, she was probably off buying croissants for breakfast, for which there'd be no honey or jam. There was never anything in her refrigerator. He smiled indulgently; she'd be back soon, he'd pretend to be still asleep so she could pretend to kiss him awake. Perhaps she'd return to bed; it had happened before. Greg closed his eyes again and dozed. It was still very early.

He woke again at seven but Micaela still had not returned. Perhaps she'd gone for a run before the deli.

He climbed out of bed and took a long, hot shower; the apartment had one of those dishpan showerheads, and the water tumbled onto him in an obliterating waterfall. He switched it to cold and gasped through a full frigid minute.

He emerged, panting and refreshed, glanced regretfully at the tumbled bed in which now, clearly, there would be no reprise of last night, and dressed in yesterday's clothes. Micaela should be back any minute. She'd boil water for instant coffee, they'd eat, their hands would touch, they'd make plans for later, then he'd return to the hotel to change and get on with his day, which he expected to be satisfactory on one level, but gut-wrenching and generally pretty distressing on another.

Greg knew he'd need Micaela tonight, her understanding, her warmth in bed, and her reassurance that yes, he'd done the right thing, that he really had no choice, did he.

No choice at all.

★ ★ ★

On his way to the front door of the apartment to see whether the *Washington Post* was waiting on the mat outside, Greg found a note on the coffee table.

"I won't be back. Mrs. Saavedra comes at 9:00. Best if you were gone by then."

Nothing about what a wonderful evening, and how she couldn't wait to see him again. And certainly no croissant and fresh coffee in his immediate future, only a visit from Mrs. Saavedra, whoever she might be—someone Greg had no particular wish to meet either.

So he departed as instructed, leaving a note of his own, equally cryptic, on a yellow Post-It that he stuck to the center of her computer screen:

"M. C.: Very good to see you again. As the Terminator promised, I'LL BE BAAAACK! G."

★ ★ ★

Greg stepped into the lobby, briefcase in hand, hungrier than ever and fastidiously aware of yesterday's shirt, socks, and underwear slightly clammy against his skin. God, he hated being dirty. It reminded him of his college days, those nights he'd stayed over at a girl's place and then got back into the same clothes the next morning. Now, however, his wardrobe had improved exponentially, and he knew that no casual passerby was likely to notice his slightly crumpled shirt collar and glance at him askance; they'd only see a successful D.C. businessman in a fine suit, on his way to the first meeting of the day.

Steel and glass doors parted for him with a whoosh of air, and he stepped out into the bright morning, which smelled of spring blossoms.

The doorman told him to have a good day.

Greg thanked him and wished him the same, knowing that, for himself, it would not be a good day. There might be the satisfaction of a job well done, but he might also lose Ellen forever. He imagined himself seated beneath one of the historic vice-presidential marble busts in the Senate spectator gallery, gazing down upon those concentric circles of polished mahogany desks where Ellen Fischer, freshman Senator from California, would be seated on the far edge of the Democrat's side, second row from the back, wearing one of her brightly colored jackets. Then Ellen would be standing at the microphone, holding aloft that incriminating envelope, facing the Vice-President and Frida Hernandez and the banks of TV cameras: "It has come to my attention that...."

Greg would need to be very careful and come up with a really convincing explanation for his part in all this.

But he was good at being convincing. He'd tell Ellen he didn't know the documents were false, that he was just the messenger—and she'd believe him. They had both been deceived, he would explain. She might even turn to him, one of her oldest friends, in her moment of crisis.

Greg smiled in anticipation, ever the optimist, his cup always half full. Perhaps, after all, the day would end well.

8:00 A.M.

Normally Ellen enjoyed her early mornings. The apartment on B Street N.E. that she leased from her friend Senator Patricia Shaw of Arizona, although a basement space, stretched from the front to the back of the house with a sunken brick terrace off the bedroom facing the sunrise. At this time of year the terrace was bathed with light, and Ellen would often take her coffee outside and drink it while tending her plants—if she didn't walk down the block for breakfast at Jimmy T's café. This was a residential neighborhood, quiet with not much traffic, and sitting in her little yard, she could almost believe she was in the country. The location was convenient too, just six blocks from the Hart Senate Building, and frequently she would walk to work, especially on a pretty morning like this. She seldom needed her Ford Escort, which shared garage space beside the house with Patricia's Camry. When moving about the city during the day, she'd invariably be driven by a staff member; returning home late and after dark, she'd be escorted by a member of the Capitol police—though this was about as safe a neighborhood as you could get, always plenty of cops around, patrolling the streets or parked watchfully on street corners. The Attorney General of the United States himself lived in a modest, blue-painted house three blocks away.

Today, however, Ellen didn't welcome the morning.

She sat in her yellow terry bathrobe on the edge of the bed, unrefreshed from her shower, staring through the French doors at the early sunlight falling on tubs of red and pink impatiens and hanging baskets of fuchsias—the ballerina type of fuchsia, her favorite with its wide white skirts spread over a bell of purple petals—but unaware of the sunshine and the flowers; aware of nothing but uneasiness and doubt.

It made no sense really, this uneasiness.

She should be brimming with confidence. Last night Greg had given her the ammunition, which screamed from those damning documents from the Bayshore Medical Clinic and Emerson Middle School, with which to demolish her opponent.

Frida Hernandez, just one step away from achieving one of the highest legal positions in the land, was an abuser of children—and she, Ellen, could prove it.

All she needed to do was stand up there and declare *child abuser*—just two words—and Hernandez would be history. Then, hopefully, that empty seat on the Supreme Court would go to someone more worthy. Carmela Ochoa, for instance, was waiting in the wings, a talented Latina lower-court judge; she was a Republican, true, but with a far more centrist record. She would be fine.

Better yet, the attention generated by Ellen's whistle-blowing, and its appalling cause, must surely carry her own Child Protection and Enforcement Act through on pure momentum.

So why, wondered Ellen, aren't I rejoicing? What's wrong with this picture?

If only I had more time, she thought.

But time was passing relentlessly, minute by minute, and still she'd come to no decision, even though she'd fretted all through the past sleepless night, alternately favoring Vicente Aguilera's advice to take Greg's gift and run with it, then recalling how passionately Derelle had urged the opposite course.

"She's not a child abuser," Derelle had said. "I've been there, only a lot worse things happened to me...." Derelle cautioned not to do anything that might jeopardize the legislation. "Don't make waves," she had begged. "Don't do anything to risk it not passing."

Vic had countered that with Hernandez discredited—*shamed*—the bill on protecting children would pass in a flash.

There was still that third option, of course, which Ellen had almost taken last night: to pass the dilemma on to the chairman of the Judiciary Committee.

She still had time to call Senator Leary.

So why didn't she?

She stared distractedly into her closet, at her row of neat suits, dark pairs of slacks, and bright jackets. She needed a plan, a course of action, before she could become energized. Her clothes—all the red jackets in the world—offered no inspiration at all.

When the phone rang, she didn't want to answer it—but it was her personal, private number known only to her staff and close friends.

"I sure hate to bother you at home, Senator"—Diane from the office, who was usually first to work, watering plants, collecting and distributing mail, brewing coffee, and humming as she worked—"but this woman's been trying to reach you. She's left five messages already and she just called again. She wants to talk with you right away. She says it's about the Hernandez confirmation. I have her cell number."

"Does she have a name?"

"Micaela Calder."

Ellen almost dropped the phone. She knew Micaela Calder, Satcher worker bee, had helped Greg track down Bianca Rivas. A cold, hard fist closed inside Ellen's stomach—it would not unclench even as she reasoned that, if she'd forgiven Greg for his role, however unintentional, in precipitating Josh's death, she should likewise forgive Micaela, who'd just been doing her job.

★　★　★

Micaela's voice sounded tired and tense, exactly as Ellen felt herself. "We need to talk. It can't wait. Can we meet somewhere right now? I don't want to talk on the phone."

What was going on here? Ellen reminded herself that Micaela and Greg were rumored to be lovers, very likely true. Micaela was beautiful, and Ellen knew Greg well enough to know he would never let a beautiful woman who worked for him get away. The last couple of years, however, Micaela seemed to have dropped out of sight. Did they still work together? Were they still lovers? Friends? Enemies?

"I'm not sure it's a good idea," Ellen said.

"Please. It's important. It's about Professor Hernandez and today's vote."

"Look," Ellen said, "forgive me if I'm dubious."

"I know, but believe me, this is not business as usual. If I put it in context, it would be like Deep Throat in reverse."

Ellen sat there nonplussed, staring at the phone, recalling those nights so long ago watching the Watergate scandal unfold and the arguments over the identity of the secret informant to the reporters, code-named Deep Throat. "I'm not sure where you're going with this," she said at last.

"Please," Micaela said. "Trust me."

Ellen reluctantly said, "I'll meet you at Jimmy T's in ten minutes. You know where it is? If you're there first, take a booth in back."

What was she getting into here? But Jimmy T's would be safe, neutral ground.

Ellen dressed, fast, no time to fuss about clothes now. She pulled on workaday charcoal slacks and a matching short-sleeve knit top, scanned her row of jackets, decided what the hell, today was a raging red day, and chose the scarlet one. She slipped into a comfortable pair of low-slung black shoes, thought, Hell no, the woman's tall, and changed to high-heeled boots, giving her at least three more inches. She usually didn't much favor cosmetics, but this morning she carefully made up her face to cover those dark sleepless circles around her eyes. She might feel like hell, even spacey with exhaustion, but she wasn't going to show such a face to Micaela, or the rest of the world. To be doubly sure, she slid on a pair of oversize sunglasses.

8:45 A.M.

Jimmy T's was a handy corner coffee and meeting spot across from the Capitol Hill grocery store, a kind of club for the locals. The breakfast rush was over, most of the regulars having already hustled through their scrambled eggs, pancakes, and newspapers, and departed for their various government offices.

Micaela Calder sat alone in a rear booth wearing dark glasses, jeans, and a pale blue tank top. A black leather fanny pack was slung over the back of her chair. A plate with three croissants was on the table. She nursed a mug of coffee in her long-fingered hands, hunching over it as if she was cold. "I got these," Micaela said of the croissants. "I didn't know if you'd had breakfast."

"Thanks. I did, actually." Ellen slid into the seat opposite her. The waiter, knowing Ellen well, brought a fresh pot of steaming coffee and placed it on the table beside her.

Ellen poured for herself, topped up Micaela's mug, and came directly to the point. "So you want to talk with me about the Hernandez confirmation, in a reverse Deep Throat capacity. What does that mean? You're a journalist."

"I'm not a journalist anymore; I didn't like the ethics. It seemed best to start over. Now I'm working for these people." Micaela extracted a card from her fanny pack and pushed it across the table. "It's a think tank. It's not political."

Ellen studied the card, The Future Mobility Institute, green on white, triangular logo showing a highway diminishing to infinity, an address in Chevy Chase, Maryland, *Micaela Calder, Associate,* reflecting that anybody could have a card printed saying anything at all.

She left it lying on the table. "So, tell me."

"I saw Greg last night. He'd got hold of my unlisted number and called out of the blue. He wanted to see me. He came right over, and of course I let him in. Even though I promised myself I'd never see him again."

Ellen nodded, unsurprised. She had done more or less the same thing when she let Greg into her office.

Micaela pulled the tail off a piece of pastry, turned it in her fingers, and set it down again. Her hands were restless, her speech abrupt and nervous as she went on. "I hadn't seen him in years. He dumped me, you know, right after your husband died. He made all kinds of excuses, how Jane's father had found out about us and made him choose: either to stay with me and not only lose his family but also see his whole career go down the tubes, or leave me and keep his secure, comfortable life." Bitterly, she added, "He pretended to be so regretful, so sad about it all, but I could tell he was actually relieved. You see, I'd told him I wanted to have a baby, a normal life, with the two of us together, not just to exist at his convenience. I wanted more than just to be his utility lady.

"So he walked away—or rather, had me sent away clear across the country—and I was angry and hurt, feeling all the wretched things people do feel at those times. Then last night, more than two years later, there he was on the doorstep, still so incredibly good-looking, warm, and loving as he can be, just as if nothing ever happened between us, telling me I'm the only person he can talk to, that he needed me, making me feel like I was the only person on earth for him."

Ellen regarded Micaela with dislike. She had said nothing about Josh, such as how sorry she was he'd died, that she felt responsible. This diatribe of Micaela's, of abandonment and personal woe, was way more than Ellen either wanted or needed to know—and what did it have to do with Professor Hernandez? She said, "You don't have to tell me any of this; it's really none of my business."

Micaela tore off another piece of croissant, regarded it, and put it down too. "I do, though. It's all part of it."

"Part of what?"

"You'll see. I'm getting to it. Please, just listen for now."

"All right, then." Ellen prompted, "Go on."

"Last night was like old times. I was thinking, surely I can persuade him he's enough of his own man now, with good enough credentials, not to need Carl Satcher and Gunther Hecht, so he can finally leave Jane and come to me. He's a terrific writer; he could work for anybody. The *Times,* the *Post*—"

Ellen half murmured, "We all expected so much from Greg."

"—and I could work from home," Micaela continued, "so we wouldn't need a nanny for the baby. I was getting carried away in my thinking a bit, but that's what Greg does to you. But last night, under all that surface charm, I could tell he was worried, and even depressed, which is unusual as you probably know— you've known him a long time."

Ellen didn't respond.

"Then he said something like, if he'd had the guts to do the right thing back then—with Josh—I'm *sorry,* Ellen. I felt so terrible about my own part in what happened—"

At least she finally had the grace to admit it, thought Ellen.

"—but believe me I had no idea what lengths Greg would go to. Last night he said that sometimes you have no choice but to betray the people you love. He actually used the word *love.* He'd never told me he loved me before, you know that? Not once. And like a happy, stupid fool, at first I thought he was talking about me."

"But he wasn't?"

"Of course not," Micaela stared down at her hands. "It was *you.* All the time it was about you. And I lay there beside him and realized he'd never love me. That he'd just go on using me, show- ing up at my door whenever he's feeling upset, lonely, guilty, or whatever, knowing I'll make him feel better, and the next morn- ing he'd wake up feeling on top of the world, expect me to run out to the deli and fix breakfast, kiss him good-bye, and be there for him next time he felt like venting. Last night I finally realized I was wasting my time, that I had to forget him and just move on."

Ellen nodded, sympathetic despite herself. "But what does this have to do with Professor Hernandez?"

She watched Micaela refocus on the matter at hand. "Hernandez—I'm getting there. See, Greg and I had a lot to drink last night. And Greg told me he'd given you some docu- ments about Frida Hernandez. Records from a clinic, and from a school, too, with evidence she'd abused her daughter back in the seventies."

Ellen had relaxed her guard a little; now it slammed right back into place. "Stop right there. We're not getting into anything like that."

As if Ellen hadn't spoken, Micaela went on, "Hernandez's confirmation's today, isn't it?"

"That's no secret. But—"

"And a piece of information like that would be red-hot, right? It would kill the nomination dead."

"If such proof existed, I imagine it would."

"And finish her career."

"That too."

Micaela looked Ellen in the eye and demanded, "So what're you going to do?"

Ellen could imagine few things more inappropriate or ill-advised than this meeting and wondered for the first time, cursing herself for not thinking of it before, with a glance at that black fanny pack, whether Micaela was carrying some recording device or even wearing a wire. This could be some kind of entrapment, typical of Satcher, even though she couldn't yet imagine what form it would take. She rose to leave. "That's enough. We're not going on with this conversation."

Micaela reached out as if to grab Ellen's sleeve. "Please, give me one more minute," she pleaded. And, noting Ellen's glance at the fanny pack and correctly interpreting it, she said, "This is just between you and me. I swear to you."

Ellen gingerly sat on the edge of her seat, poised for flight.

"It's common knowledge," said Micaela, "that you don't want Frida Hernandez on the Supreme Court and have done your best to block her appointment. And now you seem to have been given the perfect weapon to eliminate her. Don't bother to deny it, Ellen. I *know* you have those documents. But you can't use them."

Ellen took a large swallow of coffee, cooling by now and bitter tasting, and thrust her mug away. "You said, *seem* to have been given. What does that mean?"

"That those documents Greg gave you are phony. That you're being set up."

Ellen regarded Micaela through narrowed eyes. "What makes you think so?"

"Because Greg told me."

"And you believe him?"

"Of course I believe him. Why should he lie about something like that to *me*?"

"But why would he tell you in the first place?"

"Like I said, he needed to talk. He wanted to confess. He'd stabbed you in the back just about as deep as he could go. You see, it was all a put-up job between him and Satcher and Hernandez; you'd make this wild accusation, it would turn out to be false, and it would be *your* career and credibility down the tubes, not hers."

"Ah." So who was lying now? Ellen gazed deep into Micaela's eyes. She'd learned to read faces from the early days of the Children's Alliance, and it had stood her in good stead forever afterward. All her working life, it seemed, people had wanted something from her or wished to conceal something from her. She'd been lied to by the best, been scammed and conned, inevitably made mistakes and misjudgments, but through it all, over the years, she'd learned to know the truth when she heard it.

By now she could read people very well—with the exception, apparently, of Greg.

"Senator," Micaela was saying, "he'd even betray *you* and he loves you. No wonder he felt guilty. Which is when I realized there's *nobody* that man wouldn't betray. And I remembered that time when Greg went after Josh—his best friend—so desperate to find dirt he even made up a terrible story about him having the baby with that woman—"

Ellen felt the world tilt and seem, for a second, to stop completely, without sound or sight. Then Micaela's face swam back into focus, and the café clattered on around her once more. "Baby?" she said. "Whose baby?"

"Josh's—I mean, the child he was supposed to have had with his client's wife, and—"

"I can't stand this."

"Listen," Micaela's voice was frantic now, high-pitched and urgent. "It was all a lie, Ellen, I swear it; just one more lie. That woman did have a child, Greg met her—*please* don't look at me like that—but there was no way she could have been Josh's. She was way too young."

Ellen said at last, "Greg told me about the woman Josh had been seeing, but he never said anything about a baby."

"He'd have thought he didn't have to. But he told Josh. He told him the night that Josh—"

"You mean he actually allowed Josh to think he had a child? I don't believe it."

"That's why I got away from it all, away from him. That wasn't the way I wanted my life to be, groveling in the mud to bring down a good man."

Ellen said bluntly, "But you were part of it. You helped Greg."

"Dammit, yes, I did. I'd have done anything for Greg, back then. I made myself forget about ethics and truth. Frankly, I always thought that woman Bianca Rivas was lying through her teeth. All she wanted was money. Lots of money." Micaela began savagely to pull flaky pieces of pastry apart, roll them into balls, and crush them between her fingers.

"But I never knew the part about the baby," Micaela continued, "that Greg had made up that story. I only found out last night. I swear to God. And I swear that Greg Hunter is out of my life for good this time. I should never have opened my door. I was too goddam weak. But I'm not weak anymore. It's not too late to stop more harm based on lies. It's not too late for me to do something right. And to make things up to you, so far as I can." Micaela raised her eyes again to stare directly at Ellen.

Ellen drew a long, deep breath. If Micaela was lying, she was the greatest actor in the world. "I believe you. I'm glad you opened your door that last time." Impulsively, she reached for Micaela's hands and pressed them between her own. "I thank you more than I can say for coming to me; it can't have been easy."

"Oh, it wasn't so hard in the end. This was the final straw, you see—once I realized that, I knew what I had to do. I had to grow up." Micaela gave a wan smile and rose. She had eaten nothing of the pastry she'd demolished and hadn't touched her coffee since Ellen sat down. "I'd better be going; I'm late for work and I need to go back home to change. I just ran out of there—didn't want to wake Greg. I didn't want to talk with him again."

"Will he be gone by now?"

"He better be." Micaela offered her business card once more to Ellen. "Please take it. You can always reach me there if you need me. Or you can call my cell number."

Ellen nodded and pocketed it. "Maybe we'll talk again, when all this is over."

"I'd like that. And I'm glad I got to you in time." Micaela stood up, a sad woman who had turned a major page in her life. "I'll be thinking of you this afternoon. Good luck."

"Good luck to you, too," Ellen said, and meant it.

★   ★   ★

Ellen was running late. She drove herself to the Hart Building and was waved through the checkpoint, smiling mechanically at those nice Capitol policemen—*Morning, Senator, beautiful day, Senator*; both of them so cheerful—and parked in the underground garage.

Her office was full of people, everyone in movement. She was followed to her door by Vic Aguilera, Derelle, and David, her communications director, all clamoring around her—*We have to sit down, need to talk, you must decide, flooded with calls, best time for a press avail—*

"Let me have ten minutes," Ellen said. "Alone." She firmly closed the door on them.

Then she paced the big room, pausing in front of the tall window facing Constitution Avenue to gaze once more at the Supreme Court building. She thought about Hernandez as one of the nine justices working inside there, perhaps for the next twenty years, maybe longer.

During the past twenty-four hours, Frida Hernandez had assumed three distinct faces. The first Frida was an upstanding professor of law, highly credentialed, highly principled, and undoubtedly qualified, regardless of her personal agenda, to be a member of the Supreme Court.

The second Frida, vicious and sadistic, had abused her only child. She was a criminal. She should have been incarcerated. Heaven only knew what other acts of cruelty she had gotten away with—and what she might be capable of once in a position of such power.

But if Ellen was to believe Micaela, as instinct told her she must, the third Frida had not abused her child, but instead had plotted with Carl Satcher and his minions to throw a spitball, as Shirley Lester would say, not merely into Ellen's life but into the confirmation process and the future of the country. Which in itself was an act of calumny beyond reckoning.

Just as well that she had not reached Senator Leary.

Just as well she hadn't left a message.

And now, yet again, Ellen wondered exactly *why* she had not left a message with Senator Leary last night. In order to protect her source? To protect Greg Hunter? Surely not.

She clasped her hands behind her back and turned to gaze at the poster-size picture of Josh.

And it worked like magic. Almost at once her mind cleared and her course seemed so obvious. It was really quite simple.

Ellen hadn't left a message for Desmond Leary because, deep down, she'd known all the time what she should do. There was only one way to go.

She must meet with Frida Hernandez privately, show her Greg's documents, and give her the chance to explain.

And Hernandez had a lot of explaining to do.

10:45 A.M.

An hour later Ellen left her office transformed, her scarlet blazer replaced by the long, loose-fitting black jacket she kept hanging in her office bathroom, her boots exchanged for rubber-soled loafers, her hair tightly bound behind her head.

She walked down the lobby, looking neither right nor left, attracting no attention, her footsteps soft and quick, and crossed the atrium with its monumental Alexander Calder sculpture, black and jagged and over fifty feet high. The artist was presumably unrelated to Micaela Calder, but it was a strange coincidence on an already strange day. Then she took the elevator down to the little subway train that hummed gently back and forth on its magnetic track between the Senate office buildings and the Capitol.

The train was not crowded; Ellen had the small open compartment to herself. It was a pleasant ride, clean and well lit and, unlike a regular subway, unadorned by advertisements and unmarred by graffiti. Its only decoration was a line of state flags along the track in order of admission to the Union, and Ellen's eyes would customarily seek out the California grizzly bear, right there in the middle, and the New York flag, dark blue, with its emblem of justice and liberty.

Justice and liberty—I'm doing my best, she told Josh. I swear I'm doing my best.

Frida Hernandez was waiting, as arranged, in the Capitol crypt, its many pillars supporting the gigantic dome high above the underground circular space. Gazing at those pillars, Ellen imagined the weight of the thousands of tons of stone immediately above her head and felt her shoulders sag. The professor didn't appear to be burdened, however, she stood ramrod straight among the milling tourists, feet angled like a dancer directly upon the compass stone marking the geographical center of Washington, D.C.: left foot in the NW quadrant; right foot pointing NE.

She acknowledged Ellen with a frosty half-smile. "I almost didn't recognize you. I've never seen you wear black."

"Nor have many other people, so with a bit of luck I'm invisible," Ellen said, thinking how, hopefully, they'd excite no curiosity, just two women walking decorously through the halls.

"This had better not take long," Hernandez said sharply.

"I hope it won't, too," Ellen said, "but it will take as long as it has to."

Hernandez threw her a quizzical glance. She was wearing a stylish suit of black and white houndstooth check, which Ellen knew, with a twinge of satisfaction, would produce a seasick shimmer later this afternoon on television. One of Satcher's publicity people, or Carl Satcher himself, always impossibly telegenic, all geniality and teeth and perfectly made up, should have advised her what to wear. But Satcher would neither notice nor care how Hernandez looked or dressed. He wouldn't see her as a person at all, merely as a vote on the Court. *His* vote.

Hernandez, matching her longer stride to Ellen's, asked, "Where are we going?"

"My hideaway."

Most Senators were assigned a private room of their own in which they could conduct a meeting one-on-one or hold a small conference in conditions of strictest privacy. The more senior the Senator, the finer the room. Ellen, so junior, rated a small plain room, with no windows, in the back of beyond.

"It's a long way," Hernandez said as they walked.

"Everything's a long way," Ellen said. She was still struck, not just by the weight but by the sheer *sprawl* of the Capitol, and its extraordinary diversity. The historic sections with their lofty ceilings and arching pillars, gorgeous tilework, chandeliers, murals, and huge oil paintings would give way in an instant to mundane gray passages and unadorned walls only to return, unexpectedly, to historic grandeur and chattering tour groups.

Ellen hadn't used her hideaway for several months, and while mentally rehearsing her dialogue with Hernandez, she was also hoping she wouldn't get them both lost. Once she had taken a wrong turn and had emerged unexpectedly into a long corridor lined with desks where men and women were working. She'd had no idea who they were or upon which department she'd inadvertently stumbled, and had hastily withdrawn.

But so far they seemed to be on track.

They passed the old and seldom used Senate library, a musty, poorly lit repository of dim shelving and outdated books consulted only when necessary for reference to times long past. They moved along old twisting corridors, past endless closed doors, turning left, right, and left again, Hernandez often seeming to be on the verge of speech but invariably changing her mind, Ellen growing slightly anxious again, surely they should be there by now, but there was nobody to ask for directions, and even if someone did come hastening down the hallway, they wouldn't know where the hideaway was anyway. That was the whole point.

But here, at last, was that unassuming brown door obscurely set in an angle beside a spiral staircase that curved down and down toward the bowels of the earth. Ellen opened the door onto another hallway, small and narrow, with three more doors left, right, and center. Her hideaway was on the right. She ushered her unwilling companion through the door into darkness.

Ellen switched on the light. The room was furnished with a rectangular conference table and six plain wooden chairs, a wall-mounted television set, two banks of phones, an old oak desk with a black leather swivel chair, and a small refrigerator containing, if she remembered correctly, bottles of spring water and a couple of glasses.

"Please sit down, Professor." Ellen pulled her swivel chair from the knee hole of the desk, and adjusted it to its maximum height so they'd sit eye to eye. She paused to study Frida Hernandez directly for the first time, seeing a pleasant, even good-looking face, intelligent dark eyes beneath sweeping black brows, a high-bridged nose, and wide mouth.

Certainly it wasn't the face of a woman who would savage her only child—although, Ellen thought with resignation and years of experience, was there ever such a face?

She said formally, "Thank you again for seeing me at such a time."

Hernandez glanced pointedly at her watch again. "You said it was urgent."

"Extremely." Ellen opened her briefcase, removed the manila envelope, and laid it on the table between them.

Hernandez's gaze flicked from the envelope to Ellen's face, but she said nothing.

It was very quiet.

Ellen broke the silence. "A couple of hours from now, Professor, you are expected to be confirmed as an associate justice of the United States Supreme Court, barring a filibuster, which appears to be unlikely. However, some information was provided to me yesterday evening that has direct bearing on these proceedings. I have been wondering what I should do. I have not, so far, disclosed this information to the Judiciary Committee, the Senate leadership, or to anyone in the executive branch. I decided the right and fair thing to do, what I hope someone would do for me, was to give you a chance to explain."

Frida Hernandez stared down at the envelope, which she made no move to touch.

"Please open it," Ellen said. She leaned back in her chair and watched the woman opposite her take out those damning reports, glance at them—quite clearly she'd seen them before—and quickly lay them down again. Ellen asked, her voice gentle, "Do you recognize that material?"

Hernandez looked up, acknowledgment in her eyes, but she didn't speak.

"I see you do. Incidentally, the point of meeting in my hideaway, just to reassure you, is that we can speak candidly, personally, and off the record, with no staff around, and no interruptions. No cameras outside this room. Anything said here can stay here."

When Hernandez still remained silent, Ellen continued, in tones of quiet confidentiality, one woman to another. "I was never able to have a child, Professor. I would have loved a child more than anything in this world; I would have given up anything—but it was no use. Instead, I've spent my life trying to protect other people's children, as many as I possibly can. Children are precious, they are our immortality as a species. I've never had firsthand experience of being a parent, but I know that a child can be both a joy and, at times, an enormous burden. I'm aware that under certain extreme circumstances the most loving people are capable of monstrous behavior. I've seen it happen, and I've worked with the traumatized children of abusive parents; children who, sadly, are more than likely to grow up abusive in turn. It's a tragically predictable cycle."

Then Ellen leaned forward, hands flat on the table, and looked directly into Frida Hernandez's eyes. In a voice like a whiplash, *"Tell me, Professor—are you a child abuser, like those records say you are?"*

Ellen heard the hissed intake of breath and watched those strong hands clutch at the table edge.

After a long moment of echoing silence, Ellen said, "I didn't think so. I've never believed you hurt your young daughter. You treasured and nurtured her, didn't you? Those so-called records are lies. You know why I never truly believed the evidence of my own eyes? Because one of my most trusted aides taught me how to read the face of an abuser. And I trusted my instinct because she taught me well—out of deep, painful experience.

"However, I was supposed to believe what I read in these documents, and knowing my feelings on this particular issue, it was a pretty sure bet that I'd go over the top with rage, rush into action, and directly and immediately reveal the information on the floor of the Senate to oppose your nomination." Ellen paused, watching Hernandez give the slightest nod of confirmation. "I was supposed to believe this evil, to forget the idea of a filibuster—which would have stopped you—and instead to blow the whistle on you."

Ellen went on, "Later, of course, when my challenge was found to be without cause and the documents forgeries, I would be perceived as a raucous and possibly unstable mudslinger. I'd be discredited, and my liberal colleagues' own issues would be tainted by their association with me. And you, Professor, would be a hero— a Supreme Court Justice, after garnering God knows how many votes. Now, Professor Hernandez, *please*"—Ellen was half tempted to place her own hands over those clenched, white-knuckled ones, just as with Micaela, mentally cursing Carl Satcher and his darkly insidious aura of corruption—"*talk* to me. You see, I never really believed you did those things." She swiveled her chair toward the refrigerator—the room was small enough so she didn't need to rise—found the water and glasses, and poured for them both.

Frida Hernandez's hand closed over the glass and shook slightly as she carried it to her lips. She drank deeply, patted her mouth with a tissue from her pocket, nodded, and spoke for the first time. "Of course you're right."

Ellen prompted, "It was a setup."

Hernandez nodded in agreement.

"How was it done?" Ellen asked.

"The original documents are authentic school and hospital records." Hernandez's eyes now carried a nostalgic gleam, and a note of pride crept unmistakably into her voice. "Flora was an adventurous child, you see; very physical—she could climb trees like a monkey. We had a tree house in the yard and the neighbor kids would come over. One time they were up there playing a bit too rough, and Flora fell and hit her head. I took her to the emergency room; she had a mild concussion and some bruising. She was okay soon after. And another time, it was quite true, her fingers got caught in the car door one afternoon during carpool. Poor Flora. That other mother said she was very brave—didn't cry or anything."

"And the burns?"

"Those weren't burns; they were poison oak blisters. She'd been on a field trip—I remember it well, would have liked to be one of the parents driving but I never did have time, one of the things I deeply regretted. They went to the Audubon Canyon Ranch at Stinson Beach to see the birds nesting. Some of the kids did some exploring on their own. You don't notice poison oak in the spring because it hasn't turned red yet. Flora had a bad reaction, but she didn't tell me because they weren't supposed to go down that particular trail. I didn't know anything about it until they called me from school. I was ashamed; of course I should have noticed—but I was always so busy. She needed cortisone treatments. It took forever to clear up."

"I understand. So the documents themselves were legitimate, but the contents were tampered with. So easy just to add 'Suspected child abuse; notify authorities.'"

"It seems to have been quite easy."

Ellen paused for thought. She went on, "You know, polit-
ically, you and I stand on different sides of almost every issue
and we always will. But we can respect each other's points of
view, or the right of anyone to a different point of view, and
the freedom to express it. That's the nature of democracy."
Then her voice hardened. "Some of us, however, have no such
respect, merely contempt. They'll do or say whatever it takes
to push their particular agenda. One of those people is your
friend Carl Satcher. Former Senator Satcher is not concerned
with the rights of the people; he's motivated purely by personal
greed. He's a man who can never, *ever* have enough—of
anything. He perceived my husband, Josh Fischer, as someone
who'd stand in his way. Josh had already done that once, you
know, with Satcher's EastPac Development scheme—and Satcher
was determined to ruin him. When I beat Satcher—and what
a shocking surprise *that* must have been—he came up with this
scheme to get rid of me forever. No surprises there—lying,
cheating, and destroying come naturally to him. But Professor
Hernandez—can you explain to me *how he persuaded you to go
along with it?*"

Hernandez drank more water. Her hand was no longer shaking, and she appeared resigned. "I never knew the details or
exactly what they were going to do. I just gave them the records
they asked for. They told me it was for the greater good, and that
basically the ends justified the means. You understand," she went
on wearily, "that my views on abortion, gun control, and environmental regulation might have been considered too far right, even
by some moderate Republicans. And if, as expected, you led the
charge against me—especially if you had launched a filibuster—I
was done for."

"I see."

"They said it was how the game was played."

"I can imagine them saying that," Ellen said drily.

"They persuaded me how, as a Supreme Court justice, I
could be a voice for the sanctity of life, for the family, for the
future of humanity."

"And at the same time you'd be a tool to be used by Carl Satcher, in his pocket, owing him everything, for as long as you sat on the bench."

"I didn't think of it that way."

"I'll give you the credit and believe you."

"And I have to tell you there was another factor." Frida Hernandez's fine dark eyes sought Ellen's, for the first time with total frankness. "I can't expect someone like you to understand, but it has to do with being a first-generation American, raised in a poor neighborhood by parents who can barely speak English. Even though you've pulled yourself up by your bootstraps to a position of great respect, you're a lawyer and a professor at a most prestigious university and people look at you like you're really something—sometimes you can't quite believe it. You're sure they're pretending, that what they're really seeing is an imposter, just a puzzled little peasant one generation away from a dirt floor and chickens scratching on the step."

Ellen waited for her to continue.

"Not Carl Satcher, though; never him. He always treated me like I belonged. He welcomed me, courted me, and, I have to admit, God help me, he flattered me. He can be a very charming man, you know."

Ellen thought of that cruel voice in her ear: *You know you only got elected because that son of a bitch husband of yours died at just the right time.* "I'm sure he can be—when it's to his advantage."

"And with me, very clearly, it *was* to his advantage. So there you have it," said Frida Hernandez, sitting quietly, straight backed and projecting an aura of solid dignity that Ellen had to admire. "You know everything now. What do you plan to do about it?"

"Me? Nothing. But *you are.*" Ellen rose to her feet and rolled her chair aside. "You can't use the lines in here—but I assume you have a cell phone with you?"

Hernandez nodded.

"You're going to call the President and give some reason—health? family?—for asking that he withdraw your nomination."

"And if I agree to do that?"

"I will not go public with this information. Of course you won't be a member of the Supreme Court, but you'll remain dean of the law school at Berkeley. Your life will go on as before, and people will think even more highly of you. They always do when someone leaves the arena of their own free will."

Frida Hernandez sighed deeply and leveled an enigmatic look at Ellen from beneath her dark brows. "I don't think they expected this of you. They expected you to go public with it."

"That's what they would think. But I don't think like them."

"No," Hernandez agreed, "I can see that." And, slowly, "I told them a long time ago not to underestimate you, Ellen—I mean, Senator—"

"Ellen's fine."

"Thank you. They should have listened to me. I'll make that call now."

Ellen said, "I'll wait for you outside. You'd never find your way out of here on your own."

★   ★   ★

Back in her office, Ellen released her heavy fall of hair. She pushed her fingers underneath, massaged her scalp, and studied herself critically in the bathroom mirror. The interview with Hernandez had actually had a tonic effect upon her. She no longer felt or looked exhausted but taut and keen, pumped with adrenaline. Just as well, too, since she'd need all the help she could get for her next interview. Ellen shook her hair out one more time then tied it severely back again behind her neck. She did not remove her black jacket.

Derelle tapped on the door and leaned in. "What's going on?"

Ellen didn't reply, just, "Get me Osmond Ford on the phone, please."

Derelle gave her a sharp look but knew better, in view of Ellen's mood of directed purpose, than to ask why her boss needed to speak to the Republican chairman of the Senate Judiciary Committee. "Right away, Senator."

While she waited, Ellen stared into Josh's face again.

She told him, *We're pulling it off, so far.*

12:00 NOON

Senator Ford's hideaway was very different from Ellen's: palatial, much higher, with a window offering a bird's-eye view down the Mall. It was furnished with a decided eye to comfort, with an antique desk, leather armchairs, a Persian rug, and on the wall an oil painting of mountain goats grazing in a high meadow backed by tall crags and dramatically threatening clouds, which Ford told Ellen was an original Bierstadt.

Osmond Ford, senior Senator from New Hampshire, was extremely well tailored in navy flannel, a pink shirt with crisp white collar, and a navy tie with some kind of yacht club insignia on it. Tall and imposing, he was in his mid-sixties, with a full head of white hair and a ruddy complexion derived from a variety of expensive outdoor sports. He was soft-spoken, courteous, a kindly aristocrat, the kind of man to inspire instant confidence and trust. One tended not to notice the coldness of his light gray eyes.

In so many ways Ford was the eastern counterpart of Carl Satcher. The two men were similar in physical build, influence, and power. Beside Ford, however, Satcher would appear crude.

Now, a good host, he pulled out one of the comfortable chairs for Ellen, for all the world as if they were dining at an exclusive restaurant or, more precisely, a gentleman's club that allowed women on certain social occasions. He asked, "What can I get you to drink?"

"Water, if you have it."

"Sparkling or plain?"

"Sparkling."

"Ice and lemon?"

With a half smile, "On the rocks."

He smiled thinly in return, offered the drink in a cut-glass tumbler, and served himself the same.

They faced each other across the polished walnut table, and Ford passed Ellen a coaster, requesting diffidently, "Would you mind? It marks so easily. I've thought of having a glass top made, but I much prefer the look and feel of wood. Don't you?"

"It's certainly a lovely old piece."

"Georgian."

Ellen knew that was particularly antique and special and thought wryly of her own utilitarian conference table.

She drew a deep breath. It was noon. Soon, the floor of the Senate would be packed as Senators gathered for debate on Hernandez.

"Well, now," she said, laying her manila envelope on the gleaming surface. She gave him a minute to examine the documents, then explained how they were forgeries.

Throughout, Ford's expression of quiet attention did not vary, nor, beyond a cursory glance, did he examine the reports, which he replaced in their envelope and slid back to Ellen's side of the table. "An ugly story," he said, rubbing thoughtfully at a small blemish on the side of his chin—the only imperfection, Ellen thought, in Osmond Ford's entire person. "Can you trust your staff to keep it quiet?"

"The two top staffers who know part of the story have been sworn to secrecy. They would never betray me."

He nodded, knowing the blood oath senior staff have with their Senator. "I see." Ford's arctic eyes regarded her keenly. "You undoubtedly realize that if what you say is true, and in view of the circumstances I believe it is true, you hold some singularly inflammatory material in your hands."

Ellen glanced down at her hands, small and freckled, the nails clipped short with clear varnish, where they rested upon the envelope. She agreed, "Without a doubt."

"So in your opinion, what should be the outcome for Professor Hernandez?"

"In my opinion? Candidly? I think she trusted the wrong people. She didn't forge any records herself, but she did turn over documents that she had good reason to believe might well be tampered with so that the reported facts would be misrepresented. From what I understand, she was persuaded by a group of prominent people—you know them—to collude in this scheme by appeals to her most deeply held convictions, and convinced against her better judgment that this was a normal part of the political process. Putting the best face on it, these were very dirty tricks."

Ford said, "You're being charitable, Ellen, considering you were a hair's breadth away from being a human sacrifice. But you didn't answer the question."

"Well, Osmond," replied Ellen, "as to her future, if matters are handled properly, with nobody else involved, I believe she can return to Berkeley and continue her distinguished career and her duties as professor and dean."

Ford knitted his long, patrician fingers. Then he took a thoughtful drink of water. "She'll be under a great deal of pressure to reveal those personal reasons for which she withdrew her nomination."

"But she's under no obligation to reveal them. And if she's sensible, she'll take a long summer vacation, perhaps even visit her daughter in Venezuela. By the time she returns, her fifteen minutes of fame will be long over, and the press will have moved on to the next juicy story."

The gray eyes didn't waver. "And what about you, Senator?" Ford asked. "You must have considered breaking the story yourself—in view of the potentially destructive situation you found yourself facing."

"Of course I considered it."

"And concluded?"

"That my offering this information to the media would do no one any good whatsoever."

"Not even you?"

"Not even me. I'd be a three-day sensation, but there could easily be a backlash, and dirt might cling just by association. I don't want that." She didn't tell Ford that as long as she kept their dirty little secret, they'd think twice about destroying Josh's memory and her political future.

She regarded him steadily. "I plan to be around for a long time, Senator—provided, of course, the good people of California continue to want me."

The thin lips twitched as if amused. "They said you were feisty."

"They've always said that." But no longer *cute,* Ellen thought.

After a brief silence, watching her stuff the manila envelope back in her briefcase, Ford remarked in studiedly casual tones, "I understand you have a bill coming up in committee shortly."

"The Child Protection and Enforcement Act."

He quoted, "'Whereas too many American children are suffering from neglect and abuse; Whereas the future of our country is in our children....'"

"Well said, Senator."

"I would be honored to add my name as co-sponsor," Ford said. He drained his water and rattled the ice cubes. "If you'll accept that."

They held each others' eyes in mutual understanding. After a long moment Ellen said, "Thank you, Senator."

He nodded, gravely courteous. "And my thanks, also, to you."

★ ★ ★

Ellen slowly traversed the galleries, stairwells, and corridors in a near trance, feeling she had just played and won a game of high-stakes poker. Of course she had held the winning hand, but even a winning hand, played against a master, was of uncertain outcome.

What a very smooth, smart operator Ford was; how well he'd played out their match, even to reciting her bill.

I never had to spell it out for him, she thought with intense gratification. He knew exactly what I wanted, he knew what I could do if I didn't get it—and that my story would do damage where he didn't want any damage done. Also, he knows I may well be in the Senate for the long haul, and on his committee, and that there'll be other issues where he'll need me. With this shared experience under our belts, I think he has a new respect. Josh had once said, "Politics is not for the faint of heart," and now she understood why.

Ellen's heart was still racing. Her head felt both spacey and wired, her body not quite her own. She needed to be alone, to get away from the voices and clamor, and even from her own staff. She had set huge wheels in motion and now there was nothing more she could do except let it all play out.

Knowing no one would recognize her in her nondescript black jacket, dark glasses, and tied-back hair, Ellen turned off her cell phone and walked slowly down the Capitol steps and through the quiet leafy streets to her apartment, imagining what Osmond Ford would be doing. He must first reach the nominee, Hernandez herself, to confirm her decision. Then he would attempt to reach the President, and failing immediate contact, would call the Vice President or the White House Counsel.

Ellen closed the front door behind her, proceeded directly to the bathroom, and turned on both faucets of the tub, tossing in bubble bath crystals. Stepping into the deep, hot, fragrant water, she stretched forward to switch on the small TV sitting on a shelf beside the window, then leaned back to watch the debate on Hernandez's nomination on the Senate channel.

There would be no floor votes while the debate went on, so Ellen wouldn't be missed. How long would it take for Osmond Ford to reach the President?

Ellen soaked and watched and listened almost drowsily as proceedings opened with the Pledge of Allegiance and a prayer from the Chaplain, and her colleagues began debating the nomination, alternating Senators favoring and opposing the nomination.

The water had long ago gone cold when Ellen climbed from the tub, pulled on her yellow terry robe, and padded restlessly into the living room. It was after three-thirty. How much longer?

Chewing nervously on some crackers—she hadn't eaten since the early breakfast with Micaela—she watched the debate unfolding on a larger screen.

★　★　★

Just before four o'clock, the Republican Senator speaking in support of Professor Hernandez stopped mid-sentence as he was handed a note.

It's happening, Ellen thought. This is it.

"I yield the floor to the Majority Leader," the Senator said quickly, somberly, stepping aside.

Ellen watched the Majority Leader stride toward the rostrum, a tall spare man carrying a folded paper in his hand. She waited as he settled himself behind the microphone at the front of the chamber.

"It is my sad duty to read the following statement from the White House," he began. In measured, deliberate tones he released the bombshell: "For personal reasons, Frida Hernandez has asked the President of the United States to withdraw her name from consideration as an Associate Justice of the Supreme Court."

"*Yes!*" whispered Ellen emphatically in the quiet calm of her living room. "Go on! *Go on!*"

"The President is extremely saddened by this development, but expects to have a new nominee shortly. In light of this unanticipated development," the Majority Leader concluded, "I ask unanimous consent that we end this debate and adjourn until tomorrow morning at ten o'clock."

So it was done. It was all over.

★ ★ ★

Ellen dressed once more in her anonymous black outfit, left the house, and headed in the direction of the Capitol, still not quite ready to go back to her office.

She sat down on her favorite bench, facing the Capitol dome with the Supreme Court at her back. Raising her arms above her head she stretched mightily, taking a long, deep breath.

"We did it, Josh!" she cried aloud. In case passersby looked askance at this woman sitting alone on a bench yelling to herself, she took the cell phone out of her bag, turned it on, and held it casually to her ear as she told Josh everything.

Then Ellen leaned against the back of the bench, noticing for the first time that the dogwood had burst into flower—why had she not noticed before?—and that the air was soft, fragrant, and entirely delicious with the first real promise of summer. The late-afternoon light was golden, starlings chattered in the bushes, and the pigeons were no doubt cooing amorously among the high cornices and parapets.

Ellen smiled with the languid satisfaction of a job well done. She'd like to sit here, let the world stream on around her, and just watch the men and women trudge past her bound for home, not sparing a glance for the small, ordinary woman sitting alone making phone calls.

When her phone rang, her first giddy feeling was that it was Josh calling her back from another world. And why not? Almost as miraculous things had happened today.

But of course it would be the office. Well, just this once they could wait.

Ellen put the phone in her bag and gazed at the dogwood and the last frothy pink of cherry blossoms.

The phone rang again.

Damn. Of course her staff must be going nuts, wondering what the hell was happening, where she was, and what she was doing—and had she heard the news.

"Hi," she said, flipping it open, "I'm on my way."

And a familiar voice exclaimed, "So I got you. Finally!"

★ ★ ★

First came a wave of anger; then Ellen laughed out loud—the first raucous, honest laugh she'd had in a long while. She'd forgotten how good it felt to laugh.

Greg didn't sound enraged, as she might have expected, merely curious. "Do you realize what you've done?" he asked.

"I sure do."

"I'm finished."

"Is that supposed to upset me?"

"Look, I had no idea—"

"Don't make it worse, Greg."

"But you must understand—"

"What's to understand, except that you'd sell anybody, even the people you say you love, down the river?"

"It isn't like that. Ellen, trust me. I—"

"Trust you? Are you out of your mind? Listen, Greg, I know *exactly* what you did." After a pause, "I not only talked with Hernandez, I talked to Micaela."

"I see." A longer silence. Then he said, "Please believe me, I had no choice."

"You had a choice. You just don't want the consequences of the choice you made," Ellen said. "Micaela told me everything, you know. She told me how you let Josh think he had a child. How could you *do* that?"

"We had no idea she wasn't Josh's daughter," Greg said. "That woman Bianca lied to us. And the girl certainly looked the right age."

Ellen said, "Listen, Greg, stop. I felt sorry for you once. You'd had bad breaks and a sad time growing up, and I thought you really could be something if you'd ever manage to look beyond yourself. I forgave you for things I never should have. Well, eventually people run out of forgiveness. Even me, your gullible college pal."

"If it's any satisfaction to you," Greg said, "I've lost everything."

"No satisfaction, no feelings at all," Ellen said. "I'm over it."

"Carl Satcher's booted me out. My father-in-law won't speak to me. Nor will Jane. I already have messages to call her lawyer."

"Poor Greg. All that in one afternoon! And you expected it to be me going down in flames."

"Don't be so hard on me, Ell. My career's over and so's my marriage."

"I don't blame Jane a bit. You cheated on her. You didn't even try to make her happy."

"Because of you. I've always loved you. *I* couldn't be happy without *you*."

"Stop it."

"And Ellen, I know you can't see it now, but you really don't belong in politics. It's not for you—"

"I'm hanging up now—"

"I'm going back to Surprise Bend for a while—"

"Good-bye, Greg."

"Wait!—and I was thinking, now that everything is out in the open between us, and I'm going to be single, maybe we could get together later on. You have my cell phone number."

She couldn't believe her ears. "You're something else. After they made you, they threw out the mold!" Ellen cut him off with a quick, light stab of her finger on the END button, his plaintive cry "ELL——" ringing in her ears. She sat watching her phone, half expecting it to ring again right away, but it remained silent and she let out a long, soft breath.

In a certain way she felt a gnawing sadness. Part of her past was cut away, leaving behind a big, empty space. She'd cared for Greg once, maybe even loved him, but she'd loved a Greg who had never really existed, and now she felt nothing for him at all. She didn't care if he went back to Nebraska, stayed with Jane, or got divorced. She didn't care if she never saw him again. Josh was gone. Greg was gone.

But life goes on, like it always somehow does, thought Ellen, sensing the beginning of a new personal freedom, and a new energy and excitement about her job. She breathed in the dogwoods one last time, smiled at the hurrying people, and some of them smiled back.

It was spring, after all.

At last Ellen called the office. "It's me," she said. "I'm on my way in."

6:00 P.M.

They were all waiting for her as she stepped through the door, her entire staff, and they raised a lusty cheer and a clamor of declarations and questions: Thank goodness she was back. Where had she been? What was going on? So much was happening!

Indeed it was, according to the stack of messages and the bank of telephones, which showed a solid line of flashing red lights—reporters calling for her comment on Frida Hernandez's withdrawal. Did she want to make a statement?

Well, of course she did.

She told David to send out a press release. "Say something like: 'Senator Ellen Fischer said tonight that she respects the decision of Professor Frida Hernandez and trusts that she made the right choice for her family.

"'Fischer further said that this unexpected turn of events gives the President the opportunity to nominate a candidate who will bring not only diversity but more balanced positions to this critical post.'"

David said disbelievingly, "And that's it?"

"You can polish it up, the way you do, but that's it."

Then, seeing them staring at her, Vic Aguilera, David, Derelle, Diane, and all those other wonderful people, so loyal to her, and loyal to Josh, she felt her face break into a wide, wide smile. She wanted to hug them all.

"I don't know what's been going on," Vic said in awed disbelief, "but just in the last hour we've had calls from five Republicans asking to be added as sponsors to your bill."

So Ford got to them already, Ellen thought; he works fast. And, she thought with reluctant admiration, those conservatives certainly run a well-oiled machine.

Her face beaming with satisfaction, Derelle said, "You'll get your legislation through now, no question."

David asked, "Do you want to tell us what happened?"

Well, of course she would like to, she'd love to tell them, but she wouldn't. "I guess Osmond Ford just saw the light."

Derelle nodded. "*Right.*" Ellen noticed her exchange a glance with Vic, then both look away.

"Well, he's a very smart man." Ellen shook out her hair again, then stripped off her black jacket, rolled it up, and tossed it to Diane. "Would you mind hanging that awful thing up for me and bringing my red one? No, my hot-pink one, with the silver buttons."

"A pleasure, Senator."

"So what's next?" Derelle asked.

"What's next?" said Ellen, putting on her pink jacket, once more the brightest comet in the Capitol. "What's next is a friendly call to the President recommending Carmela Ochoa for the Supremcs. But that's for tomorrow. Tonight, we're celebrating.

We're going to dinner, all of us. We'll go to Marty's and stuff ourselves with the best ribs in town—and it's on me!"

Derelle said, "Another stellar decision, Senator," and together they headed out onto Constitution Avenue, the Supreme Court building gleaming at them in the last of the sunset.

ACKNOWLEDGMENTS

This novel has been seven years in the making. It would not have come to life without some wonderful people who were there for me when I thought it would never happen.

First and foremost, my agent, Fred Hill, who was introduced to me by Rick Patterson. Fred never gave up on me, and his ideas were important and right on the mark. In addition, he introduced me to Mary-Rose Hayes, my co-writer. Mary-Rose and I clicked, set our egos aside (hard for a Senator) and made it happen.

Without Chronicle Books and my editor, Jay Schaefer, I wouldn't be writing this acknowledgment. Jay had faith in us and made our story come alive. I also want to thank everyone in the publicity department at Chronicle Books for working overtime to make sure that readers not only knew that we had a good story to tell, but also that we were offering an insight into the complex and rough world of politics.

I also thank the people of California who, over the past twenty-five years, have given me the honor of serving them in several offices. In so doing, they allowed me to make—hopefully—a positive difference in their lives, and also placed me in this most fascinating arena called politics. Without them, of course, I could only guess about a world that is now so much a part of me.

And to my family, who once again endured another project with understanding, love, and some very good advice.
——Barbara Boxer

My warmest thanks, first and foremost, to Senator Barbara Boxer, whose talent and energy are phenomenal, who is the best possible writing partner, and who has opened so many doors for me that I never dreamed I'd pass through. I want most sincerely to thank my agent, Fred Hill, for bringing us together, and Jay Schaefer for his editorial expertise. I also acknowledge, with gratitude, all those who have provided help and advice along the way, especially Maitland (Sandy) Zane of the *San Francisco Chronicle,* and Howard Diamond and George Benetatos for their insights as Alameda County public defenders during the 1970s.
——Mary-Rose Hayes